SILENT TEARS

A Novel

by

Etta Smith Padrick

with

Gloria Padrick Arnold

Copyright © 2020 Gloria Padrick Arnold

All rights reserved.

ISBN: 9798650874164

For My Family

CONTENTS

Part 1: 1895-1925   3

Part 2: 1925-1932   170

Part 3: 1933-1934   319

Part 4: 1934-1938   471

Etta Smith Padrick wrote SILENT TEARS when in her late fifties and sixties. She lived from 1914 to 2016.

Etta was an enthusiastic genealogist and relied heavily upon past relatives for her book character's names. However, this book is one of fiction and the characters are a product of the author's imagination and in no way resembles anyone living or dead.

Also, the style in which SILENT TEARS was written is strictly her own.

SILENT TEARS has been published posthumously.

The front cover was designed by Gloria Padrick Arnold.

PART ONE

1895-1925

Another hot day thought Em Carroll as he stood leaning against the back door in the early morning hour. The crops had been without rain for more than two weeks and were becoming withered and dry. He turned his gaze to the sky.

"Well, Lord, you said to make our living by the sweat of our brow. I can't sweat that much, so please give me some material to work with. No offense, Lord, but some rain would sure help an awful lot."

He could hear Lukatie in the kitchen busily preparing breakfast. The odor of the frying fatback reached his nostrils, causing his stomach to growl to the accompaniment of hunger pains.

His gaze wandered over the fields stretched out before him. The earth was warm; he could smell it and he loved it. But for some reason he couldn't make it pay. Over three thousand acres were his, thanks to his progenitors. Through all the battles and hostilities of man and nature, they had somehow managed to retain the land. The first Carroll to receive a grant of land had worked hard, bought slaves and more land, often trading livestock for large parcels of land. "Land poor, that's me," thought Em. "I guess they wouldn't be too proud of me, their descendent. I haven't improved the land or made it pay."

The old plantation house was destroyed by fire during the Civil War and the house Em now lived in was built after the carpetbaggers had descended. Em turned and looked at the weatherbeaten, unpainted, clapboard house. There were two sections to this house. The front section contained four rooms with a porch across the front. A hall ran from the front door through the middle of the house to a back door. The back door opened onto a covered walkway which led to a second section. The second section housed the dining room, kitchen, and pantry. Three large spreading live oak trees provided the only beauty about the place. They let the sunshine in during the cold months and in summer shaded the old house. A flat weatherbeaten board that the children used for a swing seat hung lazily between two chains attached to the largest limb of the tree near the back of the house.

Em hated the old house with a passion that bit into his soul. It killed all the joy of planning and living. He was completely depressed with no thoughts except to make enough to keep the taxes paid on his land. There was never any money left for future planning. Instead of John Emsley Carroll, I should be named John "Broke" Carroll.

His brother, Kinyon, was smart. After their parent's death, Kinyon took five hundred dollars from the estate and left Em with ten dollars and a clear deed to the land. Kinyon had left satisfied in the knowledge that Em would never let the land go.

Em worked the negroes hard that summer and himself even harder. Some hard years passed before his marriage in 1895 to Lukatie Smith, a nurse, who lived twenty-five miles away in Wilmington, North Carolina. Em thought she was the most beautiful brown-haired woman he had ever seen. With lustrous dark brown eyes, she was a nubile woman who wore clothes to perfection. He hadn't known how she would take to his way of life, but he knew he must have her. He loved her. He pursued her. He won her.

The tenth of July, 1897, their first son, Benjamin was born. Two years later on the first of October, 1900, Lucinda came to stay. Miles added another mouth to feed and a squirming body to clothe when he arrived the twenty-fourth of May, 1902. Nearly six years passed before Meda endeared herself to the family as child number four on the fourteenth of September, 1908.

A new miracle seemed to occur with the birth of each child. It was as if Lukatie had a world all her own with each child she carried. As the years passed and the children came, he continued to love her tenderly and yet, passionately. He didn't know her 'mother world' and he knew he could never penetrate it. When the last child, Meda, was born, he kissed her gently on the forehead, whispering, "I love you."

"Love you." she murmured, smiled weakly and drifted off to sleep. Looking down at her, Em thought, All of creation is a miracle and giving birth is the greatest of all.

He had felt concern because there were so many years between Miles and the baby. Almost six. It seemed like more because Miles was so large for his age. Em had sat by Lukatie's bed a long time after the delivery even though Doctor Wesson had said she was just fine. Promising to check back the next morning, the doctor had shaken his head and left him alone with her.

Em moved to the steps and sat down as he began to reflect on the years prior to his marriage. Memories continued to flutter through his mind like the falling leaves of autumn, tumbling to make clear patterns of life where they touched.

Kinyon and Em were standing at the grave side of the gentle man who was their father. Thrown from his horse, Roan, who had reared at the sudden appearance of a rattlesnake, John Emsley Carroll, Sr., died where he fell. The whinnying of the horse had brought Kinyon and Em running from the field just in time to see John's head crushed under the horse's hooves. Kinyon ran into the house and grabbed his gun. He fired repeatedly until Roan lay dead beside his master.

Unable to speak, Em had pointed to the snake, and Kinyon had fired once more.

"I thought Roan…My dear God, look what I've done. I've killed Roan," moaned Kinyon as he looked at Em, then stared at his father's dead body in shock.

Putting his arm around his brother, Em had consoled, "It was an accident. You didn't see the snake and Roan did kill Papa, even if he didn't mean to. Don't blame yourself."

Just a month earlier, they had stood thus with their father beside them and watched their mother laid to rest. Samantha Spooner Carroll had been a good, hard-working woman. Keeping a spotless house, she often said, "We may be poor, but that is no excuse for being dirty as long as a pot of lye soap is in the making." With six tenant houses on the land, she tried teaching those inside the same principles, to no avail.

Watching Kinyon and Emsley Carroll one could only wonder at the love, respect and faith they must have felt for their father and mother now lying side by side. Kinyon, two years older than Emsley, in an embracing movement with his arms, his face impassive, had said,

"All is done."

Heavy with grief, they had turned from the grave as young Preacher Robert Murray came up to shake their hands.

"We all loved them, too." he had said with compassion.

Struggling for control, Kinyon had acknowledged his consoling remarks and moved to leave. "Excuse us now," he had said to those immediately around them and started the half-mile walk back to the house.

The negro families living on the plantation had fallen in behind them, taking up the chants Kinyon and Em had so often heard in the cotton fields. The black voices had combined in a steady dirge, occasionally adding, "Praise de Lawd. Whut we gwine ter do now?"

"Oh, Lawdy, whut will heppen ter us?" rang out another thin voice. They had huddled into a group, moving as one body.

Their wailing had finally penetrated Em's sorrow. He had turned and, with as much control as possible, had stilled their lamentations, telling them that nothing was going to happen. They would continue on as before as long as they wished. Only now, they would work for Mr. Kinyon and himself.

In a deep voice, easily recognized, one of the men had said, "Praise de Lawd. Amen." Then he had stepped forward, saying, "Thank you', Mister Em." It was Thankful Mathias, one of the few who had managed to learn to read and write. Kinyon and Em had often helped him with his attempts. What they had learned at school, they had taught him. Thankful had been quick to learn and when the new white school had been built and the Negroes had been given the use of the old one, he had attended for eight years. Although he had been large enough to be much help to his folks, they had permitted him to attend school even though they thought a Negro was wasting his time trying to obtain an education. "'cause white folk weren't gwine ter give 'em a decent job no how."

"How wrong they were!", thought Em as he sat there waiting for Lukatie to call him to breakfast. It wasn't just Negroes, he mused, plenty of white people felt the same way.

Em remembered the Sunday following the death of his father. Kinyon had gone with him to church.

As they left to walk back to the house, Penelope Sholar had hurried up to them.

"Kinyon," she had said, in her little girl breathless voice. "Mama said I should invite you and Em to come home with me for dinner." When no acceptance came quickly, she had said, "You will come, won't you? I want…I mean, we all want you both to come." Putting her hand on Kinyon's arm, pleadingly, she had looked to him for a reply. Em had waited, saying nothing, to see if Kinyon would accept. Thinking of how a home-cooked meal would taste, he had volunteered, "It's alright with me, Kinyon." Later, Em realized he had said the wrong thing as Kinyon had accepted the invitation.

Em began to laugh as he thought of the way Penelope had used every feminine wile in the book to attract Kinyon. A real atavist, that one, he thought. He had heard how her grandmother had talked her grandfather into a later afternoon walk when a storm was threatening. Her grandfather had met them at the door the next morning with a shotgun, announcing he was just going hunting. The wedding took place a week later.

Lukatie stuck her head out of the door. "What's so funny?" she asked while looking around. Laughing again, Em said, "Just thinking back to something that happened years ago, even before my time."

"Well, you come eat breakfast and tell me about it, so I can have a good laugh too. I guess I'd better call the children so they can eat a warm breakfast." she said smiling.

She crossed the walkway and entered the front section though the screen door, thankful to get out of the kitchen. It was so hot and just six o'clock. She hoped the heat wouldn't make the children cross today.

Walking down the hall, she knocked on the

thin walls, calling, "Benjamin, Miles, Lucinda, Meda, up for breakfast. Hurry now."

Back in the kitchen, she dished up the hominy grits and fat back. Over each helping of grits she poured a spoonful of hot fat grease from the pan. And egg would sure taste good with this, she thought. But I better save them to sell. We need so many things.

Em took each plate to the table in the dining room. As Lukatie took a pan of hot biscuits from the oven, the children came sleepy-eyed through the door taking their place at the table. They all bowed their heads as Em thanked God and blessed the food to the nourishment of their bodies.

After breakfast, Lukatie said, "You can start pumping water for the washing, Benjamin, and you wash the dishes, Lucinda. And see if you can't clean up the kitchen better than last time."

"But I have to go, Mama."

"Then go, the dishes will be here when you get back. The best laxative you ever have is washing dishes. I do believe it's good for you. I'll let you do them more often."

Miles began to giggle and Lukatie turned to him.

"And Miles, I do believe you could gather up some kindling to start a fire around the wash pot. Meda, you can help Miles."

"Me too little, Mama."

"I guess maybe you are, Honey," Lukatie smiled at her youngest child, thinking how hard they all had to work, even to the youngest. Em had helped Lukatie bring in a large tub of water to set on the hot stove to heat while they ate. Now, she absent-mindedly picked up a knife and piece of lye soap and started flaking off the soap into the warm water to dissolve. It was soon good and hot and they took the tub out to the wash bench against the live oak tree beside the pump bench.

Lukatie had insisted on filling in the well and driving a pump when the children were born. She didn't want to be constantly worried that one of them might crawl up on it and fall in and drown. The pump was her one luxury.

Em and Thankful came walking into the yard as Lukatie was stirring the last pot full of clothes. She was glad she was about finished the heat was sapping her energy. She stepped back from the pot and used her apron to wipe the perspiration from her face. the men walked over to the pump bench and pumped some cool water to drink.

"Yasuh, Mister Em, it's rain from heaven alone thet's gwine to hep us'n. I hope it comes soon'n nutures the fields fo' w'en all starves," ventured Thankful.

"Yes," said Em. "This prolonged drought is taking its toll. It seems this heat will never end. Sure wish we could save some of it to mix in with next winter when we really need it."

Lukatie dipped the clothes out of the wash pot with her long stirring pole, watching the hot water drain back into the big iron pot. As she put the clothes in a small tub, Meda came running around the house and pulled Lukatie's dress.

"Mama, Mama, Miles is cursing."

Lukatie picked up the clothes to rub them once again on the washboard in order to remove stubborn stains before rinsing and hanging them on the line.

Meda pulled her dress again. "Mama, Miles is cursing."

"He is cursing, you say. Well, what is he saying?" Meda was hesitant. "What is he saying?" repeated Lukatie.

Looking at her Mama, Papa and Thankful, Meda said, her eyes wide, "He's saying, cuss, cuss,

cuss." She ran back around the house as fast as her little legs would carry her, as though the laughter of the three was chasing her.

"The only thing this weather is good for is to dry clothes quickly," remarked Lukatie still laughing as she watched the sheets stir in the hot breeze.

"You shore is rite," agreed Thankful.

"Thankful, how is your grandfather this morning?"

"Aw, he's alrite, Miz Carroll. Since his blindness, he don't do nothing, but sit around."

"I guess it would be awful hard trying to do work when you go blind at his age. He's pretty old, isn't he?"

"Yassum, he wuz a slave, but he don't kno' jes' how old he is. Here, let me help yo' with dat tub."

"Did you ever know your father?"

"No, mam, afeared I dinen't. He wuz kilt by a jealous man thet wanted my maw."

"What happened to the man?"

"He wuz hung."

"Oh…"

Em finished pumping fresh rinse water for Lukatie. Then he and Thankful walked over to speak to his grandfather. He tried to make it a point to speak to the old man, as everyone called him, every time he saw him sitting outside with his chair propped against the wall. The old man was out every day, weather permitting. Em's warm thoughtfulness was sincere.

"How are you today, Old Man?"

"Mistuh Mathias," corrected the old man.

"Sure," responded Em, "Is it going to rain this afternoon?"

"Noope. I'se feeling' too peart."

He spat tobacco juice out to the side of the

porch. The juice landed in a patch that was hard and brown from the build-up of layer after layer of repeated spats that never missed the same spot more than a couple of inches in any direction.

"Getting better all the time, Old Man."

"Mistuh Mathias," he corrected again, "Yas, I hits de bull's eye eva' time."

"I don't see how you do it."

"Tak's practice, Mistuh Em. Yassuh, hit tak's practice, shore do."

"Well, Thankful, if we're going fishing, we'd better get started. Maybe we'll catch a bream or two for supper."

"Thet Thankful could throw a bare hook in de river n' cotch a fish," said the old man.

"Afeared I'se not dat good, Gran'pa. I do put a worm on de hook," laughed Thankful.

Em laughed and off they went.

"How I'd lik ter go," thought the old man. "Hits been a long time since I'se cad ma' pole ter de river or felt de warm plowed 'arth. I kin't eben enjoy goin' down thar'n seeing' hit no more."

Back at the house, Lukatie was continuing to direct the children's activities.

"Benjamin! Lucinda!" she called. "Don't forget to chop some stove wood and fill the box in the kitchen, son. Then go break off some black gum toothbrushes and you children chew them good. Lucinda, powder up some sage and mix a little myrrh with it and a fourth cup of honey to use on your teeth to help clean them."

"Do I have to, Mama?" groaned Lucinda.

"Yes, dear, you have to."

Two days later the rains came. The river was up and roaring. It looked for several days like the weather would clear, then another frontal system would come along and rains would pour again. This pattern continued until finally the sun broke through in all its brilliance, giving the world a greatly appreciate bath of gold.

In the fall, Em took the cotton to the warehouse in Campton. The Negroes had worked side by side with him to save the crop after the rains had nearly destroyed it. There was less than last year. The land seemed to yield less each year. Even with less cotton it still took several trips to get it all to the warehouse. He left his wagon and horses at the livery stable and went by train to see Kinyon. He visited Kinyon every year and always felt guilty at leaving Lukatie behind. But with the children and all the farm chores, it was impossible for her to accompany him.

"Bless her," Em thought. She always encouraged him to visit his only brother. As an only child, she missed not having any family herself.

As the train pulled away from the station, Em settled in his seat for the short ride. Kinyon had settled in Landridge City fifty miles from Campton after leaving the farm.

Asking for work at Blunt Mills, Kinyon had been hired immediately. The work was hard, but Kinyon had learned so fast that he had soon been working throughout the mill, wherever he had been needed most. He had soon decided that this work was no harder than the endless chores on the farm. At least at the end of the day, he could go to the boarding house and relax, if the other boarders would only stay sober. They were certainly a noisy lot when they drank.

It hadn't been long before James Thomas Blunt had become aware of the capable young man employed in his mill. Kinyon had seen Mr. Blunt pass through the mill on numerous occasions. At times his daughter had been with him, and Kinyon thought she was the prettiest girl he had ever seen. He had been puzzled when Mr. Blunt had summoned him to the office one day. Mr. Batchelor, the secretary, had waited while Kinyon washed up.

"What's this all about?" Kinyon had asked.

"I don't know, but feel sure it's nothing to be alarmed about," Mr. Batchelor had responded. As they entered the office, Kinyon's eyes quickly took in the room. Several young girls in white blouses were sitting behind their desks, busy with a mass of paperwork. They had looked up and smiled with interest when they saw Kinyon, dropping their eyes back to their work as the men passed by. A few pictures were hung on the white walls which were lined with filing cabinets. One picture was of a large, gray-haired, dark mustached man. Must be the founder of Blunt Mills, Kinyon had thought. He had reflected on how drab the main office had looked as he followed Mr. Batchelor into another adjoining office.

He had been surprised at the spacious tastefully decorated room. It wasn't a fussy room, but was light and airy. A large mahogany desk with the most comfortable looking leather chair Kinyon had ever seen dominated one end of the room. The floor was carpeted in plush green wool with matching drapes at the windows. He had been afraid that if he walked in he would sink to his ankles and also dirty the carpet with his shoes after walking on the dirty oily floor of the mill.

Mr. Blunt had been standing at the window and had turned as they entered. Seeing Kinyon hesitate, he had smiled and had said, "Come, Mr. Carroll, and be seated over here." Indicating a chair near the desk. He then thanked Mr. Batchelor and dismissed him.

"What kind of man is this, calling me Mr. and thanking his hired help?" Kinyon had wondered.

Mr. Blunt turned to Kinyon and said, "I

suppose you're wondering why I've summoned you. I'll not keep your waiting. I've noticed your work in the mill, how quickly you learn. For the past month I've been observing you."

"So that is why he's been in the mill so much," Kinyon had thought.

Mr. Blunt went on to say, "I've looked over your application and want to know why a man with your education is working in a mill, and out in the plant at that. Why didn't you try banking? There are any number of better paying jobs you could have gotten."

"A straight truthful answer is what he wants," Kinyon had thought. "Well, Mr. Blunt, I came from a farm the other side of Campton. My father owned over three thousand acres. He saw to it that my brother and I were both educated. At his death I took the cash that was left and signed my half of the land over to my brother, with his agreement, of course. He still lives on the farm. I came to town and this is the first place I asked for work and was hired.

"I suppose that was after you lived it up on the money," casually remarked Mr. Blunt as he had eyed Kinyon. Kinyon's expression had become passive. "No, sir, there was only five hundred dollars. I put it in the bank and I've added to it when I could."

"Sorry, Mr. Carroll, I shouldn't have said that. You must care for your brother a great deal to let over fifteen hundred acres go for no more than that."

"I do, I love my brother. I would do anything I could for him. I don't care for farming, but I wouldn't want anyone other than our family to own our land. I knew he loved the farm and would never leave it."

Mr. Blunt was impressed as he listened to

Kinyon, he liked the young man. He had heard of the Carroll's of Campton and what they stood for, but he hadn't known that this man was of that family.

"Now, Mr. Carroll, do you plan to stay with Blunt Mills?"

Feeling more at ease, Kinyon had replied, "I like learning. I feel like I know the operations and repairing of the looms. I've been a section hand, grinder, winder, worked in the dye room, shipping and others. I feel I know the operations of the mill on the other side of this door."

"That brings us to why I've asked you here. How would you like to know the operations of the mill on this side of the door?"

Kinyon had not been able to hide his astonishment.

James Blunt had crossed the room and opened a door. "This was my office before the death of my father. Afterwards I had to take over the running of the mill. Since my only child is a daughter, this office has remained empty. Until now I haven't found anyone I felt had the capability to sit behind that desk. I'm offering you that job. I need someone who cares for the mill and will run it for my daughter when I'm gone. If my judgement of you proves right, as I feel it will, a lot of power will be placed in your hands. Will you take the job, Mr. Carroll?"

Kinyon had hesitated, thinking of Mr. Batchelor.

Reading his mind Mr. Blunt had interrupted. "I suppose you have noted that Mr. Batchelor is getting old. Not much difference in his age and mine. He doesn't want the responsibility. He will be invaluable to you. We both agree that we need young blood that will get things done and be here much longer than we can ever hope to be. Well, Mr.

Carroll?"

Momentarily stunned and filled with humility, Kinyon had straightened to his full height and looked Mr. Blunt in the eyes.

"Yes, sir, if you feel I'm the man for the job. I'll do my best to live up to your expectations of me."

"Fine." Mr. Blunt had replied. "Since today is Thursday, why don't you take the rest of the week off and prepare yourself for your new job. Report to work Monday morning at eight. I'll meet you here and show you your duties. In the meantime I'll have the office cleaned and aired for you. Until Monday morning then, Mr. Carroll."

"Thank you, sir." Kinyon had turned and left the room. The girls had giggled as he left.

That had been more than seven years ago. Kinyon had married the beautiful, exciting and vibrant Jane Blunt. They had three children and lived in the Blunt mansion on top of the only hill in Landridge. As president of Blunt Mills since the death of Mr. Blunt a year ago, Kinyon was happy. He was an unusual leader and often he could be found in the plant fixing a loom instead of in his office.

Once a section boss asked Mr. Batchelor, "Is he putting on a show?" Shaking his head Mr. Batchelor said, "No, I don't think so. He enjoys it. I used to think he was ostentatious, but I'm inclined to think it is just his way to relax when he is keyed up."

Em found Kinyon at the mill. The train often stopped there to drop off a box car to be unloaded and loaded again. Em left the train and wandered through the mill until he found Kinyon. Kinyon greeted him heartily and walked with him to the office. Later as they relaxed in Kinyon's home, Kinyon again offered Em a good job at the mill, even hinted at training him as a vice president. Em was tempted but turned down his brother's offer.

"I can't leave the land and the tenants," thought Em. He almost wished that the tenants would leave and force him to take Kinyon's offer. He certainly couldn't run the farm without help.

When Em returned home on the train the next day, his thoughts dwelt on his brother's offer. By the time the train neared Campton, however, all his thoughts had returned to the farm, his family and the tenants.

The tenants were always as glad as Lukatie when Em returned. She missed her husband. But to them it meant pay for the long hot summer's work. He had Thankful to keep a daily record of each one's work. He took the book along with the money in a cigar box to the pump bench and called out the name of each family and payed each father and son according to the hours Thankful had recorded. Often the father would want to take the son's money but Em meant for each worker to have his own earnings if only to hold until he was out of sight.

Abner Tootle's family was the first called. Em let each man and woman see the book and for those that couldn't read Thankful was there to read out their earnings and their deductions for things they had borrowed during the winter months. Some of the negroes were thrifty and could manage, others still needed someone to measure out their pittance as you would govern a child. Some would never be out of debt to Em because they spent what they made at Roxie Freeman's tavern. They were the ones that grumbled. Andrew Jackson Smith took his family and left one fall. "Sour asses," thought Em, but he never tried to stop them, nor did he take other tenants into their house.

Within two months they were back, broke and begging for another chance.

"I'se a 'udder failure, Mistuh Carroll," said Andrew. Em nodded toward the house without saying a word. He turned and walked slowly to the store house.

Andrew, watching him go, wondered if Em was agreeing that he was an 'udder failure or giving them the house back. He turned to Nancy and told her and the children to go on to the house.

"Pa, we'en haint chilluns no mo'. We's grown ups," complained Lebtia, straightening up to her full height. Her breasts stood out on her thin frame like a couple of corn seeds on a flat board.

"Yore purty smart, huh?" Andrew turned to Hyrum and Hinton. "Boys, tak' yore maw and dis young'un to de house for' I whupp her. Now, de passel ov yo' git."

He turned and followed Em to the store house.

Em handed him a bag of beans, flour, coffee, sugar and a stand of lard. Remembering it would soon be hog-killing time, he took down a slab of fat back and handed it out to him. Pointing to the collard greens still growing in the garden he backed out of the storehouse, locked the door and walked to the house as he heard Andrew's "Sho' 'preciate hit, Mistuh Carroll."

At one time or another they had all tried leaving. Em never tried to stop them. They always came back; he wished sometimes they'd stay gone.

Em worried about the houses, not just his, but the tenants' houses too. All were about to fall down. There never was enough money left at the end of the year to buy a bundle of shingles let alone build houses.

All the houses were infested with rats whose stench penetrated into the houses from the attics. Roaches and ants were bad especially during the summer months. All Em could do was worry, fight the pests and continually lose. The one thing he didn't want to lose was this land. He just couldn't. He loved it. It was his life. Even though some of the negroes worried the hell out of him at times, he felt that farming was the greatest life on earth.

It was getting dark and he was ready for his supper, bed and Lukatie in that order.

In the morning Em would start the fire in the stove, feed the stock and take in the wood while Lukatie did her early morning bathing which was a summer ritual, then she'd prepare breakfast. He stood at the closed door talking as he watched her bathe from the basin of water she brought in each evening before retiring. First she washed off the soap. Then soaping the cloth again she rubbed gently around and over each breast. As Em watched her, he had an almost overpowering urge to take the cloth and finish bathing her. God blessed his woman with a beautiful body and he loved every inch of it. Having four children hadn't hurt her looks one bit.

"I've got work to do and I'd better go while I'm still able to walk out," he stated as he left the room smiling, remembering her remarks as she turned her back to him last night exhausted and ready for sleep.

"What a session," she had murmured.

*****

William Heath owned the farm adjacent to the Carroll land. Since he had no family he offered his black tenants the opportunity to purchase small parcels of land as homesteads.

Roxie Freeman and her brother Noah lived on one of these small farms left to them after the death of their parents. Their father had killed himself with hard work trying to pay for it, and it still wasn't quite paid for. A week after their father's death their mother had died of a heart attack.

Roxie was a thinker and a doer. "But what can I do alone," she thought. One thing for sure I don't intend to lose this place. She looked at Noah slumped in a chair and could feel her temper rising.

"I'll put up on hulluva fight befo' I'll lose dis place, Noah. Iffen yo' warn't so damn lazy'n hep paw mabbe he'd be alive ter day," she yelled at him.

"Aw, Roxie, whyn't you' lay offen me. I hep paw w'en he tolt me ter," said Noah, pushing his big frame lower in the chair.

"Why did he allus haft ter tell yo'? Yo' kno' dere wuz work ter do," she said harshly.

"Yo' sartin'ly air full ov pepper ter day. How'd I kno' what had ter be did iffen I ain't tolt? How, jes tell me, how?"

"Iffen yo' don' git busy 'n start doin' sum work 'round heah we's gonna lose dis place," said Roxie.

"Thar y'go gittin' iffy, jes tell me whut yo' wants don' 'n I'se gonna do hit," Noah declared.

"Yo'll do hit or hav' one helluva empty belly. Jes mak' up youre mind which hits gonna be," said Roxie as she walked out of the house.

She walked down to the riverbank and looked back up the hill. Noah was one of those people that had no initiative of his own. Condemning him wouldn't solve her problem. For two hours she stood there thinking. She looked at the house. There was one long room across the front. A fireplace stood at one end and a bed rested at the other where her mother and father had slept. Two smaller bedrooms had been built across the back in addition to a large kitchen for cooking and eating. The hill had been dug out and leveled when the two rooms and kitchen were added. She moved back to the house calling to Noah. He sat lazily rocking on the porch. She felt so disgusted she gave him a swift kick on the leg.

"Wake up!" she yelled.

"Wal 'm gosh, Sis, I wuz just waintn' fo' yo' ter tell me whut ter do," grimaced Noah, rubbing his leg with one hand and his eyes with the other one.

"Yo' cum 'round bak' we's got sum talking' 'n plannin' ter do. Cum on now."

She turned and walked around the house passing the back door of the kitchen. Noah was right behind her.

"Noah, yo' know; paw want'd us ter hav' a good home 'n he built dis one goodern most colored folk hav'. Hits up ter us ter finish payin' fer hit. But de two ov us kain't do de work de foah ov us did so we's got ter find a 'nudder way. Do yo' kno ov enyways we's can do hit?"

"No, Sis, yo' kno' I don'. I can do whut I'se tolt ter do, but I kain't do much thinkin'," said Noah digging his toes in the sand.

For a minute she softened toward him, then started talking slowly.

"Noah, see how Pa built de kitchen 'gainst the hill. How hit touches de house here side ov de pantry 'n curves out fo' 'bout aw dozen feet 'n touches de house again. Thar whar he leveled hit ter git the rooms built."

"Yas, Roxie, I see's dat," he said very precisely.

"Do yo' think yo' cud build a room ova in dare? No need ter floor hit, hit's a secret room. Drop de roof 'n cover de 'hole thang wid sod. Den cut a door through de pantry ter enter hit. Den mak dem shelves dat turn. 'Member how we's seed one 'n dat movin' pitcher show dat time?

"Uh-huh."

"Wit shelves 'n front lak' dat no one pokin' 'round wud eva see hit wuz a door."

"Yup, I kin do dat 'n no one kin eva see eny ov hit. But why, Sis?" Noah scratched his head wonderingly.

"I kin answer dat by askin' yo' one more question. Noah, do yo' kno' how ter build 'n operate a still?"

Noah beamed, "Yas I do! I sit many a nite w' ol Ed Curlee fo' he died. I do kno' all 'bout hit, I hep him a lot."

"Good," said Roxie, "that is de way we saves our hom."

"Likker! WooEeee! I neber wud hav sech a notion as dat."

"And yo' keep yore mouth shut."

"I kin do dat too. What iffen sumbody cums 'round wantin' ter kno' what I'se doin'?"

"Jest stop yore workin' 'n cum 'round front. Iffen yo' har enybody. Noah, be shore 'n cut good strong beams 'n rafter 'n put dem real close tergether 'n use the tin Pa left in de barn ter do' de top. By puttin' de rafter close tergether de tin won't rattle iffen it get walked on 'specially ater hits nailed down 'n sodded good. Be shore 'n cut a hole in de top fo' de smoke stack 'n put plants 'round de openin'…better yet we's kin put maw's big black warsh pot ova hit 'n eva 'time yo mak' a run, I'll wash clothes. That will 'count fo' de smoke. Folk will allus drink 'n de woods air full ov people wantin' a place ter go 'n we'd gonna give 'em one."

"Yo' said hit all plain, Roxie. I know'

'zactly whut yo' want." Without another word, Noah walked to the barn, got the ax and saw and headed for the woods.

Two months later Roxie and Noah moved their parent's bed out of the big room. Tables, chairs and a bar Noah built were moved in. Roxie's Café was opened on the river front.

She was proud of Noah. He had worked long hard hours. They both had. Later Noah got Ed Curlee's still and move it in.

"No need fer hit ter go ter waste. Ed didn't need hit no mo'," stated Noah.

Roxie's Café had been open about a month when Sheriff Ply came in. he walked around looking. Roxie asked him if there was anything she could help him with. He turned and stared at her for a second.

"You got whiskey in here, gal   "Nope, kaint yo' read de sign outside, hit say Roxie Café. Dat means food, Shariff."

"I don' believe in signs, gal."

He went to the kitchen and started pushing things around and not finding anything, he went in the pantry and started moving jars.

"I thank you've gone far enough, Shariff. Pots 'n pans don' break. But thet food Maw 'n me worked hard ter can will break 'n yo' start throwin' hit 'round 'n sumbody mite find yo' floatin' down de rivah. Now, hav' yo' got a search warrent?"

"Lotta spunk, huh! I like women with spunk," he laughed, "What are yo' serving today?"

"Noah went fishin' yesterday so we's got fish, rice, fried taters 'n slaw. Got sum back sweet taters too iffen' yo' lake."

"Gimme some of all of it I'm good 'n hungry."

Roxie fixed the plate and brought it out.

"Whar yo' want hit? At de table or de counter?"

"The counter will be fine; that way I can see yo' better. Yore a good looking yellow gal."

Roxie ignored him.

"Whut do yo' won't ter drink?"

"Whiskey," said Ply.

"Water or coffee. Tak yore choice," she said.

"Aw, come on, Roxie, I'm dying for a drink."

"Yo' may be rite," she flung at him over her shoulder as she walked to the kitchen. Returning with a cup of coffee and a glass of water she set them down in front of him.

Sheriff Ply threw back his head and laughed.

Roxie walked back toward the kitchen.

"Where you going," he called after her.

"I'se a kitchen to straighten' up thanks ter yo'. Leave thirty cents on de counter w'en yo' leave."

"Aw, Roxie, I don' pay for food places I eats at. I'se a public servant."

"Yore no servant ov mine. I didn't hire yo'. Yo' eat heah, yo' pay." She stated matter of factly. "In fact, hit will suit me fine iffen yo' stay away frum heah," she added.

Startled for a second by her frankness, he gave a small laugh.

"Yassuh spunk, thet's what yo' got, filled with red hot peppered vinegar," he continued to laugh.

He looked like a toad on the stool to Roxie as she looked through the kitchen door. Short and fat with hog jowls and small greedy eyes. Always willing to take something for nothing. But if his integrity was questioned, he'd pay with an insulted air. Noah walked in and stood against the wall saying nothing just watching him. Sheriff Ply felt his integrity being questioned. He reached in his pocket and set thirty cents on the counter.

Noah walked around the counter, picked up the money and dropped it into a drawer he had built under the counter. He was very proud of that drawer and counter. He was also learning to change money. Every morning they sat down with some money and Roxie would buy things at different prices and he would give her the change. He was slowly proving that he could reach some heights of success. He walked through the kitchen and out the side door.

Noah was a big man and an honest one. He also knew when to keep quiet. He tended the still right under everybody's noses and they never knew it. Whiskey was never sold in the café. He stashed it outside and those wanting a drink would ease out to get it. Not a person, black or white, would tell they could get a drink there and no one knew where Noah got it from.

Sheriff Ply finished his dinner and called out to Roxie.

"That was shore good, gal. How 'bout yo' and me usin' one of them rooms ova thar now?" Pointing to the bedrooms they kept locked ever since they found a couple in one of them one night.

"Yore crazy man. Ain't no man goona peg me till I'se married ter him."

The sheriff did a belly laugh and hollered over his shoulder as he left, "I'll be seein' yo'."

"Yo' needn't bother," she mumbled.

Shortly after the sheriff left, Noah returned to talk to his sister.

"Roxie, Mr. Heath ask me ter take Miz

Curlee ter de train stashun ter fetch her granson."

Later Noah came walking around the corner of the house with a little boy in tow.

"Roxie, dis here is Seth Kirby."

As she walked over to the four or five year old youth she reached out to rumple his curly hair and said, "Hello Seth, I here you hav' come ter live with your granmaw."

"Yassum, I s'pose 'cause nobody else wants me."

He mopped his forehead with the tail of his over-sized shirt.

"Poor little fellow," she thought as she gathered his frail little body in her arms.

*****

The church door opened and the congregation filed out. Reverend Murray walked to the door and shook hands with the people as they left the building.

Charity Murray closed the piano and joined those lingering outside. "It's such a lovely day to be outside. I see the children are all enjoying it," she remarked to no one in particular as she watched the running and playing among the trees. One bunch of boys were at the corner of the church on their knees shooting marbles.

"Miles," called Lukatie. "Get off your knees. Just look at the knees of your knickers."

He put his chubby hands on the ground pushing himself up. Once on his feet, he started pulling at the seat of his pants.

"What's wrong with you, Miles? Honey, stop pulling at the seat of your knickers."

"I can', Mama, I got itches in it," he

whimpered. His little face turned up to look her straight in the eye.

Lukatie brushed the sand from his hands and knees with her handkerchief to hide her frustration.

"Come, your father's waiting for us."

As the last wagon load left the church yard, Charity turned to her husband. They walked along silently to the parsonage at the back of the church. Folk used to invite them home for Sunday dinner when they first came to Campton, but after the four children had been born in rapid succession the invitations had dropped off.

"Robert, why don't we have a big dinner spread one Sunday after church?" Not waiting for an answer she went on. "The men could put up tables on Saturday. There would be no rushing home, and, of course, no one would expect us to bring a basket of food."

"Oh, I see my wife is after a free meal."

She smiled showing her uneven teeth. "But, Robert, it's spring and so nice to be outside."

"Then why don't you get out and plant a garden and flowers like the other women do." Looking at Charity's dejected expression, he laughed.

"I'll put it to a vote next Sunday and see if they'd all like to."

"Thank you, Robert. I'm sure they will." She was positive that if the preacher suggested it they would.

The church was about a mile from town and farmers as far as ten miles away came there to worship. The church was on an acre of land given by Em's grandfather with a clause written in the deed that if the church was ever discontinued the land reverted back to the Carroll property.

The Carroll land had nearly three miles of

road frontage and the land ran all the way to the river. A cart path which was the boundary line between the Carroll and the Heath land had been cut through the woods to the river.

Across the road from the Carroll property was the Stewart Henderson land. Stewart always wished he had the river bordering his property as Em did, although he could go and come to the river as much and as often as he chose. Stewart felt lucky that he still had the beautiful old plantation house.

Stewart had often offered to help his friend Em. They grew up together and attended the same college. He also knew from the day that Em had come home and introduced Lukatie as his wife that he had to find a wife exactly like her or he'd never marry. She was the most desirable woman he had ever seen. His initial comment as he took her hand and smiled into her eyes was, "Now, why didn't I see you first?"

At the market Stewart's produce would sell while Em's, just as fresh and good as his, just sat there. It seemed that buyers thought that living in the big house made his produce better. As a result, Stewart got richer while Em sold only a little and got poorer.

It hurt Stewart to see Lukatie doing without, living in poverty, and having one child after another. He guessed that it would have been appropriate if he and not Em was the father. Being the godfather of Em's children brought no great sense of personal satisfaction.

The Carrolls had too damn much pride to let him help. When Em took the produce back from the market, Lukatie had to work that much harder to can it. She couldn't stand to see anything wasted. A few times when Em had been sick he had taken the produce from both properties and had sold the entire load. Today had been such a day.

"What in hell did you do, buy it yourself?" asked Em.

"No, I didn't...I wouldn't do that, Em."

"I know. I understand exactly. But I don't know what to do about it." His friend and neighbor had succeeded where he had failed.

"Let me help," volunteered Stewart.

"No. We'll manage, but thanks for the offer."

"Then I'll leave so you can rest. Hurry and get well." He placed Em's money on the center table. At the door he turned.

"All right if I go down and take a swim? It was a hot ride to town and back."

"You know it is. You also know you don't have to ask. Better take a swimsuit. Lukatie is down there with the children."

Stewart felt happy as he rode down the path to the river with thoughts of swimming with Lukatie.

The swimming hole was a cove recessed in the river. Many years ago, the Carrolls had cleaned it by taking out all the cypress trees. The water there was clear and beautiful.

He found Lukatie with the children gathered around her sitting at the edge of the water gazing up in a tree.

"Oh! Uncle Stewart, you frightened our robin away." cried out Meda.

"I'm sorry, honey, maybe if we're quiet he will come back," Stewart said as he stepped down from the buggy. He took his swimsuit and went into the hut to change.

As he came from the hut, Meda greeted him with a great splash of water.

"Welcome to splash down," laughed Lukatie.

Looking at Lukatie and laughing happily, he

grabbed Meda and throwing her on his back swam out into the river and back. He loved every minute of it and he loved this family. Often he came down and swam with them on Saturday and Sunday afternoons during the summer months. But Em had always been there.

"This is nice," he said to Lukatie. He thought to himself. "Em has almost everything, at least the things that really count."

Lukatie felt the envy in his voice and thought, "He is rich and has everything but a wife and children." The words he had spoken when he first met her invaded her mind. Silently and somewhat guiltily she looked at him. He was handsome in a rugged sort of way. His cheekbones were high, face a little broad with deep set blue-gray eyes, black hair and thick black eyebrows and lashes. She wondered if there might be a little Indian blood somewhere in the past. He was six feet tall with broad shoulders and a muscular body.

"Stewart, you should get married, you enjoy children so much. You need a family to spoil."

"I doubt that I ever will marry," replied Stewart. He wanted to add, "since I can't have you." But feeling thankful for the friendship they had he felt he had better not say more.

"This is so cool and refreshing I hate to end it, but I have to get back to Em. He may need something."

"He was fine when I came by."

"It has been a while now so I'd better go, Stewart. Come on girls, let's get dressed."

They went into the hut that had been built many years ago for the very purpose it was now being used. They usually just left their suits hanging there ready for the next swim. The boys begged to stay with Uncle Stewart. He agreed saying he'd bring them up with him later.

"Have a good swim?" Em asked her as they came in.

"Yes, it was much cooler than here at the house. The boys are coming later with Stewart. It's still springtime and already too hot. If this is any criterion, what will summer be like?"

"Hot, I guess, it usually is. I think I'm getting well, I'm sure hungry," Em laughed.

A week later Em told Lukatie he had heard that Mr. Pierce had some hogs soon to farrow that he wanted to sell. "Thought I'd go over and buy a couple." As he hitched "No Name" to the cart, Benjamin and Miles came from the house and asked where he was going.

"I'm going over to Mr. Pierce's to buy some hogs."

"May we go with you, Papa?" they asked in unison.

"I suppose so if your mother doesn't need you."

Mr. Pierce was in the yard when they rode up.

"I hear you have some hogs for sale."

"Yep, shore do. Cum I'll show dem ter yo' 'n yo' kin decide iffen yo' want 'em or not."

Em and the boys looked at the hogs and pointed to two of them. "Mr. Pierce, we'll take those two."

After some dickering about price, Em paid for the two hogs.

"Thank yo'," said Mr. Pierce as he put the money in the bib of his overalls pocket and walked away.

"Just a minute, Mr. Pierce, how am I supposed to load these hogs?"

The old man turned, hooked his thumbs in his overalls and spit.

"Wal now, thet's yore problem. Thar're your hogs." He turned and walked away.

"Damn old smart ass. Boys, get a rope from the cart." They threw a noose around one of the hog's neck.

"Atta boy, Papa, you got one of them," shouted Miles.

The hog jerked, twisting the rope around Em's leg throwing him in the mud, the hog ran pulling Em through the mud and manure. When he finally got the hog stopped all you could see was Em's nose protruding out of his mud-plastered face. The screaming and laughter of the boys as they tried to help prompted the pig to greater efforts. Finally, they got the pig tied and into the wagon. The boys grabbed another rope and started chasing the other pig. Em, seeing the direction the pig was going and thinking that he could head it off, raced up the slope only to have the pig run between his legs throwing him right back into the mud and manure.

"You damn cantankerous four legged old bastard," he yelled.

The more he wiped his face with his hands and shirt sleeves the worse his face was.

Miles and Benjamin had never heard their father use foul language. This time there was no laughing. Each handed him the big bandanas they had in their hip pockets.

When they reached the road leading to the river by Roxie's Café, Em turned and headed straight for the water. Noah was standing in the yard laughing at a bunch of negro boys trying to get a mule into the water to baptize him.

"Cum on yo' damn mule, git in har. Yo' needs baptiz'n. Us wants ter mak' a chritian outa yo'."

They pulled and tugged but couldn't force

the mule into the water. They finally gave up and released the harried animal, defeated.

"Go on! Git yo' stinkin' ol' mule. Won't let we'en baptize yo', yo' kin just go ter hell."

Noah's nostirls began to flare as he slowly turned his head looking at Em still sitting in the wago.

"Dem is de stinkin'est hogs I'se eber laid eyes on."

"They aren't the only thing that smells," laughed Em beginning to see the humor of the situation as he stood there plastered with mud and manure dropping out of his ears, nose and eyebrows. He walked down to the river and waded in clothes and all washing off as good as he could.

When he got home, Lukatie walked out on the porch. "I see you got the hogs. Looks like they are about ready to drop." The smile that was on her face froze as her gaze went to Em.

"Pew! What an odor!"

Lucinda stopped swinging Meda and they walked over to the wagon.

"Papa, you stink!" they said wrinkling their noses.

"Well, since I've been drug through mud and manure in a pig pen and plastered with it, I've every g-gosh damn right to stink."

"Em!" exclaimed Lukatie.

The boys were both trying to tell Lukatie what had happened but couldn't speak for giggling.

"You whippersnappers. Do your laughing later and get to that pump bench and pump me a tub of water to wash in. Then let off steam by pumping another tub full to soak these clothes in. Now get!" snorted Em.

They boys looked at each other and started

a giggling fit that grew into gales of hysterical laughter. Em picked up a pan of dirty water from the wash shelf and threw it at them missing them as they dodged it and ran to the pump bench.

Lukatie, laughing inwardly went into the kitchen to prepare dinner. She picked up a jar of peas and beets to add to the leftovers and went over to the window and looked toward the forest as the food was warming. With all that timber, why do we have to live like this, she wondered. Em could build a dozen houses and never miss a tree. Or would he? She believed he had counted every one of them. To Lukatie, it was just a forest doing no one any good.

*****

The first time Kinyon and Jane came to stay for a weekend, Lukatie was on pins and needles. Lukatie fixed their bedroom for Kinyon and Jane to sleep in. Lukatie then slept with the girls and Em slept with the boys.

Rich Jane had taken it all in stride. She was amused at the way the Negroes and neighbors had gasped at their new Rolls Royce when they drove up in the yard. It was blue with wire wheels and had a spare mounted on the side. The day was warm so they had folded back the top. They wore dusters to protect their clothes and Jane had a scarf tied under her chin to hold her hat on.

"That is a horseless carriage," said Andrew Jackson Smith knowingly as the other negroes had gathered around. They all looked at him with respect that he should know so much.

"Yep," he spit tobacco juice out of the side of his mouth. "Saw two or three wilst I wuz gon' on vacation," he said as he enjoyed his new-found popularity.

Kinyon took a few minutes to speak to all the negroes and shook hands with most of them.

Miles ran through the house calling, "Mama, Papa, they're here." The brothers shook hands both talking at once. Lukatie stepped forward extending her hands which Jane took warmly.

"I'm Lukatie and, of course, you're Jane. Do come in. You must be tired after motoring down. I know the roads aren't very good and so dusty." Jane was impressed with Lukatie's beauty, warmth and charm. Jane liked her and quickly sensed that she would always make the best of any situation.

Kinyon walked over to Lukatie and took both of her hands in his. "It's a pleasure at last to meet my brother's wife."

"And I to meet you and Jane," she smiled.

Jane thought to herself that if the time ever came that she had to live like this she could prove equal to this woman. She had heard so much about Lukatie from Em on his visits and was amazed at the way Lukatie's personality had imposed itself on the atmosphere around the house.

Jane was taken across the road to where the old plantation house had once stood. She was awed by the beauty of the surroundings. The curved drive was kept clean. All that it needed was to rebuild the big house. She could vision the house in all its splendor and could imagine elegant carriages drawn with the beautiful matching horses as the wealthy plantation owners came calling.

Jane said to Kinyon as they strolled away from the others. "Just look at all the beautiful azalea bushes, the sturdy magnolia trees and camelias. It would take so little to get the grounds in condition again. Kinyon, could we…?" Kinyon reading her line of thought quickly stopped her.

"No! We couldn't. This is Em's place. If anything is to be done, it has to be his idea and his doing it."

"How can a man with his education not see his surroundings. Is it possible he can shutter all the ugliness out of the mind and eyes and be satisfied?" she asked wryly looking toward the house.

"Jane, we each have to solve our own problems, but we must first realize that they exist. In the meantime, it won't hurt you to experience how the other half lives. I lived most of my life here."

"I'm not complaining, Kinyon," replied Jane with the rebuff showing in her voice. "I don't have to live here. I just feel sorry for a woman like Lukatie. I like her."

"I'm sorry, dear, that was uncalled for. I shouldn't have spoken like that. Guess I still have a feeling for the old place." Changing the subject, he said, "Say, did you notice the long log building way over there in back of where the manor once stood? It's really in better condition than any other building on the place."

"Yes, I took it to be the old slave quarters."

"Right. Some smaller buildings are gone. It's used for storing the cotton now. After lunch I'd like to take you down to the river. You might like to go swimming."

"Sorry, Kinyon, I didn't bring our suits," she said happily. Glad of a legitimate excuse not to go. She certainly didn't want to go in an old river swimming hole. They had always gone to the seashore.

"Oh, yes, you did. I put them in the bag. You just wait. You're in for a treat."

Jane was even more astonished when she saw what Kinyon had carelessly called the old swimming hole. She noticed the graceful slant of the hill on the right as they approached the cove. What a beautiful setting to build a summer home, she thought. Since Benjamin, Lucinda, Miles and Em were along she said nothing.

Lukatie stayed at home needing rest more than a swim. Moreover, she had supper to think about.

Jane thoroughly enjoyed the refreshing swim and the good-natured bantering that accompanied it.

Kinyon and Jane left the next morning after breakfast. In noisy confusion they drove away in a whirl with Jane holding on to her hat even though it was securely tied with a scarf under her chin.

After they left, Lukatie went into the house to restore the living conditions to their natural state. She beat out the imprint left by the bodies of Jane and Kinyon in the feather bed, pounding with all her might and fluffed out the right places. As she put on clean sheets she smiled with amusement as she remembered Jane's surprise and delight at the bright colored sheets and pillowcases on the bed.

"Who but you, Lukatie, would have ever thought to make colored sheets and cases. They really make the room cheerful. People have always thought they could only be white. I shall try it and match my spreads and drapes," Jane had stated.

The week before Kinyon and Jane had come, Lukatie had taken her egg money and bought paint for the inside of the house. She worked hard to get the rooms painted, blue to match the blue flowers in the sheets in their room. Yellow in the girls' room and green in the boys' room. The living room was white. She knew it would soon flake off but for now it looked much better. At least it had permeated the cracks in the ceiling and either subdued or chase out the rats in the loft. The musty smell had disappeared, but she knew it was only a matter of time before it returned.

Lukatie looked out of the window toward the spot where the great manor had once stood. An early morning mist had settled over the land making the trees, azaleas and camelia bushes look unreal. She sat down as she looked and could imagine herself swimming through the mist taking swift smooth strokes with her hair floating behind her. Swimming on, looking, searching, rushing, wishing she could make it a reality. That it would be there this time. The big house. Her Blue Bird trimmed in white.

There were a million dreams within the all-embracing one. But dreams aren't real. There is the gloominess of awakening. The knock at the door bought her back to reality. It was little Seth Kirby. He had only been four years old when Noah had brought the little orphaned boy home to Roxie. Seth was nearly white although his parents and grandparents had been relegated to the negro community. He was mulatto but one could hardly tell.

"Miz Carroll," he gasped out of breath. "Mistuh Brown say kin yo' cum quick. Hit's Miz Brown's time. Whut eber that it."

"Hurry on back and tell them I'm coming and for Chuncy to have plenty of hot water ready."

"He don' got de watah biling, Miz Carroll."

"Then you just run on home. I believe you

have helped enough."

"Yassum," replied Seth, shaking his head and mumbling as he walked off, "Whut I don' hep do?"

As Lukatie approached the house she could hear the groans of Lura who was about to give birth to her fourth child. "Lura is too frail to be having children," thought Lukatie. "It is hard enough on the healthy ones. She should have a doctor."

Chuncy met her at the door. "She mity uncomfo'table, Miz Carroll."

"I'm sure she is, Chuncy." She walked over to the bed and took Lura by the hand smiling down at her.

"You're going to be all right," hoped Lukatie. "Just bear down to the pain."

Lura knew Lukatie was there and was glad. But some awesome inertia was in her making her reserve all strength to fight for deliverance of the tiny unseen human she knew to be within her. She responded only to pain and had no will to speak.

"Bear down to the pain, Lura, like you were constipated."

This wasn't as easy as the other three had been. She felt some invisible thread was holding the baby back. If the thread would only break. She felt strange, nearly unconscious until another pain ripped through her body and snatched her back.

"Please let go. Oh, God, let go," she pleaded silently, "break the string, please." The pain lessened and she floated away on a big cloud. She would float up to the mountain top. She had never seen a mountain. She had only heard how near heaven they were. Maybe her cloud would take her that near to heaven. "Oh, no, there is the children and Chuncy. I have to stay here to care for them. I can't fail them now."

Lukatie felt her brow and put a cold cloth on her forehead.

Malitha Casteen and Lula Golden came quietly into the house and urged Chuncy to go outside while they aided Lukatie who was grateful to have their help.

"This is woman's work," said Lula.

"Preciate yawl comin'," Chuncy said as he left the room to sit on the steps.

Lukatie let them relieve her while she guided the deliverance. Like the links of ancestors that chains one generation to another so the links of pain were welded together growing longer and longer until finally Lura could rest as one great pain came then subsided.

It was the next day before Lura opened her eyes. The bright sunshine made her close them quickly. She felt thin, so thin and weak, and could feel a cool wet cloth being placed on her brow. She tried opening her eyes again.

"Chuncy," she called, but her voice was just a weak whisper.

"Praise b'ter Gawd," with tears in his eyes he took Lura's small frail hand in his. "Praise be ter Gawd."

"Looks like the fever has broken," said Lukatie.

"Yassum, praise be ter Gawd," repeated Chuncy.

"M' baby, I'se had m'baby; won' sumone tell me what m'baby is?"

"Yo' baby's rite heah," said Malitha. "I'se holdin' hit."

"Boy or gal?" Lura asked weakly.

"A lovely girl," smiled Lukatie as she held the tiny wrinkled brown baby so Lura could see her. Lura's weak smile was reward enough for the three women who had taken turn fighting for her life.

Lura slept again breathing regular and normal. The next morning she awoke feeling a little stronger. With the passing of each day a degree of strength returned.

"We's hav' ter name our girl, Chuncy. She's foar day's ol' now 'n with no name. Tain't rite. We's kain't je' baby all her life. I shore want's her ter hav' a name whut's fitten fer de queen she gwine ter b'." beamed Lura.

"Dat's 'zactly whut she gotta hav'...a name wit' sum sance ter hit." agreed Chuncy. "Seem lak I wuz sorta favorin' de name of Kate fo' Miz Lukatie Carroll seein' as how withouter her hep yo'ens mite," Chuncy choked. "Well, drat hit yo' ens still with me. Praise be ter Gawd."

"Wal, den she gwine hav' thet name iffen dat's whut yo' wonts. But whe gwine hav' a nodder one in front ov hit. I names her Winfred Kate iffen dats all right wit yo'. We's kin call her Winnie. Hit sounded kinda lak de winner she gwine b' 'n git a edycation 'n mount ter sumpin."

With a piece of lean back bone in her hand, Lukatie covered the pork barrel, locked the smoke house door and went to the house. She boiled the salt out of the meat, drained off the brine and added fresh water. When the meat was tender, she thickened the broth with corn meal. Then she beat an egg, adding a little sugar and vanilla which she poured into a glass of milk. She took them over to Lura and urged her to eat.

"I don' feel lak I'se kin eat a bit. I'se got so much miseration insides me. Iffen I eats I mite puke hit outen me," moaned Lura.

"I don't think this broth will make you sick. Just eat a little now and in two or three hours take a little more. You have to gain strength to care for the baby."

"When you need milk for the baby, send Eliza for it, and if you need anything else or me, send one of the boys. Now, Chuncy, feed her while it's warm or do you want me to do it?" asked Lukatie.

"I'se glad ter do hit. I mite hav' ter whup her ter git her ter eat, but I'd fo' sartin lay hit ter her iffen she don'."

Under Chuncy's loving scolding's she grew stronger and her determination that Winnie should have a better life grew with her strength.

"Miz Carroll, we's named de baby 'n sho' hopes yo' won' mind. But noin' yo' 'n preciat'n yo' hep, we's 'thout as hot us'd name our baby, Winifred Kate."

The surprise showed on Lukatie's face. "I'm touched. I really am. Thank you so much for giving your baby a part of my name." Her eyes began to feel moist and she didn't want to let go in front of these people who looked to her for strength. "If there's nothing else I can do now, I'll go tend to the pot of lye soap I'm making. It will need stirring."

"We's all right now, Miz Carroll."

They watched her go, but Lura and Chuncy had seen and understood.

Walking across the field toward home, Lukatie repeated the baby's name. "Winifred Kate." She had never really liked her own name. Yet Winifred Kate did sound kind of nice.

Lura remarked to Chuncy as she watched Lukatie through the window. "Thet woman is a pure ol' evaday saint. Whut mak' no pufession outen doin' good deeds. All de time tryin' ter mak' udder folk lives a mite better. Shore fitten ter b' an angel. Shore is."

Lula and Malitha dropped by to see Lura. "How is Lura holdin' out, Chuncy?" asked Malitha.

"Wal, she cranked 'erself up 'n holdin' out purtty good." They laughed as they entered the room and found Lura propped up in bed nursing Winnie.

"She full up ladies, but she still yet won'ts ter hang on ter de ninny, de precious lamb."

"Ain't dey all lak' dat?" said Lula.

"Has she opened her eyes yet?" asked Malitha.

"No, I magin de lite still hurts her little eyes."

"Fo' long she'll be gawkin' et eva thang 'n yo'll b'wishin she'd close dem eyes 'n go ter sleep." said Lula.

"Shore b' de truf," put in Malitha.

They decided they better not tire Lura out, said their goodbyes, and left.

*****

On a warm July Sunday, Stewart Henderson drove down to pick up William H. Heath for church. William's wizened face belied the fact that the older man was very agile and mentally alert. His bald head and beaked nose gave him an owlish appearance. William didn't go to church for religious purposes. There just wasn't anything else to do. He did enjoy the association of the people making him very assiduous in attendance. Neither was he an old-world wizard or he'd never have allowed the colored folk on his plantation the chance to buy his land. A fair-thinking man, he felt they had every damn right in this cursed world to it.

He chuckled as he thought of the fight he,

Em and Stewart had put up to get a school for the colored. They felt empathy for their problems. Em had struck out for better schools for all children, black and white.

William could see Em now as he stood there and spoke for equal and quality education. He had said, "I think it's time for members of the school board to change their thinking, act big in the field of education. Our children need and deserve better schools they should have the security of better education. There is no reason why we can't carry on as good an educational program here as they do in large cities. If we want a better world to live in then we have to change and help out children to improve by getting them better schools and teachers."

"Well," Mr. Williams had interrupted, "I don't mind going along with doing all I can for our children; but the colored, that's what you're suggesting, isn't it, Em?"

Em had spoken quietly. "It seems improbable that you men have such shortsighted vision that you can't see the problems facing us here. These people have to learn and it's an injustice to not permit them to do so. We should help these people develop themselves. They need pride in themselves. It would be cruel to limit their world to this small part they are in. I don't think we should hold them back; in the long run the price might be too heavy to pay."

"It disturbs me that we are supposed to be leaders of education, yet we seem to be controlling it for the white only," William Heath had interjected. "No wonder the young colored are restless and filled with cynicism. All they can see ahead for themselves is hardships like their parents have had."

"But, it could give them a false view of

their future," Mr. Williams had interrupted. "Supposed after they get the education no one will give them a job?"

"You could be right especially around here, but they can go north and find plenty of jobs. Whether they do or not, they are like other young people. They want to learn, to get ahead and should be given the chance and find the joy of reading a good book. I want my children to have natural training, read books and novels and study anything that will add fire to their imagination. I want them to know about the world, to feel untrammeled and free to expand. And all others should have the same opportunity. I did say all," Em had said emphatically.

Not to be out done, Mr. Williams had said, "You know those that left lived in the state of poverty that was downright cruel and shocking."

"That's just what I'm getting at," Em had answered. "They had no education so they couldn't find work and get jobs. The old negroes know and accept the fact that education had passed them by, but they want it for their children, and I for one don't blame them."

"Well, at least they are happy," Mr. Hart had spoken. "They wouldn't know what to do with anything if they had it. They don't want anything else."

Stewart had listened quietly. "I'm just fool enough to believe God intended for everyone to have an education, Mr. Hart. If they are so happy, why don't their faces show it. They certainly don't express the joys of living."

"Aw, they're all just a bunch of melanous clouts," Mr. Williams had sourly interjected.

"I haven't wanted to get personal," Stewart had said, "but those clouts as you call them have broken their backs and spirit, I might add, giving you a soft life."

"What!" Mr. Williams had responded. "Who had a softer life than you! You surely work negroes."

"Yes, I do. I also pay them a living wage."

"Dear Mr. Stewart! I, too, pay my negro workers." Mr. Williams had replied testily.

"You've asked for this, Mr. Williams. Why are they never out of debt to you? I often hear my negros speak of your workers never being out of debt to you, and that's why they can't leave your co-called employment."

While Mr. Williams had sputtered, Mr. Heath had spoken. "How do you expect to condition them to life's good things if you don't show them the way. Times are changing and they will be lost by the time they become adults without help. We must understand this changing world we live in. We think because we're stuck off here in one little corner there isn't a big wide world out there that is progressing. The question is, can we progress with it or sit here and go backwards. Nothing is permanent. There is only advancement, change and growth and we must grow with it."

"Just where will we be if the negroes up and leave us," Mr. Williams had exploded.

"Now that's a truly selfish question," Em had said stoutly. "We won't have that problem during our life-time. Where one leaves there are always two to take his place. I still say we're guilty of blind apathy and concern when we fail to do all that's possible to better educate all children. We cannot be indifferent to their needs. Let's hope we can rectify the mistakes of our ancestors instead of living in their rut."

"Educate them and they will become unruly, ungovernable and arrogant. They will resist us on every count. You'll never keep them on the farm to work for us," Mr. Williams had blurted out trying to have the last say.

Em had completely ignored him and left the meeting followed by Mr. Heath and Stewart.

The board had voted for a new school for the white children and to renovate and add rooms to the present school for the black children.

Driving into the church yard, Stewart remarked to William, "You certainly have been quiet on the way over."

William smiled and answered, "I was rehashing our battle to get the school for the negroes. Now you'd think the whole idea was the school board's."

"The important thing is they got a better school. I'm sorry to say one or two on my place have said they aren't going, but I'll talk to them. I guess Mr. Williams will never speak to us again," chuckled Stewart, "as if I give a damn."

"I'm in complete agreement." grinned William.

"You know Campton is a town run by a pile of near-sighted jerks whose greed has kept outside industries away. What might have been one of the largest cities in the state is not much more than a fly speck on a map."

They entered the church and sat down on a bench near the back where it was most crowded. Preacher Murray came in and stood behind the pulpit, while his wife, Charity, took her place at the antiquated organ. He stood there silently looking over the congregation, and at the empty front rows until they became fidgety wondering what was wrong this morning. Finally, he spoke with a long drawl.

"Brothern and Sisters in the name of the Lord," he said looking first to the right then to the left then at the door as Em and his family entered. Seeing the back full, they walked to the front and sat down.

"Well, now," prefacing everything he says, "Here is one family not afraid of God. They didn't hide in the back row. If you out there aren't afraid of God then move quietly to the front as we stand a sing the opening hymn."

While they sang, the congregation slowly moved filling the front seats. Stewart wasn't about to move since he was sitting where he had a good view of Lukatie sitting on the end of the aisle.

Preacher Murray was saying something about "Your most powerful weapon is your moral and spiritual strength," as Stewart's mind drifted over to Lukatie. He began to amuse himself by mentally taking off each piece of her clothing and redressing her in all the finery he'd like to see her wear. A satisfied smile played at the corner of his mouth as he envisioned each piece of clothing being removed. His audible sigh resulted in a punch in the ribs from William's elbow. Next, he dressed her as a can-can girl. Nope, he was smiling broadly to himself, she's too much the lady for kicking up her heels. His eyes wandered over to Charity. He'd try it on her. As his mind took off her clothes and he saw bulges around her middle and the fatter ass she kept hid under her full long skirts. He redressed her so fast he swore she turned on the organ stool and looked straight at him. It was all he could do not to laugh out loud. With some effort Stewart brought his mind back to the preacher who was saying, "Shall we take a vote on it?"

"Why in hell can't I keep my mind where it's supposed to be," thought Stewart. "So I'd know what I'm supposed to vote on."

"Now, then, all who want the picnic next

Sunday after church out in the yard raise your right hand."

Stewart was the only one to raise his hand. Red crept up his neck and flooded his face, just like oil up a lamp wick. "When I goof it, I go all the way," he thought.

"Ahem! Well, next, all who want the picnic and the church to be at the Carroll swimming hole, raise your right hand." All hands went up.

"That's where it will be then. We'll all bring our picnic baskets and go to the riverbank at the regular church time. If the thunder is roaring, we'll wait until the next Sunday."

As usual, the preacher stood at the door shaking hands with each one as they left. As he shook Stewart's hand, he remarked, "Glad you enjoyed the sermon today, Mr. Henderson."

"Yes, yes, very good," mumbled Stewart as he hurried away to his car, followed closely by a laughing William.

"That was sure a long sermon," said William still laughing.

"Oh, yes, but if I come, I want to get my fill."

"I do too but I don't want to be gorged. By the way, where were you this morning, Stewart?"

"Just being imaginative, William. Trying a few new approaches and ideas. Some of them pretty damn good, too." He answered with a propitious smile his eyes brightening.

"Oh, this picnic is going to be an austere event," laughed William.

"At least we should hope to enjoy a modicum of pleasure."

"The food should be good, and you, Stewart, can watch Lukatie in a swimsuit." At Stewart's startled expression, he added, "Don't look so surprised. I've known for years how you felt about her."

"I'd fight tooth and nail for her if I thought there was a chance, but there isn't. Em is her whole life. I love him too or I'd do my damnedest to get her." He stopped the car in front of William's house and said, "This, my friend, is where you get off."

"At least you're honest about it," said William as he stepped from the car.

The day of the picnic dawned clear with soft warm breezes. The early morning fog already banished by the sun's rays.

"I'm glad we won't sit in the hot church today. It will be much cooler at the river," Lukatie said to Em as she packed the picnic lunch.

"It will be a nice change," said Em as he helped Lucinda clear the table of the breakfast dishes.

Carts, surreys, buggies and wagons drew up among the trees on the riverbank.

The hum of voices filled the air, causing the animals of the forest to scamper off for quieter territories, protection and the chance to search for food unhampered.

Blankets were spread on the ground for women and children to sit on while men leaned against trees as Preacher Murray stepped up on a stump to deliver his sermon.

Baskets of food brought from the wagons soon covered the planks supported by saw-horses as make-shift tables.

She's so gentle, prim and kind, thought Em, as he watched Lukatie unpack their lunch. Unknown to him similar thoughts were also running through Stewart's mind as he took the large cooler of lemonade from his buggy and brought it over to the end of the table where Lukatie and Em had placed their food on the table.

"My feeble attempt at doing something to contribute to the dinner," he laughed.

Lukatie laughed also as she raised the lid off the cooler. "Looks delicious," she stated as she viewed the ice and lemon rind floating on top.

"Look, Em."

"Sure looks refreshing like a real thirst quencher. I'm ready for a glass right now."

Preacher Murray blessed the food so they could partake of the bounties of life placed before them.

*****

Looking at the pan of figs she had just finished picking, Lukatie said, "I've come to one conclusion."

"About what?" asked Em.

Setting the pan on the table, she scratched her arms vigorously, "Those fig leaves itch me to death. God really meant to punish Eve when she gave Adam that apple and he dressed her in fig leaves."

Lukatie had Lucinda under the eaves of the house getting jars out to be cleaned for canning.

"There's a black snake under here, Mama!"

"You know very well it won't hurt you. Just leave it alone and get the jars. It's after rats."

"How many jars you want, Mama?"

"All there are. We will be needing them so you may as well get them out."

"Oh, goodness, damn," groaned Lucinda. "I'll be here all day."

"What, dear, I can't hear you."

"I said I'll get them all."

Lukatie turned when she heard running feet. Hulda Casteen came up with tears streaking down her face.

"Oh, Miz Carroll," she cried. "Maw sent me ter fetch yo'. We'ens just found Paw side of de path 'n de bak' woods ter Roxie's Café. He was stone drunk 'n hit look lak' a wood rat et his lag plum off. He jes' a mo'nin."

"Run on back and tell your mama I'm coming."

Lukatie called Em from the barn and told him what had happened.

"He must have drunk so fast that he put himself in a trance," Em stated. "To let a thing like that happen is unbelievable."

"Better send Benjamin down to Stewart's and ask him to phone Dr. Wesson to come out here."

Benjamin heard and jumped on No Name riding him bareback.

When they reached the wooded area every negro on the place was standing around gawking. Rats scuttled past their feet hiding in the roots of trees waiting to get at Alonza's leg again. Thankful threw bark at them and cursed. "The damn sons of bitches! Oh, sorry, Miz Carroll." He apologized as Lukatie and Em walked up.

They turned with an instinctive surge as one big body toward Em and Lukatie for guidance.

"Well," exploded Em. "Are you going to let him lay there all day? You gawking bunch of..." He caught Lukatie's eye and stopped short. "Pick him up and take him home." He turned to Malitha and said, "Stop that blubbering, sniveling and wringing your hands and get on home and clean the table off to put him on. Put a clean sheet on it and get plenty of hot water on. Dr. Wesson will soon be here."

"Good God," exclaimed the doctor when he

saw Alonza's leg.

"He was a mo'nin 'n dey giv him more likker 'n he pass out." groaned Malitha.

"Malitha, I suppose you realize this leg will have to come off."

"Yassuh, I allows as how hit mite. Oh, lawsy." she moaned. "Do whut yo' kin ter hep him, Doctor."

"Can you assist me, Mrs. Carroll? It won't be pleasant."

"I'll do my best, Doctor Wesson." "Dear Lord, give me strength," prayed Lukatie. "I don't mind helping to bring your little ones into the world, but to help maim one of them for the rest of his life is more than I feel I can bear."

"Em will you get everyone out? Especially Malitha, it will be too painful for her to watch."

When they were all out Doctor Wesson turned to Lukatie. "Mrs. Carroll, he is still out cold. I don't know if it's from the liquor he drank or the shock. I'm going to give him a tetanus shot. You stand by with the anesthetic and assist when you can but watch his face and if he starts to come to, give him the chloroform. He's out so cold I might be able to do this without giving him anything. If I can he won't be as sick. This is the worst dipsomania case I ever saw."

The doctor's hands were fast and sure. Lukatie handed him his instruments as he called for them keeping her eyes on Alonza's face as much as possible. He didn't flinch once. The Doctor was bandaging the stub just below the knee when he moaned once and blacked out again.

"That does it." he stated. "Mrs. Carroll, will you ask a couple of the men to come in and move him to his bed. Tell Malitha to come in. I'll give her instructions. You look kind of pale. You better stay out there. I'll finish up in here."

Lukatie smiled. "It's just the sadness of losing a leg, Dr. Wesson. I'm fine. I've seen worse."

"I'll hire you anytime you say the word."

"Thank you, Doctor, but Em wants me to stay home with the children. I'll tell them to come in."

Once outside she also told Malitha she was going on home, but if she needed her to send someone.

Walking home beside Em she couldn't help thinking of the time she could work at the hospital and get good pay for what she just did free. Em wouldn't hear of it. He didn't want his wife working for pay. No, blame it all, he'd rather I'd kill myself for nothing. I wouldn't think of taking pay for things like this. But working regularly at the hospital would be different.

Em, walking quietly along, watched Lukatie out of the corner of his eyes. She looked tired. "She works so hard for other people. Her hands are always busy bringing goodness and comfort to the sick that need her service," he thought proudly, "my wife."

Lukatie broke the silence as they passed Thankful's house. "That was a terrible thing to happen to Alonza. It will be rough on him when he sobers up and realizes what has happened. I just hope he doesn't get a fever. Plagues have started from rats."

"I don't think he will get the plague; he's too preserved in alcohol to catch anything. He was foolish to drink so much. He sure traveled the route to nothingness." He shook his head, the thought was blinding in its reality. "To have a leg taken off and not even need chloroform, beats all."

The old man was sitting on the porch drowsing in the past. His craggy face rousing occasionally on a snore. He awoke fully when he heard Lukatie and Em talking. "Howdy, Mistuh Em, Miz Carroll, nice cool day hain't hit?"

"Fine and dandy," replied Em. "How are you today, old man?"

"Mistuh Mathias," he corrected, "I'se rite pert t'day."

"That's nice to hear." said Lukatie. "I'd better go on to the house and see if Lucinda got all those jars out."

"She's rather tired," Em said to the old man as Lukatie walked on. "Has anyone come by and told you about Alonza?"

"Nope, whut dat man don' now?"

"He just got so stoned last night he passed out on the path to Roxie's Café. That is where he was found this morning with a leg nearly eaten off by rats."

"I reckon hit'll heal 'n he'll fill his gullet full ov rot gut ag'in'."

"No, the doctor had to remove his leg."

"Oh, Lawdy, jes' as shore as termorrow is terday w'en hit gits heah, he be at that corn squeezings again, Mistuh Em. I use ter tak' a nip. Got nothin' ag'in takin' a nip fer de stomach sake. But gittin' stupefied is jes' too much. Yassuh, too much."

Em agreed adding that so many make the mistake of thinking they can drink enough to satisfy the sense. "Liquor isn't the answer and the sooner they find it out the better. I wonder what Alonza will do or say when he comes to and finds his leg gone."

"Go git drunk I guess," offered the old

man.

"Let's hope not. Maybe this will cure him. I hope so, anyway." said Em as he left.

"Oh, Gawd, how kin my man work fer us'n him wif' outen two legs ter stand 'n de field on. Law me, 'n us wit six chillums. With nothing to do but wait for Alonza to sleep it off," Malitha went and sat down on the steps. She dreaded for Alonza to wake up and find out the mess he had gotten himself into. She watched Lula Golden walking across the field toward her. She's a nice quiet lady thought Malitha. Keeps mostly to herself.

"Heer'd ov yore troubles, Malitha. Cum ter see iffen I kin hep any."

"Nuttin ter do, but wait. He's still out cold. But thanks for de offer, Lula." She cast her eyes down and traced the hieroglyphic tracts the chickens made in the yard.

"Guess yo' be'in so busy yo' did en't seed thet hawk flyin' low round here, did you?"

"Nope, hain't seen him. Guess he's lookin' fer Alonza's lag," said Malitha as she looked up at the sky.

"Yo' kno' dey got a skim ova de eyes durin' dog days 'n kain't seed a dadburn thang. I'se sure glad dog days air ova. Minds me ov Ed Curlee's funeral."

At this remembrance Malitha started laughing.

"Jes' leave hit ter yo' ter cheer a body up, Lula."

"Hit wuz funny, warn't hit? Eva body a sorro'in fer ol' lady Curlee when de preacher raised his eyes ter heabn' 'n ask de Lawd ter tak' dis dear departed soul 'n a big ol' hawk swooms rite down 'n de preacher yells, "thar goes a damn buzzard. Git dis man 'n de ground 'n shovel lak hell for' he picks his skinny ol bones clean." Sumeone said, "Dats only a ol' hawk, preacher, yo' better git sum eye specs."

"Eva budy stop sniffen' ter look, den de pore ol preacher beg eva budy ter 'scuse him. Thet wuz sump'n." Malitha slapped her thighs laughing. "Pore ol' lady Curlee's eyes got biggern a sasser."

"Yeah," laughed Lula. "Thet pore ol prwacher hem'd 'n haw'd. Allowed as how hit jes' slipped out. Den he jes' say Amen."

"He got a mouth lak a cow dat preacher has," said Malitha. They both laughed.

Lula got up, rackon I orter git 'n de field afore hit gits too hot iffen I kain't hep yo.

The sun was already hot and bright. It caught in the sand of the fields and threw off reflections that were blinding causing the workers to squint so hard the tears ran down their sallow cheeks.

Earthy Tootle looked up at Lula as she paused to dry her face pushing the big straw hat to the back of her head. She remarked to Andrew Smith, "Looks lak a eel'ephant cumin down a flight of stairs backward."

"Yup shore do'," he laughed. "She so wide iffen somebody hollered haulass she'd hav' ter mak' two trips." Their shoulders shook with laughter.

The older women, dressed in gingham, cackled like geese as they waddled down the rows of cotton laughing and joking as they worked the fields.

Lukatie spent the latter part of the summer canning. Her work table was so loaded at times she was sure she could hear it groaning. Em would swear he could also hear it.

"Oh, it's the legs in those tin cans filled

with water slipping." she laughed.

"Goes to show the table is so loaded the legs spread and that's groaning."

"We wouldn't have to put those cans of water under the legs if it wasn't for the ants getting into everything."

"They love sweet things, too." Teased Em as he patted Lukatie on her rear.

She dodged another pat saying, "even that doesn't keep them off the table."

"You just can't hide sweet honey somehow all things are found," he laughed giving her another pat.

"Em! I think we'd better get the grapes picked today. They are plenty ripe. That will take some of the sauce out of you."

"Killjoy," he laughed, "but you're right. I'll go get the negroes started and come back to you."

"Oh, are you going to help me make jam and jelly and grape hull preserves?"

"Nope, I'm going to make wine. I supposed, at least get the barrels filled to start fermentation." He always gave enough to the church for the sacrament each year.

"You heard, children," called Lukatie as they sat over their breakfast. "And you know your jobs."

They all groaned. It meant more jar washing, wood to get in and picking what grapes they could reach.

"Me too little," said Meda. "Me play."

"You bring me jars," said Lucinda.

"Let's make a game of it and see who can pick the most. That way we'll get through fast," laughed Em. He dreaded it too.

Lukatie knew Em was kidding her about getting the negroes to pick, but they usually came when they saw them. To help meant grapes for their own jam and jelly. There was nothing better than a good hot biscuit with jam in the dead of winter as they sat around the kitchen range.

This would end the canning until hog-killing time when she would put up some pork.

When Lukatie had taken all the cooled jars off the table and stacked them in the pantry, she called Em and the children. "See what we've done. Just look at all the food. We'll eat good this winter," she said proudly.

"You've done yourself proud, dear. It's a marvel what hands can do." Em glowed with pride. The children grunted and ran out to play.

*****

"The wind's a restless thing this morning. One minute's it's so strong it would tear the clothes off your back and the next minute it doesn't stir a hair on your head." Em announced as he came in for dinner.

"I keep hearing it blow up then become quieter," Lukatie said as she glanced out of the window. "Think you will finish picking the cotton today?"

"Oh, yes, we're about through so we'll finish easily before dark."

"Aren't the negroes going to stop for dinner?" she asked.

"Of course, I told them to finish out the row and take a break," he said in a matter-of-fact way.

As Lukatie set the table the wind picked up again bringing the voices of the negroes singing as they worked. She liked to listen to them.

O iffen pore sinners culd but kno'

> How much fo den I'd under go
> Dey would not treat me with contempt
> Nor cuss me we'en I says repent

The wind died down and a murmur was all she could hear. They ate silently, each lost in thought.

"I guess you'll soon leave to take the cotton to the warehouse and go see Kinyon," stated Lukatie as she rose from the table.

"Suppose so. Guess I'd better get back to the field." He picked up his time book. "I guess this will be the last entry for this year."

The wind had picked up and she heard the negroes singing again.

> Gibe credit now ter what I says
> 'n mind hit til de judgment day
> Ov God I'se sent constrained ter go
> Ter call pore sinner high 'n low.

She heard the happy giggles of Meda as she walked to the side door of the kitchen to throw out the dish water. She dried the dish pan and went to the porch as she heard Stewart's voice.

"Well, hello Stewart," she greeted. "What brings you around?"

"Nothing in particular, lovely lady. I was just down for a last swim before it gets too cold. I was wishing you were there with me. It was lonesome."

She half laughed, "Wasn't it a little cold?"

"Not until I came out of the water and the wind struck me. That was enough to make me tingle like I feel when I look at you."

He was trying to shock her with his brash talk. She could feel her face turning red. It made her angry because she blushed.

"Honestly, Stewart, when are you going to stop such talk?" she tried to laugh it off.

"Now that you ask," he hesitated as the color rose in her face again. "Probably when they plant me good and deep. Warm is my heart when I look at you, Mrs. Carroll." He bowed low and mounted his horse.

She waved her hand, helplessly laughing. He pulled on the reins and as he rode off. He threw his head back in a hearty, healthy laugh.

She sat down on the steps listening as the singing drifted in from the fields.

> Woe is I iffen I refrain
> Fum go'en forth in God's great name
> A full dispensation I hopes ter receive
> 'N my best friend I often leaves.

Meda called, "Mama, come swing me." Lukatie absentmindedly walked over to the big oak and started pushing her. Wondering about Stewart. He was like a naughty child teasing her, or was he teasing? She was glad she didn't know for sure. It would ruin a delightful association. He is so much fun. She knew she loved Em, but he had never had the knack to tease, or make light, or kindle the spark of laughter. He couldn't make fun over the little things in life as Stewart could. The negroes had found it. Even in their dire poverty they would complain one minute and laugh the next.

She listened again to the singing. Some songs were happy, Alleluia songs, while others sounded so mournful that they reached down to touch the soul. She probably wouldn't hear them again until next year at cotton planting time. Sometimes they sang when they gathered around the pump bench to wash.

Lukatie hadn't known when she had insisted that the wells be filled and pumps driven that they would turn out to be the gathering place for the old to talk, the children to play, and the young to court.

>Though sulty climes yet dusty 'n wide
>I'se ben d'recked by m' only guide
>No coolin' streams kin quench m' thirst
>Though I fum won't has turn ter dust.

They sure have a lot of verses thought Lukatie as Meda called out, "Mama, I'm slowing down."

"So am I, sweetheart," she said as she gave her another push, turned and walked into the house to do her long-neglected mending.

As she sat darning socks and sewing buttons on a shirt for Em, she couldn't help thinking how different he is from Stewart. She wished he would bother to bring out the laughter in her as Stewart did. Maybe the difference is being a wife, she sighed.

Em was fussing about the entrepot prices when Stewart rode up.

"What are you exploding about?" he asked.

"The prices of cotton. I believe they want us to give it to them at the entrepot. It's up only two cents above last year and with labor costs up. Ends won't meet."

"Em, if you can hold your cotton until the first of December, I believe the prices will be up a little."

"Maybe I'll do that. I don't see how they can be any lower."

*****

Em held off selling until December and found cotton up two-tenths of a cent. "Hold off until January; prices are bound to better," encouraged Stewart. Em decided not to hold off any longer and sold the first week of December taking his annual trip to see Kinyon.

He watched the countryside as the train raced along. The beauty of it enthralled him. Yes, he told himself, there is a God. All this beauty didn't just happen. It was created. In fact, it was placed in the hands of man to work with. Am I being foolish trying to hold onto my part of it? Why? I'm not improving it. He was glad his thoughts were brought to an end as the train pulled along side of the mill. He saw Kinyon's car and left the train.

After dinner, Em mused, if he were home it would be after supper. He went in the library and sat down in a chair near the window draping his leg over the arm and started talking slowly to Kinyon.

"I see something new has been added to the household."

"What?" asked Kinyon in surprise.

"The new maid. What happened to Nellie?"

"Oh, she was put in full charge of Penny Sue, Everett and Carlton. They are a handful now. We got Milla to help with the general housework and kitchen when it's needed."

Milla had served at the table that evening. She was a lovely girl, coal-black hair, aquiline nose, bright dark eyes behind half lids with endless depths. She moved swiftly like a flowing stream ready for action waiting to be subdued. Her pale olive skin was flawless. He noted that a man with average length fingers could easily encircle her waist. Em found her fascinating to watch and found it hard to keep his eyes off her.

He wondered if she was deliberately brushing his shoulder with her arm as she served him or if it was an accident. She was most desirable and the physical attraction he felt toward her was overwhelming. He had married the only other woman he had felt such desire for. He would just leave in the morning and that would be that.

But Em didn't leave and each night she entered his room. She came to him and lay in his arms soft and warm-blooded, full of passions that once awakened were demanding and possessive. He had violated his marriage vows after seventeen years of faithfulness to Lukatie. Guilt began to flood his feelings and he knew he must leave.

The day was unusually warm for December. Lukatie decided she would take a walk. It was getting so lonesome without Em. She wondered what was keeping him. He had never stayed more than two or three days. A week passed and the negroes began asking about their money. She was running out of excuses.

She started walking down the road but turned into the woods toward the old manor site. The big straight pines had a stirring grandeur. It was neck-breaking to look up to their tops. It was as if they were protecting their land, their home for hundreds of years, their majesty placed by none other. Even the mighty oak seemed so short beneath them as if asking for protection too.

She heard a steady rhythm of horse hooves and as they came near, she turned and saw Stewart smiling as he approached and dismounted. She held out her hands to him. He came forward bareheaded, a happiness shining on his face. taking her outstretched hands in his, he held them until she became self-conscious and gently withdrew them. He raised one to his lips before he let it go.

"I saw you turn in and I followed. I hope you don't mind." He said.

"No, it's always nice to have someone to talk to especially on such a beautiful day."

He smiled crookedly, "A beautiful day, a beautiful lady. What more can one ask for?"

She turned quickly hoping to hide her flushed face.

"You've always wanted a house here, haven't you, Lukatie?"

"Yes, oh, yes, Stewart, so very much." She turned to him so sharply that she lost her balance as her foot struck a root and stumbled into his arms.

"How clumsy of me. I'm so sorry," she murmured as she withdrew from his embrace. He smelled so good and clean. For one moment she had felt so warm and protected. Maybe unknowingly that was where she got her strength to live as she was in the old house. She felt she could leave it and go to the protection of Stewart and his home if she chose to.

"The pleasure of holding you even for a moment and by accident, dear lady, is always welcome. I'll say this now, dear, and never again. I think you may have already guessed that I love you, and if ever you need me, I'm forever at your service." They gazed into each other's eyes.

"You mustn't say these things," said Lukatie breaking the gaze.

Under his smile, he looked tired. What a strain he must be living under to have felt this way so many years. She had never seen this serious side of him before. When he had talked of his feelings for her, it had always been in a joking manner. She so desperately wanted the old Stewart, the one who kidded and made her blush and laugh.

"I know you love Em. I wouldn't want you to dishonor your marriage. I'm not thinking that. Please don't let this change our relationship, Lukatie. I couldn't bear that." He had returned to his quiet relaxed way. He smiled wistfully and touched her cheek with his fingertips.

"The weather is looking stormy. You'd better get back to the house." He reached over and kissed her on her forehead then threw back his head splitting the air with happy laughter just as thunder rolled in the heavens. Flashes of lightening suddenly flashed out so sharply that she felt each flash was aimed at her.

"Get going, dear. Take the short cut through the woods. I'll watch from the road to see that you make it okay. With Em gone, I can't go with you. It might cause talk." Not waiting for her comment he jumped on his horse and rode off.

He sang to himself as he cantered his horse.

> Into each life there come the time
> To travel down the road of love.
> The fire burn deep and needs release
> Only you can fill the void, my love.

His voice broke as tears slid down his cheeks to blend with the softly falling rain.

As Lukatie hurried home, she felt a warm glow. Stewart had so tactfully told her of his love for her, then reverted back to his old self so quickly she wasn't sure he had even said he loved her. She smiled and rubbed her fingertips on her forehead. She loved him too, but not in the same way.

The rain was falling and seeing the old man sitting on the porch she spoke to him.

"Do you think we're in for a bad storm, Mr. Mathias?"

"Howdy, Miz Carroll, yassum, hits gwine ter weather up purty bad. I kin feel hit in m'bones. Hit's gwine ter be bad dis time. I aches sumpin' awful."

"I hope the children get home from school before the storm really breaks."

"Yassum, I shore do too. Mistuh Carroll not cum home yet?"

"No, not yet." She said. Lukatie longed for Em to come home. "Doesn't he know I need him?" she thought. "My bed is so empty and lonesome at night." She felt that every damn negro on the place was talking about his long absence.

The wind blew harder as Lukatie hurried home. As she reached the house, she could hear Benjamin's voice coaching the horse along and the buggy soon rolled into the yard.

"Hurry and barn the horse, Benjamin, and all of you get in the house before the storm really breaks."

She went in the house to check on Meda, who was still sitting on the floor cutting out paper dolls from a catalog just as Lukatie had left her.

All evening the hard winds blew. The temperature dropped so fast that the rain was half ice. It fell with such malevolent competence that it seemed to know exactly where every hole in the roof was and aimed directly at it.

"Maybe we had better have an early supper," said Lukatie to the children. "We'll dash down the porch to the kitchen and while I get a fire going, you go feed the stock, Benjamin." The icy fingers of winter had really hit. They all hovered around the old kitchen range. The rain and ice had turned to snow. Just that afternoon they were comfortable outdoors in only a sweater around their shoulders. The swirling flakes drifted through the roof and melted as they fell on the stove.

"Since your father isn't home, we won't do very much cooking."

The resinous lightwood had responded to the match with a burst of flame and the kitchen was good and hot when Benjamin came in and said, "Mama, there is an old man and woman at the back door. They look drowned and frozen."

Lukatie went to the door. "Yes, what can I do for you?"

"Ma'm we's plum froze 'n hungry 'n wet ter de bone. Could yo' please tak' use in fer de night. We's tuckered out. We'un kain't go 'nudder step withouten sum rest 'n food. We's on our way ter Landridge ter our son's. He work 'n de mill thar." Said the old lady.

Four sudden and sharp flashes of lightening made Lukatie gasp, feeling sure it struck something nearby.

"Come into the kitchen where it's warm and we'll see what we can do." She stated shakily.

She did wish Em was home. What in the world could be keeping him? She turned to Lucinda.

"Dear, put two more plates on the table while I see if I can find some dry clothes that they can put on."

She was back shortly with the clothes. "They are old and patched but they will be dry and warm," she said as she handed them to the old couple. "You can take them in the pantry there and change while I dish up some supper. There is a pan of warm water there on the stove you can take along and wash up. When you're finished, come on in and eat."

When they had washed and changed, they didn't look so old. Lukatie judged them to just past the peak of middle age.

"Have a seat there at the side of the table." Lukatie said, indicating the two empty chair with her hand. They sat patiently while Lukatie blessed the food, and passed it around. "Help Meda with her serving, Benjamin."

"Sure, Mama."

There was fried fatback, peas and potatoes that Lukatie had canned, some left-over collard greens and some hot biscuits. There was also a small amount of butter on the butter dish. As the old man reached for it, the old lady turned to him and said, "Don' eat de butter, deah. Save it fo' yore breakfast. Hit will b' good on hot grits."

"Yo kno' I don' lak grits, dey mak' my mouth feel all quickie." All the children turned their eyes to Lukatie who shook her head. So the butter was left untouched.

"I am Mrs. Carroll and these are my children, Benjamin, Lucinda, Miles and Meda. My husband is visiting his brother in Landridge."

"Yassum, we wuz tolt down de road, two houses bak' dat yo' sho' would tak' us in."

"The Sholar's place," thought Lukatie. They or no one else knew of her vow never to turn away another soul in need. She thought again of the time she had found the old man eating out of the slop pail. The memory still made her feel sick to her stomach which prompted her to say, "Eat up there's plenty more in the pot."

Lucinda went to the kitchen to fill the bowls again after the old folk had emptied them the first time around. Worrying about her own supper, she stuck her head around the door facing and said, "I thank you there isn't so much more in the pot."

"Oh, you're a funny, you are." teased Benjamin.

When supper was over, Lukatie said, "I guess you noticed the cot in the pantry. You're welcome to sleep there."

The woman said, "de two of us kan't sleep on one cot. We'un kin use yore bed 'n yo' sleep there since yore husband hain't ter home."

Startled for a moment, Lukatie said, "No, I sleep in my own bed. I have another cot folded against the wall in there that I can put up. You will be warm there since the flue is against the pantry wall and you can keep a fire going in the stove and lay your clothes around on chairs so they will dry."

With the dishes washed and put away and the cots fixed, Lukatie told them good night and went to the front part of the house locking the doors. Something she never did when Em was in the house. She supposed the couple was all right. They looked harmless enough but then you couldn't tell how deep a dog could bite by his bark either. She still didn't know their names. Oh, well what's in a name.

The snow had ended but the rain continued through the night. The wind shook the house so hard Lukatie thought it would fall off its foundation. She slept little and was thankful when morning came bringing with it a hushed world and bright sunshine streaming through the windows. Benjamin called from outside.

"Mama, come look at the chimney." The top was leaning about a foot and a half away from the roof of the house.

"Maybe your father will come today and fix

it. Good thing we have a tin roof on the house, shingles would have blown away for sure."

"Mama, I bet I can fix it." Without waiting for Lukatie to answer, he went on to explain. "I can put a flat board against the chimney and take a stout pole and prop against it. Then climb the ladder and hit on the pole until it forces the chimney back into place. Then put hooks into the house on each side of the chimney and get that heavy chain out of the barn and link it from one hook around the chimney to the other hook and it will hold it in place. Should I try it, Mama?"

"We do have to have some heat in the house," thought Lukatie as she looked at her fifteen-year-old son with pride. "Yes," she thought, "It just might work."

"You go ahead and try it if you like while I cook breakfast and get the old folk up. They should be on their way."

Lukatie entered the kitchen and it was still warm. She shivered as she hurriedly put some wood in the old iron range hoping it would catch fire from the few embers still in the fire box. Then she knocked on the pantry door to awaken the old couple.

"It's a beautiful day for traveling. Hurry up while I fix some breakfast and a lunch for you to take along."

She first noticed the empty butter dish on the table, then checked around, all the food left over from the previous evening was gone. She opened the pantry door and the old couple was gone as was a jar of jam and the clothes she had lent them. She then checked the breadbasket. Gone were all the leftover cold biscuits.

She noticed with amusement that the cots were left straight and orderly.

*****

Two weeks from the day he left, Em came riding into the yard. He wondered if the guilt he felt was showing in his face. He thought, "How can I work myself out of the quagmire in which I have been wallowing and still keep Lukatie's love?"

The children had just walked home from school and came rushing out to greet him. Well, at least they still loved him. Benjamin showed him the work he had done on the chimney. "Good thinking. I couldn't have done better myself," praised Em. His eyes watched the door for Lukatie.

She was in the kitchen cooking and stayed there. He finally went in the house. There was an uncomfortable silence between them for a moment. "Couldn't leave the food to burn," she offered as he stood there. "Hope you had a nice trip." She felt like slashing out at him, but didn't dare. She wanted to say a lot but held her tongue because of the children.

Things were strained between them for a long time. Em's only excuse for staying was to be by Kinyon if he needed him. He told of a man working in the mill who was trying to stir up trouble for higher wages. "That brother of mine has a prodigious memory, calls everyone in the mill by name. He was shrewd, intelligent and constantly one thought ahead of the men he talked with which was just about everyone of them."

"If he's so smart why did you stay around so long? I'm glad he got them straightened out or I'd spend the rest of my life without a husband. What annoys me is your apparent devotion to him after he walked off leaving you stuck with nothing but this forest hell."

There, she had told him what she thought of his forest and wished she had done so long ago. As he walked out of the room, she added, "I still feel there was more than just the mill that kept you there so long."

Em paused not turning, then walked on out of the house. "What can I say? he thought. She's right. Right down the line." He got the two man-saw out and called to Thankful. "After I pay the men, let's go cut some firewood."

"Yassuh, sho' could use sum."

They were gone all afternoon. The next morning, they took the cart and brought up the wood they had cut. While Em worked he worried about the strain between him and Lukatie. "She has every right to be upset. I'm guilty as hell and know it. But right or wrong there had to be a change and it can't be for the worse. There is no way for things to get worse unless she leaves me. O, God, don't let her do that," he moaned. "I love her, I always will. I've sinned and I admit it. Don't make me pay for it by losing her. I can't hurt her more by telling her. There has to be another way."

"Yo' alright, Mistuh Em?" asked Thankful.

"Yes, it's just that it's cold out here. Guess we've worked enough for today. I've had it."

"Yas, sir, I'se willing." Thankful said and they headed home.

"It's sure cold. Hoar's frost hugs the ground like crystals," Em said as he entered the living room and backed up to the fireplace.

Lukatie smiled. She had taken extra pains to look her best when she dressed that morning.

Encouraged by the smile, he said, "You're looking very beautiful, Lukatie." His eyes pleaded as he spoke in a quavering voice. "Don't you know how much I love you, need you. I told you I was sorry about staying away so long. I did wrong. I didn't realize it at the time, but now I do. Honey, nature didn't make me perfect. For our sake, I wish it had."

Lukatie was shaken and rose from her chair to walk into the circle of his arms. He held her tightly.

"Oh, Em," she cried, "How I've missed you."

"Stop shivering darling or are you quivering," he teased as he kissed her. She vowed silently she would never mention those two weeks again to him if she could help it.

Even so, the guilt lodged in Em and caused him to provide her with only sporadic companionship. Only when his desire could not be contained. But his love grew deeper and more sincere until next to God he worshipped her. He wished he could do more for her and give her lovely things like Jane had. But instead of things getting better, they seemed to get worse and the house was beyond anymore patching.

"Dear God, what can I do," he prayed. With the passing of time, Lukatie's trepidation about the change in Em began to thin. She was dubious but tried to carry on her life in her quiet dependable way.

*****

One week before school let out for the summer. Miles was feeling devilish. "Gosh," he thought, "I haven't done anything mischievous since I stole the clapper out of the school bell." Just at the close of recess he went in the privy. Quickly stuffing the hole full of paper, he struck a match to it and ran to his room easing himself quietly into his seat. He quickly opened his book and started his arithmetic problems.

"Sarah Banham, what are you doing to upset the whole class?" asked Miss Moody.

"I couldn't help it, Miss Moody. Honest. Look." She pointed to the smoke coming out of the vent stack of the privy that was making perfect smoke rings by this time.

"Where are the Indians," piped up a small voice.

"That's enough," said Miss Moody. "Quieten down all of you."

Miles didn't expect all this commotion. All he wanted was to burn the stinking thing down. He should have realized it was cement and wouldn't burn. And there it was making beautiful smoke rings. He tried to giggle like the rest of the class and act surprised. Instead he felt the color crawling up the back of his neck and flooding his face as all eyes turned in his direction remembering he was the last one to enter the room.

"Miles, are you responsible for that?" asked Miss Moody pointing out the window.

"Yes, Ma'm."

"Well! I've never known anything so reprehensive. Of course, you know we'll have to visit your parents this afternoon."

"Yes Ma'm."

"You can write. I like to start fires, five hundred times on the black board. Write." She commanded.

Miles didn't say a word when he got home. He just disappeared into the corn crib where he could watch the house. He didn't have to wait long for he soon saw Miss Moody waddling down the road. She was so short and fat the children had all dubbed her duck-butt.

Lukatie met her at the door. "Woe is me," thought Miles. He continued to watch until he saw her leave half an hour later. Then he heard his mother calling him.

"Aw shucks, I may as well go and get it over with." He snapped the twig he was holding and threw it down as he walked into the yard.

"Why did you start a fire in the hole in the privy, Miles?"

"Well, aw, Mama, it stinks. I just wanted to clean it out, sort of."

Lukatie broke out in a big laugh throwing down the switch she had in her hand.

"Miles, don't you ever do a thing like that again. And if you tell them at school tomorrow that I didn't punish you, I'll beat you twice as hard."

"Yes, ma'm. I'll tell them I thought you were going to kill me, which ain't no lie."

"Isn't a lie," correct Lukatie. She chuckled as she walked back in the house.

Saturday the children all begged for a picnic at the swimming hole to celebrate the end of school.

The wagon was packed and they were ready to go as Stewart with Miles on the back of the horse came riding into the yard in a gay mood for a picnic.

After playing in the water with the children, Em sat on the bank until lunch time watching the others. Stewart was busy teaching Meda how to swim. Then he moved to help Lukatie spread the lunch.

"It's always a pleasure to go picnicking with you and sink my teeth into a piece of your fried chicken, Lukatie," said Stewart. "Right, Meda?"

"Right, Uncle Stewart."

As Lukatie was slicing the cake and passing it around Stewart said, "If you don't mind, I'll just have another piece of chicken for dessert," he winked at her smacking his lips.

"You may have both," laughed Lukatie.

Feeling lazy after lunch, Em decided to go fishing. He got the can of worms he had slipped under the seat of the cart and took a pole from the hut.

"Anybody for fishing?" he asked. Hoping there wasn't. He didn't wait to see and walked along the riverbank to a nice secluded spot. He put a worm on the hook, found a good tree, cast his line in the water, then sat down settling in against the tree for a good nap.

He was almost asleep with a blissful half smile on his lips when a redheaded woodpecker landed on the tree and started rat-a-tat-tat, sending vibrations through the tree. Em jumped to his feet in a daze. He threw his hat at the bird, yelling, "You damn redheaded bastard. You don't have to scare the fool out of me." At the same time, he noticed that his fishing pole was taking a dive toward the water. He jumped on it with both feet as it hit the ground. It was jerked so hard, he almost fell in the water. He was so mad he just picked up the pole and started walking up the bank. The pole finally stopped jerking and Em walked back to the water's edge and there at the end of the line lay the largest bass he had ever seen. He caught four more then walked back to join the others.

He could see Stewart still playing in the water with the children. "Crazy man, rather play with children than fish," he thought, "maybe that's because he doesn't have any of his own. He should get married."

"Fish tonight," called Lukatie as he came

toward them, beaming over his catch. "Join us, Stewart. Looks like there's plenty." He had eaten at the Carroll house almost as often as at home when he and Em were growing up. He accepted graciously thankful for a few more hours with Lukatie. "She's as uncomplicated as her fried chicken, chocolate cake and hot biscuits." He thought.

When they rode up in the yard they were greeted with a very young puppy. He scampered up the steps behind Em, his warm brown eyes fixed on him as if to say, "I'm yours. I'll stay if you'll let me." His tail beat against Em's leg claiming adoption. Then he sat down and gazed up into Em's face. Em laughed, reached down and patted him on the head, saying, "He's just a tiny baby of a thing. A puppy like you must have an owner. So you just hang around, someone will claim you soon."

The dog ran around Em's legs with great gusts as if he knew he had just been given a home.

"Engaging rascal, aren't you. Maybe you just want my fish."

The others had gotten out of the cart and stood watching.

"Oh, ain't he tiny," exclaimed Meda as she ran up the steps and sat on the porch. She threw her arms around the wiggling dog.

"Can he be mine, Papa, please? What is his name?"

"Why don't we call him Regal until his owner shows up?" suggested Benjamin.

"Now that is taken care of, let's take care of these fish, son. Grab us a knife and pan and come on to the pump bench."

*****

"The summer is sure passing fast," thought Em while pumping a bucket of water for the kitchen. Then he noticed a colored woman stumbling down the road. She had a bundle in her arms. She looked so frail. Her clothes were dirty and dusty. She was barefooted and her feet looked swollen, cracked and bleeding.

When she saw Em she turned into his road. "Please, Mistuh, hep me," she pleaded as she stumbled into the yard and sank to the ground. Zarilda Mathias had also seen the woman and walked over getting there just as Lukatie came out of the kitchen. "What a dolorous, painful, enervating-looking woman," thought Lukatie.

"Poor thing, she's exhausted," Lukatie said. "Let's see if we can't get her inside."

Zarilda reached for the bundle in her arms, but the woman held on tight. "My baby, my baby," she moaned.

"No one will hurt your baby. Here, let my daughter hold it while we help you into the house," said Lukatie as Lucinda walked up. "She daid, my baby daid," the woman moaned again.

"Den let me tak' hit so's we's kin giv' hit a propah buryin'." Zarilda reached again for the bundle.

This time the woman gave her the child. They all looked at the baby thin and breathless. "Why hit kain't b' mor'n a day ol'," exclaimed Zarilda. "How about that. Naval cord 'n all still attached."

"Good heaven, leave it as is and bury it all together. Don't let anyone else see it," said Lukatie.

Thankful came up and quickly took in the scene. He picked the woman up and took her into the pantry room. Lukatie went in the house looking for clean clothes to put on her. Zarilda then gave the baby to Thankful with instructions to get Myrtle and Abraham Barnes to go with him after the preacher and give the baby a proper burial.

When Lukatie returned to the pantry, Zarilda had the woman undressed and almost bathed. Her back was scarred and welted where she had been beaten. She looked to be about thirty years old.

"Look ahere, Miz Carroll."

"I wonder who beat her like that, Zarilda?"

"I don' kno' but dey sho as sortin ort ter b' kilt."

It was a couple of days later before they learned the woman's name was Lovie Morris. Her parents had beaten her because she had gotten pregnant by a white man. A negro would marry you, but no white man will. They told her to get out and never let them see her face again. They wouldn't even let her get her clothes.

"How did they know the baby's father was white?"

"I wux afreared not ter say so whin my time wus near."

"Where are you from, Lovie?"

"Jest across de line ova'n South Carolina."

"You mean you walked all that distance. That must be over a hundred miles from here."

"I ketched a ride on de back ov a cart from a place called Leland ter Wilmington and walked de rest ov de way." She was alert looking thin woman. Her eyes large and round. Full lips and hair less kinky than most negroes.

"Where were you going, Lovie?"

"I wus trying to get ter Richmond, Virginia ter my married sister's."

"It would take a stronger person than you

are to walk that far."

"I knos' thet now, Miz Carroll. I don' kno' how I kin eva pay yo' fer all yo' done fo' me. Kin I work ter pay yo'?"

"You don't owe me anything. I try my best to help anyone I can that is truly in need. Lovie, I'm very sorry about your losing your baby."

"I trys ter think hits fer de best, Miz Carroll. Alone lak I am, no place to go. How could I keer fer a baby. But m'arms shore feel empty. I longs fer a baby ter holt 'n coo ter 'n I think ter feed."

"Milk coming down? Better keep it milked out, you could get a fever because of it."

"Yas'sum, I shore will."

Lukatie was looking out the window as they talked and saw Thankful coming.

"Well, Lovie, it looks like you've really made a conquest. Thankful is coming. He has come inquiring about you every day since he brought you here."

"He's mity nice, but a man lak him cuddn't see a woman lak me ater whut I'se don'."

"Well, Lovie, the real mystery lies not in the person or what one has done, but how the other person looks at it."

Lovie had been with the Carroll's a week when Lukatie went into the kitchen to start breakfast and found a fire already going in the stove and breakfast started.

"You shouldn't be up doing this yet, Lovie."

"I couldn't sleep. M'tits were hurtin' so I got up ter relieve m'self. Hit ain't hepn' much."

Lukatie took a flour sack from the kitchen drawer. "Here, Lovie, fold this and bind it around your breasts good and tight."

Em entered the dining room and headed for the kitchen when he heard a soft knock on the porch. He paused. "It's hardly daybreak. Who in the world can that be," he wondered. He went back to the door listening as he heard running feet and could barely make out a figure disappearing around Thankful's house.

He almost tripped over a box sitting on the porch. He looked down upon a sleeping baby with a note scrawled in large unsteady writing. He could barely read it in the dim dawn of morning.

"Yo' sired her. Now yo' raise her. Her maw died w'en she were born 'n she needs a home. Yo' tak' good ker ov her. She's one week old."

Em stuffed the note in his pocket and started running after the disappearing figure. He realized the futility of catching the man when he heard a horse running hard. He stopped dead in his tracks as the impact of the message fully sunk in. Taking the note out of his pocket he read it over. Then took his knife and carefully cut off the first seven words and put them in his pocket to destroy later keeping the rest of the note in his hand he returned to the house.

"Dear God," he prayed, "what have I brought upon us?"

Hearing the commotion, Lukatie came to the door. "What is it? What in the world is going on?" she called to Em as he walked back into the yard.

A whimper attracted her gaze. She walked over to the box.

"My Great God in heaven! A baby!"

She picked up the box and took it to the dining room table. It was an earth-shattering impact to Lukatie as they looked at the baby and Em found himself looking into the miniature face of Meda. He handed Lukatie the note in his hand.

Meda names Didge

"We'll take her to the orphanage," he said.

"Oh, no, you won't!" snapped Lukatie. Asserting herself she said, "We'll keep her. Maybe her folks will think it over and come back for her."

They both knew no one would ever come but the words could never be spoken.

Em kept insisting on the orphanage, but Lukatie was defiant. "Dear God, does he think I'm blind."

The children getting up for breakfast came in and saw the baby.

"Oh, a baby, a real live baby," whispered Meda. Then she got excited. "Didya ever see such a pretty baby, didja, Mama, didja? Can we keep it, Mama?" "What's her name?"

"Well, dear, I guess you just named her. Suppose we call her Didge until we learn her real name. Maybe someone will come for her."

Lucinda, Benjamin and Miles had kept quiet. Now Lucinda spoke.

"But, Mother, I didn't know you were…"

Lukatie stopped her with her eyes and shook her head. "Here, read this note. She was left on the porch. This means she was born the twelfth of August, 1912. Lucinda, dear, go into the house and get a little cotton and the alcohol, some of Meda's baby clothes and flour sacks for diapers. Benjamin, will you get a pan of warm water, soap, cloth and towel, please."

They all watched fascinated while Lukatie bathed the baby. Em had left the room when the children had come in. Now Meda slipped away and came back just as a diaper was about to be pinned on the baby. She held out a can of baby powder left over from her own diaper days. They all laughed.

It was a moment to cherish as they all

stood around looking at the baby. She was all porcelain pink, a contented gold red haired moppet that formed ringlets around the glowing pink face of the week-old baby. Lukatie raised her eyes and met the ache in Lovie's eyes as she stood in the door taking in the scene before her.

Lukatie picked up the baby, cotton and alcohol and walked over to Lovie. Laying the baby in her arms, she handed her the cotton and alcohol and said.

"We have a hungry guest in the house and I think you're just the one to do something about it. Wash your nipples good with the alcohol and give her breakfast while I finish cooking ours."

"Yas'sum," beamed Lovie as she disappeared into the pantry.

They all listened to Lovie cooing over the baby. "There is one happy soul here today," thought Lukatie.

There was never any talk of Lovie leaving and as her strength returned, she took on more and more work around the house and farm.

Em's overactive thoughts were playing havoc with his mind as he tired to figure out ways of getting the baby placed in the orphanage. He argued that he just couldn't feed two more mouths and a dog.

"Stop it, Em! There is plenty of food canned here and you know it." Retorted Lukatie.

"Well, they have to have clothes and shoes."

"With all the things Jane brings there will be plenty for Lovie and I can sew for Didge. Stop worrying about it. We can't get rid of that baby." She stated emphatically.

"And why can't we?"

"It would break the children's hearts; they all adore her as much as if she were their own sister."

Em just grunted and walked out of the house. "How much has she guessed?" he wondered. He decided to call Thankful and go fishing. There he could do his best thinking.

He had qualms about holding Didge, but Lukatie would put her in his arms every chance she got. "Here, hold her while I change the cradle," she'd say. "She will wiggle off the bed." "I wish she had died with her mother," thought Em. "Oh, no, I don't wish that. But they could have just placed her in an orphanage home to start with and we'd never have known the difference."

Lukatie wasn't just sure when she became aware of it, but she started having headaches. When they became progressively more severe, she went to see Dr. Wesson.

"Migraine," he told her. "What are you nervous about? Or what is bothering you?"

"I really don't know, Dr. Wesson."

"I always thought of you as always the buoyant, earthy, leveling influence, ready and able to handle any situation but evidently something is getting to you. Is it the two new members of the household?"

"Oh, so you've heard?"

"Yes, you could send the woman on to wherever she had started and put the baby in the orphan home if it's going to affect your health."

"No, I can't do that."

"Why not?"

"They need us...and...I have to have them." "Oh, dear God!" she thought, "How can I turn Em's child out? How could he have done this to me?" Her eyes were bright with tears.

"Here, Mrs. Carroll, take this capsule and go home and lay down, completely relax. Let the woman prepare dinner for you."

"Thank you, Dr. Wesson, I'll try to follow orders." "How can I rest," she thought, "Preparations have to be made for Kinyon and Jane for the weekend."

When she got home little Seth Kirby was standing in the yard.

"I'se cum ter see th' lil' baby," he announced. Looking her straight in the eyes, he grinned a beautiful toothless grin.

"She lak me, her maw 'n paw don' want her."

"Her mother died, Seth. It wasn't that she didn't want her."

"Oh, her paw daid, too?"

"I guess something has happened to him. Come on inside and see the baby then run along home. Mrs. Curlee will be worried about you." Seth gazed into the cradle that Lukatie had Benjamin get out of the barn and cleaned up for the baby.

"Whut's 'her name?"

"We call her Didge."

"I'se gwine tak' keer ov' her w'en I grows up, Miz Carroll, so's yo' kin rest. She sho' purty 'n dat's de truff."

"That's a nice thing to say, Seth. You run along home now. I have a headache and must get some rest."

"Yas'sum, I'se gwine cum agin 'ter see her." He called out as he left. He became a regular visitor and was holding Didge's hand when she took her first step. He was good with her.

The next day, Malitha came by to see the baby.

"My she sho' air purty, Miz Carroll. Yo' gwine ter keep her?"

"Yes, I supposed so. Of course, that will be up to Mr. Em. How is Alonza getting along? I hear he has made himself a peg leg."

"Yas'sum, he sho' did, he gits 'round on that thang goodern a two-legged man," she chuckled.

"He's given up drinking, too, I hear."

"Perzactly whut he don'. Losin' dat lag sho' cyored him. He's afeared iffen he don' he mite lose de udder lag."

"I'm glad he's not giving you any more trouble."

"All de trouble he eva gibes me now is a lot ov lip 'n internal exercise." She chuckled on the way out.

The next few days it rained and Lovie was hanging wet diapers all around in the kitchen and dining room to dry.

Em walked in. "Phew! What a stinking odor."

"You ought to be use to it by now."

"I may be used to it, but that doesn't make me like it." He turned and walked back outside.

"Lovie, it might help to rinse the wet diapers out before drying them."

"Yas'sum, Miz Carroll, I'll do thet."

Jane and Kinyon came for their end of the season visit, bringing bolts of sample material with them. They were shocked at finding Lovie and Didge there and listened with interest as the story of their being there was told to them.

"Lukatie, you amaze me more and more every time I see you," said Jane. She couldn't hide her astonishment.

For the first time, Lukatie could go swimming with Jane. Thanks to Lovie taking over all the work.

"Go along now, Miz Carroll, yo' needs ter relax 'n enjoy yore family."

It was the first time Kinyon had ever seen her out of all the long skirts. He knew she had a trim ankle and a pretty face, but was totally unprepared for the wet radiant Lukatie in the clinging swim suit she had made out of material he had brought her.

"You could get rich designing, making and selling swimsuits, Lukatie, if you make them fit everyone else like they do you," Kinyon said. She smiled and blushed.

"Well, I'll be. Em, where did you say you found her?" Before Em could answer, he continued. "A nurse in a hospital. The place where everyone loses his dignity and modesty and she can still blush. A queen, indeed."

"Remember, please, I was a nurse, not a patient." She laughed. Jane and Em were laughing uproariously at Lukatie's embarrassment and Kinyon's delight in making her blush.

Lukatie turned to Jane, "Don't let me forget I have something for you before you leave." She had worked hard on some sheets and pillowcases hand-stitched with a white embroidery design. They were made of the pretty blue percale material Kinyon had brought on their last trip. When Jane saw them, she was delighted.

"Too bad I can't sew like you can, Lukatie."

"I'm sure you could if you ever needed it."

"I should learn. Kinyon is always splitting his pants between the fly and inseam, so I could fix them."

"How does he do that?"

"I don't know, he surely isn't that big. I don't believe," she laughed as they reached the porch. She handed Kinyon the sheets and cases.

"Beautiful," he said, looking at the transformation of what he thought was just plain blue material. "But then that is why I make the material. Lukatie's life will never be flat and mundane. She's too busy and has too many interests." He added.

"Guess I'd better get in the kitchen," smiled Lukatie. "Miles please take in some wood."

After the evening meal, they all sat around talking. The general colloquialism being dull, Kinyon suggested he and Em take a walk.

"I've tried to get you alone ever since we arrived and I saw the baby."

"I'm aware of that," replied Em.

"Then you're also aware that I know the parentage of the baby."

"I guessed as much. Does Jane know?"

"No."

"I'm sorry Milla died. Kinyon, I didn't love her. Attracted, yes. She came to my room without an invitation and it happened. I found it hard to leave but, believe me, it was only physical attraction. I'm truly sorry."

"Jane accused me of it for a long time until Milla finally convinced her it was her boyfriend's and as soon as he found a job to support her they were going to get married. In her seventh month she left us."

"We have another older woman now. It was she who told us Milla died. She let us think the baby died with her. Now I know it didn't."

"Will you tell the woman you know the baby lived?"

"No, I think it best not to. She's leaving us too."

"Thank you, Kinyon."

They continued to talk and walk with Kinyon doing most of the talking and Em asking questions. About an hour later they returned to the house.

"After that walk I could inhale another piece of your chocolate cake, Lukatie." Laughed

Kinyon light-heartedly.

"Bless him," thought Em, for seeming so gay after the seriousness of their conversation.

Loaded with the usual canned foods, Kinyon and Jane left for home Sunday morning.

"Kinyon, it would be wonderful to have a summer home down on that hill by the river. Why don't you ask Em to give you that land back? He doesn't farm it."

"Nothing doing, I took all the money even if it wasn't much. At the time it seemed like a lot compared to living on the farm. I left him with nothing but that land and I won't have it back."

The simplicity of his character was filled with honesty. He was zealously upholding the standard of his convictions.

"But Kinyon, when the children are old enough they would enjoy the swimming hole so much," she pouted. "Anyway, half of that place should be yours."

"The children are old enough. They could enjoy it now if you cared to bring them. I just hope your over-protection of them isn't going to make them grow up to be spoiled selfish children, thinking they are better than other people, just because they are lucky enough to have a little more. Now stop pouting, beautiful, and let's enjoy the ride back home."

"Where would the children sleep if we brought them?" asked Jane.

"Lukatie would just put up more cots, simple as that." He answered. "I've seen the bedrooms and halls lined with cots and we children had the greatest time of our lives."

"All right, next time they come. Thank God they can at least get a bath in the river."

Kinyon chuckled heartily. "You really get

to me, Jane."

"I shouldn't be too hard on her. She never had to live like this," he thought of the awe he felt when he married her and went to the big palatial home to live. Big marble entry, marble fireplaces, big glass doors opening onto terraces all around the house. Their own bedroom with large glass doors opening onto a private terrace. He had never seen so much glass and so many rooms.

She had been mighty good about coming home with him. She never complained. In fact, she seemed to enjoy it. He'd have to give old man Blunt credit. He hadn't spoiled this daughter of his. Once he had asked if using the outhouse bothered her very much. "Haven't you heard," she quipped, "everybody used them before electricity."

*****

Stewart's parents had died in a train wreck while on their way to New York to visit his oldest sister, Elda, years ago. Elda had raised their younger sister, Titia, who had miraculously escaped injury.

On his return home after a month's visit with them, he heard of the baby left on the Carroll's porch and went over.

"Why didn't you tell me there was another one due. I would have stayed home to give you moral support, or maybe hold your hand," he teased Lukatie.

"Nut, you can always give me the lift I need."

They had reached the cradle. Stewart looked down at the baby.

"Good heavens," he said apprehensively.

"Oh, Stewart, you notice it too. She should have been carried under my heart, not someone else's." She broke into tears. Stewart put his arms around her to comfort her.

"I wonder if Em realizes what a remarkable woman he has?"

It was with considerable pain that he abstained from speaking of his feelings for her again. He had kept silent for so long, she often wondered if he had ever told her he loved her.

"Go ahead and cry, dear. Get it out of your system. You'll feel better," he said as he caressed her head as it lay against his shoulder making her very aware of his arms around her.

"I must not take comfort in another man's arms," she reasoned with herself withdrawing from his arms.

"The sad thing, Stewart, is to watch Em when he is around her. It breaks my heart to watch him. He can't even reach out and claim his own child."

"It hurts me to see what he's done to you, Lukatie. You don't have to take all this. I'll always be over there waiting."

"No, Stewart, don't. I'm learning to live with it. Em doesn't know that I know she is his. In fact, she's a very dear child and no trouble. Lovie takes care of her."

"That's the colored woman who lost her baby?"

"Yes, she is a lot of help. Stewart, I think we should adopt the baby."

"Adopt her! You can't mean that."

"I have to mean it. How can I put Em's child out? Please give me the encouragement I need to mean it." She pleaded.

"The old lucky stud," thought Stewart. "I suppose you're right. What does Em say?" he said questioningly.

"Nothing. He had admitted to nothing. We haven't even discussed it. He either thinks I'm blind or doesn't remember how Meda looked as a baby. I feel sure this baby's hair and coloring are just like his mother's. Most of the older folk around here are gone and maybe those that are left won't remember."

"I remember and so will William and most of the old negroes. They won't let on though."

"Stewart, I wonder if you realize how much I value your friendship. You've always been around when I've needed understanding and compassion. Thank you for letting me unburden my feelings."

"Any time, dear. If I can help, I'm glad. After all, that's the only time I can get near you," he smiled teasingly.

Lukatie walked over to the mantle and took a couple of aspirin from a box.

"What are those for?" he asked.

"Headaches. I seem to have them all the time lately."

"I can see why. I'll run along now so you can get some rest."

When he left, Lukatie went outdoors to watch the negroes picking cotton. "They are so graceful and rhythmic," she thought.

There is so much talk of farm mechanization she wondered how the farmer living as poorly as they were could afford to buy the machinery. "In fact, if it comes to that, what will the negroes do?" she mused.

"They don't sound worried now though as they sing. Taking up the song where they left off a year ago," she mused, humming with them.

I draws no penchion whilst heah below

> Ter pay m' charges as I go
> I'se gwinin' fo'th on m' own expenses
> Trust'n de Lawd for' m' defense.

"So much has happened in the past year," she thought. She felt the headache beginning again. "Guess I'd better go rest before it gets too bad. The ache never seems to go away completely, just dulls down then flares up again." She continued to listen to the singing as she walked back to the house.

> Through creeks, 'n riv'as deep 'n wide
> Both hi 'n swift I walks or ride
> Oft rollin' cur'ants culd beat wit' force
> 'N many time turn me fum m' cose.

Such faith they have. I seem to have lost all of mine. After taking more aspirin, she sat down to rest while Didge continued sleeping. She felt so tired.

Suddenly the baby cried out.

"Oh, no! I can't get a moment's rest. There is nothing wrong with her lung power." She forced herself out of the chair and walked to the bedroom door. To her horror a rat was scampering out of the cradle. She grabbed a broom and took a swipe or two at it as it crawled through a hole.

Blood was all over the baby's foot. Looking close, she found the rat had bitten the baby's little toe half off.

"Oh, Lord, why have I been burdened with another child," she cried aloud in anguish as she grabbed the child up and ran to the kitchen. Lovie saw her and ran in to help. They cleaned and bandaged the toe.

"Lovie, go clean out the crib. Then stay with Didge while I board up the hole the rat went through. You just can't kill the darn things. They are everywhere: in the house, the attic, under the house and in the woods. The old houses are so depreciated they can get in and out as they darn well please. I wish the place would burn to the ground. Then something would have to be done." For a second her mind raced through the timber standing straight and tall just outside the window.

"And, Lovie, dry her. Her wetting machine seems to be working overtime."

"Yas'sum, Miz Carroll, law me, law me dis pore chile," groaned Lovie. "She lak m' own."

That night Lukatie got on her knees and prayed for forgiveness for her evil thoughts. "They say out of deeds grow our character, but I feel my thoughts and words counteract any good I might do," she thought as she crawled in bed.

She yearned for Em to turn to her, to hold her close and comfort her. She felt it was little to ask for taking care of his child. Yes, and to make love. She needed so very much to know that she was still a desirable woman. "Strange, I should be the one to shut him out, not the other way around," she thought.

The next morning, she approached Em about adopting Didge.

"Absolutely not," objected Em. "And the sooner she is put in an orphanage the better for all of us."

"I think you'd better reconsider. I don't intend to give her up. Neither do I intend to raise a child I can't claim. Don't expect me to understand why you are acting and behaving as you are. You act as if I'm a stranger to you. Em, I don't understand you anymore. What have I done?" she cried.

"For goodness sake, Lukatie, cut it out.

You haven't done anything. You can't expect a honeymoon to last forever. I just don't see how I can afford another child, another negro and a dog. Three more mouths to feed. All the houses are in deplorable condition. I haven't the money to fix them up. They aren't worth fixing even if I had the money. It worries me sick, that's it. Yes, that's it." His long tirade over, he felt relief at finding an excuse.

"Well, guess I'll get Thankful and go fishing if I can tear him away from Lovie."

"Yes, you do that. You go fishing." She said sharply.

When Em came back from fishing he was told they had received word that Preacher Murray's wife dropped dead.

"What happened to her?" he asked.

"She had a heart attack right after dinner."

"I'm sorry to hear that. Guess we'd better go pay our respects and see if we can do anything for them. Take some food maybe."

"I've got Lovie frying a chicken and I just finished baking a cake. I suppose others will take something, too."

Em gave the eulogy at the funeral. Lukatie's heart went out to Preacher Murray although she had never particularly liked the man. Preacher Murray thanked everyone and when offers were made to take the children until he decided what he wanted to do, he stated "We'll stay together. Sena can cook and I can help. We'll make out."

Unknown to those present his decline of their offers wasn't because he loved the children as much as he loved the attention he received because of the fact that he was willing to sacrifice all to keep his family together.

SILENT TEARS

"What a wonderful man." Said one lady, sniffling. The other ladies joined in with their crocodile tears as Lukatie called them.

"I don't understand why they are carrying on so," thought Lukatie. They had all talked about Mrs. Murray. No one had liked her. She had been unfriendly, reserved, and had always sat around with a sanctimonious expression on her face. "True, her family will miss her and I shouldn't have such thoughts," she rebuked herself.

*****

Nearly a month later a new family moved near town. No one ever really knew them well. The Bolton's were loners and sequestered themselves. They never returned a social call and people soon left them alone. Mr. Bolton found work with Heywood Lumber Company. They had a son, Hezekiah, and a daughter, Mary Ann.

Soon after their arrival, people began missing things around town and on the farms. No one ever thought to connect the disappearance of their belongings with any member of the Bolton family. Mr. Bolton was well-liked at the lumber yard and soon heard of the things being stolen.

One evening at supper, he said, "Hezekiah, do we have to pull up stakes and move again? You said when you got out of jail in Florida you would behave and we could all start a new life. Already I'm hearing of thefts in the town and on the farms."

Mary Ann jumped up from the table and ran from the room in tears, words trailing after her.

"I can never have friends." She shouted. "I'm afraid you will steal the clothes off their backs or their virginity." The door slammed.

Hezekiah raised his eyebrow and continued eating. Then he spoke to his son. "It shames me to say it, but you're wicked. I can't throw my own son out so why don't you just leave and give us peace."

"Perhaps something will miraculously awaken my fretful, self-indulgent ill-tempered, ball-faced self, but until it does, Pop, shut up and leave me alone." Hezekiah smiled coldly, finished his supper and left the house.

"Oh, Henry, what can we do? We can't even make friends. Mary Ann's life is miserable. Why, oh, why was such a child born to us." Cried Lena Bolton. "Ours is a house of darkness, a purgatorial gloom."

Hezekiah was obdurately cruel, his behavior vile. He deserved the appellation "wicked." He had been guilty of every sin committed and capable of thinking up new ones. He only gathered close to him those of his own ilk. Be they white or black so long as they were evil and corrupt as himself. Filled with cowardice and deceit, they would band together and steal from stores and homes in town or would raid small farms. They usually left the large plantations alone because there were too many negroes around them which increased their chances of getting caught.

Lovie had been with the Carrolls a year when Thankful, who had been courting her seriously, asked her to marry him.

"Is hit alrite iffen we's marries up?" she asked Lukatie. "I mean yo' won' mind? I jus' be rite ova thar iffen yo' needs me."

"Of course, it's all right, Lovie. Thankful is a fine man. I wish you both all the happiness you deserve."

"Thankful is gwine ter talk ter Mistuh Carroll. Waunts him ter witness fer us. Yo' too, iffen yo' can."

Thankful was also asking Em about cutting some timber for adding a log room to his house.

"Guess I'll go along and help him to make sure he only cuts what can be used." Em told Lukatie. "I sure hate to see the trees cut." Many friends came to help Thankful add on the room and within a week it was finished. Lukatie gave Lovie material to make some dresses, underwear, sheets and pillowcases. Lovie was thrilled with the beautiful things when they were finished.

"Ah do decla'ah ah feels lak ah blushin' bride, only de blush don' show." They laughed happily.

Two weeks later they were married. Em went to the wedding, but Lukatie had to stay home with Didge.

"I'm sorry, Lovie, I did want to go, but you see Didge has a temperature. I think I'd better stay with her."

"Yassus, she is sick. Ah'll drop in ter morra ter see how she is."

Lukatie put her arms around Lovie. "I do hope you'll be very happy, Lovie."

Every house was buzzing with excitement. All who could were going to the wedding and to Roxie's afterward. The cry was, "Come on to Roxie's. They're having a shindig tonight for Lovie and Thankful."

"Whur yo' goin?" asked Malitha Casteen as Soloman ran out the door.

"Ter de café ter cyore m' lil' ol' cold." The words bounced back as he ran down the steps.

Em and Mr. Heath went to the party out of respect for Thankful and Lovie. They made their excuses and left shortly after the wedding ceremony.

Clarkey Brown jumped up and yelled, "I

wants sum action, man. I'se a rite ter sum after workin' in de field all week." The place was filled with free love and knowing looks.

With a nod from Elijah Golden, one dark brown rather pretty girl of seventeen shimmied over to Thankful and said, "Well, alrite, man, git wit hit, let's dance," As she danced around him all eyes were on Thankful and Lovie. Thankful gulped down his drink, caught Lovie by the hand and pulled her to her feet and started dancing. Everyone laughed so hard they were holding their sides or doubling up and slapping their thighs.

The girl shrugged it off and danced over to Clarkey Brown like a serpent. She seemed to prefer the men from the Carroll farm to those of her own group at the Heath farm.

"Well," she smiled down at Clarkey.

"You bet," he jumped up and stepped in swing with her. They shortly disappeared.

Within the first year a baby boy was born to Lovie and Thankful. "He will not wear de name ov Thankful," Thankful said firmly. "Ah stands firm on dat. It's a woman's name enyhow. How 'bout de name ov yore paw?"

"No! I neva wants ter heah his name as long as I lives." Declared Lovie. "How 'bout yore paw or grandpaw?"

"The ol' man?" Thankful was doubtful.

"Why not? Gilbert Mathias wuld b' a nice name. De ol' man wuld feel proud. He has so little in life. Iffen not him, den yore paw."

"Ah don' kno' m' paw, Lovie. He was killed fore him and my maw culd git married. My maw neva loved anudder man."

"I'se so sorry. I didn't kno'."

When tiny Didge saw the baby she beamed and pointed at him. "Gick, Gick." Young baby Gilbert Mathias was called Gick for the rest of his life.

When Lukatie returned home after Lovie gave birth to the baby, Lucinda asked, "Mother, why do you knock yourself out trying to wait on others? You know it's thankless."

Without hesitating, Lukatie answered, "I find helping others to be one of the greatest joys there is."

"Why don't you charge when you go deliver a baby and sit up all night. Nurses do and you're a nurse."

"When I do something for someone else it plants a seed of happiness in my soul to know I've been of service. You wouldn't cheat me of that, would you?"

"No, but you need so much, yet you are always giving."

"Giving is the seed of contentment, dear. Someday you will understand."

Roxie was busy in the kitchen. Saturday was always a busy day. Negroes simply did not like to work on Saturday. They either went to town or came to her place, usually doing both.

It wouldn't be long before the place would be paid for. Then she could take it easier. Mr. Heath praised her every time she took him a payment.

"I'm glad to see you are doing so well, Roxie."

"Thank yo', Mister Heath. I'se not afeared ov work. Noah heps a lot. He works real hard."

"You making whiskey on that place, Roxie?"

"Why, Mistuh Heath!"

"You could slip me a bottle once in a while," he laughed. "I do know old Ed's still disappeared. You just be mighty careful, you hear. Sheriff Ply's a nosey old boy. Wouldn't want you in any trouble."

"Yas'suh, thank yo' Mistuh Heath."

"Now whar is dat Noah. He could brang me in sum wood."

"Noah," she called.

Sheriff Ply cleared his throat as he walked in. "Caught ya's alone, huh? Heard yo' call Noah. So guess he ain't heah. Yore a humdinger, girl."

"Yore a nuisance," she snapped and started to close the kitchen door. He stuck his food in the door jam. She let go of the door and put both her hands on his big pot belly and shoved with all her strength.

"Yo' git yore foot out ov dat door fo' I stomp yore toes off." She said coldly. Noah appeared from the pantry.

"Hey," Ply said suddenly upon seeing Noah. "I was only funning. Jes fix me a plate and I'll eat 'n be on my way."

Noah stood in the doorway, arms akimbo as Roxie prepared the plate. Ply didn't know if Noah was going to strike him or not. "Sure, I would arrest him," he thought, "but not until I'm hit. If dat big lummox hit me I'd go clear through the floor."

Noah walked over and sat at one of the tables looking at the paper while the sheriff ate. When he finished, he belched a few times. Noah was feeling nervous. He had almost walked out of the hidden room with the sheriff in the kitchen. "It's a good thing Roxie shoved him when she did." he thought. "She called so I thought it was safe to come on out." He wiped the perspiration from his forehead.

Sheriff Ply glanced over at Noah feeling annoyed at him for being there.

"Yo trying ter fool sumbody into thinkin' yo' kin read that paper, boy?"

"Yore damn rite I kin read hit. I'se been goin' ter school 'n Roxie has been hepin' me."

"Well, ain't thet something. A wise-ass, huh?"

"A man wantin' ter git married has ter have sum larning', Roxie said so."

"Yo' wantin' ter git married, boy?"

"Sheriff, my name is Noah 'n I do wants ter git married. I'se plenty ol' 'nough ter tak' a wife."

"Yo' know whut to do wit her if yo' git her?"

"Guess I'll learn."

"Who's the lucky gal?"

"Lebtia Smith. I ain't asked her yet."

"That girl! Why, boy, any man around can sleep with that one."

"Not ater I marry her dey won't."

"Shore ain't choosy, are yo', boy," he laughed as he went out. He got on his horse and rode away. His deep laughter rolled behind him.

"So yo' wants ter git married, Noah?"

"Yas. I sho' wuld lak ter iffen hits alright with yo, Roxie."

"Hav' yo' courted de gal?"

"Nope, jes seen' her w'en she cums ova heah wit' de udder boys. She de one I'se picked out."

"Jest like that, huh? I suggest yo' court her 'n den mak' up yore mind iffen yo' want ter marry her."

"Iffen yo' say so, Roxie. I kin dance wit her 'n tak her outside lak de udder fellows de 'n ask her."

Roxie threw up her hands helplessly and went back into the kitchen. "It's a shame to be twenty-four years old and that innocent," she thought. She didn't really know what sex was all about herself, but had a darn good idea. She had lain in bed as a child and trembled as she listened to the squeaking bed springs in her maw and paw's room. You'd think they were running a fast footrace.

There was singing and dancing with much rhythm that night. Several young men sat in a corner strumming either a guitar or banjo. In the middle of the room several couples were clinched together swaying and humming in the darkness of the room.

Hannabella Golden, her mouth hanging open showing buck teeth with spaces between them, was moving around alone. A stripling of a girl was dancing alone in an ill-fitted sleazy dress. She looked stupid with her large black eyes rolling around. She was shimming like a dollar bill blowing in a swift breeze.

"That's rite, honey, shake dat thang. Look at thet gal go." Called out Solomon Casteen.

"Shet yore fat mouth," she snapped back.

Jesse Tottle sat watching her. "My gosh," he thought, "It would take a large tub of hot water and a pot of lye soap to wash her ugly away." He felt sure she had taken a bucket of ugly pills. "But," he thought, "I could throw a bag over her head and…huh…" Marble jaw, a short nervous fellow with a jutting chin, looked around to see if anyone was watching. Satisfied, he rose and stumbled over a chair as he started toward her. "Damn!" he thought as all eyes turned on him.

There was nothing to do but go on and ask her to dance. After a couple of dances, they slipped out the door and headed down the bank of the river.

"Dar goes Marble Jaw and Hannabella," laughed Solomon.

"Whyn't yo' go home 'n tak' a bath 'n whils't yore at hit, wash yo' mind," quipped someone from the corner of the room.

SILENT TEARS

"Who said dat?" yelled Solomon jumping up.

"Hit don' matter who said hit. Dar'll be no fightin' in heah. Noah!" called Roxie.

"Aw shucks kin a fellow hav' any fun?" Solomon pushed back his chair and left.

"Thet's de way hits don'," thought Noah as he took in the action with interest wondering where Hannabella and Marble Jaw were now.

They danced until the sun filtered through the smokey hours of dawn. Everyone was exhausted when they picked up their guitars and banjos and headed for home.

"We'se cooled down de earth tonight now hit's time fo' rest," Hinton Smith said. His words came out as something slightly nasal as the door closed behind him.

Roxie and Noah cleaned up the place. Then she took a pan of water to her room, bathed and put on her best dress and hat and called to Noah.

"Ready, Noah?" He had taken a swim in the river and came in and dressed. "I jest kain't tak' those whore baths," he said.

Roxie straightened his tie. "Do yo' kno' whut a whore bath is?"

"Wal, no, jest heah de fellows talkin'."

"Then watch whut yo' say befo' udders," she chided.

They locked up and left for church.

Sunday was her day of rest and she always took a nap Sunday afternoon while the café remained closed.

*****

"How time flies," thought Lukatie as she watched Seth swinging five-year-old Didge. He really meant it when he said he was going to take care of her.

Malitha came close enough to call Seth. "Yore gran'maw sent fer yo' ober ah' hour ago 'n yore still heah. Now yo' git yore lil' wite ass home. Git now afore I frap yo' one."

"Oh, I'se gwinin'," shrugged Seth as he ran toward home.

From the beginning of her life, Didge had an insatiable appetite for learning. With the help of Lucinda, Benjamin, Miles and Meda, she knew the alphabet and numbers to a hundred. She knew to take letters and put them together to make words, although she could only handle small words.

She would make Seth play school with her and then mimic Lucinda as teacher. Using a stick and writing in the sand, she taught Seth the alphabet, demanding that he learn it. She talked about next year when she would go to school and shamed him for not wanting to go. In the fall he went in self-defense.

His teacher was Azariah Pope. On the first day at school, Seth opened the classroom door slowly. Mr. Pope, standing near the window, looked up from the paper he was reading.

"Come, come in. What can I do for you?"

"I wont's ter cum ter school."

"What is your name?"

"Seth Kirby."

"Will you come over to the desk?" He walked over and took his chair as Seth approached him.

"You are in the wrong school, aren't you?"

"No suh," said Seth. "I'se a negroe."

"You'll have to bring proof if you expect to attend here."

"He's a red bonner. That's whut he is." Called out a boy in the back of the room. With this clue, the whole class took up the chant.

"Red bonner! Red bonner! Red bonner!" They

began patting their feet and clapping their hands in rhythm.

Rising to his feet, Mr. Pope said, "See this?" as he shook a ferula stalk over his head. "I'd hate to punish any of you, but I intend to have order one way or another in this room at all times."

A subdued hush fell over the room as Mr. Pope looked around the room and glared into each child's eyes.

He said, "Then what are you, third row, fourth seat, and you first row, second seat, and you, and you," he pointed out about half the class. By this time you could have heard a pin drop. Mr. Pope paused, looking over the class, then continued.

"Don't ever let me hear those words again in this class or on the school grounds. Take a seat, Seth."

It was in the midst of this introduction that Seth began his first day of school. He learned fast. Playing school with little Didge paid off. But it was a hard cold, unfeeling road full of knocks and bumps that he traveled, and he continually drew on courage he didn't believe he had.

After two years, Mr. Pope said of him. "For one so young and starting so late, he has sounded values than most boys, and has the will to succeed. His mind is open and fresh for learning."

Seth had gone home that first day furious with the world. He didn't want to go back to school but he knew he would. He had picked up a rock as he walked along the cart path and in fierce anger had thrown it wildly into the woods as if to rid his body of all frustrations.

Something fluttered and lay still. He ran

to look and there lay a dead rabbit. He picked it up and ran home showing the knot on the rabbit's head as proof of his story.

From then on, he pitched rocks every time he saw one and later became pitcher for the school baseball team, winning every game he played in. Slowly, he began to make a name for himself in baseball.

Mr. Heath loaned Seth books and offered to help him. Many evenings they sat at the kitchen table with the lamp turned high and studied. Seth soon advanced to the head of his class. He caught up the years he had lost and forged ahead. In time, he was insulated against the hatred directed toward him because of his white skin and settled into a falsified calm.

Mr. Heath also taught Seth trapping, taking along a skinning knife and rifle which he gave him. "Not that we want to be an anarchist as it seems, but there is so much poverty that you have to do a lot of things to even exist. You can sell the pelts, Seth. It will help you get the money to get through school."

At first Seth objected to killing the animals, but before long it had become a pattern to him. It's just a necessary means to an end he would tell himself.

He took his pelts to Deaver's General Store until one day when he went in while Mr. Deaver was boxing some furs to mail to the furriers, he noted the address. When he got home, he wrote the company and asked if they would handle his furs.

"Indeed we will," they wrote back. From then on, he boxed and shipped his own furs, receiving a check for twice the amount paid him by Mr. Deaver. His trap line ran for miles along the riverbank and in the wooded areas of any farm that he had permission to use. He was up early every morning to check the traps before going to school. He caught muskrat, racoon, otter, beaver, weasels, skunks, rabbits and squirrels; tails and all. He trapped only in winter when the pelts were at their peak. Seth also kept up his yard work and stable duties for Mr. Heath. He soon became an expert at earning and managing his earnings.

Em watched the brilliant splashes of color reflected on the drifting clouds as dawn erupted outside the window. The beauty of it only brought the dread of another day. He was more tired than when he went to bed and now another long hard day of work lay ahead of him.

Maybe when he sold cotton this year, he could buy Didge some art materials. She was showing signs of becoming a very good artist and such a talent should not be wasted.

He didn't want to adopt her, but Lukatie would never let him rest until he did. And he would before he'd ever tell her the truth. He had to go into town today. Maybe he'd look into it and have it over with.

Lukatie stirred beside him. How he yearned to reach out to her. She was almost as beautiful now as the day he married her. Here is where one's inner resources lie, he thought watching her through half-closed lids.

Not realizing Em was awake, Lukatie slipped out of the bed to take her morning bath. As she bathed she watched Em's face through the old worn mirror on the dresser. He was watching her. Her eyes were gentle as they met his in the mirror. Understanding this man gave her strength and a sensuality which could have flame instantly had he so desired. It had been a good marriage from its inception, until his long trip to Kinyon's. She wondered how long he was going to punish the two of them for his sin. She had married him for better or worse and it never entered her mind to leave him. But, damn it, she didn't have to love his forest hells. And she didn't intend to go through the rest of his life unfulfilled.

Em watching thought, "She is beautiful, so much woman. I'm a damn fool. I've excommunicated myself from her. How could she have ever loved an old farmer like me anyway? I have to find out if she still wants me," he thought. "I've tortured myself and her long enough. I can't blame her if she tells me to go to hell. It sure has taken saintly patience to put up with me."

He got out of bed as she finished bathing and was reaching for her clothes. Walking up behind her, he placed his hands on her arms. Their eyes met again in the mirror. Hers were filled with so much love and wanting, he felt he should kneel down to her. "Oh God," he cried as he gathered her in his arms, "Forgive me for being a fool, sweetheart."

She put her arms around his neck and pressed her body tightly to his, placing a warning finger over his lips. "Don't call the man I love a fool," she whispered.

Em carried her back to the bed.

*****

Lukatie watched daily for a letter hoping for one from Benjamin. She still wasn't over the shock yet and could vision him as he had walked into the house nearly a year ago to announce that he had signed up in the army and was going to France. It was the summer of 1917. She didn't know much about war and didn't want to. The thoughts of her son fighting some place in France horrified her.

His letters always mentioned Didge. He hoped she wouldn't forget him. Lukatie often talked about him to Didge in an effort to keep his image alive in the child's mind. "I hope by the time I get home she will legally be my sister." He wrote.

After each letter, Lukatie pleaded. "Em, please let's adopt Didge before Benjamin gets home. She will go to school next year. Please, Em."

It never entered her mind that Benjamin would not come home. Two months before the end of the war, the message had come. A telegram, so cold and callous. "We regret to inform you, but…" Lukatie fainted and was incoherent for two days. She was in a state of shock with only the names of Benjamin and Didge spoken clear enough to be understood.

Stewart came and sat with Em. His heart was breaking for the woman he loved and for his lifetime friend. Lovie was there, taking care of the household duties. Her love and concern for Lukatie were evidenced by her tender care.

Later, when she was better, Em told her that the army would bring Benjamin's body home if they wanted it. There would also be a monthly insurance check for about twenty years from a policy that Benjamin had taken out.

"No! He wanted to go. If it's all right with you, let's leave him there. Let the bones lie in their grave. I don't feel I can go through this again. I don't want the insurance either." It was agreed, but the checks came and were banked.

When pictures splashed the front pages of the newspapers announcing armistice, with the parades and celebrations going on in New York, Lukatie looked with little feeling, numb to it all.

Em admitted, at least to himself, that he was something of a dreamer, hoping things would happen that couldn't without a push.

"I suppose it's time to be a doer as well," he thought. His father had worked hard, his mother had done without to give Kinyon and him a good education, even college. Kinyon had done well. "Me?" he thought, "Nothing! I can't seem to leave the farm. Something holds me here." He kicked the dirt and the dust floated up into the air settling a few feet away.

He looked up as Didge came running through the yard. As he looked at her, he thought, "Nature plays the damnedest tricks on people. Guess I'll make Lukatie happy and adopt her."

That week they signed the adoption papers. "Now, Em has his child," thought Lukatie. "I hope he can relax." He didn't and began to withdraw more and more into his shell.

"Is Papa a thimit, Mama?" asked Didge one day.

"A what?"

"A thimit. That's what I call Regal when he's running around without direction. I call Winnie, Elva and most of the girls one. They don't know what they want to do."

"Do you, Didge?"

"Oh, yes, I want to be an artist."

"You're willing to work long hard hours at it?"

"Oh, yes, but I don't think it will be hard," she called as she ran out.

"A thimit, indeed," thought Lukatie. Leave it to a child, especially that one.

Lucinda came in and announced that she had gotten a summer job at the new dime store in Campton.

When Em had time, he took her to work in the buggy or had Miles take her.

"Do you like working there?" Lukatie asked.

"I think I will when I get used to standing all day. It is interesting seeing all the people that come in there."

"Wouldn't you rather be a nurse?"

"No, Mama. What has it gotten you?"

"I think the word is gratification, dear, and that is reward enough."

Lucinda had grown into a lovely auburn-haired girl, with deep blue eyes set in an almost round face that shone with vitality and health. She was a very graceful five foot six inches and carried not an ounce of extra fat.

She loved the silk stockings and slippers she wore on Sundays, thanks to Aunt Jane. They were a welcome change from the long dark cottons and high-top shoes she wore during the week.

One day at work, Lucinda was in the rest room when one of the other girls came in. "She's an odd ball," thought Lucinda as she spoke to the girl.

"Hello, you're Prudence Lee, aren't you? I'm Lucinda Carroll."

"Yes, do you like working here?"

"It's all right, I guess." She finished combing her hair and returned to her counter.

"Hum," mused Prudence, "She sure is pretty and shapely."

Lucinda worked on the cosmetic counter and had to pass near the hardware counter whenever she went to the restroom or stock room. Prudence would see her and follow. One day, upon finding Lucinda alone, Prudence had reached over and briefly touched her on the breast. At Lucinda's startled withdrawal, she quickly apologized and left the restroom.

Later Prudence handed her a note saying she truly was sorry she acted so impulsively and hoped that she would forgive her. "You looked so pretty and desirable that I fell in love with you and had a desire to know you better." She ended the note by asking if she would meet her some evening after work just to talk.

Lucinda ignored the note outwardly, but inwardly she warmed toward the girl. Two weeks and four notes later she agreed to meet her.

"Let's go to my apartment after work. I'll fix supper for us."

"It will have to be tomorrow evening. I'll have to tell Mama." She didn't feel elated about going home with her, but she seemed so lonesome.

"Mama, I'm having dinner tonight with Prudence Lee. She works on the hardware counter. So, let Miles pick me up in a couple of hours after work."

"It's nice you have something to do. I hope you have a nice evening."

"Thanks, Mama," she called as she dashed out of the door.

Dinner was good and Prudence outdid herself to make her comfortable.

"How can you afford a place like this on your salary?" Lucinda asked.

"The house is mine, left to me by my mother. She also left a bit of money. I live in these two rooms and rent out the rest of the house. This big house was too lonesome alone, but when Mama was alive, we had a gay time playing all over the house."

"When you were a child, you mean?"

"Yes, yes, of course."

"Then you don't have to work?"

"No, I do it to pass the time and to keep busy. Say, when the weather is bad, why don't you stay over with me?"

"Thanks, maybe I will. It would save getting wet in that leaky old buggy."

After a few more suppers, Lucinda mentioned to her mother that when it rained Prudence had asked her to stay overnight.

It poured all the next day and Lucinda went home with Prudence that evening.

"We'll have to sleep together since there is only one bed. Hope you don't mind?"

"No, I'm used to sleeping with Meda all the time."

"Do you want to sit up late or go to bed early?" asked Prudence.

"If it's all right, I'd just as soon get a good night's sleep so I'll feel like working tomorrow."

When dinner was over and the dishes done, Prudence told Lucinda to look on the bed where there was a gift for her to use when she stayed overnight.

"Save you the trouble of bringing anything along since you never know when it will rain."

"Oh, how beautiful." She held the nightgown in front of her and whirled round and round. It was a soft blue satin trimmed in lace with tiny satin covered buttons down the front. Then she noticed how nice all of Prudence's things were, all very tailored and expensive looking.

"Maybe you'd like to take a bath and put it on." Suggested Prudence.

"Oh, yes, I've never bathed in a real bathtub in my life."

They were settled in bed when Prudence turned to Lucinda and said, "I could bring you real joy if you will allow me to."

"What do you mean?"

She kissed Lucinda and touched her breasts.

Lucinda caught her breath with a sharp intake. Encouraged, Prudence continued.

"They are nice and round. I thought they would be. Has anyone ever touched you before like this?"

"No, I...I don't understand your meaning."

"That's because you're pure. I thought you were when I first met you."

Prudence unbuttoned the night gown slowly and folded it back from her body and said.

"Mama and I used to have a lot of fun like this before she died. It's been lonesome without her."

She put her mouth on Lucinda's breast and her hand on her thigh slowly easing along her body. Lucinda tingled all over and had a sudden urge to run from such a strange feeling, yet she was helpless to move.

"We can take turns with each other if you like. But it really doesn't matter. Here, I'll show you."

In the spring a new store manager was sent. He arrived on a Monday. When Lucinda went in on Saturday, he was impressed with her efficiency as well as her good looks. Within the month he was asking her for a date.

"Mama, the new store manager wants to date me."

"Do you want to date him?"

"I don't really know. I've never given much thought to dating. A few boys at school have asked me for dates. I said no and thought no more about it. They just didn't interest me."

"Dear, does this man interest you? He is an older man. Didn't he say he was twenty-nine?"

"Yes, Ma."

"His experience might be more than you can handle. I won't tell you, you can't see him, just be on guard. We have talked about sex but talking is a lot different than action. Some men are very forceful and some are gentle. They will all try you to see how far they can go. Just be careful, dear, and don't lose your high ideals. No man is worth it. This family believes in marriage and when you reach the point where you desire to go the whole route with a man and he doesn't offer marriage, you know he is only out to ruin your life." Lukatie smiled. "I don't mean to preach, dear, just take care."

"Mama, he has only asked for a date."

"I know, but he may ask for another date, then another. It is better to say all this now than later."

The next Saturday, Prudence attempted to get Lucinda to meet her. Lucinda said she couldn't because it was Didge's adoption date and they always made a big day of it. "Just like we do on birthdays."

"Well, all right, but that had better be what it is. If I ever catch you out with a man, I'll kill him and you too if I have to. Don't think I haven't noticed Mr. Rue hanging around you."

Lucinda was startled; this was something she had never anticipated. She felt a chill run down her backbone. She walked over to the mirror and started putting on the pale pink lipstick she liked to use. For the first time, she noticed the lipstick marks all over the wall especially around the mirror. It was a blaze of red, orange, and purple tints made by finger marks from smoothing on lipstick. "What a mess. I wonder why I never noticed it before."

Through the mirror she saw Prudence watching her.

"Put on some lipstick yourself. You sure

need some and do something with that hair. Funny, I never noticed before how much you look like a man." Agitation flowed through her words.

Seeing the hurt look on Prudence's face caused her to feel annoyed at what she had said. Turning she walked out of the restroom and went quickly to her counter. She was shaking and felt ashamed of the advantages she had allowed the girl to take with her body. Thank God, it was one-sided, and she had never reciprocated. She began to feel sick and wondered if she was going to vomit.

Just then a little old lady wearing a black hat and coat with horn-rimmed glasses sitting on the bridge of her hawk nose approached the counter and asked if she would show her some hair nets. Thankful for the diversion, Lucinda picked up one each of several brands and showed the lady. She finally chose one and asked, "are there any holes in it, dear?"

"Why, yes, Mam. It's full of holes."

The minute the words passed her lips she thought, "Now I've done it. She will report me as giving her a smart answer and I'll get fired." Instead the little lady laughed and said, "yes, it is and that was a good answer. I'll take it."

"Thank you, Mam." Lucinda took the money, dropped the net in a bag and handed it to the little lady smiling at her.

The manager had walked up and was standing at the end of the counter. "You look so nice when you let that smile creep up into your eyes."

"Thank you, sir," she smiled as she busied herself straightening up the nets.

A week later it was raining when Lucinda finished her word. Lukatie had not sent Miles for her.

"I will not go to Prudence's house again,"

SILENT TEARS

thought Lucinda. "I can't stand her mauling over my body again. I must have been out of my mind." She started walking toward home.

"Lucinda," called Prudence. "Are you going to the drug store before we go to the apartment."

"No, I'm going home."

The store janitor came and rolled up the awning. Ignoring him, Prudence said, "Miles didn't come. You can't get home."

"Oh, yes, I can. I can walk."

The janitor went back in the store.

"Come, now, Lucinda, it's raining too hard. Come on now or I'll cause you a lot of trouble."

Mr. Rue walked out of the store and locked the door. Turning he saw the two girls and said, "Didn't your brother come for you, Miss Carroll?"

"No, sir."

"Can I give you girls a ride home? I'm going out your way, Miss Carroll, and it will be no trouble. My car is right here. I came out earlier and snapped the curtains in so it's dry inside."

"Thank you, Mr. Rue. It would be a long, wet walk home."

When he dropped Prudence off at her home, she slammed the car door. "Good night!" she exploded.

"My, my, having trouble, Miss Carroll?"

"That, that girl, she…oh, I just don't like her. I'm sorry, Mr. Rue. I should not have expressed my feelings so."

"People have a right to their feelings which brings me to mine. Miss Carroll, I'd like to call on you, if I may? There's just one problem though."

"Oh?"

"Managers aren't supposed to date the girls working in the store so we can't be seen together."

"You could fire me," she laughed.

"I'd never do that," he said as he drove into the yard. Turning, he looked at her a moment. "You're so pretty. I'd like to take you places to show you off. May I come in and meet your family?"

"Yes, if you'd like to, but they won't be expecting company."

Lukatie was surprised to see them. She had automatically taken for granted Lucinda would stay over with Prudence. After introductions were made, she asked Mr. Rue to stay over for supper.

"May I go to work with you, Lucinda?" asked Didge.

Lukatie responded in Lucinda's place. "You'll have to grow up first, dear."

Didge thought for a minute and said, "then, Mama, will you grow down so you can play with me?"

"That child will go places. She's a thinker," laughed Mr. Rue.

He became a regular visitor at the Carroll home. He knew Lucinda was poor to work for such meager wages and that her living conditions were below the borderline of poverty. As he looked around the farm, the vastness of it astonished him. "To have so much and at the same time so little. Was it poor management? Did they place their value in other places and things? It wasn't hard to see they were all well-educated."

Fountain Rue fell in love with her family almost as quickly as he had with Lucinda. They all had so much fun at the swimming hole. Lucinda was happy and the glow on her face didn't go unnoticed by Prudence.

Lucinda did wish Prudence would leave her alone. She was running out of excuses. She had

Miles come for her rain or shine, explaining she didn't sleep well when she stayed at Prudence's and would really rather be in her own bed. Prudence didn't like this explanation, but she didn't create an argument, for which Lucinda was grateful.

When Fountain Rue and Lucinda went riding, they kept to the countryside. One Sunday, the whole family went with them. They packed a picnic lunch and left early in the morning to drive the thirty miles to the beach and spent the day.

Lukatie sat on a blanket, which Em stretched out beside her, while the others played in the surf. She listened to the waves sing as they reached up to kiss the sun then rushed in to drench the beach and roll away leaving behind a gift of shells. She slipped off her shoes and walked along picking up the prettier shells. The waves washed up on her feet and as it returned to the ocean, she felt herself sinking. She laughed alone as she pulled her feet out of the sand and walked on. From somewhere in her mind she found herself wishing Stewart were there. She compulsively turned and started counting the heads of her family. She smiled as she noticed Lucinda and Fountain had drifted down the beach away from the others and wondered if he would someday become her son-in-law.

Walking back to the blanket Lukatie sat down and watched the white gulls against the blue silk skies spotted with white billowing clouds. So beautiful, she thought, so open, not like watching through the trees at home. Her eyes drifted back to the gulls at times flying low over the water in hopes of catching a morsel of food from the sea.

She saw the family descending upon her and began unpacking the lunch.

It was almost dark when they got home. The whiplash of the waves and the salty water had been a marvel to them. They all declared, however, that when it came to swimming the old hole just couldn't be beat.

*****

Going to town one day, Didge noticed a woman reach out to feel another's face.

"Mama, why is the lady feeling the other lady's face?"

"She is blind, dear, and that is her way of seeing the other lady. She can see by touching. She can probably see better through her fingertips than most people can see through their eyes."

"I can see good, Mama."

"Yes, you can, dear. But I'm beginning to wonder if I can. I keep having these headaches and wonder if it is my eyes. I wish I could go to the doctor and have my eyes tested, but I just don't have the money. Maybe I'll check in the five and ten cent store to see if I can use their glasses." Aspirin only made her feel better, but the pain was never eliminated, just lessened. She was taking six to eight pills a day in order to keep going and didn't like doing that.

They walked in silence awhile looking in store windows. Doesn't hurt to wish, she thought, looking at the handsome furniture and pretty dresses on display.

"Mama, why are those women dressed like that? They look so hot."

"I imagine they are dear. They are nuns. Called sisters in the Catholic Church. That is about all I know about them."

"Do you want to be a nun, Mama?"

"You really are inquisitive today, aren't you? To answer your question, no, dear, I do not want to be a nun."

"Why, Mama?"

"Because it's too hot."

Lukatie had always believed that when a child was wise enough to ask questions, they should be answered as truthfully as knowledge would permit. Having no insight into a nun's life she could only answer Didge according to the dictates of her own heart and her believe in womanhood.

"Dear, that is their religion and we should never say anything against it. To do so is to step on their pride and we should never do that. But I honestly feel it is a waste of fine womanhood. I believe that when the scriptures say we were placed here to multiply and replenish the earth, that is exactly what it means, excluding no women."

"What does that mean, Mama?"

"It means we should marry. That marriage is what God expects of us. For us to bring precious little children into the world. Like you, honey. But I'm sure the nuns must do a good service to mankind."

"Did my real mama think I was precious?"

"I'm sure she did, darling."

"But I didn't know her."

"She died when you were born. That is when you were brought to us."

"Did you know my real father?"

Hesitantly Lukatie answered. "I don't think I did, dear." "No, dear God, I'm sure I didn't," she cried inwardly. Didge gave her the look precocious children reserve for adults as she said softly.

"Do you love me like you do Lucinda and

Meda?"

Poor little darling, how deeply she feels. She squeezed her little hand as she truthfully answered.

"Of course, I do, dear. Every bit as much." Lukatie could never hurt this child because of her own beliefs and hurts. They say what you don't know doesn't hurt you. But it's what I'm sure I do know that's killing me.

She was glad when they reached Deaver's General Store so she could sell her eggs, do her shopping, change the subject and get back home.

"Look 'round fer whut yo' want, Miz Carroll. I be wit yo' in a minute."

She looked around for the owner of the voice finally finding him up a ladder oiling the big circular ceiling fan. How funny Mr. Deaver looked with his sharp pointed nose showing above the underside of his chin. She wanted to laugh. She got her egg money and left the list of groceries to pick up on her way home.

"Come, Didge, let's go to the dime store now."

Didge roamed around in the store while Lukatie went over to Lucinda's counter to try on glasses.

"Mama, you don't want those things."

"If they will stop my headaches, I do."

Didge saw Stewart. "Hello, Uncle Stewart." She called as she ran down the aisle to him.

"Well, hello there, Didge. Who's with you, dear?"

"Mama. She's over trying on glasses at Lucinda's counter."

"Come, let us get a root beer from that big barrel over there while you wait." He could see Lukatie trying on the glasses. "Had Em lost his head letting her get those things?" he wondered.

He watched until she left the counter, glad she hadn't bought the glasses. He turned his back so she wouldn't know he had watched her.

Lucinda spoke to her mother. "If you think you need glasses, Mama, then go to an optometrist."

"You know we can't afford for me to do that."

"You could use some of that money piling up in the bank from the government checks."

"No, dear, I can't," she said, dropping the subject abruptly. "I'd better find Didge and get back home. See you tonight."

"Bye, Mama, I'll be home around the usual time."

"Look who I found," greeted Stewart as Lukatie walked up.

"No, no, I found you, Uncle Stewart."

He laughed. "I believe you did at that, Didge." He didn't know why but he always felt full of laughter when he was with Lukatie. She looked tired.

"Have a drink with us."

"No, thanks, Stewart."

"Can I offer you ladies a ride home?"

"Thanks, Stewart, but we have the buggy."

"Before you leave, come over to the bookstore. I want to get Didge something." It was a small watercolor set with paper and a book of directions. Didge threw her arms around him. He dropped his arm around her shoulder. As his eyes met Lukatie's she smiled. What a nice way to bring happiness to a child, she thought.

"Oh, Uncle Stewart, thank you. May I have it, Mama?"

"Of course, you may, dear. I thank you too, Stewart. She's very good, you know. Her mother must have been very gifted."

"I'll paint your portrait one of these days, Uncle Stewart."

"I'll hold you to it."

"You're a forgiving, fascinating pigeon," he looked at her, his eyes serious but his lips teasing. "I still wish I had seen you first. You know something, I'd build you your Blue Bird."

His candor was disarming. "I think you're a bit daffy," she laughed looking into his eyes.

"Come, Didge, we have to hurry."

"What's a Blue Bird, Mama?" asked Didge that night at the supper table.

"A blue house I've always wanted, dear." "I hope she says no more." Thought Lukatie.

"Say, did you show your father the art material Uncle Stewart bought?" Looking at Em she said, "We ran into him in town today."

A few days later Lukatie heard voices outside and looked out the window. She saw Seth sitting on the steps and Didge standing beside him feeling his face. Her eyes were squeezed shut.

"Didge," she admonished.

"I'm just practicing, Mama. I may be blind one day."

"It's not at all likely. You have exceptionally good eyesight. You just learn to use it well and don't miss the beauty in all things. And you go home, Seth."

"Yes, Ma'm."

"Seth, I'm not mad at you."

"Yes, Ma'm."

The following Saturday, the whole family rode into town. They would talk to friends, window shop and wait until Lucinda got off from work.

"Are we going on an excursion, Mama?" Didge wanted to know.

"You might call it that."

Old man Mathias sat in his chair propped against the wall as usual, leaning his head back, his eyes closed, listening as everyone left for town. It was hot and perspiration ran in deep rivulets across the deep-set furrows of his forehead.

Sitting there alone he muttered to himself, "Whut a long hot stuffy Sattidy eva one ov dem damn negroes goin' ter town. Wouldn' wok on Sattidy iffen dey life depends on hit. Don' kno' why fo' dey shore hain't got no spendin' money 'n dey leaves me here all by m'self. I kain't ebn h'ar a breeze a stirrin'. But I'se 'har'n sum feet arrunin'."

Ira Golden caught Lebtia Smith in front of the old man's house and started necking her, trying to pull her into the hedge.

"Sto dat, fo' sumbody see us."

"Eva body gon' ter town. Cum on gal I'd shore lak' to pleasure yo'. Cum on now." He tried enticing her into the bushes again. She motioned toward the old man.

"He...oh, yo' kno'. He's blind as an old coot."

"Nuttin' wrong wit' his h'arin'."

"Then keep yore mouth shut." He closed it with his own running his tongue into her mouth. She squirmed as he continued to pull her toward the bushes.

"Cum on, hit's really great stuff."

The old man with his eyes half closed thought, she rite I can h'ar 'n thar ain't a noise within fifty miles I don' reck'niz. I hain't lived dis long fer nuttin'. He half smiled licking his lips as he savored his memories, listening to the sounds beside the house.

Henry Casteen, returning from town, saw

Ira. "Yo' didn't go ter town?"

"Nope."

Then Henry saw Lebtia disappear around the corner of the house. With a mirthful wink, "Did yo' buzz her man?"

"A co'se. Hit wuz her fust time, too."

"Fust time, my foot, How did she fool yer lak thet. Must be yer' fust time iffen yo' don' kno' bettern thet."

Ira took a swing at him, "Cut it, boy, doz'en men already had her, so why fight 'bout hit?"

"Mebbe I jest up 'n marry up with her fo'sum other man gits her. I still say I'se fust."

"She mite not wan' ter marry up with yo'."

"She let me hav' her fust, didn' she?"

"So yo' say, so yo' say. Believe whut yo' lak!"

The old man just sat and listened, remaining quiet. He knew much of the goings-on around him. He had had his day, some of them rough, but he had always redeemed himself. He had the scars to prove it. A smile lit up his face, showing his toothless gums. One would think for sure his nose and chin might meet if he smiled a little harder.

"No, look thar yo' dang fool y' woke de ol' man." Ira glared at Henry and stalked off toward home.

The old man was remembering the time he had gone coon hunting with a bunch of men. Alonza Casteen had gotten drunk and passed out. Catching a coon they cooked and ate it. Then remembering Alonza laying over there drunk they rubbed their hands around the greasy pot and then over Alonza's hands and around his mouth. He started coming to and wanted to know when they were going to eat. "I'se hongry," he lamented.

"We et, Alonza, yo' et. See yo' got grease all around yo' hands 'n 'round yo' mouth."

Alonza looked at his hands and licked his lips.

"Ya's rite. I'se got hit all ova me, guss I'se et alright, but I'se shore hongry as hell to jist et."

"Cum on, le's get home. Git up, Alonza." They all stalked off.

*****

All the women were commenting on the sermon as they came out of the church.

"All I got out of that was for the wives to keep their nose out of their husband's business." Said Lukatie.

"Heck, I already knew that and I'm not even married," answered Lucinda.

"Then you've learned a lot for one so young."

"I've a good teacher, one who sets examples," laughed Lucinda. "Mama, I'm thinking of getting married when I finish my year of business school. Fountain has an offer to be transferred to Richmond, Virginia to manage a larger store in the middle of June. He wants me to go with him. We don't know how to work it out. He could be fired for dating a girl in the store. He's going to discuss it with you and Papa this afternoon."

"Lucinda, why don't you quit work? Then you wouldn't be a girl working in the store. That is, if you want to marry him."

"I think I do, Mama. But how can I be sure? Where do you draw the line between love and physical attraction so you know which you feel or if it's both? You know, sex."

"Dear, sex is a nutriment that can give life and should only be used between married couples. Love and sex are not the same. There is sex without love. Yet sex is the final climax of real love. Marriage has to be more than satisfying the emotional or physical needs."

"The man one marries is not always the perfect person you think he was. They become less and less the person you thought them as the years go by. The demands of married life often change the woman too. But with those years, you're hopefully blessed with the grace to live with it. Dear, if you feel Fountain is the man you want to spend the rest of your life with, then marry him and be happy and tell him today you have to quit work."

"We have never felt right to spend the insurance money the government has sent since Benjamin's death. Maybe now is a good time to use some of it."

"Thank you, Mama. Thank you so much. You seem to always have the answers." She put her arms around her mother just as the others came out of the church.

Fountain came that afternoon in a nervous cold sweat. Em decided to let him sweat it out. Fountain got out of the car. As he walked around it, he was bareheaded wearing a loose swinging duster coat. "What a striking, handsome man," thought Lucinda as she watched him slip out of the duster and throw it on the seat of the car. He vaulted up the steps two at a time.

"Miss you when I don't see you early every morning," he said as he sat down in the porch swing beside her. "At least Saturdays," he added.

"I declare, Fountain, you're so nervous I don't think you even know which month it is."

"I do too. It's the marching month. The last day of it too," stammered Fountain.

Em threw back his head laughing. He had a hardy laugh. Fountain and Lucinda laughed too. Fountain relaxed.

"I guess you already know I plan to ask your permission to marry Lucinda, Mr. Carroll."

"Yes, she told us. She decided to work a couple more weekends and quit."

"Then you won't get in trouble dating me," teased Lucinda.

"You can tell your grandchildren you fired her so you could date and marry her," grinned Em.

As Em and Fountain discussed her future, Lucinda's mind closed them out, lost in her own thoughts. "I'll be glad to get away from the girls in the store," she thought. "Most of them have minds so low they are in guttural disorder and think everyone else is the same. They are a bunch of thimits as Didge would say. I only hope I don't have trouble with Prudence. I've tried to break it off with her easily but firmly."

She put off telling Prudence she was quitting until the last possible minute. Then one of the other girls told her. She walked up to Lucinda's counter.

"I want to see you in the restroom. Now or I'll make a scene."

"I haven't time. I have to leave this counter straight," answered Lucinda.

"I'm not just talking to hear myself. You come now." She turned and walked away. As a woman walked up to the counter, Lucinda waited on her then went to the restroom.

"You thought you were pulling a fast one, and I wouldn't learn you were leaving, didn't you? You dirty bitch!" blasted Prudence.

"Name calling will get you nowhere,

Prudence. I told you some time ago I was through with you and it's time you believed it."

"This is the thanks I get for being your friend and showing you the finer things in life. Well, you won't get away with it. I'll tell everyone what you are, especially Mr. Rue. I've seen the way you look at each other."

"You tell anybody anything you want to. But when you do, just remember you're telling on yourself too. I can talk also. I believe I have as many friends if not more than you do. If you want to lose your job just place a doubt in Mr. Rue's mind and he'll fire you. He can't fire me, I'm quitting anyways. How would you like for me to tell what you said went on between you and your mother. It wouldn't paint a pretty picture, would it, Prudence?"

"I'm sorry, Lucinda, please don't leave me. I love you."

"In case you're not aware of it, I left a long time ago. Just remember, the only way to keep me from talking is to keep your mouth shut."

"Yes, yes, Lucinda, but please don't…"

Lucinda left Prudence's plea hanging in midair and went back to her counter. Visibly shaken, she tackled her work vigorously to cover her confusion.

"My, aren't we working hard." Lucinda looked up to see Fountain standing at the end of the counter smiling at her.

"I want to leave everything in order for the new girl. She'll have enough to do learning where everything is." Why does he have to show up now, she thought.

"I'll miss you," he quipped with a mirthful wink.

"Within a month you might tell me to get lost," she teased.

"Maybe in a couple," he teased back and walked on.

Lukatie spent the next month making gowns, slips, dresses, a couple of suits and last of all the dress Lucinda was to be married in. They had decided to have a quiet wedding at the church. Lucinda didn't want the traditional wedding gown, just a nice plain white dress with a sweetheart neckline and long sleeves, a fitted bodice with a skirt that flared slightly with three-inch lace just about the hemline, and matching lace around the sleeves and neckline. She decided on a white wide brim hat with net and orange blossoms tucked around the brim. White pumps, purse and gloves would complete her ensemble.

The evening before the wedding, Lukatie, Lucinda and Fountain visited Preacher Murray with their license and explained that Fountain was being transferred to Richmond and they wanted to get married after church. Would he ask everyone that cared to remain for the ceremony?

"I'd be happy to unite you children in Holy Matrimony," he lied. Sunday morning, he was nervous throughout his whole sermon. It was noticeable and everyone began wondering what was wrong. He cut his sermon short. The eyes of the congregation turned questioningly to one another and they started to leave. Only the closest friends knew the marriage was to take place.

"Just a minute," he said, "I have an announcement to make. I have been asked to perform the wedding of Miss Lucinda Carroll and Mr. Fountain Rue this morning so they can leave immediately for his new job in Richmond, Virginia. All wishing to witness the ceremony remain seated. Others should leave quietly. All are invited to stay." There was an audible gasp through the room. All stayed.

"Mr. Rue, will you please come forward and stand to my left." Fountain left the back of the church where he and the Carroll family had come in unnoticed after the service had started. He walked slowly down the aisle. Preacher Murray cleared his throat loudly. "Mrs. Carroll, will you and the children come down front and sit?"

"And now, Mr. Carroll, will you and your lovely daughter stand at the back of the church and walk down the aisle while Sena plays "Here Comes to Bride."

"She is indeed lovely," thought Em as he held his arm out to his daughter.

Before her death, Charity Murray had taught her daughters to play the organ. As Sena played she wondered if she would someday walk down the aisle like Lucinda was doing now on the arm of her father. "Pa certainly can't marry me and walk me down the aisle too. Looks like I've got a problem."

The thoughts made her bang out the last notes hard and loud.

"I'll catch it now," she thought as all eyebrows shot up. Not realizing to what extent her problems would reach she sat there lost in her own thoughts.

Prudence slipped in and sat down in the back unnoticed as all eyes were on the bride.

Sena was suddenly brought back to the present as her father was saying, "I pronounce you man and wife, you may kiss your bride, Mr. Rue."

Preacher Murray watched as they kissed, then he turned and walked down the aisle to the door as others gathered around them. He felt guilty as he remembered his thoughts of going to court Lucinda Carroll. He stood there burning with desire and couldn't help himself. The

Carrolls interrupted his thoughts thanking him, and Fountain slipped him a ten-dollar bill as the preacher handed him his marriage license.

"Thank you very much," Fountain said.

"You're welcome," he said, clearly flustered.

Lucinda smiled at him as she turned and left the little white frame church. The congregation followed them to the car. Fountain had already snapped the curtains in so their suitcases, clothes and gifts wouldn't fall out of the car.

A few people found out about the wedding even though they did try to keep it a secret. Fountain had told the new manager the day before the wedding and he told the girls in the store. The manager had brought out the gifts from the girls and slipped them in the car before going into the church. Only Fountain knew who he was.

The new manager was the only one to see Prudence slip in just after he had arrived. He watched her as she cried through the whole ceremony. Lucinda saw her as she was leaving the church. The girls exchanged enigmatic glances. Prudence's eyes showed hurt and pleading. Lucinda thanked God she didn't see her before the ceremony. Feeling safe now, she smiled at Prudence and walked out of the church. She and Fountain said their goodbyes to the family last and drove off.

Meda standing beside Miles watched them drive away and remarked, "I'll escape from farm life, too, one of these days."

"Why, what's wrong with farm life?"

"Look what it's doing to Mama."

"What has it done? She seems perfectly happy and content. I know she wants a better house, but what has that to do with farm life?"

"Oh, Mama is like a willow tree that bends and sways with the wind. She's flexible, capable, responsive to changing conditions and always there. I'm not like that."

Lukatie turned to see who Lucinda was frantically waving to as they were leaving. She saw Lovie, Thankful, Zarilda and a few of the other negroes standing down by the road waiting for her to pass.

"I'm so glad you came, but why didn't you come in? You know you were all invited." Em chided gently.

"Yassuh, but we jest thout as how we'uns could stand out heah 'n watch. Our baby shore was perty." Said Zarilda, her eyes glistening with tears.

Fountain drove silently for a couple of miles. He stopped the car and turned to Lucinda. "Any regrets?" he asked.

"Oh, no!"

The smile she turned on made his heart leap with happiness. He loved this girl and wanted her love more than anything else in the world. He took her in his arms and kissed her. "I do love you so much, Lucinda Rue. We'll drive until dark then stop at a hotel and get into Richmond tomorrow. We'll start looking for a house or apartment the next day."

He pulled her close to him as he started the car.

"He didn't ask if that was all right with me," she thought, and aloud she asked "How can you afford all that and this car? You must have made a large salary."

"Not really, I'll make much more in Richmond. An uncle of mine died just before I came to Campton and willed me the car and over ten thousand dollars. I've saved it. He had no family and I was his favorite nephew."

"Oh," was all Lucinda said.

It was getting dark when they reached Royal Mount, found a hotel and unloaded the car. Lucinda had been curious about the few gifts. Her mother had made many things for her and the family had given her a hundred dollars. She knew it was the money they all called Benjamin's and she hated to take it.

"No telling what you'll need so take it," Em said.

She was already missing her wonderful family, even little Didge. What a happy child. To get them off her mind she turned to Fountain.

"Let's open the packages."

"Can't that wait," his voice got lower and more intimate as he continued talking. "We've got to clean up, go out and get dinner and go to bed." At her startled look, he added. "So we can get an early start in the morning. The roads are so bad we can't travel fast. If we have to pay farmers for many more toll roads, we'll be broke."

Back in the room after dinner, Lucinda said, "I still don't intend to sleep until I've opened the packages. After all, there aren't that many of them." She went straight to them as he opened the door. The last package she opened startled her. Fountain seeing the expression on her face said, "Honey, is something wrong?"

"Oh, no!" her voice trembled, "This, this gown. It's so pretty and there is no card in the box." She was thinking, "Damn Prudence." "She did this deliberately. Giving me a gown just like the one she gave me the first night I spent with her. Well, damn her soul, I'll show her."

"You're mumbling honey. What is it?"

"Nothing, guess I'm getting tired. I'll

just use this gown tonight and not bother to unpack my things."

She picked it up and went to the bathroom. When the tub was full she stepped in. As she did so the door opened and Fountain walked in undressed and stepped into the tub with her.

"Mother always said wash together and be friends forever. I want your friendship and your love," he teased as he reached for her.

*****

When Em sold his cotton in the fall, he bought Didge a good set of oils, brushes and canvases. It cost more than he thought he could pay for it, but he's just have to cut someplace else.

"Is she really that good?" asked Kinyon.

"She's good. With the proper materials she could be great."

"Then let me send her some good books on art, charcoal and paper."

Didge was so excited she threw her arms around Em.

"Oh, thank you, Papa, thank you."

Em stood straight as a pine tree. He finally put his hand on her shoulder.

"You're welcome, child. Now, go paint." He turned and walked out of the house.

Didge studied the books absorbing all her little mind could hold. She went to the small library in Campton and read everything she could find on the great artists. She had a prodigious memory that could retain nearly everything she read.

When Kinyon came in the fall, he brought her more canvases, a book on oils and a variety of brushes. He also brought gifts to the other children.

"It seems we should bring her a doll instead of paints." Remarked Jane.

This trip they brought the children, Penny Sue, Everett and Carlton. They loved meeting their cousins and adapted to the change of environment like ducklings taking to water. They made a path chasing each other through the kitchen into the dining room and back on the porch until in desperation, Lukatie said, "Do your running and playing outside. I can't even hear if my cooking is getting done."

The older boys made pop guns from alders and whistles from reeds.

Meda made Penny Sue corn husk dolls with corn silk hair. "That sure is an odd-looking doll, Cousin Meda."

"Yes, I suppose it is." She then busied herself making a bean bag which they tossed for many hours of fun.

While Didge wore them out getting them to pose for her, she marked a spot on the floor where their chair was to sit so they could take a break and come back to the exact spot. They enjoyed it and were surprised at the good work she was doing. A teacher at school was trying to guide her, but she was doing it mostly alone. All the teacher could do was criticize not correct.

"On our next trip, you can do a portrait of Kinyon and me," said Jane.

"You'll have to stay longer than a weekend if I do. I could do you in charcoal, then work from that. At least, I could try."

"Sit down, Aunt Jane, and let me see what I can do." She worked swiftly for half an hour then at the bottom of the picture she wrote in Jane's coloring. She handed it to Jane just as Kinyon walked in. They looked at it silently for a full minute.

"Didge, your work is beautiful. Do you know people will pay big money for work like this? She did this in half an hour, Kinyon." Later, Jane asked Em and Lukatie, "Did you see the charcoal sketch Didge did of me?"

"Yes."

"Em, you said she was talented, but we had no idea she was that good. Tell them what we talked about, Kinyon."

"With your permission, both of you, when Didge finishes school, we'd like to send her to Europe and France. Maybe there she can get the best training in art."

"No! Didge will stay home," said Em. "It's unthinkable."

"But what an opportunity for her," stated Lukatie.

"I'm sorry, dear, and thank the two of you, but Didge stays home."

"Just for one year, Em, please," begged Jane. "She has such talent. Anyway, this is long-range planning."

"Her talent won't be wasted," Em was recalcitrant and the subject was dropped.

Jane had every intention of approaching Em again when Didge finished school. In the meantime, she would just wait.

Without meaning to, Didge heard the whole conversation.

"Why, oh, why?" she cried out and ran from the house and down the river road. Regal followed bouncing joyfully along.

"Oh, God above," cried out Lukatie. "The child heard us. Maybe I'd better go after her."

"No!" said Em. "You know the woods are her retreat. She'll be all right. She will go sit on her thinking stump and when she has thought it all out, she will come back. You'll see. Come on, Kinyon, let's walk."

They walked in silence awhile before Em spoke.

"You know I can't let her go, Kinyon. Alone with no guidance for a year or more."

"There's a teacher in Landridge that is good, but not as good as one of the European teachers. Perhaps you would allow her to come and stay with us."

"Yes, I'll think about it. I'll really consider it seriously. I know I can trust her with you."

Regal nuzzled Didge. She patted his head and he looked up at her affectionately, sighed and lay down at her feet and slept contentedly as she sat down on her thinking stump. She pulled her knees up under her full skirt hugging them close to her and stared dully at the reflection of the trees in the water.

Her inner thoughts crowded her mind. All it could say was, "Why, why, why?" She felt as empty as the clouds that drifted appearing to dissolve in the skies.

The tears were running down her cheeks when Seth saw her sitting there.

"Thinking again," he teased.

Wiping her eyes on her skirt, she lowered her legs and told him what she had overheard while he listened quietly.

"Don't let the tears in your eyes blur your vision, little one. If you don't demand your rights people will walk over you. But wait until you're older."

"What rights?" she said vehemently. "They took me in, adopted me, and raised me, and are sending me to school. They could have sent me to an orphanage. I repeat, what rights? It's like getting a horse; they say, whoa or go, and I obey."

"The rights of another human being."

"It's like battling for survival or fighting to exist. Call it what you like. Papa's hard on me for some reason."

"Many problematical things require attention, don't let it upset you. Just take a deep breath and eliminate them, one by one. Just don't let it get you down," Seth said quietly. "You do know that when you're eighteen, they can't stop you if you want to leave. There are laws."

"They can stop me by just saying no. Mama would let me go in a minute. It's Papa."

She looked up at him and thought. "Who ever said the eyes were the mirror to the soul knew exactly what they were talking about. Seth's eyes are the mirror to my heart. I see myself lost completely in them. When I look at him, I feel like…she looked out at the water…like the tide is dragging me under. Is a thirteen-year-old girl supposed to feel like this?"

Realizing the darkness was closing in, she looked around at the dimness of the forest and the lazy river.

"Funny," she said, "How purple it looks in the twilight."

"What?"

"The forest."

"It's getting late," he held out his hand. "You'd better get home before it gets dark."

She could feel his grip and prayed he'd never let go as he pulled her to her feet.

"I'll watch you to see you get home safely. Remember, little one, don't let dreams pile up in your head. Make them a reality by achieving," he said with irrefutable logic.

He moved with the grace of a cat and was soon out of sight.

The shadows of the trees gave a terrible grotesque beauty as they fell around her. She felt so alone and quickened her steps. Regal's low growl warned her of someone on the road ahead. She found herself looking into the cold empty eyes of Hezekiah. Violent emotion showing in each harsh line of his face. "He makes my skin crawl," thought Didge.

"Well, well, look what I've found," reaching out his hand.

"What are you doing here?" she snapped bewildered, drawing back out of reach. Regal moved in beside her. She was scared, but thankful to know Seth was nearby in the woods. "I warn you. Stay away from me and get off the Carroll land." He grabbed her and Regal growled and started barking just as they heard whistling in ← Seth? the distance drawing nearer from the direction Hezekiah had come.

"Sorry, young lady, I didn't mean to startle you." He left the road and cut across the woods. And ?

Next morning as Jane and Kinyon were leaving, Jane placed her arm around Didge's shoulder and said, "Honey, you've a good clear mind. You see beauty and create it. Continue to work hard and when you're finished school, Uncle Kinyon and I will try again."

"Yes, Ma'm. Thank you, Aunt Jane."

*****

The next Sunday at church, Preacher Murray told the congregation the parsonage was too small for his growing family and Sena was getting too old to sleep in the same room with the boys. A young woman needs privacy, so could they build another room on for her. Clearing his throat, he said, "larger donations would help. I just want you to give it some thought during the coming week. Now I'll give my sermon for today on repentance."

"Ought ye not to repent and tremble before God and know that you can only be saved through Christ."

"First he asked for money, Christ didn't ask for money. Now he's calling himself Christ," Hezekiah yelled. "Are you Christ?" The congregation gasped, astonished.

"No, I'm not Christ. I'm his servant, doing the best I can to teach as he taught."

"Oh, I'm a great reformer, I am," laughed Hezekiah.

"You will be condemned to eternal damnation and burning fire if you don't repent."

"Lord, spare us," Hezekiah bent low in a genuflection position, laughter bubbling over.

Choosing to ignore him, Preacher Murray continued in his unctuous voice, "We were given this country in which to worship God. Don't let the dream of our country fade. It was established to the Glory of God, that man could settle here and worship as he sees fit. We have to understand the past in order to speak with sureness of the future, and repentance through Christ. We're given the scriptures to help us do that. We cannot do as we might please." He paused and looked at Hezekiah. "Unless we please to do right by all those with whom we come in contact. Salvation depends on repentance, baptism, truth and honesty. It must become our law."

Hezekiah rose, an amused look on his face and walked out laughing.

SILENT TEARS

The road of the mind turns weird curves at times and when Hezekiah's mind turned that curve, his mind was darkened and he cares none for his actions.

He got on his horse and rode past the Carroll home looking it over. "Nothing in there," he thought, "worth stealing." He saw Lebtia Smith in her yard. Riding over he said, "Hey, why ain't you in church like all the rest of the heathens?"

"Didn't feel lak goin' dis mornin'."

"Your folk gone?"

"Yes."

"Left you all alone, huh?"

"Dat's rite."

"May I come in?" He got off his horse throwing the reins in a bush.

"Don' tink so, yore a white man."

"Girl, don't you know the difference between the black and white isn't color, it's an element of society. It's true, you know. You mean those white Carroll's don't come buzzing you?"

"Nope, dey keeps ter dar own. Dat's why I allus lak livin' har."

"My, my, come on in, honey. Where is your bedroom?" He took her by the hand and pulled her roughly into the house.

The room was bare with just basic essential items needed for existence. There were stools, chairs, an old bureau, a table and a stove. Behind the door was a bed. He started to unbutton her dress and she pointed to the door leading off the end of the room. They entered.

"Peel," he said.

"Yo' pay now! Dar is no free samples har."

He laughed and threw a quarter on the dresser. They both undressed.

"Kind of pretty, but skinny." He said.

Later he dressed, walked over to the

dresser, picked up the quarter and turned and looked at her. With a flip of his thumb he tossed it into the air, caught and pocketed it. Without a backward look, he walked out of the room and out of the house.

"Yo', low-down common wite trash!" she screamed. "I hope sumbody shoots yo' head offen yo'!"

Everyone left the church hurriedly to avoid speaking of Hezekiah. On the way home, Lukatie said to Em, "Wonder why Preacher Murray wants the extra room? The two boys could sleep in Sena's room. It's large enough and the two girls could share a room. Those rooms are large enough for two full-size beds."

"Maybe he's thinking of marriage again."

"I can't imagine any woman marrying him. He has always been repulsive to me. His little eyes, pot belly, greasy hair and a breath that smells like last night's slop jar makes me wonder if he drinks."

"Now, now, don't be too hard on the man, honey," teased Em.

"I can't help it if I don't like him. Let's start going to church in town, Em."

"I don't see how we can do that." Em was surprised at the inflection of dislike in her voice. She never expressed dislike for people. It wasn't her nature to do such a thing.

The following Sunday it was decided to have an old-fashioned box supper at the church to be held on Friday. The purpose of the supper was for the parsonage building fund.

*****

Briant Roberson swore when his 1924 Dodge touring car came to a halt." Where in the world

SILENT TEARS

am I?", he thought disgustedly. He got out of the car to check the gas tank. He walked to the right side and raised the hood, touched a wire or two and put the hood down. "I don't know a damn thing about a car motor and the weather's as hot as the devil," he thought to himself. Looking around he saw a young boy riding a beautiful buck skin horse. Taking his handkerchief from his pocket, he signaled for the boy to stop.

"Can you tell me where I am?" he called.

"Yes, sir. You're near Campton. It's just around that curve a little ways," said Seth.

"Is there a garage there? My automobile has broken down."

"Yes, sir. It's about half a mile from here."

"Is he any good at fixing an automobile?"

"Yes, sir. Mr. Tartt's very good. He can take a block of wood and a mallet and in no time at all restore a bent fender to its original form. And take an engine apart and put it back together as good as new."

"If you're going that way, would you please ask him to come out here and help me? I'm a salesman and my automobile is full of samples and I hate to leave it."

"I'll tell him, but you may have to wait awhile. If he's busy he won't come until he's finished with what he's doing."

Briant walked across the hot dusty road and sat down beneath a large oak. At least that was better than the hot road and even hotter car. Three hours later Mr. Tartt came in an old truck with an engine that sounded smooth as a sewing machine.

"Yo' de fellow dat wants yore jitney fixed up?"

"I'm the fellow."

"Whut's wrong wit her?"

"If I knew, I'd fix it and wouldn't need you," Briant snapped wiping sweat from his face. He was tired, hot and agitated. The stupid chump, asking stupid questions.

"Thar, thar, son. I'll git yo' goin'."

"Purty thang," he said, eyeing the automobile. "Government man through her t'other day wit one jes lak hit. Buyed gas at m'place." Pulling out a plug of tobacco and a knife, he cut off a chew and put it in his mouth.

"Hav' a chew?" he offered holding out the knife and tobacco to Briant.

"No, thank you, Mr. Tartt. Will you please see if you can fix my automobile? I'm in a terrible hurry."

"Kno' my name, huh?"

"The boy told me. I'm Briant Roberson."

"Oh." He got in and tried to start it, then looked under the hood. He poked around for half an hour while Briant sweated.

"Well, I'se seed whut hit was. I'll pull yo' inter de geerage. Fuel line stopped up, I guess. Doubt if I kin git hit fixed ter day." He took a chain from the truck and looped it around the axle. "Now I'll hook on ter m' truck 'n yo' git 'n and steer yore aute'bile whilst I pull yo'."

Briant sat there behind the truck looking ahead as if in an angry dream. "This can't happen to me. What will I do in this hick town tonight?"

"Man, could I use a drink," he remarked to Mr. Tartt when they were parked at his barn he called a geerage.

"A man needs ter do a little whisky-nippin' once 'n a while ter re-vitalize a body."

"Know where I can get one?"

"Nope, don' drink m'self not good fer

business."

Briant would have laughed if he hadn't felt so desperate. He didn't like to deviate from a set schedule.

"Sure you can't fix that now?"

"Nope, yo' need a new fan belt too. I'll hav' ter order hit from Wilmington. I'll telephone fer hit 'n hit'll be har 'n de mail termorra."

"Any place around here I can spend the night?"

"Yep. Maw kin put yo' up. On yan side de road. Cum on."

Sounds like a runaround to fatten his wallet, thought Briant.

"What about my things in the car?"

"Tak' whut yo' need fer de night. Rest will be safe. Put in yore curtains iffen yo' lak."

Briant found Mrs. Tartt to be a pleasant, plump short round faced woman, with her thin white hair combed straight back and rolled into a bun on top of her head.

"Why," he thought, "does a fat woman like a thin short scrawny man like Mr. Tartt or visa versa? Guess it would be a problem for two fat ones to get together."

The room he was given was clean and airy. The furniture was old, but that didn't matter. He was only going to spend one night in it and hope to never see it again. While they were eating dinner, Briant asked.

"What does a person do around here for entertainment." He turned the lazy-susan in the middle of the large round table helping himself to more beans. The food was simple but very good.

"Wal, we'ums visit around de neighbors and gossip. Go ter church on Sunday. Sum ov dem got crystal radio sets, but dey hain't much ter dem.

Say, dey's a box supper dat de church down de road 'bout a mile at six o'clock ter night. Yo' mite lak ter go ter thet."

"What in the world is a box supper?"

After they explained a box supper to him, he went out and sat in the shade of a great live oak tree. Later he walked back into the town he had earlier been towed through.

He was rewarded with a smile or two from girls working in the dime store. He brought some razor blades and was about to ask the dimpled girl at the counter for a date when he remembered the box supper. "Why not try something new," he asked himself. "Indeed, why not?"

He went back to his room and shaved at the mirror over the dresser. He used a pan of water dipped from the kitchen stove reservoir. "I'll get there early enough to watch the boxes taken in so I can get a good-looking country girl to eat with," he thought. "After all, I'm good looking. In fact, handsome in a dark sort of way. With black hair, brown eyes, tall and slender," he told himself as he preened in front of the mirror like the cock he was.

He told the Tartts he was going out to the box supper and with his coat slung over his shoulder, he started walking down the road.

When he reached the church, Preacher Murray introduced himself. Briant explained himself and car trouble saying the Tartts had said he might enjoy the box supper.

"I'll just stand out here in the cool until it starts."

"Fine," said Preacher Murray. "I'll go back inside and start getting things ready."

Briant watched as several women came with beautiful boxes wrapped in crepe paper decorated with bows and flowers. Then a surrey rolled up with five people. A very distinguished blond looking man held the reins on a beautiful black horse. With him were probably the wife, two daughters and a son or was the fellow with the girl? He felt the zing of his neurons when he saw Meda and prayed to God the fellow wasn't her date or husband.

Three boxes were handed out to the young man. Damn, thought Briant, which one belongs to the beautiful young girl? I'll just have to buy one of them and take my chances. He made a mental picture of the three boxes as they were taken in. He followed them in sitting as near as he dared to Meda.

The bidding soon started. It seemed to drag along at first with husbands mostly bidding on the wives' boxes. Occasionally a young girl's box would pick up the interest of the young fellows as they counted their pocket change each time they upped a bid. Then the preacher picked up one of the Carroll boxes and the bidding jumped.

Huh, thought Briant, they can't know which box belongs to whom. They are either a well-liked family or it's good food. He was about to bid when Didge turned to Lukatie and said, "Mama, Uncle Stewart is bidding high on your box. He likes your fried chicken." Maybe getting in with the mother would be best he thought as he called "Five dollars." No box had sold higher than fifty cents so far.

All eyes turned on the stranger. "Six." Called Stewart. Briant let him have it at ten dollars. He bid on one of the other boxes and got it for five dollars. As the boxes were sold, they were handed to the fellow that bought it until all had been auctioned.

"Ladies, claim your gents and go to supper," called out Preacher Murray above the chatter in the church. There was a rustle of skirts as they all moved around. Didge and Meda turned and looked at Briant then down at the box. They moved down the aisle. With a splash of a smile, Meda moved on as Didge stopped beside Briant.

"I'm Didge Carroll. You bought my box."

"I'm Briant Roberson. I'm glad I bought your box, pretty lady," he beamed at her. "I'll be happy to eat my dinner with such a charming young lady."

"How did you happen to be here?" asked Didge.

"My automobile broke down. Mr. Tartt has to order a part for it from Wilmington so I have to wait till tomorrow to be on my way. They told me about the box supper, so here I am."

"Where were you going?"

Deciding the next question would be, why where you going there, what kind of work do you do, etc., he thought he might as well give her his life's history and be through with it.

"I'm a salesman of ladies ready-to-wear dresses. I'm heading to Charlotte, North Carolina then on the Columbia, South Carolina, Atlanta, Georgia and all the towns in between and possibly down into Florida. My father owns the dress factory."

"Is business good?"

"It is if I work hard and place a lot of orders."

"How do you like my dress? My mama made it. She makes all our clothes. She even makes Papa and Miles' shirts."

"Maybe we better hire her to design for us. The lines of your dress are plain and complimentary, well fitted. In fact, you're a beautiful family." His mind was quickly turning pages in reverse as he smiled at Didge and picked up a chicken leg.

"Your flattery might get you an introduction to my sister. I see you can't keep your eyes off her."

He took a bite of chicken, startled at her frankness. Then the young man is a brother, not husband or date. He didn't know why, but he felt happy.

"You know everyone is watching us. That's because you're a stranger here. They're wondering what we're talking about, too." She laughed as her eyes roamed around the room.

"We'll keep them guessing, all right?"

"Thank goodness you bought my box instead of that Hezekiah Bolton that bought Meda's. I don't know what he's doing here. He's no stranger, but he never comes to church unless it's to make trouble. He's a thimit, he is!"

"A what?"

"A thimit, that's what I call a nothing person. No aim, no direction in life. I think he's hypocritical." She gave a disgusted sigh.

"That's saying a lot. Everyone's life is meaningful."

"Not his."

Briant took another look at Didge. "What have we here?", he thought, as his mind raced back to the questions she had put to him. How at ease she was. About thirteen or fourteen at the most, he'd guess.

"What do you plan to be when you grow up? Or haven't you decided yet?"

"Oh, yes, an artist. Do you have a pencil?" She picked up the lid to the box lunch. She straightened out the corners while he took a pencil from his inside coat pocket.

As he finished eating she was sketching.

The pencil was jumping from one hand to the other.

"Ambidextrous," he thought.

"Bet you wish you had gotten Meda's box," she laughed as she handed him the box top.

He nearly choked on the piece of cake he was eating as he looked himself in the face.

"I'll believe anything else you say, beautiful lady, and I'm glad it was your box I got."

Lukatie, Em and Stewart walked up to them.

Didge introduced them, adding, "Mama, he thinks his father should hire you to design for his dress factory. He likes the fit and simple lines of our dresses."

"Thank you for your expression of approval," smiled Lukatie.

"You're welcome. You're a very talented family," he offered as he handed Lukatie the sketch Didge just did of him. "When she asked for my pencil, I thought she was fixing to ask for my address," he teased.

"She is good. Maybe when she's older she can find an outlet for her art."

"You speak with an accent. Is New York where your father's factory is?" asked Em.

"Yes, sir, it is."

"If you'll excuse me, I'll help clean up. It seems everyone has finished. Nice meeting you, Mr. Roberson." Em nodded as he turned away.

Stewart could see Meda was having a hard time with Hezekiah. They seemed to be arguing. He walked down the aisle. As he drew near he heard Meda say, "I told you I'm busy with my studies and don't have time for dates."

"I know school is out, Miss Carroll. You mean it's me you don't have time for."

"It isn't necessary to stop learning just

because school has recessed for the summer." Retorted Meda.

"Pardon me," said Stewart as he leaned across a bench. "Meda, your mother said she wishes to see you if you've finished eating."

"I've finished. Excuse me, Hezekiah."

She took Stewart's arm. "Thank you, Uncle Stewart."

"You bet, even if I did lie in church."

"I believe the Lord will forgive you that one."

"I could see he was giving you a hard time and thought you needed an easy way out, Honey."

"He scares me. He has the coldest eyes I ever saw."

"I'll join them so it will look like Mama sent for me." She squeezed his arm and went over to the family taking Miles by the arm.

"May I present my sister, Miss Meda Carroll, Mr. Briant Roberson," said Didge.

"Hello, Mr. Roberson. Nice to have you with us," she smiled.

Lukatie saw Hezekiah glaring at them and before Briant could acknowledge the introduction, she said, "Miles, why don't you, Meda and Didge take Mr. Roberson to his room while we help straighten up here. We should be ready when you return."

"You might find a surrey hard riding after an automobile, but even that beats walking," teased Didge.

Em walked over, "Nice to have you join us this evening, Mr. Roberson." Turning to Lukatie, Em said, "We better get busy so we can get on home."

As they left the church, Hezekiah turned a cold chilling smile on them. He went out and mounted his horse and rode about one hundred feet behind them all the way to the Tartt home.

In the surrey, they were feeling worried and told Briant of the thefts that had taken place lately and of Hezekiah's actions in church.

"Would you mind stopping at the garage and let me take my sample cases out of the car? They might be safer in my room."

"Be glad to," said Miles.

Didge laughed. "See what I mean, Mr. Roberson."

"I do believe, I do, young lady. May I call on the family tomorrow? By the time Mr. Tartt gets my automobile fixed, it will be too late to keep any of my appointments. I'll wire them to expect me Monday."

"Maybe you would like to go to the swimming hole with us in the afternoon. We all go every Saturday and Sunday when the weather permits," said Miles.

Briant turned his head toward Meda for confirmation, but in the musty darkness she could feel rather than see the plea in his eyes.

"I'm sure the family would be glad to have you join us in a swim, Mr. Roberson."

"Then I'll be glad to come if you'll give me directions."

"That is easy," chirped in Didge. "The church is the beginning of the Carroll land. Just go on down the road about one and a half miles. Ours is the first house."

"Good heavens, do you own the whole countryside?"

"No," said Miles, "Our ancestors settled here on a land grant. It seems there was no end to their supply of money. They bought out every landowner who would sell or trade a horse and plow until they acquired about three thousand acres. I checked it out at the courthouse."

"My," Roberson shook his head in amazement. "That is a vast amount of land."

"We'll be looking for you tomorrow," said Miles as they dropped Briant off at the Tartt house.

Hezekiah was in the road waiting. He called out to Meda.

"Miss Carroll, I guess your mama made you ride home with the stranger. That's all right. I understand. Will you talk to me now?"

"No."

"Say no more, Meda. Hezekiah, you are blocking the road. We'd like the pass." Called Miles.

"Oh, would you now?"

"Watch out, Miles," whispered Meda. Miles reached down and took the whip from the floor of the surrey. Standing up and leaning forward as far as possible, he stung the rump of Hezekiah's horse with a quick jerk of the whip. The horse bolted and took off down the road.

Em and Lukatie were waiting when they returned to the church. They all laughed as they told of their encounter with Hezekiah.

"I hope that is the end of it," Em said solemnly. "But he's a bad one. He's carnal, sensual, devilish and I do believe the devil owns his soul. Mind you, that's what I believe. Too bad. I think his family is nice. Everyone is beginning to think he is behind all the thievery. I hope not for their sakes."

"Em, how awful," said Lukatie, quite moved.

"For some reason, they act like they are afraid to make friends. How is Mary Ann at school, Meda?"

"She keeps to herself. She talks some but never gets friendly with any of the girls. She seems afraid to join in. You know, kinda holds back."

"What a lonely life they must all live. It must seem like an illness having a strange boy like him," said Em, ending the conversation.

Saturday, they got the weekly letter from Lucinda. It was full of news of the new house Fountain was buying.

That afternoon Briant's car was fixed and he went looking for the Carrolls. When he saw the first house on the left after he passed the church, he felt apprehensive. This can't be where a family like that lives, but I can stop here and ask. As he drove up in the yard, he saw Miles putting a basket in a wagon.

"Just in time," he called. "Hope you brought a swimsuit?"

"I sure did. Hope you told your parents I was coming."

"We did. Mama fixed a picnic supper for us to eat by the river. Uncle Stewart is coming, too. He lives in the big white colonial house on the right. It seems our house was the only one to burn down during the Civil War."

"Oh, Mr. Henderson is your uncle?"

"No, he's our Godfather, but we grew up calling him Uncle. We only have one uncle and he lives in Landridge and is president of Blunt Mills since Mr. Blunt's death. He is Papa's brother."

Briant, like Fountain, couldn't help but wonder what was wrong that the plantation house had never been rebuilt.

Surprise struck him forcefully when he reached the old swimming hole. They all laughed at him. He was game to try any old swimming hole just to be with Meda, but this lovely place was far beyond his expectations. As they rode up, they startled a deer who disappeared into the woods.

"We often find them drinking here," said Meda, her eyes following the deer.

Briant followed in Fountain's footsteps and was in love with the whole family before the afternoon was over. He asked if he could visit on his next trip and felt happy with the assurance he could.

Stewart was amused at Briant's obvious interest in Meda, who acted her usual self. If she had any interest in Briant, it was not obvious. She played in the water splashing all of them.

Stewart teased her, "You're too big for me to throw across my back and swim out with now."

"You're too soft to try," she teased back.

Stewart made a dash for her just as Lukatie called, "Supper time."

Stewart turned and caught his breath. Lukatie was standing at the edge of the water. The wet suit she had made was clinging to every curve of her body. "A goddess," he thought, "How could I ever stop wanting her?" He ducked his head under water as if to cool his thoughts.

"Come, children," he said when he surfaced.

"That's an easy way out," Meda laughed as she swam for shore, aware that Briant was watching her. He swam over beside her. "You look mighty pretty all wet and shimmering, you little blue-eyed redhead. Too pretty a picture for a man to think of leaving." His face burst into a grin. She liked the grin. It was infectious and she smiled back.

They were all famished.

"I'm eating like a glutton," laughed Briant. "I'm starved after all that swimming."

"That happens to all of us every Saturday," Em informed him.

Stewart, standing beside Lukatie at the end of the picnic table whispered behind a chicken thigh, "think he will fit into the family?"

"I hope not. I'm losing them too fast."

"Right," said Em, who had overheard.

Stewart came by early the next morning to say he had received word that Elda had a heart attack and that he was leaving for New York.

"Anything we can do while you're away or to help you now?"

"I was wondering, if you're free, could you drive me to town to catch the train and bring the horse and buggy back. I think they will be better here than at the stable in town since I don't know how long I'll be gone. Festus is tied up, but I can phone him to come get me when I get back."

Lukatie laid her hand on Stewart's arm, "I hope she's well by the time you get there. Give her our best wishes for quick recovery."

"Sure will," he patted her hand and he and Em left, Lukatie turned back into the house thinking, "I never knew his sister Elda, Em did. She was much older and had gone to New York when I came here."

On his return trip, Briant stopped by again. His intentions were transparent after a few more visits.

Meda was tall, five foot seven inches to be exact, and moved easily and softly. She had the grace of the animals of the forest. Living on the farm bored her. She had desires that needed satisfying and simply didn't see the beauty around her that Didge was painting.

Meda felt Didge exaggerated her paints, and she told her so. Looking at a painting one day, she said, "All that beauty isn't around here."

"Oh, yes, it is," defended Didge and would

delineate the painting to Meda.

"Well, I just don't see anything around here like that," she shrugged, and walked out of the room to dream her own private thoughts.

Marrying a traveling salesman from New York is one way of getting away from here. Thinking of New York thrilled her. It must be an exciting city, so large, so much to see and do.

Briant had his own apartment in New York. It was more convenient to the night life he wanted. He was a free liver and a private person. He felt it was wasted time to drive out to Long Island after work every day and to get up so early every morning. When he wasn't on the road selling, he worked in the office with his father, learning the business that he would someday own. He often dated the secretary who had visions of marrying him and the business. She wasn't exactly sure when she began to feel his lack of interest in her. When they worked late, he would take her to dinner and a movie and always came to the apartment afterwards to make love. Sometimes he spent the night slipping out in the early morning hours.

She had gone all the way trying to please him. But lately when he took her home, he would say goodnight at the door and using the excuse of tiredness would turn to leave without even a goodnight kiss. She could feel everything she wanted slipping through her fingers.

"Who is she?" she yelled after him one evening.

He whirled around, "What do you mean, Priscilla?"

"Exactly what I said. Who is she? Your indifference tells me there is someone else and I don't like it. Do you hear me?" Her voice was nearly shrieking.

"Keep your voice down. Do you want everyone in the building to hear you?"

"I don't care anymore. You think you can disgrace me and walk out. You know I love you and lately you ignore me."

"If I've hurt you, I'm sorry. As for disgracing you, that takes two. I've never told you I loved you and you know it."

"Who is it then or what is it?"

"There is no one else, not now. Does that answer your question? I'll see you tomorrow at the office," he turned to go.

"I'm not sure you will," she retorted.

He paused, "Suit yourself. Maybe you would like to find another job at that."

She was at work that next day. Briant raised his eyebrow, said "Good morning," and went about his work. Two days later he packed his samples and as he left, he paused at his father's desk.

"Dad, while I'm away this time, try to get rid of her," nodding his head toward Priscilla.

"So, the affair's over," Mr. Roberson laughed. "I'll see, son. She's smart and it won't be easy to replace her."

"Thanks, Dad."

*****

Meda finished cleaning the house. "All right if I go to the swimming hole, Mama?"

"Sure, is Didge going?"

"No, Ma'm. She's out someplace painting."

Regal walked with her, chased a rabbit and barked at squirrels brave enough to bark back when they were half way up a tree. She swam until spent, then lay at the edge of the water to rest.

A voice spoke behind her, "I've heard of

this swimming hole all my life, but didn't know until now what I've been missing." Meda whirled around, mad because her dreams of bigger, more important things had been interrupted.

"Hello," said the stranger, a tall dark young man, in his early twenties. He looked at her with blue green eyes fringed with thick black lashes under very heavy eyebrows. His look was careful and deliberate, as his eyes raced over her.

Very rude and ugly, except for the eyes, she decided. A slight scar was on the lower part of his right cheek.

"Who are you? And what right have you to be here?" she demanded.

"I'm Madison Hinson, Uncle Stewart's nephew." He smiled and the light scar disappeared into the natural creases around his mouth, changing his whole countenance. He continued standing there in a casual insolent slouch, watching her. She rose slowly to her feet and walked out of the water. He thought, "What a most desirable girl. I wonder if I dare try." Regal ran up to Meda and stood beside her looking at the stranger.

"Where have you been?" she scolded, patting the dog's head.

"Guess I don't try," thought Madison, "At least until I make friends with the dog. Can't tell about strange dogs."

"Sorry about your mother," said Meda. "Please excuse me." She went into the hut leaving Regal at the door. When she dressed and came out, Madison Hinson was gone.

The next day Stewart took Madison to meet the Carroll family.

"We thought the change would do him good," said Stewart as he made the introductions.

"We're all sorry to hear about your mother passing away," Em spoke for the family. "We hope you'll like living on the farm." Madison and Meda never acknowledged that they had already met.

It was a warm Saturday afternoon in November and Meda walked out into the yard. It was a lonesome day. Miles was out on a date, and Didge was in the woods trying to capture autumn scenes on her canvas. Papa and Mama had gone down to the parsonage to see how the room was progressing. Meda started up the steps of the front porch to sit in the swing when she heard an automobile turn into their yard. Suddenly, lifted out of sheer loneliness, she beamed as she saw Briant drive up. He jumped out of the car and scooped her up in a bear hug swinging her around and around. Regal was romping in a delirious circle around them as he chased Meda's feet.

"Oh, I've missed you. I love you, do you hear me? I love you!" He kissed her gently for the first time. "How different," he thought, "from the kisses of passion that had satisfied the senses between Priscilla and himself." He let her slide slowly down his body feeling every curve against him. Looking into her eyes, he asked, "Meda, will you marry me? At least think about it?" He said when he saw her eyes cloud over.

"I can't think of marriage until I'm through with my business course, Briant. Then we'll see how we feel, until then..." she smiled up at him, "It's so good to see you. Will this be your last trip until spring?"

"Not if I can help it. May I see you again when I return?"

"Of course, I'd be disappointed if you didn't stop."

"Good, I've reserved the room at Mr.

Tartt's. I've also reserved it for Christmas week if I may come see you then? May I Meda?"

"Yes, you may. I'll tell Mama and Papa. I'm sure they won't mind. They walked down to see how the room on the parsonage is progressing."

"Let's ride down and get them," he suggested.

Em and Lukatie were just leaving as they rode up.

"Thought we'd come and give you a ride home," Briant said as they greeted him.

"Thanks, that's thoughtful of you," said Em.

The room at the parsonage would be completed in another week. The men of the congregation were doing the building. Em was doing his part and, like the others, would be glad to get back to his own work.

A week later it was finished, and Preacher Murray bought a bed for Sena and moved her things in.

"There, isn't that nice to have a room all to yourself and not have to sleep in with Julia and the boys?"

"Yes, Papa, but why can't Julia share it with me?"

"We'll see, we'll see," he mumbled.

That night he slipped into Sena's room and got into bed with her.

"Papa," she cried out in alarm.

"Be quiet, girl. I just get lonesome in the bed alone."

"Then get one of the boys."

"Not the same. Just go on to sleep." He turned over and was soon asleep. Sena slept little during the next month as he came into her room and crawled in her bed on six separate occasions.

One evening, Sena asked, "Where are Julia and the boys, Papa?"

"The boys begged to spend the night with the Sholars. Julia is spending the night with the Heywood children. There is sickness in the family at Landridge and Mr. and Mrs. Heywood will be gone over night. You can just fix supper for the two of us."

"Why? Those children are old enough to stay alone. They are as old as Julia."

"Guess that's it. They just wanted their friend over. Julia acts old. Got a lot of sense she has."

After supper, Sena sat down to study. "That is done for the weekend. I'm glad I'll graduate in June," she remarked as she finished her work.

Preacher Murray was sitting at the table reading the Bible. "Listen to this. It says here in I Corinthians. "I shall receive of the Lord that which he hath delivered unto me."

"Papa, he's speaking of the Lord's supper."

"In I John he speaks at great length about love. Tells us to have no fear in love. So there is nothing to fear," he smiled at her.

"Now, girl, you go into that fine bedroom I built for you and undress while I go out to the privy."

Shocked at her father's words, she retorted, "I'll do no such thing."

"I ain't going to plead with you. Your ma up and died, and I need a woman."

"Then get married."

"You tell me. Who am I going to marry? A middle-aged man with four children. I was thinking of courting Lucinda Carroll but she up and married that Rue fellow. Tore me up, it did."

"So that is what was bothering you that morning."

"Sure was. There isn't anyone else. They are either too young, too old or married."

"Then have an affair with one of them. Just leave me alone."

"Mind your talk, girl. I don't have to have an affair or get married. I've got everything I need right here." He pointed his finger at her.

"Papa, have you been drinking?"

He ignored her question and harshly shoved her toward her bedroom door, her pitiful cries fell on the silent night.

PART TWO

1925-1932

Walking along the riverbank, Seth was reminded of the times when his own survival and that of his grandmother depended partly on his mastery of the traps he placed along the river to catch game and furs. Now, thanks to Mr. Heath's guidance and encouragement, he would soon be going to Etherton College in New York.

Seth had learned that life was a pattern lived step by step. A thing he was prone to forget at times like these. As he approached the Carroll's swimming hole, he saw Didge swimming around alone. He walked over to a tree and sat down out of sight from anyone that might come along the cart path to watch her.

After watching her for awhile he stood up to walk to the water's edge as he usually did when going from one trap to another and Didge would swim up to talk to him. The water was clear and he could see her as if the water wasn't there. Her hair was like refulgent gold as the sun reflected off of her beautiful tresses. "Good Heavens," he thought, "she's naked." Seth couldn't take his eyes off her.

"How can a true God make me so mixed up. I live as a negro. Yet, I've every right to live as a white man." He looked at her again and thought, "forbidden." Adam was forbidden to partake of Eve's fruit, but Eve offered and Adam partook of it. Didge hasn't offered, but Seth knew that the feelings were there. She swam to an overhanging tree limb and reached up taking her swimsuit down. She slipped it on and headed for shore. She paused on her hands and knees as she touched bottom. She looked around feeling his nearness or was it hope. She told herself she was just too young to feel so much. Digging her fingers into the sandy water bottom she clutched a handful of sand and brought it to the surface. She splashed it back into the water furiously as she tried to rid herself of all frustrations.

She heard Seth whistling as he walked around some Spanish moss that festooned the branches of a cypress tree.

The vision he has just seen made it hard to block out the love and desire that was shining in his eyes. Although it frightened her, she sensed and understood the magnetic force that flowed strongly between them. The feeling was strange, wonderful and new.

"No," she decided, "I'm not sure I understand it completely." Her expressive eyes looked up at him. He looked down at her but didn't touch her. "Negro I. I dare not." It was a straw he reached for in vain. "It can wait," he told himself. "She's wonderfully pure and untainted. Let her stay that way until she's old enough to decide for herself. One of these days I'll reach out and see if she's there."

Remorse flooded his senses, but why should he feel such remorse for wanting her. He realized that he had loved her since the first day he saw her in the cradle.

"Hello, Seth, setting your traps?"

"No, just checking to see that they are in place. How's the water?"

"Just right but guess this will be my last swim until next summer. At least I'll be in school and not have to be indoors around Papa so much."

"Why do you say that?"

"Oh, Seth, I'm just tired of holding in. When I was little, I didn't notice so much. But now the coolness toward me is so evident."

"Has he denied you self-expression or anything else that he can provide you?"

"No, that's just it; Papa has completely

withdrawn from me. He shuts me out of his life as though I didn't exist. I feel he'd like to negate me completely."

"He's a busy man and has a lot of worries. No man could be that unfeeling toward you, little one," he smiled. Her face changed and began to glow as the flush spread to her cheeks.

"Thanks for the tidbit, which reminds me, I'm hungry and I'd better get home."

"What tidbit?" she thought as she walked home. "How foolish I am."

Seth was a regular visitor at the home of Lovie and Thankful. He could watch Didge better from there. She was growing into a beautiful young lady not as large of breast as Lucinda and Meda but to him she was perfection.

As he walked toward Thankful's, he saw the smoke curl from the old chimney. A kettle of water sang on the stove and Zarilda was busy in the kitchen as he walked in.

"What's in the pot?" he asked.

"Soup, got evathang I'se cood find throwed inter hit."

He picked up the stirring spoon and dipped up a spoonful. He blew across it for a second then put it in his mouth. He dashed for the door and spit it out.

"Damn woman," he exclaimed, "How long has that soup been warming on the back of the stove. That stuffs got a head on it."

"No good huh, duden't much tink hit wus. Bin settin' thar three or fo' days."

Shaking his head, Seth walked out the door and sat on the step.

"Soup no good," said the old man. "Shore glad yo' got ter hit fust," he chuckled.

Seth turned and looked at the old man with his back bent and neck kinked from years of hard work. He felt sorry for him. He couldn't see or read his Bible anymore. So he just sits and listens to the sounds around him. He had always loved to watch things grow, chew his tobacco and hunker down to pick cotton.

"Do you mind being so old?"

"Oh, no, hit's great. O'cose hit wus a rough road ter travel ter git har." He chuckled, making his deepset eyes look buried in his face.

"Yes, I suppose it was. You amaze people by the way you can tell who everyone is that comes by or speaks."

"Yo' sittin' thar waitin' ter catch a sight of young Miz Carroll."

"I suppose so. She's growing up right pretty."

"Don' let youthful ignorance shake yo' up. Boy, thar's a strong line betwixt wite 'n black."

"If we were meant to live in the same world together why weren't we made alike, old man? You tell me, who I am?" No reply came from the old man and Seth continued. "I'm a one-fourth black and three-fourth white bastard. Gosh dang, it hurts." His shoulders sagged and his dark brown eyes flashed as his head dropped almost to his chest then raised slowly.

"I'm more outcast than anyone." He stood straight to his full height of six feet two.

"Look b'hind yo' negro 'n whut do yo' seed? Yore b'hind dats whut 'n dats all yo' gwine eva seed iffen yo' keep tinkin' back. Dar's a hedge ova dar haint day?"

"What about it?"

"Wal, boy, yo' mak' up yore mind on whut yo' wonts ter b', 'n go atter hit. Don' run 'round 'n circles lak' dat hedge row do. Yo' reach fo' de sun lak dat witey do."

"How can I, there is so much about myself I

don't know. It's as if I wasn't in existence. Yet, I know in my mind I'm a human being, and I've got to find the answer."

The old man sat perfectly motionless staring straight ahead and spoke.

"Yo' hav' a chunce iffen yo' leave dis place. Use yore looks. Nobudy kno' iffen yo' don' tell 'em. Finish yore edycation 'n stop feelin' sorry fer yoreself. Yo' oney got one chunce. Use hit. Find sum derickion den go atter hit. No cumb heads eva gits eny place. Dey jist sit 'round 'n grumble 'bout not havin' ah chunce causin' dey's black. Trouble is dey don' hav' ah chunce causin' dey neber tried fer one. Yo' jest a tadpole now, but time yo' is gron'd up yo'n kno' de answer."

"I'm nineteen, I should know the answer now. It's…it's just that this white devil in me won't acknowledge the black blood running through my veins. If you could see me, you'd know I look as white as any man."

"Yore trouble is thet gal ober thar, yo' played with her too much. Yo' fergit dat lil' gal 'n look fer ah nudder one."

"I've been loving her too long. I can't stop now."

"Hit wus ah hot nite she wus dere jest fo' daybreak. I cuddn't sleep 'n wus har on de porch. I heered evathang that went on ober thar."

They heard Zarilda's steps moving nearer the door as she worked in the house. The old man lowered his voice. "I's gwine say hit in yore ears boy," and he continued to tell Seth of the early morning Didge was left at the Carroll home.

Em was feeling low as he walked around the house. "What an empty life. I'm going no place accomplishing nothing. I couldn't be a worse failure if I worked hard at it. I'm tired, so tired, and things are getting worse all the time.

This place should delete the tax assessor. I don't know what to do. The houses are all in deplorable condition. We're living in such extreme discomforts." Em was an open-minded, unselfish man wanting those around him to be comfortable.

His thoughts ran rampage as he leaned against the hickory tree in the back yard. "Maybe I can get together enough money for a large insurance policy to leave Lukatie, then fall off of that second-hand no good tractor I bought and let it run over me, or figure some other way to take my life and make it look like an accident." He sat there pondering the idea. It might work, but could he, a man who always believed in God, do this. After all, it would be for Lukatie and the children. They would have the money to buy the things he could never give them. Still, to take one's own life would be the cowardly way out.

Lukatie interrupted his thoughts when she walked out of the kitchen fanning herself with the tail of her apron. "It's sure hot in there," she said softly as she took in deep breaths of the fresh air.

"Come on in and eat,"...you thimit. "College sure doesn't give out diplomas for common sense," she thought then felt ashamed. But why doesn't he do something to improve things? She walked back into the kitchen and the old screen door slammed behind her. Mr. Heywood has tried and tried to buy timber from him and he won't sell it. What in heaven's name is he saving it for?

After supper they sat on the steps. It was a muggy night flushed with honeysuckle and bay laurel and distant rumbling of thunder. Lukatie glanced at Em thinking, "I'd like to stick a fire cracker under his butt and light it to get him off his ass and do things."

The promise of rain hung in the air.

"We sure need rain." Em remarked. "The fields are ankle deep in dust." It soon began to drizzle.

They went to bed earlier than usual and lay silently listening to the large rats in the attic. They sounded heavy as cats running around as if they were excited about something. Lukatie was afraid to go to sleep. How she wished she still had the relaxed feeling she once had with Em and could move closer, just to feel protected would mean so much. "I don't pretend to understand him anymore," she thought. "I'm just here if he should need me…like a servant."

She kept the house clean and tidy, but the stench of the rats made it smell like sour urine. The negro houses were even worse. They didn't seem to care if they were kept clean or not. In spite of everything, Lukatie could say clothes hung on doors or in corners. Personal possessions packed in boxes lined the walls. Some just had mattresses thrown on the floor with big holes in them to sleep on, especially for the children. The children were always full of sores or pink eyes. They were listless, which Lukatie couldn't understand because they did grow plenty of food. She knew they weren't hungry. "I think it's just laziness and a lack of desire to do better and keep clean. Maybe they just don't care."

She was thankful that there were only three or four cold months in the year. With so many cracks in the floors and walls, it was impossible to heat the house properly.

With the dawn of morning, the storm struck. A fierce wind was blowing with driving intensity, wailing savagely in its desire to destroy everything in its path. Angry tongues of lightening flashed accompanied by roars of thunder. Tree branches splintered and crashed to the ground. The house shook and it felt as if the roof was being ripped off.

Lukatie slipped out of bed and dressed without her morning bath, then went to check on the children. They all slept soundly and were completely oblivious to the thundering storm.

The storm continued to lash out in its fury throughout the entire day. Everything and everyone were drenched. Em and Miles tried to patch the roof where sheets of tin were ripped off. They used every piece of tin and planks they would find but the rain continued to pour in.

Em paused in his work to look out over the farm. He could hear the negroes working on their roofs also. He felt angry and started telling God with a variation of expletives just what he was doing to their homes and the predicament he was getting them in. Lightening struck a tree close to the house knocking Em to his knees. He grabbed for the roof top to hold on. "I'm sorry, Lord, I didn't mean disrespect. I need help. Please help me, dear God."

Lukatie felt like she was on a ship at sea when she tried to walk on the porch between the house and the kitchen. The only thing in their favor was the warm weather.

There was little that could be done and no one hurried to do it. "I hate this place," blindly thought Lukatie. "It's tragic. I can't sleep at night because of the rats. I'm filled with terror and I don't dare let the children know how I feel. No, they aren't children anymore. They are young adults and afraid too."

She sat on the old faded rose sofa in the living room and looked at the paint flaking off the wall. "How drab," she thought. A center table sat in the middle of the room with three chairs scattered around. The old organ that no one could play occupied one corner of the room. Even the children had stopped banging on it. Em's stool chair was by the fireplace. The fireplace was the focus point of the room and everything faced it.

She watched the water seeping in around the fireplace and run down the wall. Pans were all around the room. The dripping water was ringing throughout the house.

The wail of the wind continued to sound like it was trying to destroy everything in its path. That any of the rickety old buildings continued to stand was a marvel.

Meda was reading and Didge sat at the window sketching the swaying trees and sheets of rain. Leave it to her to find beauty even in disaster.

The next morning everyone was grumpy as they walked around outside looking at the damage to the house. Even the crops had been destroyed. They could replant the garden for a late crop, but it was too late to think of replanting the cotton. There was no money for more seed. The little money crop they might have had was gone.

The negroes were sullen. Thankful was the only one that didn't act like the storm was all Em's fault. Rats and ants were worse than ever. The future did indeed look clouded.

Em could only recall his fear of trying something new. His life was flat and hopeless. Maybe the spirit would move him one day, but until it did, he would wait for the desperate need to slap him in the face.

Em had always believed he should find solutions to his own problems and not worry God about every little thing. He had always prayed for others, but now he walked in the house and went into his bedroom. He closed the door and kneeling by his bed prayed for personal help to find a way to overcome his feelings and to know how to solve the dilemma he now faced.

The next morning, Em watched the children pick ants out of their molasses then sop their biscuits in the dark substance. He had seen them do this many times before when the ants got real bad and he accepted it as a way of life that couldn't be helped. Now, when Lukatie took her place at the table and stared at the ants, she remarked, "It seems no matter what I do I can't keep those things out of the molasses. I tighten the lid and keep the jar sitting in a pan of water, but they still find a way to get into it." With a sigh, she pushed the ants to the side of her plate and started eating.

Em glanced toward the window not bearing to watch her. "What have I done to her?" he thought. He looked at the beautiful tall virgin timbers. How he loved them. "Why, I bet a dozen of those things would nearly build a house. Something has to be done," he pondered. But what? Like a loud clap of thunder, it hit him. "Yes, that's what I'll do or die trying."

With a sudden movement his fist came down on the table leaving the imprint of the knife handle he was holding. He exclaimed, "Thank you, God. That does it." From that moment on the dent was called Triple D or dimensions of decision dent, with the dimensions turning out far greater than anyone dreamed.

Em wanted to make living conditions better for the negroes as well as his own family. Do they really want it? Would they take pride in a better home? What effect would it have on them? Would they be content? A thousand questions raced through his mind as he rose from the table.

The family just sat watching the change come over him, too startled, too intrigued to speak.

Em bent over in front of Lukatie, "Go ahead, dear, kick."

"Whatever for? But don't repeat that offer."

"When I think of all I've put you through because of that timber out there. I'm ashamed of myself. I've always thought it couldn't be cut or sold. All I've ever cut was a little oak for firewood and that's all I've ever allowed the negroes to cut. Why, I could sell five hundred acres and never miss it. I thought it had to be kept in the family, Lukatie. We don't have to face defeatism yet, not with all that forest out there."

"Em, calm down."

"Calm down, nothing. I haven't even started. Careful you don't talk yourself out of a new house."

Em was thinking faster than he could talk, feeling he had to get it all told at once.

"Now you just sit and listen while I think out loud. First, I'm going to get Thankful to call all the negroes' families to meet with me out there at the pump bench. I'm going to ask their help in cutting trees, sawing it into lumber, plane it and build new houses for everyone. I'll sell enough of the lumber to Mr. Heywood to get the other materials we'll need plus the food we'll need."

"Do you think all the talking will do any good?" asked Lukatie.

"I sure pray to God it will. You do some praying too. Then I'm going to Kinyon's to tell him what I have in mind. I feel he should know."

"Well, that's nice but it's your place."

"I know, but he practically gave it to me. I've always had the feeling it was still partly his," Em answered.

"I hope it's not just infectious enthusiasm, Em."

"No, I mean to do all I can."

"About Mr. Heywood, I suggest you wait until he comes to you. Remember the Sholars when they went to him. He told them the price of lumber was down and paid them about half the price he first offered them. He's tried to get yours long enough so when he comes poking around just act indifferent. Act as though you don't need to sell. You can get started with the money in the bank that is accumulating from Benjamin's insurance. God knows he can't need it, and I can't think of a better reason for using it," Lukatie encouraged.

"We'll keep this in the family, all right?" They all agreed. "I'll go talk to Thankful, then I'll catch the afternoon train to Landridge."

When he came back from Thankful's, Lukatie stood beside him on the porch watching the negroes gather with Thankful at the pump bench.

"I'd like to kick them all in the seat to get them out of their alarming, lazy and disgruntled apathy," Em exclaimed.

"How often I've had the same thoughts about you," she wanted to say but remained silent. Em took her silence as agreement.

"I guess there's too much white blood intermingled with the black and those are the ones crying out for release. It's like a dissatisfied cancer eating at them. It sure isn't Carroll blood, but Carroll blood or not you can mark my word, one of these days there will be a fighting war between the black and white. I've heard my father say it and I say it too."

"You could be right," replied Lukatie. "You children stay back out of the way." She was nervous and having a hard time hiding it. Em left the steps and walked slowly to the pump bench. "This is my estate to improve or ruin," he thought.

After the darkness of the storm, the bright sun illuminated their worn threadbare clothes. The blank deep lines in their faces accentuated as they turned up to Em as he stepped upon the pump bench. Each was wondering why Mistuh Em wanted to see them. "Wus he gwine to seel out 'n lebe allus wit' out a home?" they asked Thankful.

"Look lak de storm don' tuck cure ov fo' allus cullered folk," spoke up Abner Tootle.

"Deys nare place ter go, 'nare job ter git, special' me wif dis peg leg," said Alonza Casteen.

As Em watched them gather closer he thought, "These are all descendants of slaves. These are the children and grandchildren of those negroes that had stayed on after their emancipation. They have always had it tough and I don't blame them if they leave. But Lord how I hope they don't. I need them. I've seen the day I wished they'd all leave. Even then I don't know how I'd tend the cotton crop without them."

"Once to every man comes the moment of inspiration to decide. That decision shapes his life, be it for good or evil, progression or retrogression, right or wrong. Why did it come to me so late in life?" thought Em.

Em looked down at his feet wondering just where to start. With a sigh he raised his head and spoke slowly.

"I need your help. In helping me, you also help yourself. We can do much together, separately, very little. I am fully aware of our inadequate housing and that is what I want to talk to you about."

The visor of doubt, hope and hatred for giving them hope was across every face as they listened to Em. How could he possibly do all he was promising? They looked at Hyrum for his reaction then back to Em.

As he turned his head deliberately to include everyone, "We have always grown plenty of food here and no one has gone hungry. Each family cans, and with winter greens we eat. As you all know, the cotton we raised didn't bring in enough for next years' seed and fertilizer or shoes for our feet."

"Sartin 'not our feet, but yoren is allus prutty well shod," yelled Hyrum.

Em thought of the shoes and clothes Kinyon and Jane had brought. Thanks to them they were not barefooted. He and Lukatie had shared generously with the negroes. How easily people forget.

"Stop talking out of both sides of your mouth and listen for a change, Hyrum," Em said patiently. "You all know our houses are falling down with us in them. You can all see that. We all need so much, and I think I've hit on a way to do something about it."

"Sounds like a lot ov mouth ter me," interrupted Hyrum. Ignoring Hyrum Em continued, "First, we can replant for a late crop of food. There will be no cotton. It's too late to replant so there will be no money crop this year which leaves us free for the rest of the summer."

"Second, I don't have any money to pay you wages. So, what I'm proposing to do is cut timber enough to build us all new houses. I'll need your help and support."

In one sharp barb Hyrum yelled, "I'se not building yo' no damn house."

Em felt like he could clobber the ignoramus, but he continued. "We should get together and work. There is one proven fact: we can't sit on our ass and get comforts."

"Who gwin git dis comfort yo' or us?" asked Hyrum.

"All of us, I hope," answered Em. "You hold the answer in your hands." He told them.

"Don't rattle my door, man." Said Hyrum.

"Whose door?" threw back Em. He was really getting fed up with Hyrum, the impassive insolent lout. Damn it, he needed the youth on the farm. They were the ones he was depending on most. They are the ones with strong backs to do the heavy work. They were young and teachable. He was capable of cold controlled, tight-lipped rage. He never let go unless it was triggered by rudeness, dishonesty or defects in those he loved and trusted. Those who were capable of better even great accomplishments, never thinking he, himself, fit in this category he placed others in. Looking more at Hyrum than anyone, Em said, "Get this through your head and get it good. I'm not responsible for your welfare. If you want to leave do so now. But if you stay, be prepared to work. We've got to combine inspiration, brains and brawn and use some wisdom to reach our goal and we all benefit."

"I'll bet that made Hyrum feel lak a couple of nuts on a ferris wheel," whispered Levi Brown to Thankful.

"Thet boy's go no feelin'. Whut he needs is a good rubbin' in horse liniment."

"Ha," laughed Levi, "Hits good fer a jackass so's hit mite hep him."

Em's heart softened as he looked into their

hopeful expectant faces. But only for a moment he had to be hard. Sure, convince them even though he wasn't convincing himself.

"I'm not promising instant upheaval but hope to move along constantly with each person participating on the buildings until each is completed. It will take a lot of faith and determination, but we can do it if we pull together. The only thing I can give you for the work is a lifetime right to the house you will live in. I'll put it in writing with a clause that the first time you leave there will be no coming back and claiming the house."

"Since there will be no cotton there will be no contingency wages, but I'll see to it no one goes hungry."

Hyrum was in a sullen mood and said, "So fer yo' hain't don' a damn thang. Whut's ter mak' us tink yore gwine ter now?"

"I'm too busy to stand here swapping inane remarks with you Hyrum. I have things to settle."

"Wal, thet's a switch, hain't hit." He fixed Em with a frosty gaze as he said, "Yore words giv' us hope but whut iffen yo' kin't produce?"

Em felt naked, open and a sense of menace engulfed him. It was hard to control his temper when prejudice rears its ugly head. He felt like telling Hyrum to leave.

"Hyrum you can work according to whatever rules are decided on today or you need no longer stay on this farm. In the future we'll have no room for malcontents."

For a few moments, they felt the old fears of the unknown. They looked around them...the big oaks casting intangible shadows. They felt the presence of the ghosts of their ancestors who had worked this land. Surely it wasn't falling apart then as it is now. The blank bottomless expression on their faces hid their real feelings from Em.

He could stand the quietness no longer and said, "The measure of our ability is to think, to plan, and work together. Hostility will not bring peace and freedom; neither will it banish tension and conflict." There is a way of dealing with such things, thought Em. I only wish God would show me how.

"We can bring better living conditions into our lives if we work together. It will take joint efforts. Do we have the ability to cooperate with one another? If not, we can go on living as we are. If the answer is yes, I'll see what I can do about a sawmill and we'll go to work."

When Em finished talking, they stared at him in silence. Their heads filled with the words he had just uttered. Each was thinking, "Coud we's do all dese thangs 'n hep each udder?"

Em's hands felt so large at the end of his arms. He wished he knew what to do with them. He wished someone would say something, anything. He felt he could stand their stares no longer. At last a murmur of agreement sounded through the group. Their eyes shining brightly in their weathered faces said more than their agreement to do as he asked.

"Thank you all. It's time to stop wishing and start doing. We all have to work our butts off and hope to finish before cold weather."

Lukatie stayed on the porch. She felt a mixture of pride, love and more hope in a better future than she had since she married Em. She could still remember the feeling of disappointment when he brought her here as a bride.

Seth had come up and listened to Em.

Turning to Didge, he asked, "Can he do all he's promising?"

"Papa won't promise them anything he doesn't feel he can do. It would be dishonest and a cruel delusion."

Nineteen-year-old Seth had always marveled at the wisdom of Didge. He had to stay on his toes to keep up with her.

All eyes were fastened on Hyrum. His father, Andrew Jackson Smith, turned to him. "Son, we'd all lak ter improve our conditions. Well, wudden't we. We's tried hit out yander once 'n cuuden't mak' hit. We's doan want no han' outs. We'en kin do fo' ourse'ves har."

"Pa, I gits so mad folk allus tellin' me whut ter do. Let's face hit, Pa, we'ns air de servants of birth. We'ens up agin a brick wall."

"I doan recon' as how Mistuh Em's tellin' yo' whut ter do. Yer dree ter do as yo' please. He ask for we'ns hep fair 'n square. Doan be a damable dirt head boy. Tink. Doan be short on de supply of tinkin' tings out. Whut kin yo' gain by fightin' agin allerus. Mistuh Em jest tol' we'ns whut he kin try ter do. Tak hit er leav' hit. Iffen yo' tak hit den stand by yer chaise er leav', whut kin yo' do? Whut will you hav'? Jest ask yo'self. Why leav' de only life we'ns kno'. Wes got no learnin'. Now tink."

"I'se tinkin', Pa."

Hyrum turned to Em. "I'se gwine sta' iffen hits alright wit yo'?"

Em breathed a sigh of relief and stuck out his hand to Hyrum who shook it vigorously. He felt that if Hyrum stayed the others would.

"I'll have to hurry to catch the train to Landridge. But I want you all to know I thank you," said Em as he stepped down from the pump bench and headed for the house. He turned and walked over to the old man sitting on the porch listening.

"You feeling as good as usual today, Old Man, I mean Mr. Mathias."

"Yup, nuttin' wrong with me but ol' age 'n rascality."

"What do you think of all the building we're planning?" Em asked.

"Dat's jes fine fer de young'uns. I'se glad fer dem. Reckon I stay hare whar I'se use ter tings, Mistuh Em."

"You'll get used to a better house; you'll see." Em hurried back to the house and dressed in his best suit and left for Landridge. On the train he was thinking of his mission. "Am I nuts? I must not have a smidgen of sanity left. The idiocy of the whole idea. The vastness of it is fantastic."

Kinyon was surprised to see Em when he walked into the Mill.

"Well, brother, what brings you to town?" he greeted as they shook hands.

"You might say the storm blew me in. It has practically demolished the whole farm. I have to rebuild fast. They are planting again for a late food crop, but the houses will never carry us through another winter. I only felt it fair to let you know I plan to cut timber from the land to rebuild our house and the six tenants."

"Great!" smiled Kinyon happily. Em raised his eyebrows in surprise.

"Jane wanted to build you and Lukatie a house every time we visited. That is about all she talked about at least halfway home. I always told her no, that a man took pride in his own accomplishments, not in someone else's done in his favor."

"You're right, of course."

"Em, things just don't happen. You make them happen. I'm glad you have finally realized it. I'll help in any way I can. You know that." Em felt a little hurt and disappointed that the ones that really mattered, even Lukatie, had stood by and waited for the land to practically destroy him and had not said a word. The realization that any one of them could have told him, at least drop a hint now and then, of what to do years ago irritated him and he spoke more sharply than he intended.

"The only help I want from you is the loan of the sawmill sitting out there in the yard unless you need it. I'll go back and get the horses and wagon and haul it down there and when I'm finished I'll haul it back. And I'll sell enough timber to pay you the rent on it."

"Em I'm sorry if I said too much. I only want to help. That sawmill hasn't been used since the mill houses were built. You're welcome to it. I'll get Jim, the caretaker, to check it out and show you how to operate it. There is a planer, you'll need, too. It will probably take a few days to get it ready and loaded. While you wait you might like to look at some house plans. You've got a big job ahead of you." "It will take me a while to go get the horses and wagon."

"Won't be necessary. I ordered a new truck last week and it's to be delivered tomorrow. You can have the old one; it's in good running condition."

"I can't drive, so I'll go get the wagon."

"You can learn. There's nothing to it."

The thought of driving thrilled Em. While Kinyon was busy in the mill, Jim taught Em to drive.

It started raining again and Em was worried. "Kinyon, they can't stand more rain on the farm. I should be there."

"You couldn't stop the rain if you were there so don't worry."

"I can't help it. I was supposed to be back yesterday."

Jim oiled and fired up the mill with Em watching and helping when he could. Kinyon walked out to watch as mill hands looked out the windows. Kinyon had a paper in his hand.

"Here, Em, is a blueprint so you'll know how to assemble this thing when you get it home. Study it while the saw is up and it will be easier. In fact, you can take Jim with you to help get started."

"Won't be necessary. I've got plenty of help there." Before it was over, he wished a thousand times he had Jim with him.

"All right, you're the boss, Em. I hope you won't mind, but Jane is so thrilled she has spent every day since you've been here out getting blueprints of houses of all sizes. We'd love to go over them with you tonight if you'd like. You might find something in them you'll like. If not, you can keep looking. I tried to stop her, but she was having so much fun you'd think she was going to build herself a new house. You know she loves Lukatie like a sister and you like a brother."

"Yes, I know. It's all right, but this house for Lukatie has got to be her Blue Bird. I'll know it when I see it."

He was very surprised that evening to see how many plans Jane had found. With all the rain falling, Em was having a hard time keeping his mind on the blueprints. They went through plan after plan only to discard them. Finally, he picked up one that had three bedrooms with closet space and a large kitchen and parlor, also a smaller room for a bath inside.

"This I like."

"For Lukatie's Blue Bird?" Kinyon and Jane voiced in unison.

"No, for the tenant houses."

They let out their breath. "You had us worried there for a second." Em looked at the rest of the plans. "Jane, I appreciate all you've done, but the Blue Bird just isn't here. I will use that one plan. I think the tenants will like it."

"Excuse me a minute, Em," she winked at Kinyon. In a second, she was back. "Here," she handed him an envelope. He opened it and slowly unfolded the plan.

He studied the plan. It was a sixteen-room pillared house with six columns. Three large curving steps outside, the porch curving with the steps. A wide curving stairway inside to the second floor off the marble entry. To the left was an informal room with a marble fireplace. Beyond this room was the dining room and large kitchen. To the right of the entry was a large room with a larger marble fireplace. One large bedroom with bath on the first floor that opened onto a private terrace. It also had a fireplace. Off the dining room was a study or library. A clothes closet and powder room were tucked neatly beneath the large stairway. A fireplace was in the kitchen and off one end was a pantry as large as Lukatie's present kitchen. Beside the fireplace was a door leading to a hall where stairs would lead to the second floor. Across the hall was a door that opened to a four-room apartment. Two rooms downstairs and two rooms upstairs with bath. From the top of the stairs landing there was an entrance to the second-floor hall that led to a sitting room and five bedrooms.

The spacious attic could be used for more room, or thought Em, with a skylight for a studio for Didge. She was really good and needed room to paint. She deserves it.

Em looked at Jane. "This, my dear Jane, is the Blue Bird."

"Oh, Em, Kinyon," her glance took them both in. "I'm so happy. You know I was afraid to show you that plan. At least until you had seen all the others."

"You did right. Now my problem is the electricity."

"I believe by the time you're ready for it, you will have it. I read in the paper a month ago they have already started running lines through rural communities."

"Wonderful, then I can sell enough lumber while we're cutting to get the plumbing fixtures and electrical wiring. I'll have to hire a plumber and electrician. Guess I can find both in Campton," Em said.

"If you can't, you can still borrow Jim. His helper can take care of things here until he gets back."

"The trouble with that, the way the house is torn up, there is no place for him to sleep. I really feel worried about them with the new storm. I've been away too long. I hope they haven't lost faith in me and my promise to them," worried Em.

Going to his room that night Em met Carlton in the hallway.

"Uncle Em, are you going to build your house down by the river?"

"No, Carlton, over where the old manor house stood. Why?"

"Mother sure loves that hill by the river."

"She does?"

"Yes, sir. I overheard her tell Daddy how nice a summer house would be there. She wanted him to ask you about it."

"Oh, what did your father say?"

"He said, no. I won't hear of it."

"I see, well, goodnight, Carlton."

"Sure, Uncle Em. 'Night."

*****

Everyone was wondering what had happened to Mr. Em. He should have been home days ago. Him and his big promises. All he wants from us is yesmanship to his lip service while he goes off to his big important brother and takes life easy.

The rain had started again the night he left. Thankful went around checking on everyone. The mood of every one of the negroes was ill…almost evil in their thoughts. They could see Miles patching the roof of their house and knew they weren't fairing any better. This made them feel a little better.

Fear of not knowing and wondering what was to become of them was running strong in hushed thought among the negroes. They poked around not knowing what to do yet knowing something must be done with or without Mistuh Em.

Lukatie and Didge listened to Miles hammering on the house as they waited apprehensively for Em to return. They feared something had happened to him. Everything smelled so damp, sour and fetid. They huddled against the wall on the porch to get away from the smell inside.

Seth was wondering how Didge was fairing during the heavy rain. He knew the house had always been in bad condition. As he had grown older, he had worked more and more for Mr. Heath. He and his grandmother were living in the back rooms of the big old handsome house. Seth had made many repairs on it and helped to keep it clean and take care of Mr. Heath.

In his spare time, he still tended to his traps. The storm had left them untouched. He was saving as much money as possible to go to college. Mr. Heath had implanted within him a great desire to further his education and always in the back of his mind was the drive to equal Didge. He felt sure she would never go to college. The Carrolls would never send her since their own daughters hadn't gone. She would probably take a business course as Lucinda and Meda had done.

To escape hanging around the house, he put on a slicker and hat and went to the drug store in town to get a prescription filled for Mr. Heath. He could give Pal, the gelding, a good workout. He mounted the horse and led him through a series of sharp turns and then he let the horse have full reign and Pal ran until he was satisfied.

Since Mr. Heath had bought a car, the surrey stayed in the barn and horses in the pasture. Automobiles were sure the ruination of horses he thought as he reached the drugstore. As he walked in, he saw Mr. Nye, the druggist, talking with a strange man. Seeing Seth, Mr. Nye said, "Here he is now, just the boy you need for your team. Seth Kirby, meet Mr. Glenn Bradley." Mr. Bradley turned looking at Seth. The loose-armed, long-legged tall boy standing before him looked perfect. He stuck out his hand to Seth. "But I thought you were…," he hesitated.

"Negro," Seth finished for him. "I am, sir."

"Mr. Bradley was passing through going to Atlanta to look over a pitcher he had heard about. He needs one for the college team. I was telling him about you."

"I'm going to college in the fall so that lets me out. But there is a game tomorrow afternoon if the rain slacks. You might want to watch if you're still around." Seth handed Mr. Nye the prescription.

"What college are you going to?" asked Mr. Bradley.

"Etherton in New York City, Sir."

A smile spread across Mr. Bradley's face. "Maybe I'll see you there. I'm their coach."

He stayed over to see the game and liked Seth's swift fast ball and the number of times the men at bat struck out. He remained in the background not wanting Seth to know he was being watched. His eyes swept the crowd. They were ecstatic about the beauty of his pitching and they all breathed in unison, "beautiful." The crowd was spellbound.

The druggist had told him of the battles Seth had fought through school because of his white skin. The unusual was happening here today. Because of sickness, Seth had been asked to play on an all-white team. So far as I'm concerned his identity will remain here in Campton thought Mr. Bradley. He went on to Atlanta feeling sure he would look Seth up when he returned to Etherton College.

*****

Em and Jim finally got the truck bed loaded with the sawmill and planer. On the seat beside Em were books on building, blueprints of the sawmill and houses he had selected. Thanking them and shaking hands with Kinyon and Jim and others who had come out to help him, he drove out of the mill yard through the gates and headed home. At times he had to stop for the rain to slack. It came down in sheets impossible to see through. He was thankful that the truck had a good top on it. It was late afternoon when he finally drove into the yard and saw Lukatie and Didge huddled together on the porch against the wall.

He jumped out of the truck and made a dash up the steps and gathered them both in his arms. It was the first affection he had ever shown Didge.

"What you both must have gone through, I'm very sorry."

"You couldn't have known and you couldn't control the weather," said Lukatie. "Mr. Heath sent Seth to get us to go there and Stewart drove over to get us to go to his house, but I felt I had to stay here and try to take care of the little we had."

He caught himself quickly as he became aware of his arm around Didge and her head against his shoulder. He shuddered openly.

"How can you stand it out here. It's so damp. You'll both catch a cold." He turned quickly and opened the dining room door. "Go inside."

"The dampness and odor were so bad we couldn't stand it in the house," said Didge.

"Start a fire. Maybe it will help dry things out." "Still patching holes," he remarked as he heard Miles hammering on the roof. Em called Miles in.

Thankful saw the loaded truck in the yard and came over to investigate. He looked it over and then knocked on the porch.

"Come on in out of the rain," called Em, as

he opened the door.

"What yo' got thar, Mistuh Em?"

"A sawmill."

Lukatie, Meda and Didge looked at the blueprint of the mill that Em spread out on the table.

"If tomorrow is fair, we'll drive down into the woods and start putting it together while the others start felling trees. Tell everyone to meet here in the morning at six. We'll have to work from sun-up until sun-down in order to finish before cold weather."

"Guess that is worth missing a ball game for," laughed Miles. "Seth is pitching for our school since our man is sick."

"Should be a good game."

Thankful felt happier when he left Em than he had since his wedding day. He hurried home and told them the news. Then he went to every house. He felt good when he gave his news to the Smiths. Especially Hyrum, who was like an interloper trying to devise every insidious trick to prove Em was not honest in his promise to build houses for all. He will have to admit now that Em is trying. That is all any man can do.

Stewart drove up in the yard and jumped out of the car as Em was checking the truck for the night and started back up the steps.

"Supper," said Em.

"No thanks."

"Coffee?"

"No thanks."

"Titia wrote she was coming home for a while."

"Well, that should be good news."

"After four husbands and the fast life she lives, I'm not sure. I don't want any trouble with her here. People around here know she had been married four times, but they don't know she's man crazy."

"Maybe she has changed and will settle down," encouraged Em.

"I doubt it. She's my sister, but I'd rather she didn't come. I just can't tell her not to though. She hasn't been back since she was sixteen," said Stewart.

"I know, right after that visit she and Elda went to Europe. Elda found she was pregnant and couldn't make the trip back until the baby was born. I remember David going to visit them," remarked Em.

"Yes, and Titia married some old count and stayed. You know I never did know the names of all her husbands. Don't remember them is more like it, I guess. She is a Johnson now. They were all old and weak. She's a very wealthy thirty-eight-year old woman now."

Stewart rose to leave. "Em, I see you've got your work cut out for you. If I can help, I'll be glad to."

"Thanks, Stewart. I may call on you to read blueprints."

"Go eat. I'll see you later," said Stewart.

Em and Miles sat late into the night studying the plans from beginning to end. Em's knowledge of building was minute. Each night thereafter, they were up late pouring over blueprints and books.

The next morning was fair and beautiful. Promptly at six o'clock everyone was at the pump bench eager to hear what Em had to say.

"They look like a bunch of lost souls," Em thought. He dreaded the starting but relished the thought of the ending. Being with negroes all his life he thought he knew their thinking processes, plus their nuance of feeling, but found that he was often wrong. There had to be respect and compassion for their sensitivity. They chose to remain at the farm. They meant to be loyal and rally around the only boss they had ever known. They were trying to act as if it were pragmatically possible to go on as if nothing had changed and Mistuh Em could go on paying them for their labor. Only they knew there wouldn't be a payday at the end of the year. Instead a paper would be handed to them saying they had a home for life.

Their faces all turned to Em eager to hear his plans.

"Whut's all thet stuf' on dat truck, Mistuh Em?" asked Solomon Casteen.

"That's a sawmill I borrowed from my brother. Miles, Thankful and I are going to take it down in the woods and start setting it up while the rest of you start felling trees. It will be hard, hot work. But work is the glue that will hold us all together. There will be work for the woman as well, without them we men couldn't accomplish much. Did you replant while I was gone?"

"Yassuh, first day yo' wus gon." Spoke up Abner Tootle. "Iffen de new rain dudden't warsh away de seed."

"Good," said Em. "The women and children will tend to the gardens and have your meals ready while we build. Time is wasting. Let's get to work. Gather every saw and ax you can find. Especially the two-man saws, rip saws and buck saws. Put them on the wagon and follow us. Come on, Thankful."

The rapt expression and bubbling voices as they turned to leave showed their happiness at the thought of better living conditions.

"Oh, darn," exploded Em. The scowl on his

face etched deep in his brows as the truck came to a stop.

"Papa, it looks like we start pushing. Get out, Thankful." Miles laughed hopefully. "Maybe the truck isn't stuck very deep."

"Just up to the hub and we don't even have a shovel. I rode the ruts all the way from Landridge and didn't get stuck. Now this happens."

"This low land is always mucky when it rains, Papa," Miles continued to laugh.

"We may as well wait for the others and use the horses," said Em taking a seat on a fallen tree trunk.

There was a lot of jest and jargon when they did arrive an hour later. "That's enough lip. You've had your say. Let's get this truck out of the mud," Em said emphatically.

About halfway between the house and the river Em drove the truck over in the woods. "We'll put the mill up here about four hundred feet from the road and start clearing out every tree from the road until we have all the lumber we need. I'll mark a few of the trees that I want to put aside for special jobs while the rest of you unload the truck."

"Thar he go takin' de easy job," fretted Hyrum.

"Hyrum, I know you're the laziest man alive."

"Yassuh, Mistuh Em. I shore be, but de seat ov m' pants is de last part ter wear out."

"That's because you sleep so much," said Em as he walked off into the woods.

He loved the woods, it was joy to walk in the tall forest and see the squirrels scamper up a tree jumping playfully from limb to limb, tree to tree, traveling miles and never touching the ground.

Sometimes the deer like the rabbit would give him a daring fleeting glance and turn their white tails in his face and disappear into the dense woods peering back as they fled. I'm destroying their haven he thought as he marked another tree and walked on.

Returning to the unloaded truck, Em got the blueprints. Looking at it over his shoulder, Thankful said doubtfully, "Kin we do thet?"

"You bet we can. By jingoes, we'd better."

"Look's lak' a heap ov junk ter me," put in Hyrum.

"This junk pile is going to work for us," snapped Em determinedly as he walked over into the middle of it. This is the firebox with the boiler. Someone's job will be to keep it fired and water in the boiler to get the steam to run the mill. You can haul barrels of water from the river or house whichever is easier. It's to be kept at one hundred forty-five pounds pressure." They all looked in awe that Em should know so much so quickly about the mill.

"These large belts, pulleys and wheels are attached to the motor to turn the large saw blades. We set the log roll in place to feed logs onto the carriage tracts and those cant hooks keep the logs in place as they are being cut into lumber. This long chain in the dust conveyor is to be attached to a tall pole. It keeps the sawdust out of our way. Maybe a good place for it is over on that little hill and let the sawdust pile up there and fill in behind it."

He pointed out other parts, carriage, tracts, head blocks, set works, roller bed, standard and dogs. "There will be plenty of scrap lumber for the firebox. Now, let's put this junk pile together. Any questions?" He paused a moment thanking God there were none.

"Thankful, pick out a couple of men to help you while I read this blueprint and direct putting it together. The rest start felling the trees I've marked."

While Em was busy, Lukatie took time to walk over to the old manor site to do some daydreaming. After all that rain it seemed so good to be out. She walked around visualizing the house, her "Blue Bird" sitting there so proud. She had to admit that the house plan far surpassed anything she could have imagined. It was hard to believe it was about to become a reality.

Stewart saw her there as he was driving down to William Heath's. Turning into the lane he stopped on the wide curve in front of the place where the house would stand. Throwing his cap in the seat, he jumped out of the car.

"May I be the first visitor to the Blue Bird, dear lady?" he addressed her running his fingers through his thick dark hair.

"Oh, you've heard. Oh, Stewart, I can hardly believe it's about to happen," she exclaimed jubilantly.

"Well, it is if all that noise I hear down in the woods is any indication," he smiled. "It takes so little to make you happy, Lukatie Carroll. You're really glowing, you know. You're a prudent creature as natural as a rain drop."

"Please, no more rain for a while, thank you."

"How about as natural as a summer breeze then," he laughed. "You should have this Blue Bird and me."

"There you go again, Stewart Henderson, I just don't...," she had turned and upon looking into his face saw his teasing grin.

"You just don't what?"

"Know what to do with you."

"I could make a few suggestions," he laughed. After a moment she said quizzically, "Em tells me Titia is coming home for a while. I only saw her a couple of times. She was so young then, about fifteen, I think. Strange there were never any children from all her marriages."

"Maybe the men were all too old or she just didn't want any," said Stewart his voice dropping.

"I remember she was very pretty and she's still rather young. Perhaps she will marry again. When do you expect her?"

"In a month, maybe sooner." They were attracted to the noise of an automobile driving up in the yard of the house.

"Guess I'd better go see who that is," Lukatie turned and started walking toward home.

"Foiled again," sighed Stewart. Lukatie glanced back at him, smiling.

"I embrace her with my eyes and heart, but my arms remain empty." His words seemed to follow her.

"Dear Stewart," thought Lukatie. "I guess I will always wonder if things might have been different if I had met him first. But I don't think so."

Briant saw Lukatie walking across the field and leaned against his car until she came into the yard.

"Hello Briant," she greeted him with outstretched hands.

"Hello, Mrs. Carroll. I read in the paper, also heard over the radio about the bad storm through the Carolinas and I just had to come. I was so worried about all of you and Meda. I guess you know I love her and want to marry her?"

"Not from her we don't know it. But Em and I thought you must be interested since you continued to come see her."

When his car drove up Meda hurried to her room. "I'll freshen up," she told Didge, "while you straighten up the parlor."

"What about me freshening up too, Sis."

"He didn't come to see you, Toots."

"Oh, my goodness, my clean underpants are hanging out there on the line on the back porch."

"Go get them," said Didge indifferently.

"I can't do that. He'll see me getting pants off the line of all things."

"Oh, for gosh sakes," Didge walked out and took the pants and called, "Hello there, Briant."

"There," she said holding out the pants to Meda.

"Thanks, Toots, but did you have to call out and attract his attention to them?"

Lukatie was telling him about the new house and how busy Em and the negroes were.

Meda stood in the parlor with papers and books in her hands as if straightening the room.

"Why, Briant, what a surprise," she winked knowing he knew Didge had told her he was there.

"Come let's go for a walk while the sun is shining so brightly. I'm stiff from riding so long. Will it be all right, Mrs. Carroll?"

"I suppose so. Will you stay for supper with us?"

"If it's no trouble, I'd love to."

"Come, I'll show you the sawmill," Meda said. As they walked, she was very reserved. A sort of habitual preoccupation. Not intentional, just not knowing. She wasn't sure of her feeling for him. She was very busy trying to figure out if she could care enough for him to marry him to get away from the farm or should she wait and hope someone else would come along. It certainly wouldn't be Madison. He was liking the farm and Sena Murray too much.

Briant broke the silence, "When I heard about the storm, I was so worried about you. I had to come. Meda, please marry me now. You've kept me waiting so long. Here, I've brought you a present." He handed her a small package.

She eagerly opened it. There lay a lovely diamond ring. "It's beautiful Briant. But how can I wear it unless I am sure I love you? I enjoy being with you, but love, I don't know."

"Meda, I love you so very much. Please love me too. Wear the ring until you decide. I'm going on down to Miami and will come back by here. You can give me an answer then."

"I'll try to, Briant."

They had reached the sawmill. Em was surprised to see Briant. Briant asked if he could speak privately to Em. He told him of his love for Meda and asked to marry her.

"I'll leave that up to Meda. You seem like a nice enough fellow, but she will be the one that has to live with you. Just so she is sure."

"Thank you, Mr. Carroll. She hasn't said yes, but if she does, I'll be good to her."

They walked on down to the river holding hands. Standing on the bank, Briant turned her to face him and looking deep into her eyes brought his lips down to hers. Softly and gently he kissed her lips then her neck and back to her lips more fiercely as he gathered her in his arms. He felt driven with desire.

Feeling the urge within his body, she pushed away from him.

"No, Briant, only after marriage. I thought you knew I wasn't that kind."

"I do know it, but what difference can it

make. I want to marry you anyway."

"It makes a lot of difference to me."

"Please, Meda, I want you so. Please prove your love for me."

"Prove it," she gasped, "I haven't said I love you and if I decide I do, I'll prove it at the altar." She blushed, "Well, not there, of course."

"You are an unfeeling girl," he declared morosely.

"Not at all, just selective. Here, you want the ring back?" She held out her hand to him.

Realizing he had gone too far, he took her hand and raised it to his lips kissing the ring then her palm and closing her fingers over the kiss. She stared at him bewildered.

"I'm very sorry, Meda. I had to know. It won't happen again, darling." He reached for her hand. "Come, let's go back to the house. Promise you'll think about us and give me an answer when I return. I'll be back in about four weeks."

Meda spent the next week thinking. Then she approached Lukatie.

"Mama, what is love? How does one know if they are in love or not?" She was looking at the ring on her finger as she asked the question.

"Love, I think is the feeling you get when you are suddenly shocked into the awareness of the existence of someone else. You want to please them. Their happiness becomes very important in your life. Marriage based on physical attraction or romantic dreams is nothing but infatuation and won't last. It's so thrilling while it does last. Then you wake up one morning and find you have nothing."

"Doesn't it take that to make a marriage last, Mama?"

"I would say esteem, affection, concern for

Does Lukatie love Em? or Stewart?

one another, religion and a liking of each other and to enjoy doing things and going places together makes a healthier, steadier marriage. It takes much more than physical or emotional needs. Hostilities can and do exist between husband and wife at times and it takes loving, honest feelings of expression with each other to overcome pressures and be happy. Where there is a deep attraction also an honest feeling of liking a person, the risk of an unhappy marriage is less."

"Thank you, Mama, guess I'll have to think on it some more."

"Honey, move slowly into love. Control your emotions and enjoy each moment step by step. To rush without feeling it all is to defeat a wonderful trusting future that could be ahead for you."

Lukatie left Meda to her thoughts as Miles came in with a letter from Lucinda. She wrote she would like to come visit but the doctor didn't think she should travel. Lukatie read on, "I haven't mentioned this before because I didn't want to worry you. But I'm so unhappy. I just have to get it out of my system. This last trimester has been the hardest. I feel so depressed all the time. I wish the baby would come so I could leave Fountain. His ways have gradually killed all the feeling I ever had for him. Do you know that since the day we were married, I have never been allowed to leave the house for church, shopping for groceries or clothes or even take a walk for exercise unless he or a member of his family is with me. They have to choose my clothes, what we eat, even my baby's things. Oh, Mama, thanks so much for the lovely things you made and sent for the baby and me. I think of all the time you spent cutting, stitching and putting together the pieces. I admit I cried over every loving stitch in them. Thank you so much for loving us enough to do it."

"I don't know if the things meet with their approval or not. They are far prettier than anything they picked out and I believe they know it. I'm getting them soiled from handling them so much. Fountain did say they were nice."

"If another woman or man speaks to me, he asks what they said. Do you know I'll have to steal the money for a stamp to mail this when he goes to sleep? He reads all the letters I write and mails them himself. I hope you've been getting them. I was lucky there was no one here when your package came, and the money was in it. I hid it and will not use it until I leave, and I do mean to leave."

Lukatie's heart was heavy as she finished reading Lucinda's letter. My heaven, she thought, one daughter thinking of getting into trouble and one trying to get out. If there were only a way to make them understand marriage is no smooth road to travel. Now the family has a new worry.

When she answered the letter, she was careful and wrote only about the progress on the house, the weather, their health and Meda's ring. She expressed their love for her and desire to see them and closed the letter hoping she had said nothing to make Fountain question Lucinda about writing home without his knowledge.

"A beautiful open-topped Pierce-Arrow with New York license plates has just driven up in the yard at Uncle Stewart's," called Miles as he drove the truck into the yard.

"Wonder who it is," chorused Meda and Didge.

"Don't know, a woman was driving it," said Miles.

"A woman," they chorused again.

"Yup, women drive in the large cities a lot," he said.

"They do."

Ignoring them, Miles continued, "It sure is pretty. It's powerful. You should have heard the engine. That's the kind I'll get one of these days."

Lukatie had listened from the porch. "I wonder if that is Stewart's sister, Titia. He said he was expecting her to come. She will probably be with him at church tomorrow. I think I'll walk over and see how the foundation of the house is coming along."

"All finished," smiled Miles. "I'll walk with you."

"We will too. Come on, Didge," said Meda.

Miles started laughing, "Mama, you should have been down at the sawmill when Mr. Heywood went down there."

"Tried to get the lumber for nothing, I suppose."

"Papa said, good morning, very politely and went right on with his work. He was marking more trees he wanted cut and every time Mr. Heywood asked him about selling some lumber, he would move on to another tree. The Mr. Heywood started offering prices. Papa would just grunt and move on. You couldn't tell if his grunt meant yes or no. Mr. Heywood kept going up with the price. Said with the building boom going on in Florida, he could sell and ship every board of lumber he could get. Papa said, yep, guess you could but it looks like I'm going to need mine."

"Playing it cool, was he?" asked Lukatie as she laughed, "Go on, what did they say?"

"Finally, Mr. Heywood offered him a price for all the lumber he could spare. Papa told Mr.

Heywood he'd have to haul it out because he didn't have time to. He didn't like it, but he finally agreed to."

"Watch it on the foundation, Didge, you might fall," called Miles.

He felt himself her protector since Benjamin's death. Papa sure doesn't show any sign of feeling for her. Oh, he brought her paper, pencils, charcoal sticks and even a watercolor set one time. Didge was so excited over it she threw her arms around his waist hugging and thanking him. He just stood there like a stick was up his rear. "I just don't understand him," thought Miles watching her now with Meda. The resemblance hit him fully.

"Mama, you sure you didn't birth Didge?"

"No, of course no, you know I didn't. Why?"

"Look. Just look at her and Meda."

Lukatie looked and saw what had always been there...only now as they grew the resemblance was more and more evident. "Now what do I say?" she thought.

"I've always heard that when a child is adopted into a family it takes on the likeness of that family. I guess that is what has happened with her. Anyway, people see what they want to see," thought Lukatie. She walked off and started breaking off some dead wood in the arbor vitae.

Miles walked the curved drive with thoughts working overtime. I should have kept my mouth shut. I know Didge wasn't born to her. But can Papa be her real father? I wonder if that is why he is so indifferent to her. Yet, it isn't exactly indifference, but he sure works hard at building up an immunity. She was left at our door. Didn't her family want her? Who is or was her mother? Is keeping her Mama's way of making Papa pay for what he did?

As Lukatie predicted, Titia was at church Sunday with Stewart and Madison.

"Go to church," Titia had exclaimed when asked to join them. "I haven't been to church since I was a child."

"Then it's time you went. How better can you meet people than at church?" Stewart said.

"Do I have to?" she said turning to Madison with a feigned grimace of pain.

"I think Uncle Stewart is right. Things are different here. Anyway, there's nothing else to do. You just might learn something of value."

"Huh," Titia turned and went to her room.

She loved beautiful clothes and when she appeared in church she was dressed in the latest fashion. Her well-rounded slender figure showed them off to the best advantage, wearing them shorter than the women in Campton. The men liked it. The women swore to themselves they'd lose weight.

Titia, in her late thirties, was as blond as Stewart was dark. She was still a beautiful woman. Her blue eyes were an invitation to most men that looked into them. To put it mildly, she was susceptible to the fascination of handsome men especially if they were rich. Although she didn't need money.

After the death of her fourth husband she had more than she could ever spend unless she threw it away. She would rather make a dazzling impression on people than really get to know them. To her women were just a necessary part of things. She much preferred the company of men.

There was an expression of veneration on most faces as Stewart introduced her to members of the congregation.

She appeared a bit mollified as she greeted them. "What an actress," thought Stewart as they drove home.

"Well, that is over," voiced Titia. "I was on my best behavior, too."

"You should always behave in such a manner."

"When I look at all those plain women, it makes me glad I left here so young."

Stewart had a strong feeling of disapprobation as he glanced sideways at her.

The following Sunday at Church, Preacher Murray asked if a booth could be built for the annual fourth of July fair to make money for a new organ for the church.

"What next?" thought Em.

"It's open for discussion. So please voice your opinions."

"I'll admit that church does need one." Lukatie whispered to Em.

Em raised his hand. "Preacher Murray, we admit the church needs one, but with the building I'm doing on my place, I haven't the time to spare to help. We are trying to finish the houses before cold weather, or we'll all suffer. I can furnish the lumber for a booth if you can get other men to build it. But what do you plan to sell in it?"

"Everyone likes to eat. We could have baked goods, sandwiches and drinks. If the ladies have some handmade articles to donate that would be nice. Something like that is what I had in mind. Mrs. Carroll, could all the ladies go to your house one afternoon and plan it?"

"Why not have a kissing booth? Makes a lot of money and no work," spoke up Titia.

"Titia!" Stewart's voice was a reprimand.

"Can I help if I like the easy way out? Sorry, dearest." She murmured.

"As we sing the closing song, we'll ask the

SILENT TEARS

Sholar boys to pass the plate."

"What a brilliant assemble of deities, rich too, I hope. Pass the plate, boys, and empty it when you get here." Spoke a loud voice from the doorway.

Every head turned. There stood three men with hats pulled down over their foreheads and kerchiefs over their faces with only the eyes showing. One who appeared to be the leader was holding open a bag.

Preacher Murray spoke out while all the others remained in chock.

"You're a bunch of miscreant evil doers. Why, why it's open depredation. That's what it is."

"Man, don't you sound off. You flatulent ass. Someone should stick a pin in you and let out all that gas."

"I'll help," thought Sena, "but it should be a bullet."

Hezekiah had a sin darkened heart. It was hard to control his temper. He was having a hard time now.

"Hell, it's stinking hot in here."

"Stinking no. And if you think this is hot, it's nothing compared to the hell you'll be in if you don't repent and look to God. You're atrociously wicked," said Preacher Murray. "Why you're taking the food out of my poor children's mouths. God forgive you. What a wicked deed."

"Men like him are agents of destruction. They're putty in the devil's hand." Hezekiah said pointing at the preacher.

"Amen," agreed Sena, almost audible. Now she hated him. It was becoming an obsession with her.

Didge turned in her seat and looked the men over making a mental picture of them.

SILENT TEARS

Impatiently, Hezekiah said, "All right, you gold mouth, soft talking, pious preacher. Get a move on these boys with the collection plates." The Sholar boys had remained rooted to the spot shaking.

"All right boys, do as they say," urged Preacher Murray.

"Yes, sir," their voices rose excitedly.

The Sholar boys had worked up such a case of nerves their hands shook so bad some of the money missed the bag and fell on the floor.

"Calm down, boys, no one is going to hurt you as long as you do what you're told. Just pick up the money and put it in the bag. There that's good boys. Now, folks, all eyes to the front and sing your closing song and have prayer before you leave the church. I'll leave men posted outside to see that you do."

He stood there until the singing started then backed out and they all left turning in different directions meeting at the river on Carroll land.

"Boys, we've got to change our meeting place. With old man Carroll cutting timber, they might find our hiding place. We'll meet here Tuesday and find another place. All but you, Hyrum, you better work. We'll let you know."

They had stuffed their kerchiefs in their pockets, changed coats and took off their work hats and stuffed them in a stump. While he was talking Hezekiah was busy dividing the money as usual; he had already slipped out a handful of change into his own pocket.

"It's like an old William S. Hart movie," said Titia after the meeting. "I can't believe it. Remind me not to wear anything of value or bring any money here again." She shook her head in disbelief.

On the way home, Didge said, "You know, don't you, the talker was Hezekiah and one of the black boys was Hyrum."

"How do you know that? I don't know how you can possibly know." Meda looked at her surprised.

"The eyes, try painting portraits, you'll see."

"You'll remember eyes you've once looked into. His are clear."

The next day, the ladies came to the Carroll's as planned. Lukatie had put a quilt in the frames that morning, placing chairs around it. Needles, thread and thimbles lay around the quilt.

"With so many of us together, I thought we could quilt a quilt for the fair as we talked," explained Lukatie.

"Good idea. Are we doing it by the piece?" asked Mrs. Heywood.

"Yes."

It had a large star in the center with a smaller one in each corner. She had made the quilt top over a year ago. With no special need for it, she had tucked it away. The soft colors on the yellow background and yellow lining looked beautiful stretched out before them.

Titia, a precise articulate person, had dressed up to go over to Lukatie's.

"Titia, go back to your room and put on the oldest thing you've got. That skirt and blouse you wear around the house will do fine."

"That rag? You can't be serious, Stewart. If I change, I'll be late."

"Won't hurt if you are. You aren't going to a fashion show." "A vain woman, my sister," mused Stewart as he watched her go back upstairs.

Titia's only reason for being here was because of Madison. On a short visit home just before her sixteenth birthday she met and fell madly in love with Stephen Whitley. It was a week filled with dynamite.

Then Daniel was called back to New York. Elda seeing the closeness of Titia and Stephen decided they too should return with her husband. On learning she was pregnant, Elda and Daniel had made a hurried trip abroad. Daniel returned saying that Elda was pregnant, and the doctor said she would have to stay until the baby was born or chance losing it. She had never been a healthy woman and they had no idea she was expecting or they would have stayed home. Titia would stay with her and let Daniel know if Elda had any complications.

"Oh, yes," he answered when questioned. "I'll go back and bring them home when the child is born." Ten months later they returned with three-month-old Madison.

After the birth of Madison, Titia grew into an apathetic person wanting only material things, and these she acquired in the only way she knew of to get them. She'd marry an old man. All they could do was fondle her so she'd take her love where she could find it. Not even Stewart knew of the deception.

Titia had married a count in his seventies. Two years later he died leaving her a rich woman. After the death of her fourth husband, all of them old and all very rich, she had come home. She always spent a year or two between marriages with Elda and Daniel to be with Madison. He was the only person left now, other than Stewart, that she really loved.

She started calling Madison "My baby." He took it as teasing saying he was no baby. "You certainly aren't," she agreed.

They had gone to town a few times and ran

into Stephen Whitley. His wife had died a year earlier, and he was looking for a wife and mother for his three teenage children. He had called on Titia several times. He never forgot her and would have married her, but they were gone before he got up nerve enough to ask for her hand in marriage. Now she looked at everything and everybody from either the material or sexual standpoint.

She wouldn't even mind cohabitation if the reward was rich enough and the man interesting enough. She had become brash and no matter where she went she was outspoken, often embarrassing those around her.

The women were inclined to talk about Titia, trying to find out all they could about her. They asked Lukatie questions as they quilted.

"I wonder how old she is," one woman said. Meda overheard and paused long enough to say, "Whisper when you say that. A woman's age is her most guarded secret." She walked out on the porch as Titia drove into the yard.

With cookies and lemonade made, Meda felt she could rest before serving and sat down swinging gently in the creaking front porch swing and listened to the hammering as the men worked. Those that weren't grumbling from the heat were singing, droning what sounded like a jungle chant, lifting their hammers in unison like they were cymbals ringing out. Indigent people in need of so much and trying so hard to get it.

"Hello, Meda, I suppose I'm late."

"Not really. Go on in. They're all in the parlor except Didge and Mama. They're in the kitchen."

Titia walked in and heard her name. She paused in the hall. She didn't recognize the voices.

"How many husbands has she had?"

"About four, I suspect."

"What do you mean suspect?"

"No one really knows how many of her men she married."

Martha Sholar expressed an interest by asking, "Does anyone think she intends to marry Stephen Whitley?"

"Well, what a devine circle. I knew I was missing something by being away all these years." Said Titia as she stepped into the room. "If there is anything I like to talk about, it's me. As for my intentions, when I decide what they are, I'll keep them to myself. Furthermore, I thought we were to come here to discuss the church booth not to gossip like a bunch of old hens."

A few of the ladies making sibilant sounds sat a little straighter in their chairs. They mumbled a few "good mornings" and went on with their quilting.

"How intimidated they can be," thought Titia as she headed for the porch.

The meeting continued as Lukatie rejoined them.

"Mrs. Carroll, I brought yo' ova a mess ov branch lettuce. Yo' kin pore hot grease on ter hit 'n kill hit. Hit will b' mity good wit' hot braid 'n fried wite side."

"Thank you, Mrs. Tartt, that is very nice of you. Mrs. Heywood, could your husband furnish the nails? Em will furnish the lumber and maybe you others could get your husbands to build the booth. We women will make as many handmade articles as possible and take baked goods and sandwiches and plenty to drink."

Lukatie called Didge and Meda to serve the

refreshments. Titia offered to help. Not knowing Titia had paused as she passed the parlor door, Martha said, "I don't care what she says. There is something very tenacious between them."

"Who?" asked Mrs. Tartt.

"That Titia and Stephen."

"Oh, I doubt it," defended Lukatie.

"Stop taking up for her because she's a Henderson." Martha's scoffing voice was snappish. "You know what they always say, when a new cow goes to pasture she has to graze."

"Then we'll each have to take care of our own bull," said Mrs. Heywood with a shrug.

"Guess she made all that money on her side or maybe it was her back or however she goes about it," argued Martha.

"Ladies, I think you should drop the subject. After all, Titia and Stephen are both free should they care to go out together. If you have to talk about them, do it someplace else, please." Lukatie said firmly.

"That woman," stormed Titia as she went into the dining room.

"Who?" asked Meda.

"That Martha Sholar. She's entirely too speculative with her comments and should keep her opinions to herself."

"Oh, don't pay any attention to her. She's just a thimit."

"A what?"

"A thimit," laughed Meda. "That is Didge's name for someone she feels has no direction. For example, all Martha can do is talk about people. She really never accomplished a thing."

Titia joined Meda and Didge on the front porch after the lemonade and cookies were served. At the same moment Seth rode by on Mr. Heath's buckskin horse.

"That is what I call meat. Who in the world is he?" asked Titia. She saw the glance that passed between Meda and Didge.

"Is something wrong with thinking some fellow is neat," her voice rising to a high pitch.

"You have a short temper, don't you?" asked Didge.

"I have," she breathed deeply, "I really have."

"A short memory, too. You show interest in him and you will get talked about." Said Meda.

Titia's eyebrows shot up defiantly. "Why, for goodness sake?"

"The fellow is Seth Kirby. He tends Mr. Heath."

"So?"

"He is negro. It must be hard on him. He looks so white." Said Meda.

"Really." Titia looked irresolute appearing a little mollified as she watched Seth turn and ride into the yard.

"I see they are coming along real good on the houses," Seth addressed them all.

"Yes, they are. Seth Kirby, this is Mrs. Titia Johnson. She is Mr. Stewart Henderson's sister here for a visit," Meda said.

Seth nodded.

"She's helping us plan a booth for the church at the fair. The church needs a new organ."

"I'm out to give the horse a good workout. Good luck at the fair." He said and rode out of the yard. Seth looked like he was sitting on top of a big gold brick as he rode into the sunshine.

"He is very much a loner. He has an enormous ability to learn and is going to Etherton College this fall. They say he pitches the fastest ball in North Carolina. He'll probably make the national league if he wants it," Didge said.

"They don't take Negroes," Meda said.

"They won't know unless he tells them," defended Didge.

Titia watched Seth ride off. The palpitation of her heart increased. She barely heard the conversation between the two girls.

The scraping of chairs on the uneven floor told them the meeting was over as Didge, Meda and Titia went back in the house.

Speaking loudly Titia said, "I promise you I'll be the last to leave. I'll not give them another chance to talk about me. Not at this meeting, anyway." She smiled a sweet acid smile.

Martha, feeling guilty, left with a "humf," and the rest followed.

Titia doubled in laughter, walked to the window and watched them practically crawl into their buggies and ride away.

"Look at the old withered up hens run. I'll bet their husbands haven't taken them to bed in years. But if you take a good look at their husbands, maybe they have at that." Her laughter rang through the house. "Bye, come over." Titia left three embarrassed women still laughing.

"What a woman! Can you take her seriously?" asked Didge.

"Depends upon the emphasis and inflections on what she is saying, I suppose. Have a seat, girls, and let's finish this quilt," invited Lukatie.

Marth Sholar hurried to prepare their evening meal. Trying to work off the antagonism she felt toward Titia. She thoroughly disliked the woman.

James wasn't anxious to go in the kitchen,

but Martha was a good cook and he was hungry. He knew that after that meeting it meant talk, talk, talk. A sharp resentment went through him when he thought of Martha's big mouth. "That woman's got more mouth than a hog has ass," he thought. The thought made him feel better as he walked in.

She smiled happily at him. A smile that caught him off guard as he sat down at the kitchen table.

"Have a good meeting?" he asked.

"Oh, yes, we're all going to sew and bake and fix a picnic lunch. You know what?"

"No, what?" he asked knowing better.

"Lukatie had a quilt in and we quilted. She is going to give it to the church to sell at the fair."

"That is nice of her."

"That Titia woman was there."

"Oh, oh. Here it comes," he thought.

"What a bore. Her and her airs. She didn't do a thing. Except bring in some lemonade and cookies from the kitchen. I hear she can be had modestly."

"Oh."

"I don't know what they mean by modestly. If she can be had then that ain't modest."

"Isn't," corrected James. "Why don't you stop the gossip, Martha, and let me enjoy my food."

"Strange, I've never seen anything modest about her except her looks." Martha said quickly. "If you get the meaning. That big car, all those fancy clothes. She looks like what she ain't…isn't."

"All right, Martha, what's on your clammy little one tract mind. What is it she looks like?"

"A wench, if there ever was one," she

screeched.

James stared at her, shocked that even Martha would say such a thing.

"For gosh sakes, Martha, is that the way you keep the fat worked off your skinny nose, by poking it into other people's affairs? Jealousy is a bad thing, woman."

"James," she yelled. "How dare you talk to me like that?"

"Then shut up. I don't want to hear it."

"So, you're taken by her too. I never thought my own husband would defend a woman like that. And to think I have to work at the church with her." She began to cry.

"Then you'll know what she's doing, won't you, Martha?" James said with a sarcasm that cut, bringing on a new flood of tears.

"Damn," he got up from the table and walked out of the kitchen door. His face mellowed as he thought of Titia. Any man's fool not to desire her. "She's beautiful, desirable and the most feminine-looking woman I've ever seen except in a moving picture show. She's far beyond my reach," he sighed. "Wish I was about twenty years younger. I'd sure as hell try."

As Titia drove home she saw Seth coming down the road and slowed the car bringing it to a stop beside him.

"Hello," she called up to him as he continued to sit astride the horse.

She wanted this man like no other she had ever seen. Thoughts of Didge flashed through the labyrinth of her mind. "Why in the world would I think of her? That child?"

"May as well let a man know what you want," she decided and said, "If you're feeling lonely, I can be of service."

"What do you mean by that remark?"

"I think you know," she blushed appropriately.

"If that is an invitation to your bed, you're wasting your time. I'm not interested."

"I don't waste time. I don't think you'd be sorry either. I'm a lot of woman with a lot to offer the right man."

Feeling somewhat overwhelmed by her audacity, he said, "Lady, you sound like a fast-talking con artist trying to sell your wares. Let's just say I'm not the right man." He left her sitting there and rode off, shaking his head. "And I thought she was quiet and demure," he said aloud. "Raw, she is, raw plumb through."

He urged the horse to a faster trot.

*****

To put an end of the argument as to whose house would be built first, Em decided to build the foundation of each house. Doing the negroes houses first appeased them and gave them experience before doing his own house.

Every house was to be completely finished before anyone could move in.

Hyrum and Hinton Smith, with the help of Jesse Tootle were given the job of loading the lumber onto the wagon and hauling it to the house sites.

One day Jesse approached Em. "Mistuh Em?"

"Yes, Jesse, what's on your mind?"

"Wel', Mistuh Em, thet Hyrum he ban takin' do goud paces ov lumber 'n pattin' hit at his house. I thank yo' auto kno'."

"All right, Jesse, I know. Go on about your work and forget you told me."

"Yassuh."

On pretty days all the colored women got

together and cooked outdoors for their men. Lukatie could see them from her opened kitchen door. She smiled as she watched them around the pot laughing and talking. "They are having a lot more fun than I am," she thought.

It was Wednesday before Em caught Hyrum alone as he headed for the wagon.

"Getting along all right, Hyrum?"

"Oh, yassuh, Mistuh Em."

"That's good. Say, Hyrum, were you at the white church last Sunday night?"

"No, suh, I shore won't," he said in a wry voice.

"You'd climb a tree backward to tell a lie before you'd stand on the ground and tell the truth, wouldn't you?"

"Oh, no suh."

Em, thinking of what Didge had said…her sureness. He felt sure now too. He said, "I think you were and I'd better not ever find out I'm right."

He started to turn away, seeing Jesse, he turned back to Hyrum as he was climbing into the wagon.

"I see you are pulling out the best pieces of lumber and putting them at your family's house."

"Oh, no suh," rolling his eyes toward the sun.

"Don't deny it, Hyrum. I've walked around and seen it. Now you go get every bit of that lumber and put it all down at Clayton Golden's house. I told you we'd take it as we come to it and I meant it. Do you understand?"

"Oh, yas suh, Mistuh Em. Yas suh, I'se gwine do hit rite."

"Whut's dat all 'bout?" Jesse asked, as he jumped on the wagon.

"Nuttin'...say we'ens doin a good job. A co'se we'ns gotta move dat lumber at ma' house ober yander ter Clay Golden's."

Jesse couldn't suppress his laughter.

"Jesse, whut yo' don', tol on me." Growled Hyrum.

"I hain't tol' nuttin'. Ah feared he'd larn 'bout hit. I tol' yo' yo' ort not ov don' hit."

"Yo' dum rotten negro. Yo' shet up fo' I kills me a black bastard."

"Wal, whar I'se cum from iffen dey burrie's one negro dey allus buries two ov dem."

"Yo' shoulda stood in bed, yo' unnastan' me, man?"

Jesse ducked just as Hyrum spit in his face.

"Dam yo'." Hyrum was mad for missing him. He clucked at the horses.

"Go yo' fo' lagged bitches."

"Gaahhd," groaned Jesse, "I haint did nuttin'."

"I oughta whup yo' wit a hickory stick, no dadum hit a blackjack stick 'n tak' de meat with hit. Go, go I sa'd yo' fo' lagged bitch."

The next day Em went to town for nails, and stopped to drop off some corn to grind into meal at the grist mill.

"Seem's lak they's a lot of controversy over voting to keep the country dry or not. Whut yo' think, Em?" asked Mr. Bonham, owner of the mill.

"I think it will stay dry for a long time yet. Sure will be hard on the bootleggers, if it doesn't."

"Yup, guess a lot of stills would close down."

"Put a lot of people out of work. I don't care for drinking myself, but people will always do it."

"Guess you'll have that corn ground when I come back. I've got to go over to Heywoods."

"Yup. How's the house coming along?"

"Slow, I'm afraid," said Em as he left. "It sure would be nice to just sit and talk while I wait for the meal," thought Em.

For the first time, Em felt a sense of self-sureness. He had collected a good sum from Mr. Heywood for the lumber and deposited it in the bank. Bricks for the foundations and flues in all the houses were paid for.

As he drove the old truck up in the yard, he noticed all the men gathered around the pump bench.

"What in hell is going on here? I go to town after nails and come back to find everybody loafing."

"We'ens not loafin', Mistuh Em," said Abraham Barnes. "We's all thursty. Thet boy, Gick, hain't ban' round with de watah all mo'nin 'n we's jest got ter hav a drink."

"Get your drink and go on back to work. Where's Miles and Thankful?"

"Dey's down at de sawmill."

"All right. I'll see about Gick."

Em walked over to Thankful's and knocked on the floor of the porch as he remained standing in the yard.

Zarilda stuck her head out of the door. "Yassuh, Mistah Em."

"Where is Gick?"

"He 'n har."

"Tell him I said to get his lazy ass out here and get busy before I put my foot in it."

Zarilda giggled. "Yassuh, I'll tell him." She turned back into the house. "Yo' heered him, Gick, don't play possum wit me. Git now. Git outen har 'n do whut yo'se tol ter do. Or don' yo wan' nar' fine new house ter live in. Cood b' yo' druther go on feedin' de rats since dey don' got two ov yore toes 'n half a finger. Yo'se lak thet, huh? Git 'n fetch dat watah fo' dem men."

"I'se got de misery inside granmaw," complained Gick.

"Yo gwine get de misery outside too iffen yo don' git off thet bed 'n git."

"Sprang fever go yo' feelin' lazy, son. Sum sulphur and molasses whu yo' needs thet will get rad ov dat no-count feelin."

Mumbling to himself Gick got up and went outside. Picking up the bucket of water he started toward the men. Em watched him as he unloaded the truck.

"Gick," he called.

"Yassuh."

"You empty that bucket and fill it with fresh water. Get with it now, thirst needs a quencher."

Gick shrugged and slouched off toward the pump bench mumbling "Don' see anythan' wrong wit dis watah I pumped dis mornin'. Nuttin' wrong with hit even iffen de dog did tak a drink outten hit whils't I wus restin'."

A week later Em slipped him a nickel.

*****

The old man came out on the porch as Em finished unloading the truck one day.

"I wonder how many more days it will be until it rains, old man?" Em walked over to the porch.

"Mr. Mathias," he corrected. "I don' kno' iffen hits eva gwine ter rain again or not. Seems ter me w'ens had 'nough fer a spell."

"Seems so but the ground is already dry. We need some on the gardens."

"Dat would hol up yer buillen'."

"Yes, it would," agreed Em. He greeted Seth as he walked up with his guitar in his hand.

"Do you play that thing?" Em asked as he walked off.

"Just strum it a little," replied Seth sitting down at the steps. In his more mellow moods Seth often played and sang to relax his mind of unpleasant thoughts.

"Play 'n song for me, Seth," said the old man.

"Sure you can take it?" He started by playing "The Old Gray Mare" followed by "Red Wing." Then he played and sang "Silver Threads Among the Gold" and "After the Ball Is Over." As Seth played and sang song after song, it took the old man back to his youth when he would go to Swamp Harbor and dance and play around with the girls while he eyed Zarilda's mother. Then he was brought back to the present as Seth played an unfamiliar ballad.

Oh, oh, tonight I'll love her tonight.
I'll hold her tight then softly say goodbye
It's our last I'll say when we part
But I'll go leaving with her my heart

Oh, oh, tonight I go it alone.
There's no place that I may call home.
So, I roam and stay on the go
Now she can never again tell me no.

So, I drift from town to town
And find there is no other to compare
She's one of a kind and very fair
But what have I to give her now?

> Oh, oh, tonight, I'm going back tonight
> It's three years since I took my flight
> The bell rang, I heard footsteps, Oh, oh
> A child said, hello are you my pa?

Em had listened to Seth and was surprised. Lukatie walked out the kitchen door.

"He plays well and sings in a soft mellow tone," Em said.

"Yes, he plays it well," Lukatie said, pleased. Didge listening from the front porch. She was surprised and proud. She wished she could tell him so.

The old man slapped his thighs as he stomped his feet, laughing. Zarilda had come out on the porch laughing, "Whur did yo' git thet one, Seth?"

"Oh, I just made it up as I went along."

"Yo don' ban 'n sum budy's corn patch fo' shore. Hit pleasures me a heap ter har yo', Seth."

"I thank hit was purty 'n kind ov said," said Winnie as she came around the corner of the house.

"How long have you been there?" asked Seth annoyed.

"Long enough," she said coyly, "ter har dat song."

"Think I'd better go," said Seth as he rose to leave. I'd better beware, he thought, as he left. There is a sullen, defiant quality about her that I don't like or trust.

"Tanks fer playin' 'n singin' fer us," called out the old man. Seth threw up his hands without looking back.

"I tink he is de purttiest man I'se eva laid eyes on," Winnie looked at him lovingly.

"His back is mos' as purtty as his front."

"Tain't no man yit, still jist a bot," said Zarilda.

"He's twenty, hain't he? Dat's a man ter me."

"Sta' way frum dat boy, Winnie," warned Zarilda.

"I kin't do dat. Eva time I see's him I git me self a throat full ov heart 'n a stomach full ov butterflies. I jest kin't get him shook outer m' head 'n I try. I'se really tryin'." She turned and pathetically trailed after Seth. She was clearly lovesick.

"Dat gal's headed for trouble. Dat boy don' wan' her," Zarilda said as she went back inside to get away from the flies.

Seth cut across the swarth of woods to the café. Winnie followed the path getting there a few minutes later. As she entered, she glanced at him with an eloquent lift of the eyebrow. Seth was sitting at a table with George and Kelly Sowell of the Heath farm and Elijah Golden and Hinston Smith of the Carroll farm. They started to pass a bottle around handing it to Seth. They said, "Cum alive, man. We's livin' for now. Har tak' a drink 'n git hyped up 'n dance."

Seth took the bottle and smelled it. "Pure rot gut," he said. He handed the bottle back. "This drinking is way out leading to the brink of nothing. Look what it got Alonza. A wood peg. I want no part of it. Just count me out." He picked up his guitar and walked over to the wall and propped against it and started strumming and singing softly.

Roxie came in from the kitchen. "Git dat bottle out ov har fo' de sheriff cums in. I mean hit now. Yo' wont him to close me down so's yo' won't hav' no place ter go? Yo' kno' I don' allow drinkin' in har."

"Dat shariff cumin now," Winnie said looking through the window. "He shore is," she looked around the room.

Elijah went to the window. "Damn iffen he hain't." He grabbed the bottle and ran out the kitchen door.

Jurasa Tootle was dancing with George Sowell and laughed softly and delightedly at a sensual suggestion whispered in her ear as he bit it. She gave a sultry laugh and wiggled out of his arms just as Sheriff Ply entered the café.

"What's this, a rump grinding session," he asked.

"Why in hell don' yo' sta' way frum heah?" Roxie glared at him as Jurasa wild-eyed and frightened backed over against the wall.

Trying to appear indifferent, George said, "Whut big eyes yo' got, Jurasa." He tried laughing but no one joined in and his efforts trailed into nothing.

"Yes, among other things," put in the sheriff eyeing Jurasa.

"Whut 'n de hell do yo' kno' 'bout her?"

Sheriff Ply glared at Roxie ignoring her question.

"Who's in those two rooms, gal?"

"No one," she turned back to her work.

He walked to the end of the room and tried the doors.

"Gimme the key. We'll see."

"Lak' hell I will."

"Do you want me to go git a sarch warrant?"

"At least he kin say warrant," snapped Roxie.

"Noah," she called. When he didn't answer she turned to Seth. "Will yo' cum wit me?"

"Sure, Roxie."

Taking the key from her apron pocket she opened both doors.

"All right, Shariff, have yore darn look. Then git out ov m' café 'n sta' out wit' yore polluted mind."

"Kin't do that, girl. I'se a public servant lookin' after de interest ov the people. So, don't git all het up." All he found was two very neat rooms. Seth looked at Roxie. "Are you really that angry?"

"Angry, I'se livid with rage. He's so good at bein' mean I'se shore he invented it," she rasped.

"Don't let him harass you. He's just a lot of bull with an insidious mind."

She tried to shake off her irritation, but he was just so exasperating why should she. "I may as well wallow in it," she thought.

Noah had come in and stood behind the counter watching the usual crowds come in for the evening. There wouldn't be much money passed. They would play their guitars and sing to pass away the time. In fact, Noah usually just stood and stared at Lebtia all evening unless Roxie yelled at him to do something.

Roxie locked the doors, thanked Seth and walked over to Noah.

"Stop staring at her," she said under her breath. "Yore showin' her how yo' feel. Git out thar 'n dance wit her."

"Whut a shame. Encouraging that big dumb ox to dance," said the sheriff with feigned sympathy.

"Yeah, mebbe m' head was messed up. I don' kno, but we shall see," he walked over to Lebtia. "Shall we dance?"

"I'd lov' ter," she stammered in surprise.

After the dance, he invited her outside.

Once outside he just walked and talked and was a perfect gentleman. Lebtia was in shock, a special kind of shock, having never been treated as a lady before.

"Wal, I be damn," said the Sheriff in disbelief.

"Thank yo', Shariff, I owe yo' a drink," she sat a glass in front of him on the counter.

"Now I've got her." He picked it up and took a big drink nearly choking.

"Gol' damn water," he yelled and stormed out of the café. Roxie laughed so hard she forgot she was mad.

With a tentative smile on her face, Winnie walked over to Seth.

"Shall we dance?"

With everyone looking there was no gracious way out. Standing his guitar in a corner he started dancing holding her as far away as possible.

Not realizing they were helping Seth out, Jesse, Calvin Tootle, Abraham Barnes and his two sons occupied one corner playing their guitars, banjos, and fiddles, decided they would have some fun, switched from a waltz to a modern fast stepping tune. Some jumped up and tried to fit in a fox trot. Others caught on and started to do the Charleston.

"That lets me out," said Seth relived. He walked over to his guitar, picked it up and left the café.

"Hey, whar yo' goin?" called Winnie.

"Home."

"I bet iffen dat Didge wus har he wuddin't leave."

"Wal, she won't be har," said Roxie.

"I kno' him bettern she do." flaunted Winnie.

"I guessed as much."

"I don' mean dat way. Dat's de closest I'se eber got ter him. I could shoot dat bunch ober dar. Changin' tunes lak dat." Roxie just laughed.

Lebtia soon learned that Noah was just a big boy with a rough-tough look and a heart like a kitten.

Briant came back for his answer from Meda on Friday. She was so busy preparing for the fair she did not have time to talk to him privately. He stayed over until Monday morning so he could spend Sunday with her.

The fair started early. It was a beautiful day. The ladies had brought more than the booth would hold. As they sold articles they'd put more out until they finally got everything out. Miles had made some frames for six of Didge's paintings she felt were good enough to donate. These hung on the post supporting the top of the booth. The booths were built around the courthouse. The dance was to be held in front of it that night.

Four women installed themselves behind the counter each taking a side. Sena was there and took the first shift so she could be free in the afternoon. She hoped she'd see Madison.

The street side of the booth was heavy with baked cakes, pies, cookies, candy, sandwiches, coffee, lemonade and soda pop. The quilt they had quilted at Lukatie's along with the needlework and crochet dollies was on one side, another side was filled with handmade toys. The fourth side was beautifully arranged with children's clothing.

On the lawn in front of the courthouse near the river they were having a turkey shoot, bag racing and egg rolling. Clowns were everywhere teasing people and doing tricks.

About eleven Titia came swishing down the

street with Madison, like she owned the town.

"She's as nervous as a whore cat vying for a man's attention," remarked Martha as she watched her walking toward the booth.

"Don't talk like that, Mrs. Sholar," said Sena.

"No reason why I shouldn't, just 'cause you're sweet on her nephew. I should keep quiet." Martha quipped.

"I'm glad you told me, I didn't know I was," said Sena. "The streets are filled with gibberin' idiots and she's the biggest one," remarked Martha.

"No," thought Sena, "you are." Martha's barbs would wilt the boutonniere in the buttonhole of the ribbon cutter at the dance tonight. Madison walked around her side of the booth and asked for a glass of lemonade. Without a word she picked up a cup and filled it.

"Five cents, please."

"How about ten cents," he said handing her a dime.

"Say these pictures are really great. Don't tell me they are some of Didge's?" Madison said admiringly.

"Certainly are," said Stewart as he walked up. "I've got a very talented God child. Look how she has captured the grandeur of the cypress, oaks, river and the swiftness of the fish rippling through the water. I'll buy it." He said. "I have just the spot in my study for it." Even Martha had to laugh at Stewart.

Everyone had priced their own work and Didge had priced the paintings at ten dollars each.

"Here take twenty-five and change the price on the others to twenty-five. You'll get it too."

This fourth of July fair was a yearly event

and people came out of the swamps and flatlands like moles out of hibernation. With automobile travel the in thing, strangers were always passing through following the coast from north to south and stopping now, buying the handmade articles like they were prizes showered down from heaven.

These foreign people were amused at the dried roots and herbs for make-it-yourself remedies. One sign read...spice plants make tea in the spring to thin your blood...sassafras made tea in the winter to thicken the blood. The dried roots were tied together in ten cent bundles. They sold. "They just smell so good," remarked one woman.

Titia was alone at one end of the booth with Sena for a minute. Nodding at Martha, she said, "I guess she has had plenty to say about me."

"Yes," laughed Sena. "She said you are a whore if there ever was one. We don't pay her any mind." She added quickly. "She isn't happy unless she is saying something derogatory about someone. Ignore it. She's got maggots in her brains." Sena murmured.

"People would be much happier if they would learn to keep their mouths shut. I'll be back around noon. We are spreading lunch with the Carrolls on the riverbank and hope you will join us." Titia said.

Sena glanced at Madison and back at Titia.
"I'd love to," she smiled.

Titia knew Madison was interested in Sena. They talked quite openly and frankly with each other and that was as far as it ever went.

"Come on, Madison, let's look at the other booths." Suggested Titia.

"There she goes pursuing men like a hyena

after prey."

Sena shook her head in disbelief.

"Honestly, Mrs. Sholar, you say too much. Mrs. Johnson is only walking down the street looking at booths with her nephew."

"Humph, look how she's puttin' on fer Stephen Whitley over there standing in the door of the bank."

"Where else would he be? He does work there."

"Huh."

Titia glided along like a cloud moving on a caressing wind as if looking for a target to land on.

Stephen was watching her. She looked like a dream; one that had recurred over and over in his mind for over twenty-two years. But dreams aren't real and that is real flesh and blood floating along the street. It was like magic how she could inject so much with so little effort. I'd like to take up where we left off, but she won't have anything to do with me. He left the door to wait on a customer that had come in.

James Sholar and William Heath were leaning against the corner of the bank watching her too.

"She certainly is a hipless looking woman," said William.

"I hadn't noticed, wished you had brought my attention to it earlier."

"Gentle down, you old codger before you have a heart attack. You see a pretty woman and right away your eyes strip her down to her bottom."

"Hello," said Didge as she walked by.

"You left out something, William."

"Don't know what it could be."

"I take her shoes off too."

"Now that's the petrified truth."

"Do you still chase women, James?"

"Sure, but when I catch them, I don't know why I did," he sighed. "You know having is not as exciting as wanting," James said with a hearty laugh as he started walking off.

"I declare, James, you've got the biggest ass I ever saw on a man."

"Well," looking back at William's protruding stomach, "I'd rather pull one than push one any day. I'd better go see what Martha's up to."

Sena watched Madison as much as she dared knowing Martha would be eyeing her every opportunity she had. She liked Madison and had slipped out a few times to be with him. They had a meeting place in the woods. Madison didn't like slipping around; he saw no reason for it.

"Why don't we tell your father we want to date? It's as simple as that."

"Oh, no, Madison. He has forbidden me or Julia to date. He has the boys watch us when he isn't around. The man in the pulpit and the man at home are like two different people. Please believe me. It will have to be this way or not see each other at all." Her voice was firm.

"I'll agree to try it for a while. But I like you too much to go on and on like this."

She knew the time would come when she would have to stop seeing him. She could never marry him. He would expect her to be a virgin and her sanctimonious, preaching, hypocritical pious in-the-pulpit father had plucked her virginity. "Oh, God, will you ever forgive me for hating him so much?" she agonized. She fought him like a tigress when the children were away and carried her bruises for weeks afterward. He had enjoyed it more when he had beat her into submission. He had never beaten her in front of them. She was disobedient he had said. He would send her to bed telling the children to go to bed while he went in and talked to Sena. She must learn to obey. "But our sister is good," they would plead. "Don't beat her anymore. She would do no wrong."

"Shut your mouth and go to bed like you're told," he would yell at them and they would hurry to their rooms.

He came now walking up to the booth. The women greeted him with handshakes and smiles, while Sena stiffened unnoticed.

"How are sales?" he asked.

"Real good," said Martha. "Everything is selling like hot cakes."

"Great, maybe we'll get that new organ!" under his breath he said, "and there will be some left over to put in my pocket." Forgetting Em had been voted in as treasurer of the church. Unknowing to him, Em was taking care of that.

"What did you say?" asked Martha.

"Oh, just that I'm going over in the park and see some of the horse races."

At that very minute Em and Lukatie were over in the furniture store talking to Mr. Wilson about an organ suitable for the church.

"Em, I've got a good second-hand Hammond organ in the back I can give the church a good price on. Had it tuned the other day. I'll take the old one as part of the cost. Come in the back. I'll play it for you."

"Sounds good, doesn't it?"

"Yes, it does."

"This one is only a year old. Say, how is the house or should I say houses coming along?"

"Just fine. We start putting on the roofs Monday."

"Think you'll be finished by the fall? I was out your way the other day. You're going to need a lot of furniture for that big house."

"You're right about that." Em turned to Lukatie. "Will you step out there to the booth and ask Sena to come over here and see what she thinks of this organ?" Sena came in quietly, sat down and began to play the organ.

"Sounds like an angel from heaven playing on its harp when she plays it," remarked Mr. Wilson dewey-eyed.

"It's second hand but looks like new." Em told her when she finished. "We can get it much cheaper than a new one. But since you're the one to play it, I think it should be up to you. Don't you agree, Lukatie?"

"Yes, Em. I do agree she's the best judge."

Before answering, she ran the scales a few times to gain her composure. She knew if she spoke then she would cry. The organ was beautiful and she loved it. It was perfect. But no one had ever asked her opinion before and made her feel her decision was important. She would always love the Carrolls for that.

Lukatie saw the emotional struggle as she looked into Sena's face.

"Maybe she'd like to give it some thought before deciding. Anyway, we might not make enough money with our booth to buy it."

Thinking of the big profit he would make on furnishing Em's new house, Mr. Wilson said, "Since it's for the church, I'll let you have it for four hundred dollars plus the old organ."

"I'll speak to the congregation in the morning, Mr. Wilson, and let you know Monday when I come to town for building supplies."

"All right, Em. I'll be looking for you."

They left the furniture store and went on down to the river where Meda and Briant were holding a place to spread the lunch. Briant had acted so sweet since coming back she had said yes to his third proposal of the day.

"May I kiss you now?" he asked.

"In front of all these people? Of course not." She laughed.

Stewart, Titia, Madison, Didge and Mr. Heath with a picnic hamper joined them about halfway across the courthouse lawn. Madison managed to fall in step beside Sena.

When the lunch was spread and Em blessed it, Stewart said, "I'll eat Lukatie's chicken. I know it's better than Zilphia's any day."

"You'd better not let Zilphia hear you say that. She'll kill you." Teased Titia.

He walked toward Lukatie and Em.

"I tell you, Em, you're one hell of a lucky fellow."

"Amen," said Mr. Heath.

"No one knows that better than I do," Em said as he filled his plate with food.

"May I make an announcement?" asked Briant.

"No need to. We see your face and I'll bet a piece of that chocolate cake, she said yes," Madison said laughingly.

"I did," laughed Meda.

"When?" asked Didge, thinking how lonely she'd be when Meda married and left.

"On his next trip in about a month."

"I'll see to it that it's exactly one month. It won't be a selling trip. I'm just coming to get married. Start practicing the wedding march, Miss Murray."

Sena broke out sobbing. Lukatie held her in her arms.

"There, there, dear, what is wrong? Can I help? You know we're all your friends."

"I know. I'm all right, now, thank you. It's just that weddings are so sad to me." She said turning back to the others.

"Maybe we could find someone else to play," said Briant, concerned.

"Please don't, I'd really love to play for you and Meda."

"Then it's settled," smiled Briant softly. "After lunch could we go boat riding? I noticed they are renting boats up there," indicating the small pier further down the river.

"How about it, Madison? You and Sena come along with Meda and me."

"I have to go back to the booth and help relieve the others so they can have lunch."

"You'll do no such thing. You've worked there all morning. I haven't taken my shift yet. Neither has Titia. We'll work the booth while Didge packs up the leftovers and Em puts the hamper in the trunk," said Lukatie.

There was no way out of going so she went reluctantly, hoping her father would never find out.

They rowed down the river singing and laughing to a private spot and pulled into shore. As Meda and Briant got out of the boat, Madison held Sena back.

"No, they want to be alone."

"Oh," she sat back in the boat. "This way we can be alone too," he said. "Are you always so distant?"

"Was I, or am I. Oh, for goodness sakes, what's there to say?"

"You haven't said a word since getting in the boat."

"I was busy singing or whatever you want to call it."

"Sena, were the tears for us? I know I have my peculiarities, but I think they're nice ones," he said with a slight smile and shrug of his shoulders.

"Madison, there can never be anything for us. I only hope Papa doesn't find out about this. Why didn't you help me back there?"

"Then you didn't want to come with me?" Confusion was written on his face.

She cut him off feeling slightly dizzy. I better stop looking at the water she thought. She knew she wasn't pregnant since it was that time of the month.

"Want has nothing to do with it. I told you how Papa is. If he finds out about this, he will beat me."

"Oh, come now, Sena, you're a grown girl. Lecture you maybe but beat?"

She rolled up the long sleeves of the dress she was wearing.

"Why do you think I wear long sleeves in hot weather. I'll tell you…to hide the bruises, that's why. If I cross him at all this is what I get. See?"

He gazed in disbelief at her bruised arms and shoulders.

"He should be reported. In fact, shot."

"Good God, no. He would lie out of it and then things would be worse. I've no one I can go to and talk to. There are bruises all over my body like that. Please, Madison, don't say anything to anyone; he wouldn't stop with me. He'd beat Julia and the boys too. God forgive me, but I wish he'd drop dead."

"Oh, Sena, darling, I'm sorry things are that bad. Why don't you go to Mrs. Carroll?"

"What could she do if I did. She'd react just as you are."

"There is Aunt Titia. She is very easy and understanding to talk to. She'd pack you up in that car and take you away from here. So would I.

If you'd only come and marry me."

"And I'd never forgive myself because I know he'd take it out on Julia."

"Sena, I think you know I love you. Please run away with me. We'll get married and go to my house in New York. I've got money, but if you want me to, I'll go to work. Dad had his own real estate and loan business and he had good men working for him. They are still running the business for me. I worked there in summers and took business in college. I'll also inherit Aunt Titia's fortune. She's a very wealthy woman. Funny thing is I'm happy here. All that wealth and New York living doesn't interest me. But for you I could take it."

"Oh, Madison, dear, sweet Madison, what can I say?"

"Don't say anything yet, think about it and I'll meet you next Wednesday night at the usual place."

Meda and Briant were coming, unaware of the troubled conversation that had taken place in the boat as they stepped in laughing and gay.

Sena excused herself as soon as they docked and left them.

Martha was still in the booth when Titia and Lukatie relieved two of the women. Titia talked only with those she was waiting on thinking how glad she'd be when her two hours were up.

"You don't talk a bunch, do you?" said Martha.

"When there's something to talk about and someone to talk to I do," said Titia.

Before Martha could say more, a clown ran up to Titia, "Selling kisses, Ma'm?"

He screwed up his already comical lips. Guess I'll give Martha something to talk about, she thought, as she leaned over and planted a kiss on his lips laughing.

"One dollar, please." He handed her a dollar.

"Worth every dime of it," he grinned as he ran off.

Titia picked up the dollar and handed it to Martha. "Here, maybe this will pay for a key on the organ."

"Hump, down here, Mrs. Johnson, you're going to find out you aren't as important as you think you are. Or in the social position you think you are." Martha threw the dollar in the change box and walked out of the booth.

Titia's laughter followed her.

The day was clear and hot. Men walked around with faces slick with sweat while the ladies kept theirs dried with a powder puff.

At the booth Em was helping out. During a lull he counted the money.

"Lukatie, we've got over four hundred dollars. I think I'll take it over and deposit it in the bank. Stephen said he would be there and for me to just knock on the door."

"Why don't you go do that. I don't like the way Preacher Murray has been hanging around. He keeps asking about sales and how much we've taken in. I don't like it. In case he doesn't know it, this is church money, not his money."

"He has changed. You were right about him all along. It was hard for me to see it." Em said as Martha walked up.

"Lukatie, I guess you noticed the quilt and all of Didge's paintings are gone but one. A fine-looking woman in a big car drove up and had a fit over that quilt."

"Well, Mr. Henderson had said put the price up on Didge's paintings and on that quilt too.

So, when she asked the price, I blurted out 'thirty-five dollars' and she said, "I'll take it." Just like that she said it. Well, then she spied Didge's painting and had another fit over them and bought two of them for twenty-five dollars apiece. That is what Mr. Henderson paid for the one with the fish in it. He said it was worth more."

"So, Stewart got that one. I always liked it." Em said.

"Why, Em, why didn't you say so. I am sure she would have given it to you gladly had she known." Said Lukatie.

"Guess I'd better get over to the bank with this money."

"You're a little late. Here comes Stephen now."

"I was just going over," said Em.

"I'm going back. Just taking a breather. About sold out, I see. Got anything left to drink?"

"I'm going over to give the fortune teller a rest," said Martha and headed for the tent that was set up for that purpose.

Lukatie filled a cup with lemonade. As Stephen drank, he looked around the booth. His head hit Didge's last painting.

"Ouch!" He looked to see what he had run into.

"Have to get hit in the head to see a good thing. You know that would look good hanging in the bank."

"We'll sell it to you," laughed Lukatie.

"It is the town with the river running beside it. Say, that's the bank, isn't it?" Em looked.

"So it is."

"I'll take it. Come on, Em," Stephen said

as he paid for the painting.

Em came back in about half an hour. "Well, we hung the picture and I deposited the money in the name of the church with me as treasurer. Lukatie, the more I think of it, I believe we should let Preacher Murray go and get someone else."

"That might not be easy to do since he has been here so long."

"Where is Didge," asked Em.

"Coming down the street."

"We're going to stay and see the fireworks, aren't we?" she asked as she came up to the booth.

"Thought we'd go as soon as we're sold out," said Em.

"Oh, Papa, please, I've never seen fireworks only pictures of them in the paper or books. I would love to see the real thing."

He thought of the attempts she had made to paint fireworks lighting up the skies and falling on a dark city. Finally ending up by painting them out.

"Well, all right, I suppose we can stay."

"Oh, thank you Papa," she ran off toward the park.

"If you're too tired to stay, we could let her stay with Meda and Briant and come home with them."

"No, we'll stay. Don't you want to see the fireworks, too?" he smiled.

"Don't care if I do," she said returning his smile.

Didge found Meda and Briant sitting on the riverbank where they had their lunch. She stood there looking around and saw Seth also sitting beside the river tossing pebbles into the water. She knew he wouldn't come to her, so she'd go to him. I must paint his portrait, she thought. Right away before he goes to school. As she walked up, the shining eyes he looked into seemed opaque as though she had painted them. Yet no artist could capture the glow he saw shining there.

"Staying to see the fireworks?" she asked.

"I don't know. I drove Mr. Heath in. If he stays, I stay," he said, standing up. "Are you staying?"

"Oh, yes, it will be the first time I've seen them."

"I saw your paintings at the booth. They looked like life."

"Oh, thank you, Seth. I donated them to the church. I didn't even know you were in town. Where have you been all day?"

"On the other side of town mostly about a half mile down the riverbank fishing. I told Mr. Heath a little while ago I'd be over here."

"Did you catch any fish?"

"Enough for our dinner tomorrow."

"You'll be leaving for college before long, I suppose."

"Yes, in the fall, but I'll be back each summer."

"I'm very proud of you, Seth. You've come a long way."

"Thanks to you for goading me into going to school in the first place. You know that first day of school I was so mad and confused that on the way home I picked up a rock and threw it as hard as I could into the woods. It hit a rabbit in the head and I ran all the way home with it. We ate it for supper. That started the pitching." He laughed with sudden merriment and Didge joined in.

She couldn't take her eyes from his. The

currents surging through her senses were hypnotic. "Do Meda and Briant feel this way?" she wondered. Aware someone was coming toward them, she asked, "Seth, what are you majoring in?"

"Business. I have plans, Didge. There is something out there beyond Campton and I'm going to see what is there. I'm aiming for the top. I might not get my toes out of the sand, but I'm aiming. Oh, how I'm aiming," he declared as he reached down and picked up a rock and threw it in a smart curve into the river.

"No dream comes true without a lot of work to push it into view," said Didge.

Titia had heard the last of their conversation. "Bravo," she called out clapping her hands.

"Hello, Mrs. Johnson," said Didge. "Have you been having fun?"

"Fun in the town? Looking at the agricultural booth and live-stock, phew!" she wrinkled her nose. "Yes, I had my palm read. The fortune teller said I was going to meet a tall dark-headed man. She said I was going to a dance and this man would ask me to dance. That he was very interested in me. That cost me a dollar. She said I shouldn't be wasteful with my money. I told her I had just wasted a dollar."

"And what did she say to that?" asked Didge.

"She said it was for a good cause. Oh, yes, she said I was a free spirit. I wonder who she was. I'd swear it was old lady Sholar. But in all that fancy gypsy get up I couldn't tell. I didn't know she was so harsh and callous. I thought she and all the church ladies were friends."

"It's getting dark so if you'll excuse me, I'll go back to the booth and watch the dancing," said Didge. She went over to Meda and Briant.

"Coming to watch the dancing? It will be square dancing mostly, I hear."

"This should be a good time to learn it," said Briant as he pulled Meda to her feet. They walked through the park and over to the booth.

Seth watched them go. As always with him her withdrawal left him with a helpless sense of longing. He wished this Johnson woman would get lost. He could feel a personality change come over him in her presence and he didn't like it. The sooner she learned he was an unbendable man, the better. He remembered their last meeting.

"You'd better go over there with the crowd, Mrs. Johnson. You shouldn't be away from them in the dark."

"You're with me. I feel as safe as I want to feel."

"I'm leaving to drive Mr. Heath home."

"Seth, you make me feel invisible. Look at me. I'm human, see?" she held out her arms to him. "I'm here in the park with you. I could be over there dancing. Why don't you respond to me? No strings attached, Seth."

"No, just strong rubber bands, huh?"

She put her hands on his arms letting them slide slowly upward. She could feel his body stiffen and draw away.

"What kind of ingredients are you made of? You're so darn remote," she cried out half in anguish. "Don't you feel anything for me?"

"No," he stuck out his jaw and glared at her. He was furious. He wanted no part of this forward woman.

"If you've got to have a man, you can find plenty of your own kind to take you on."

"You make me sound like a whore."

"Don't worry, your secret is safe with me. Just leave me alone."

"You animal, you."

"At least I'm aware of my instincts and capable of controlling them and let me say here and now they don't include you, you bitch." He immediately wished those last words back.

"You'll pay for that," she said viciously.

"I'm sorry, Mrs. Johnson, but if you aren't one, stop acting like one."

"I, I'll…"

"Will do nothing and say nothing. If you do, I'll say plenty. And there are those who will believe me since they already know you so well. And they also know me." He walked off and left her standing there.

"Something wrong, Mrs. Johnson? Are you sick? People et a lot ov junk at the fair terday 'n got sick. Can I service yo'?"

"Can you service me," she broke out laughing.

"Yassum?"

"Now that is a straightforward way of putting it."

"Sorry, Mrs. Johnson, I only meant…"

"Who are you?" she broke in.

"I'm Moses Sholar."

"Sholar?"

"Yes, Ma'am."

"How did you know me?"

"At church, ma'am. I've seen yo' thar lots ov times with Mr. Henderson. Iffen yo' don' mind me saying so I think you're the purttiest lady I eva seen."

"Who are your parents?"

"James and Martha Sholar."

"Do you know anything about servicing a woman as you so aptly stated?"

"Yas, ma'am."

"Well, what are you waiting for?"

"Yas, ma'am." He said excitedly starting to undress her.

"No, no. No undressing out here."

He lifted her skirt up and put his hand on her knee letting it slide up her thigh.

"Yo' sure do feel good, Mrs. Johnson." He reached for the top of her panties and slipped them off laying her back on the grass. "Yas, ma'am, you sure feel good."

*****

Briant danced with Meda and Didge. After the dance they returned to the booth. He turned to Meda.

"Shall we try again?" he asked.

When they left the booth Em looked at Didge. "There will be no more of that, young lady."

In a thin, amazed voice she gasped, "Why, Papa? Meda's dancing, why can't I?"

"Because I said so. That is reason enough."

"Let her have fun with the others," put in Lukatie.

"Leave this to me, Lukatie."

With hurt feelings, Didge walked briskly away. A clown ran up grabbed her arm and said, "Have fun, laugh and be happy. Here and here." He brushed his fingers lightly under her eyes and from each corner of her mouth to the other. "Make them smile," he planted a kiss on her cheek and ran off into the crowd of dancers.

Seth walked up to her and asked if she had seen Mr. Heath. He noticed her warm brown eyes had lost their sparkle.

"No." she sat quietly not caring to say more.

He wondered if she had seen Titia's

advances. Reason told him she couldn't have; it was too dark along the riverbank.

"Something wrong, Miss Didge?"

"Plenty to me. Nothing to anyone else."

Seth had never seen her like this and knew something was troubling her.

"I'm the only one in our family that gets hurt," she cried out.

"Why do you say that?"

"The others can date, dance and go out for fun. Not me. I'm kept home. If Didge wants to paint that's fine. Just don't want to do anything else, Didge, because you can't."

"You sound rather bitter or is it sorry for yourself." Secretly he felt elated because she wasn't allowed to date. If she didn't date, she wouldn't fall in love and marry someone else.

"Both, I suppose. Oh, look! The fireworks are starting! Excuse me, Seth." She jumped up and ran down to the riverbank.

She's going to break her neck one of these days darting around like that, thought Seth, as he turned to look for Mr. Heath. To Didge it was a moment to cherish as she watched the fireworks. They seemed to be exploding in a myriad of colors against the dark skies. They seemed to blend with the stars, looking spectacular, then a moment later they were pushing downward like a million shooting stars defying capture.

That night sleep came hard to Didge. She could hardly wait to start painting the fireworks that exploded over and over in her mind.

The next morning in church, Preacher Murray was obsessed with the desire to get his hands on the money taken in at the booth the day before. He smiled brightly at everyone and said, "Brothers and Sisters, I hear you did real well at the fair yesterday. That means you won't have to listen to this old squeaky organ any longer. If Brother Em here will give me the money, I'll see about getting the new organ next week." He unconsciously scratched the palm of his hand.

Em stood up. "I'm sorry, Preacher Murray, but I can't give you the money."

There was a murmur through the church. "What do you mean you can't give it to me?" asked Preacher Murray.

"I took it over to the bank and deposited it late yesterday when everything sold out. It's in the church's name and as treasurer I have to sign along with you for all that is drawn out of the account. I didn't think it wise to keep all that money on hand with all the commotion that was going on last night plus the church robberies that have taken place."

"Of course, of course. That was best, Mr. Em," said the preacher with disappointment written all over his face.

While Em had the floor, he explained about the organ they had found. "Perhaps the congregation would like to take a vote on it."

While they were voting, Hezekiah rose and quietly left the church. He raised his arms in a circular movement, mounted his horse and rode home.

Hyrum turned from the tree he had hidden behind to watch for Hezekiah. "Mite as well go home. Dar's no money thar," he said to the other three waiting for him.

After dinner Meda took Briant over to see the houses. As they walked, she told him about Lucinda. "Briant, could we possible take her and the baby on to New York with us unless she changes her mind? Titia and Madison said they could use their house on Long Island. It's just sitting there empty. It will give her a chance to decide what she wants to do."

"Sure, honey, write her we'll stop over with her a week after we're married."

"But it won't take us that long to get there."

"We're going to have a honeymoon, love." He pulled her behind the new house and kissed her tenderly at first, then fiercely. Feeling her body tense, he drew back. "All for now, sweet," he laughed. "Say, these houses are really taking shape. It will be like a different place when we come back visiting."

Home was not the happy, peaceful place for Didge that it had been for Benjamin, Lucinda, Miles and Meda. All she remembered of Benjamin was talk from the others trying to keep him fresh in her mind. "It's Papa mostly. He acts like I'm not here. It's like he's afraid to like me. Oh, he'll get me things I need. I know he likes my paintings or he wouldn't buy me oils and canvases. Mama is the only one that really shows any love for me. Maybe if I run away the whole crux of the situation might disappear. But where would I go."

Thinking of the fireworks, she got out her paints and headed for the river with Regal, the second, running bravely ahead of her. It had been like a burst of creation to watch the fireworks come alive in the sky last night. "I must paint them before I forget. They aren't like a tree…always there." Regal II lay down by her thinking stump and went to sleep.

She worked with celerity while the fireworks were still fresh in her mind. "I've got it, I've got it at last." Happiness grasped her. The words were a cry wrung from her throat. With a sigh she sat down on her thinking stump and looked at the canvas in front of her. "There's a separate and beautiful life in art," she thought. "What would become of me without it? I create my own happiness through art. It's all I have," she thought.

Seth seemed to come as though magnetized when Didge was at the river. He had hung back waiting for her to take a break in her work not wanting to interrupt her concentration. The last rays of afternoon sun filtered through the trees dancing ecstatically in her hair trying to rob it of its gold when he finally walked over to her.

"Golly, Miss Didge, the Lord gathered all the stardust in heaven and sprinkled it in your hair. Then he brushed his hands into your eyes," said Seth. Silently thanking God the sparkle was back. As he walked behind Didge to look at the canvas.

"You are invading my medieval kingdom."

"Sorry, my lady. I didn't mean to intrude," he said as he bowed low. "Am I forgiven?"

Didge burst out laughing. Sitting in a squat position, he looked silently at the painting for what seemed like ages to Didge.

"Yes, you really have got it."

"So, you heard me. I feel so foolish bursting out like that. I had no idea anyone was around."

Regal II stirred and looked at them with dignity and went back to sleep. Didge automatically reached down and patted his head as she continued talking.

"Does that make sense, Mr. Seth?"

"Yes, what's with that Mr. talk?"

"The same thing that's with the Miss talk." They both laughed.

"Seth, sit for me next week and let me do your portrait, please?"

He felt incredulous at the idea. He stared

steadfastly at her, not believing she was serious. A magnetic rapport snapped between them. His manhood begging for release. Seth's face contorted in agony as he looked at her. One of these days I'll cross the finish line, he told himself. He pulled himself together grinning at her. "If you're sure that's what you want, I'll try to keep still. How about next Sunday afternoon?"

"Good, I'll see you then."

Things were in an uproar when she got home.

"Where have you been?" demanded Em.

She held out the painting.

"Oh, we should have thought of that."

"It's beautiful. It looks real," said Lukatie.

"I don't know where they think I've been all this time," she thought, shaking her head more amused than angered.

The women were busy with their gardens trying to save the second crop. No one did any house cleaning anymore. Why clean something you're going to leave, pure foolishness.

"Dese bean vines air up 'n runnin'. Yo' young'un go tie twine to 'em so's dey kin vine up ober de pole 'n tek kar yo' don' break dem," said Zarilda to all the children underfoot where the women were gathered around the pump bench doing their washing.

Lukatie wrote to Lucinda telling her that Meda and Briant would marry the first Sunday in August and would stop by to see her on the second Sunday on their way to New York. I'm telling you now so you can make your plans to be free at that time to be with them.

"Thank you, Mama," thought Lucinda. "I read you very clearly." It was welcome news. She answered it within the week.

Dear Family,

I'll be so glad when the baby comes. I hope it's on time. I guess after so many years of marriage it's time to have one.

Fountain took me to see a good movie last night. At least he said it was good. I'm ashamed to admit it, but I felt so tired I fell asleep almost as soon as it started.

I've gained nineteen pounds all in one place. I look so funny. My visits to the doctor get closer together. I hope my next visit will be in the hospital. It seems women can't have a baby at home anymore. It's crazy. I'd rather stay home. The way I'm feeling it should be over soon.

I look forward to seeing Meda and my new brother. Above all I hope they are meant for each other and will be happy. By the time they get here I should be feeling well and have things fairly settled with the baby. I'll try to have everything ready for them.

I'll close. I'm real tired and have a headache. I hope this letter makes sense. It's supposed to.

All my love,
Lucinda

The twentieth of July, she went into labor. The lack of exercise was taking its toll. She was having a hard time.

The doctor stepped into the hall and asked Fountain what the trouble was.

"I don't know," he answered.

"I don't understand why she is having such a hard time. She's suffering so much. Did she take her daily walks?"

"No, sir."

"I told you to see that she took them."

SILENT TEARS

"I was too tired evenings to go with her."

"Well, she had all day," the doctor was clearly irritated.

"I wouldn't let her go out walking alone."

"Why in hell's name wouldn't you. You talk like you've been sitting on your head."

"Is that a diplomatic way of telling me my ass is on my shoulders?"

"If the shoe fits," he rushed to the delivery room.

"She's going to need some help," he said to the intern and head nurse. "Give her ether. Mrs. Rue, bear down to the pain."

"I can't."

"Sure, you can. We'll help you. Just bear down like you're constipated when a pain hits."

"I can't," cried Lucinda, "Just leave it in there." Some dreadful inertia within weakened her will to fight. What a silly I am she thought as she opened her eyes and looked around to see the doctor and nurse laughing at her remark. She closed her eyes and that was all she remembered. She would rouse up with each contraction and immediately fall asleep again.

When awareness returned to her, a nurse was patting her cheek and saying, "Wake up, dear, wake up."

"Don't want to, just want to sleep," the words were thick and slurred. She knew her baby was dead; nothing could come from her tired wretched body and live.

"You have been sleeping a long time. Your husband is here to see you."

Fountain was sitting beside the bed wondering just how to tell the woman he loved with all his heart their baby daughter was dead. The umbilical cord had dropped pinching off the child's supply of oxygen. Her physical condition was so weak that she only lived an hour.

His own physical condition was spent from keeping the long vigil and emotional strain of self-blame. How had she stood such pain for eighteen long hours? He wept blaming himself for her pain. The doctor told him it was best for the baby, and both of them, that God in his mercy took her. Had she lived she would have been a vegetable.

Surprising enough, Lucinda did not break down. She swore to herself that never again would she go through such pain for a man as jealous and selfish as Fountain. There were tears in her eyes that she held back calmly.

When Fountain finally went home, she asked the doctor to please find an excuse to keep her in the hospital until she was strong enough to wait on herself, and to please warn her husband not to touch her for at least two months. "Please do this for me, Doctor, I need the rest," Lucinda pleaded. Thinking of his first conversation with Fountain, the Doctor agreed to do all he could.

That will give me ample time to make my plans, she thought. She asked Fountain to please pack up all the baby things and ship them to her mother. She also asked him to write them about the baby and to tell them that she would write later. "When I go home, I don't want to see them. It's hard enough as it is," she explained. When Fountain came to visit her, the next day he told her he had done as she wished.

Lukatie was in a state of shock when she opened the package and saw all the baby clothes she had lovingly stitched for Lucinda's baby. There was a direct line from her heart to her eyes and they overflowed as she automatically reached for the envelope laying on top of the tiny garments.

Meda and Didge came into the room. "Mama, what in the world is the matter with you?" asked Meda.

"You're white as a ghost," said Didge.

Their eyes glanced at the contents of the box. Didge calmly took the letter from Lukatie's shaking hand and read it aloud. The words went in through the ears and out through the skin leaving it cold and damp.

"This means she really does intend to leave Fountain. That poor baby. My only grandchild and I didn't get to see and hold it." Lukatie cried a brokenhearted woman.

"Girls, please go see to your father's and Miles' dinner. Em dropped the package off and went on down to the sawmill. They will be right back to eat."

"Sure, Mama."

Em and Miles walked up the steps as the girls walked down the porch toward the kitchen. Seeing their long faces Em asked anxiously, "What's wrong, where is your mother?"

"You'd better go in the parlor. She's in quite a state." said Meda. She motioned for Miles to come into the kitchen with them.

Em took Lukatie in his arms. "Thank God, nothing is wrong with you." He held her tenderly as a fresh gush of ears ran down her cheeks. Each tear mirrored a memory of Lucinda as a child.

"Our grandchild didn't make it, Em." Her voice was flat and dead.

"I guessed as much." He continued to hold her close as he read the letter over her shoulder.

"We can be thankful Lucinda will be all right, at least physically. Says here she has an infection and the doctor is keeping her in the hospital until it clears up."

"Do you want to go to her, dear?"

"I couldn't be with her if I did. There is no telling how long she will be in the hospital. I feel certain she will stay as long as they will let her. I know by this she doesn't plan on any more children and is going through with her plans to leave Fountain. No, I won't go. I may be in the way of her plans. I hate the very thought of divorce but in her case, I think I understand it. She lived in a prison all this time. A good one but a prison nevertheless."

"Whatever you want to do. Are you all right now? If so, I'll go eat and get back to work. I'm sorry about the baby and for Lucinda."

"I'll write to her today," said Lukatie drying her eyes.

Em's whole personality had changed. He was doing what he had wanted to do ever since he could remember but could never find the way.

"Things are going too slow, too slow," he concluded.

"Let the men do more, Em. You're working too hard. It's telling on you. The men rest on weekends while you and Miles pour over books and blueprints or are out working. Miles is young enough to take it. But even he takes some time off for dates. You never stop."

"This has been a fractious month trying to keep everyone under control. If we don't get more accomplished next month we may as well give up, Lukatie."

"You're a little judicial about them, aren't you?"

"Yes, when I'm sure they can handle it all right, I'll turn more of the work over to them. Only about two-thirds of them are viable so I must do all I can to help."

Stewart came up. "How about going down for

a swim?"

"You know you can. But I've got to get back to work. Say, make Lukatie and the girls go with you. She needs to get out. We received word Lucinda's baby died." Em looked down at his toes as his eyes began to tear-up.

"I'm sorry, Em. I really am." Said Stewart.

"I know, I've got to get busy on the house so there will be room in case she wants to come home."

Stewart raised his brow as Em walked off.

On the way to the swimming hole Lukatie told Stewart about Lucinda's decision to leave Fountain. They were sitting at the water's edge watching Meda and Didge swim.

"I feel like I'm passing the summer in limbo. It's an effort to make myself move."

"Who else could have as much stamina as you, Lukatie? I'm sorry about the baby. I know it hurts but grief is like an illness one gets over."

"True but it does take time. I can't turn my emotions on and off like an electric light. I only wish there were something I could do."

"I know that. You're a good gratuitous woman always giving freely of your time and service to others with no thought of recompense."

"Oh, but there is, service turns my day into something special."

"You're one of the nicest, warmest, and gentlest of human beings. The pity is there aren't many more like you."

"Are you trying to lift me up in pride? You will, you know, if you keep talking like that."

"Truth is truth and you do have a rare capacity to care about others."

"Stop it, Stewart," she laughed.

Little Mary Casteen was sitting on the

steps when they returned to the house.

"Hello, Mary, how are you today?"

"I'se gotta bile on my knee. Maw sant 'm ter yo'."

"Well, let's have a look at it," Lukatie smiled. "Wait right here and I'll get something to put on it."

Stewart waited too. Lukatie hurried back. She cleaned the boil with alcohol, applied salve and bandaged the knee.

"The boil has about reached the maturation point. In a day or so we should be able to get the pus out. Mary don't pick at it and leave the bandage on. You come back tomorrow."

"Yas'sum." Mary stared at the bandage, stood up and walked off stiff-legged.

"She will be the center of attention." Lukatie told Stewart who laughed with her as they watched Mary cross the field.

"See, I was right. You do have so much compassion for other people." Lukatie smiled.

"It makes me feel comfortable all over when I do something nice for someone."

"Not just nice, Lukatie. Everyone under your guidance is clothed in love. And you're loved in return."

Didge came out of the house and placed her arm around Lukatie's shoulder.

"See," said Stewart as he rode out of the yard.

"I didn't mean to run you away," yelled Didge.

"You didn't. I was leaving," he laughed.

At last the houses were ready for the roofing to begin. Em assigned three men to each house showing them how to use a chalk line. He told the men he was pleased by the way they were all cooperating. "I know it's hot, but let's have no dawdling now. This means survival for all."

He was moving from house to house encouraging everyone with whom he came into contact.

At the Smith house he noticed Hyrum messing with the shingles turned up around the chimney. "Don't worry with that Hyrum. Go on to something else. The flashing will take care of it." "It would be easy for a fellow like Hezekiah to lead him around," thought Em. "I firmly believe, Didge is right about him. Proof is another thing."

"Dis sun is mummifyin' 'm." complained Hyrum.

"Having a warm house to live in next winter will make up for the heat now. If you get busy and finish it."

"M' feets hurt."

"Why, you haven't stood on them all day. It should be your ass hurting." Em said with irrefutable logic as he walked away.

"I'se gwine to conjure up sumthin' again dat man." The thought comforted Hyrum.

It was hot. The sun was high overhead...a beaming boiling streak which hit those on the roof tops like a steady flow of hot steamy air from the steam box of the sawmill. They tied bandanas or rags around their foreheads for sweatbands. They were doing a very good job on the roof tops as each shingle was nailed in place. It should never leak thought Em.

"Keep up the good work, boys. You're doing fine." Em would say in passing not waiting for conversation. He always believed in giving the devil his due and a little encouragement never hurt anyone.

Didge flashed through his mind. "I can't help it," he thought. "I've built up such an immunity, I don't know how to change. I don't know how to relent. I can't. It would never do. The rest of my life will be lived in subterfuge evading the truth of her birth."

He looked around from the top of a roof top taking enormous pride in his surroundings. His lonely and austere nature gave thanks as he lifted himself in pride for his accomplishments. He smacked a fist into his palm as he looked at the line of houses. The houses were all facing the road that led down to the river and Roxie's. Each house had nearly twenty-five acres of land surrounding it. He had given Thankful the chance to pick the site he wanted for his house.

"Think I'll tak' the site near the main road, Mist' Em. On the river wuld be nice, but ah don' wan' to be near dat café. Too much noise ober dar."

When Didge went to the river the following Sunday with paper, charcoal sticks and an easel in her hands, Seth was waiting. Seeing his surprised look, she explained, "I have to do preliminary sketches of you first and transfer it to canvas. Then if you can meet me here next weekend, I'll do the actual painting."

"Oh, I see I've got a lot to learn," he chuckled softly.

"How about sitting on the stump, Seth, and I'll get started." She did three quick sketches, profile, three-quarter and front face view. Seth took a break between each one.

Didge decided on using a red underpainting thus a red-faced Seth glowed out of the picture.

"Why red?" asked Lukatie questionly.

"I read where the early 18th century artist, Allen Ramsey, in his figure compositions used red as an undercoating for skin. I thought I'd try it."

"Why doesn't Seth come here and pose

instead of your going all the way to the river?"

Didge laughed, "He's bashful. He won't pose where anyone can see him. He's shy of the least bit of importance. If you happen to walk down that way don't let him see you or I'll never get this finished. It will take a few more sittings, anyway. It's slow work. I can only do so much and wait for it to dry."

"Too slow for me. I'd never paint. I like doing things I can do in a hurry and be finished," said Meda.

"Mixing turpentine in the oils helps them dry faster. Well, I'm done," said Didge.

Meda shook her head. "I don't see how she does it. I just haven't that kind of patience."

"It takes training and discipline," said Lukatie.

"Doesn't it bother you knowing she is in the woods alone with Seth, Mama?"

"My heaven, no. Seth would never harm a hair on her head."

It was a pleasure on this bright summer day to walk along the path with Regal II racing around her feet. Again, Seth was waiting. A quick bubble of built-in laughter erupted as she saw him standing by the river.

At the house she had decided on the full-face sketch. He was pleased because he could have the joy of watching her work.

She would usually sing or hum a little tune as she painted. Now she was bursting with song. At last she was painting Seth. One large strong hand rested on his crossed arms with the other hand tucked in between arm and body. "He has strong features. I must not get his lips too full especially the top one. They are almost thin," she thought, as they broke into a smile over large even white teeth as Didge looked up.

"Wipe that smile off your face," she teased.

"I feel a little absurd sitting here so rigid."

"Relax yourself. It will show in the portrait. Just don't change your position." She smiled into his flashing dark brown eyes. His straight blue-black hair was parted on the side and combed back. He was a well-built man. Hard work had seen to developing muscular arms and broad shoulders on top of his six-foot frame.

She tried talking or singing to keep him relaxed. Her voice tinkled with exuberance matching the expressiveness of her hands as she worked.

"Just remember one thing, Seth. A portrait will not look like a photograph."

"Not usually, but yours probably will."

"Afraid not. I hope not. They aren't supposed to." She looked into his eyes. Her body thrilled with an utterly new kind of feeling not yet invented meant just for the two of them. Her soul responded to his like a river floating a tree branch that gets caught but with the rising tide moves on. She increased the speed of her brush strokes to help put such thoughts out of her mind.

Within her eyes lay the dark promise of mystery. Never before had anyone looked at Seth with so much love to offer.

"We need, we must talk about our lives. There is much that has to be said," Seth said gently in a low-keyed voice.

She looked a trifle shaken and drew a deep hard breath. Shadows and sounds broke through her thoughts. She tore her eyes from Seth to look wildly over her shoulder. It was the whole family, including Stewart, Madison, and Titia, coming down for a swim. They came chatting and laughing with their usual comradery, all walking over to see the painting.

"I'll buy it," said Titia, cutting her eyes at Seth.

"It's far from being finished," Didge said, feeling that Titia would never get it if it was.

"That is a very good likeness," grinned Meda.

"It isn't fair everyone can see it but me. She won't even let me peek." Laughed Seth.

"Not until it's finished," Didge laughed impishly.

"Come on Stewart, we came down for a swim," said Em.

"I hope we haven't disturbed you too much, dear," said Lukatie.

"No, Mama, it's getting too wet now. I can't do much more until it dries some."

"You've really done a lot," said Lukatie remembering the red face that had magically disappeared.

"We may as well stop, Seth, see you next week. Same place, same stump."

"Right," he said as he moved toward a path through the woods and was soon out of sight.

When they had all gone in the hut to change into their swimsuits Didge sat down on her thinking stump. She looked down the river where it rounded the bend and flowed far out of sight. Sitting in her favorite spot seemed to ease her very soul, her mind traveling the out-lying roads of thoughts. Suddenly her thoughts were distorted by a rush of bodies splashing in the water. Titia was trying to throw half the river at Miles.

"The thimit," thought Didge. "She's obviously making a play for him. It's just as obvious he isn't interested as he swam out beyond her reach and stayed. She does everything she can think of to attract men." Didge gathered up her art supplies and went home.

Meda awoke early on Sunday morning and lay in bed listening to the birds greet the day. My wedding day, she thought. I should feel excited and filled with anticipation of happiness, but I feel nothing. True to his word, Briant had come Friday and was to meet her at church this morning. They would be married as had Lucinda then they would leave. Briant wouldn't tell Meda where they were going to spend the week.

"I wish the new house was finished so you could be married in it," said Didge. "Aren't you excited?"

"Nope."

"You're not?" she shot upright into a sitting position on the bed.

"I would be, but I'll never marry. Papa will see to that. He won't let me date or even dance. It's a good thing I like to paint because that is all he will let me do."

"Wait until you grow up a little then you can do all the things you want to do. Guess I'd better finish packing."

As Sena played the wedding march, Meda dressed in a white traveling suit of linen, moved down the aisle holding Em's arm like she was about to step onto a dance floor and do a fast foxtrot.

Lukatie raised her eyebrow. Then as Em took his seat beside her and Preacher Murray started the ceremony, words floated away with no meaning as she retired into her own meaningless private world. "For better or worse, health or sickness," she half listened, "I pronounce you man and wife."

It was over. The step had been taken. There

was a satisfied smile on Meda's face as she turned. Lukatie felt shock. "Merciful God, where is the happy glow that should be there. Something is remiss in this marriage. I permitted myself to believe it was truly a marriage of love." At the car she kissed Briant and then Meda. Slipping an envelope to her, "Give this to Lucinda when you see her. But don't let Fountain see it." It was a note and money to help her once they left her in New York.

"Bye, dear, and Meda, please be happy."

Meda got in the car as she waved to everyone. As they drove off Miles turned to Didge. "Well, I guess you're next, little sister."

"No such luck."

"I don't know," she shrugged. "Maybe Papa can tell you. Anyway, you're next, little brother. It's time you brought a wife home," she teased.

"He's a prize," said Mrs. Tartt.

"Prizes come in popcorn boxes too," answered Em, his eyes fastened on the disappearing car.

Lukatie watched until they were out of sight as she thought, "We never know when we take a step today what change it will bring into our lives tomorrow or just how it might affect our lives in the future."

"Are you going to tell me now where we're going? I see we're heading south instead of north. Why?" asked Meda.

"We are going to spend the week at Carolina Beach. I've rented a cottage. We will lay in the sun, play in the surf, swim in the ocean and eat seafood to our hearts' content, among other things," Briant laughed exuberantly.

"Why not a room instead of a cottage?"

"I wanted privacy, something we've had so little of. Do you mind?"

"No, not really if that is what you want."

"That's what I want."

"You should have told me. You see, I didn't bring a bathing suit."

"Glad you didn't. We'll buy one first thing in the morning. How about one of these wool one-piece, very short ones with the sunback and get you out of the rompers."

"Briant!"

"Oh, they were fine for the swimming hole, but not the beach."

They reached the cottage in the late afternoon. Meda loved it. After supper they walked along the beach. Taking off their shoes, they waded in the water. Laughing as the waves swept over their feet, they paused long enough to watch the sunburned children build sandcastles, clawing out sand to make mud pies that wouldn't hold together, and digging tunnels with the fervent zeal of childhood. Meda felt a great desire to join them.

They picked up shells straying farther along from the cottage than they realized. As they walked back the moon came up shining bright and beautiful. Meda was breathless as she watched it cast silvery streaks across the endless waters.

"Didge should see this and paint it."

"It's so beautiful it takes my breath. I could look at it forever."

"You can't, my love." He took her in his arms and kissed her as he had wanted to ever since the first time he had seen her.

She suddenly wanted to shrink back or run away. "I mustn't show I'm frightened," she thought. "Not now, not ever." She walked quietly back to the cottage with his arm around her.

She unpacked her bag hanging her clothes in the closet. "We have three bedrooms," she laughed. "One apiece and one for our things."

"Ha, we'll only use one," he said as he pulled off the bedspread.

She took a gown from her suitcase. "I won't be long," she said, as she closed the bathroom door.

He started to follow her and remembering her tenseness walked over to the window looking at the moonlight glitter on the water. He unbuttoned his shirt and removed it as he slowly began to undress.

Meda tried to keep her mind on what she was doing but couldn't. "Will it be painful or boring? I'm so tense, I must relax." Her mind started racing madly asking herself question after question all with the same meaning. "How can I get out of this? What have I let myself in for? Is this love? I could say the excitement started my period. No, I mustn't pull any tricks. I must be honest. It's just my nerves." She placed a smile on her face, removed the gown she had put on and with it trailing in her hand she opened the door and walked into the bedroom.

Surprised, Briant looked down at her as she threw her gown across the bedpost. She could read the desire in his eyes and for the first time could feel herself responding as he slipped off his pants and picked her up. Holding her close he walked to the bed, murmuring, "Waiting never filled the bucket. You little bundle of joy, you're as anxious as I am."

Long after Briant was asleep Meda lay quietly beside him listening to the strange sounds of the night. "How different the roar of the ocean sounds from the singing of the forest.

What will the sounds of the city be like?" she wondered. She thought of her mother when they had been too noisy in the kitchen as children, "Out! All of you, out! Before dinner burns up. I can't hear my cooking, so I'll know when it's done." "My mama cooking by sound," mused Meda as she finally dropped off to sleep.

It was late afternoon when they reached Lucinda's the following Sunday.

"Let me look at you, Meda. How you've grown. It's been eight long years." They embraced as if they would never let go.

"Lucinda, Fountain, this is my husband, Briant Roberson."

"What a glamorous looking blue-eyed redhead," thought Briant as he greeted them. "Little sister sure grew up."

"Come in and tell me about the family," said Lucinda.

"Mama is well but grieved as we all are over the loss of the baby. They are all worried about you and hope you are feeling much better."

"How about the house? Is it about completed?"

"You won't believe it when you see it. It's so big and should be finished within five or six more weeks."

"You can stay with us a while, can't you?" Lucinda pleaded.

"Just overnight. Briant has to get back to work," Meda smiled.

"Oh, please, make it two nights at least, can't you, Briant?"

"I suppose we can." He answered.

"Thank you. I haven't been with my sister in so long a time."

After dinner, the men sat on the porch talking while Lucinda and Meda washed dishes.

"I've a letter that Mama said to slip to you."

"Give it to me tomorrow after Fountain leaves for work. I especially wanted you to stay over another day so I could pack. I couldn't do it with Fountain home all day. I'll do all I dare tomorrow then finish up when he leaves Tuesday morning. Then leave here forever." She shuddered openly.

"Has it been that bad?" Meda put her arms around Lucinda.

"I like Meda's husband; he seems like a fine fellow," remarked Fountain as they prepared for bed Monday night. He studied every inch of her body to impress her curves into his mind. Even noting the mole an inch from her navel. He had kissed it many times and was impatiently waiting until their next fulfillment. Another week, at least, the doctor had said.

Fountain said goodnight unaware she was planning to leave the next day and this would be his last night with her.

In the next room, Meda and Briant were talking in low tones.

"Meda, Fountain said he would wait until after we leave to go to work so he could say a proper goodbye. Now what?"

"Oh, no," moaned Meda.

"Look, we'll get up early and you can tell her we'll leave and come back at ten. We'll forget something."

"That's a great idea, Briant!"

"He seems like such a square fellow that really loves his wife. I hate doing this."

"I'm sorry to put you through this. But I don't know any other way to help her. She has lived in this prison of a house for over eight years. You read that letter from her."

"Yes, and I wonder if she could be exaggerating a little."

"Absolutely not, can't you see how jealous and possessive he is? We've had no time alone at all for woman talk."

"I did notice that."

When they returned at ten the next day for the suitcase they left behind, Fountain was still home.

"I saw your case and waited. I figured you'd come back for it."

They put the bag in the car.

"Well, goodbye again." As Meda hugged Lucinda again, she whispered, "two o'clock."

"If we left anything else just ship it to us," said Briant as he shook hands with Fountain again.

"Let's go downtown and park where we can watch the store. When he goes in, we'll go back and get her. This delay is awful, we'll have to stop overnight somewhere, won't we?"

"Yes."

"It sure will be hot sitting in the sun."

He laughed, "I tried that one time."

"When was that?"

"The afternoon of the box supper."

Meda laughed, "The Hezekiah night, huh? Hey, look there goes Fountain into the store. Let's go."

When they returned to the house, there was a strange woman sitting on the porch.

"Do you understand now, Briant. There's the watch dog." Meda grabbed a kerchief and tied it around her head and put on the dark glasses she had bought on the beach.

"You stay in the car, Briant," she said as she jumped out of the car.

"Howdy, Ma'am," she said as she walked up

the steps. "I'm from the Salvation Army to pick up some suitcases of old clothes we were called about."

God bless her heart, thought Lucinda, as she heard from the open doorway.

"Come on in, Miss," she called. "I'll have these things ready in a few minutes." She almost burst out laughing when she saw Meda.

"Here, Mother Rue, will you move this box of stuff onto the porch?"

"I didn't know you were giving anything away. Does Fountain know? Some of the nieces could use them."

"Not these, anyway, they are already promised."

"You're not giving these good suitcases away?"

"No, I didn't have any more boxes. They will return them tomorrow."

"I guess I'd better phone Fountain about all this."

Lucinda jerked the telephone out of her hands. "You'll do nothing of the kind. Just tend to your own business for a change."

Meda took two cases out to the car, "Get the motor started, Briant." He packed the cases in and started the car.

Lucinda placed the letter she had written to Fountain on the dresser as she picked up her purse. At the door, Meda said, "Ma'am, if you can bring that case to the car, I won't have to come back in for anything."

"I'll take it," said Mrs. Rue, "Seems like a lot of stuff you're giving away."

"I'll take it. I've already got it in my arms," said Lucinda.

She had been guarded night and day for eight years and meant to end it somehow this day.

I just can't take any more of Fountain and his mother.

Mrs. Rue sat down on the porch as they arranged the boxes in the back then Meda got in the front and Lucinda jumped in beside her calling to Mrs. Rue, "I'll help them with these things and get my suitcases. Start Fountain's dinner if I'm not back in time." They drove away leaving Mrs. Rue stammering on the porch.

"I suppose she wants to make sure she gets her suitcases back," she consoled herself as she sat back rocking. "Fountain won't like it," she thought. "He's going to be mad."

"Lucinda, Briant's apartment has only one bedroom. We plan on looking for a larger place as soon as possible. In the meantime…"

"That's all right. A sofa, even the floor will do fine. I just thank God for you both for getting me away from there."

"Here, Lucinda, is a key to a beautiful house on Long Island that you can use for as long as you want it. No one will know where you are," Meda explained.

"I don't understand. Whose? Is it your parent's place, Briant?" asked Lucinda.

"No, it is Madison Hinson's and Titia Johnson's." She raised her eyebrow quizically as she fingered the key. "They are Stewart Henderson's sister Elda's son, right? Titia always lived with them. Elda practically raised her. I remember now."

"Yes, they are with Uncle Stewart now for an indefinite stay. They insisted we bring you the key and take you there, said Meda. "They said to tell you not to worry, they will never tell you are there."

"What good friends! Madison and Titia must be as wonderful as Uncle Stewart is," Lucinda said. Her voice broke, as she fell wordless.

"They are special people," said Meda.

"What a beautiful place," exclaimed Lucinda as they drove into the yard the next day.

"You'll stay here with me a few days until I get used to it, won't you?"

"If you want us to," said Briant. He thought his family home was large, but this was a palace in comparison.

Lucinda opened the door and went in. They placed their bags in the entrance hall and looked through the house. A huge ornate fireplace with intricate design occupied one end of a huge room.

"Must be a ballroom," said Meda. "I didn't know there were houses like this anymore."

Smaller replicas of the fireplace were found in the parlor, library and dining room. The windows in all the downstairs rooms were covered in beautiful velvet drapes. They found glass double doors opening onto a side terrace with steps leading into a formal garden.

"Oh, my, look at this. I've been told they were rich. But you would never know it by their actions," said Meda.

As they turned back into the house, they were met by a woman of about sixty years in age.

"Oh!" exclaimed Lucinda. "I didn't know anyone was here."

"I'm Delia Cox and this," she pointed to the door as a man entered, "is my husband. We take care of Mr. Madison and Miss Titia's home. You must be Mrs. Rue and her sister and her husband, the newlyweds."

"Yes, but how in the world?" Meda stopped at Delia's smile. "Miss Titia telephoned that you would be coming."

"We were sure stopped dead in our tracks. She forgot to tell us about you two," said

Briant.

"You all just come with me and I'll show you to your rooms. You must be tired after your trip."

"I think I'm too excited to be tired. New York is so big," said Meda.

"You'll be staying, too, for a few days, won't you, Mrs. Roberson? She'll need you for a while."

"If it won't be any trouble. We thought we'd stay with her a little while. She has been through so much," said Meda.

"Yes, I know and I'm sorry. I too lost my only child but that was years ago."

Meda and Briant stayed with Lucinda two weeks. The second day after their arrival, Mrs. Cox approached Briant about inviting his parents over to meet their new daughter.

"There is absolutely no reason not to use this place. It's empty too much. It will be nice having a dinner party again. I'm used to it and love it."

"What does a person say after an offer like that?" laughed Briant. "Yes," said Mrs. Cox. "Invite as many as you like. How about next Wednesday at eight? Just let me know how many people you want to meet your beautiful bride." Her eyes began to dance with excitement.

"How about everybody in the world," he teased.

"Let's narrow it down to about half of them," she laughed.

"Really, Mrs. Cox, there would only be my parents and the salesmen and their wives. Traveling for my father's business, I don't have time to acquire close friends. Especially the kind I'd want to meet my wife," he winked at her. "When Meda and Lucinda come downstairs, we'll see what they think of the idea."

There were about thirty at the dinner party. Lucinda helped Mrs. Cox with the preparations. With only the serving left to do she went to her room to bathe and dress.

Meda dressed in the white dress she had worn in the wedding and met Mrs. Cox at the top of the stairs. Mrs. Cox turned to Briant. "If the guests arrive before we get down just say your wife was detained at the last minute. Come, dear."

Meda followed her into Titia's room. "What a lovely room. How did she ever get drapes and carpet to match so perfectly?"

"She has a gift for decorating. Come, we must hurry. Take off that dress. It's nice but this is a very special occasion."

On the bed lay the most beautiful soft green ciffon over slipper satin dress that Meda had ever seen.

"Slip into this, quick. It will be perfect with your hair."

"But…" Meda hesitated.

"Orders from Miss Titia. She told me to take care of everything. You might say all this is a wedding present from her. The dress is yours. You might say she's a woman with a strange appetite, but she is good and generous. But I wouldn't advise anyone to try using her or take advantage of her or they will wake up finding they've been had. She's shrewd." Laughed Mrs. Cox.

"The low round neckline calls for pearls and matching earrings. Your white pumps will do fine. Now your beautiful gold hair. Sit down in front of the dresser, dear."

Meda followed orders quietly. Mrs. Cox draped a cape around Meda's shoulders and stuck some irons in a lamp she lit for that purpose. With deft fingers she piled her hair upon the top of her head. Forming curls around her face with the warm irons, letting a cascade of curls fall down the back of her head.

"I never dreamed I could look like this," said Meda, as she whirled in front of the mirror.

"One more thing," said Mrs. Cox. She took a string of pearls from a case and fastened them around Meda's neck handing her the earrings to adjust to her own comfort.

"But Lucinda," said Meda in a concerned voice.

"Don't worry. She has a dress that is just fine. She bought it to wear to a dinner the store managers had."

The door opened and Lucinda came in.

"Oh, Lucinda, you look beautiful," cried Meda.

"So does my little sister."

"Oh, here's perfume," said Mrs. Cox.

"The one thing I forgot," said Lucinda.

"If you'll excuse me, I'll go help Mr. Cox."

"Mrs. Cox, thank you so much. I wish I could adopt you," said Meda as she embraced her.

"I thank you, too," said Lucinda.

"You're both welcome," she beamed as she left the room thinking that Meda was just too pretty for her own good.

"Since you're the bride, you go on downstairs alone, Meda. This is your night. I'll come in a few minutes."

"I'm too nervous. They are all strangers."

"Don't worry, dear, Briant is there. Take a deep breath and go," urged Lucinda.

Meda descended the stairs slowly seeing a bunch of girls around Briant kissing him and embracing him with shrieks of girlish pleasure. The office girls, she thought, smiling. One girl was hanging on as if her life was anchored to Briant.

He pulled her arms from around his neck and walked over to Meda reaching for her hand. The girl's eyes flashed, and her jaws tightened.

"What in the heck was that?" Meda asked in an undertone.

"The one in the office I told you about."

"Oh, her. Poor thing."

"You're the incredible one and a flower of loveliness. I could crush you in my arms."

"Not now. Later, my dear," teased Meda, enjoying her role.

She was aware of the pride and tremor of his voice as he introduced her to his parents. She hugged them timidly.

"I always knew you had good taste, son, but you've picked the beauty of womanhood," said Mr. Roberson.

"You just made my evening, Sir," said Meda warmly.

"It's so nice to have a daughter and such a lovely one," said Mrs. Roberson. "Briant has told us so much about you. We feel we've known you for months. I'm so sorry I was ill at the time of your wedding. I did so want to attend."

"I thank you and hope you're feeling better now." Said Meda as Lucinda entered the room. "Come, Lucinda, and meet Briant's parents."

Meda greeted Priscilla pleasantly as if she had never heard the name before.

"I'd like to write her obituary," thought Priscilla.

Meda had a special ability to relate to people and was soon at ease. The dinner was served with elegance and soft music coming from the radio in the ballroom. Afterward there was dancing at one end of the huge room.

"You really have a captive audience," whispered Lucinda.

"Guess it runs in the Carroll family…that salesman can't stay away from you. Go ahead, dance and enjoy yourself for a change."

"I feel like Cinderella," chuckled Lucinda.

The last guest left by midnight and when Lucinda and Meda headed for the kitchen to help clean up, it was spotless.

"How in the world did you do all of that and continue serving drinks?" asked Meda.

"Practice, dear," Mrs. Cox said from the door off the kitchen leading to their quarters.

All of a sudden it struck Meda how much this house was like the one her father was now building.

"How many rooms are in this house, Mrs. Cox?"

"Seventeen including our quarters."

"We'll retire now and with all my heart I thank you for the wonderful dinner. Please rest in the morning." "We shall," said Meda.

As they ascended the stairs, Lucinda asked, "Why did you ask about the rooms in the house?"

"Tell her, Briant."

"Well, the home your father is building, your mother's Blue Bird, has fifteen rooms and laid out a lot like this one. Only the ballroom and parlor here will be a parlor and informal sitting room there, with marble fireplaces instead of the ornate ones that are here."

"I can't believe it. It sounds fantastic. How can he afford to do it?" asked Lucinda.

"I thought Mama had written and told you."

"She hasn't told me anything like this."

"He's selling timber and getting rich doing

it. Maybe we shouldn't have told you. Perhaps Mama and Papa wanted to surprise you when you go home. Papa is building all new tenant houses, too. He's like a different man."

"I'm happy for them. But I can't understand Papa selling timber like that, the way he loved those woods."

"The house was falling down. He had to do something," said Meda.

As Lucinda undressed, she thought, "that explains the money Mama sent. I hated to take it knowing it must be her egg money. I'll write tomorrow."

*****

Titia, in a restless mood, decided to go over to the Carroll's and see the houses being built. Driving up in their yard she called out, "Anybody home?" Didge walked out of the kitchen door.

"Hello."

"Come on, let's walk over and see the new houses. I hear five of them are finished."

"Will it be all right, Mama?"

"I suppose so," Lukatie answered from the kitchen.

Em was so tired he had a bone-deep ache all over. He knew the others were tired too.

He yelled, "Come alive now. Climb out of your rut and get busy. Come on now. Get the lead out of your ass."

Titia applauded.

In exasperation Em turned, "Run along now. One thing we don't need around here is women."

"What are you? Some new breed of men," laughed Titia.

"Didge," he glared.

"Yes, Papa, she wanted to see the finished houses."

"Then go look at them and stay away from us. We're busy working."

"Titia, all the houses are alike. We'll look at the second one. Papa doesn't want us hearing their rough talk."

"These are ready and very nice tenant houses. I think," said Titia.

"I see they've got the heaters in. Maybe they'll keep warm this winter," said Didge.

They came back to the Carroll house. The radiators were in each room with one in the attic room fixed up as Didge's studio.

"It will be a beautiful house of antebellum design," said Titia.

"Not as pretty as yours and Madison's house in New York. Meda and Lucinda write like it's a palace."

"Not really. Only a couple more rooms than you'll have here, dear. If you count your studio, then only one more. About three of our rooms are a little larger, that's about all."

Titia walked over and looked out of the window as Seth rode by on his horse. "Didge, I find it very hard to believe he's negro, don't you?"

"No, I grew up here and I've always known it. He is mulatto, his mother was mulatto, his grandmother too. His father is white although no one has ever known who he is. I'm told everyone thought she was carrying Jeff Batt's child. She wasn't, but he loved her and tried to marry her, but she wouldn't have him. She ran away and went to her aunt's in Washington. When Seth was about four, she ran off with another white man. A couple of years later the aunt sent him here to his grandmother who raised him and still curses his unknown father. That is all I know about it."

"What does he do for a living?" asked Titia.

"He traps. He and his grandmother take care of Mr. Heath. When Mr. Heath doesn't need him, he sometimes does odd jobs for other people. Mr. Heath is getting old and needs someone. He treats Seth like a son. The only child he had died of colitis when it was a year and a half old," Didge said.

"How long has Mrs. Heath been dead?" asked Titia.

"Before I was born. Why the interest, Titia?" questioned Didge.

Titia laughed, "He could go north, and no one would ever think he was Negro. Why on the seashore getting a tan is the popular thing. You should see people lying around on the beaches trying to see who can tan the darkest. They are much darker than he is. Half the night too some of them lie there." She laughed as if at some private joke. "Although I fail to see how moonshine can tan their bottoms."

"Oh!" uttered Didge.

Titia was gross, and knew it, but got mad as hell if anyone said so. She was warm, clever, calculating and game, especially if the game was in bed. "Maybe I've said too much," she thought.

Didge asked, "Why did you marry all those old men?"

"Because I had to develop a background and I like all that they had."

"But what kind of love life could you have with old men? I'm sorry, Titia. You needn't answer that."

"I'll answer, you're old enough to know what the heat of passion is all about. Love or sex, if you will, is one of the normalities of nature, sweetheart. Free people are the only ones that know what to do about it. Sex without guilt is much better than spending the rest of your life feeling guilty with a lacerated conscience, such as, should I or shouldn't I? To know only one man is to play only one record," Titia elaborated.

"It doesn't bother you what the women at church and in the neighborhood think?" asked Didge in awe of her frankness.

"To hell with these self-centered narrow-minded stuffy old women. I'll dare to live my life exactly like I want to and to hell with the consequences. Anyway, why worry over consequences that never happen?"

"Aren't you afraid you'll pay heavy one of these days?"

"No. I admit I'm sexual. I look for entertaining satisfying men. You can't escape from yourself through marriage. You are what you are, my dear."

"Is she for real?" thought Didge. "She would corrupt Satan. If I could be like her, I could give my love to Seth but then he would have no respect for me."

Titia smiled sardonically. "Society would call me a female failure. But I say I'm a woman that knows how to live and get the most out of life. Are you shocked?"

"Maybe. I still think marriage would be better."

"Yes, marriage is better. You have a cloak to hide behind. But if I can't get marriage, I'll take what comes after."

Didge shrugged, "Glad I don't feel that way about it." She soon learned Titia was a frantic, helpless bore. All she cared to talk about was men. As she watched her drive off, Didge thought,

"What a pity to be so man crazy or sex crazy". Thank God I could never be like that."

That night Hyrum was very busy as he moved everything in his home to the kitchen. After Hinton took his parents and sister a mile away to sit half the night with the family of a dead friend. He then took oil-soaked rags and set them on fire and slipped out of the kitchen door and headed for Roxie's.

Didge was sitting in the dark on the back steps thinking of her conversation with Titia when she noticed the flicker of a light in the Smith's house. She watched as it got brighter.

"Papa, come quick!" The urgency in her voice brought Em and Lukatie hurrying out the door.

"What do you want?"

"Didn't the Smiths go off? Look at their house."

"Good God, Didge, run get Thankful. Blow the whistle, Lukatie." Soon every man, woman and child that could pump or carry water or wet rags was putting out the fire. It was soon under control.

"Mistuh Em, cum here," called Thankful from the door. He pointed to all the furniture piled in the kitchen.

"Hyrum, I'll bet he didn't go with the others."

"Nope, he shore didn't. I seed him headn' ter Roxie's a few minutes ago." Said Solomon Casteen.

"Where did the family go?" asked Em.

"Dey went ter set with a dead friend ter hep change de cold watch jars dey has ter keep packed around de man til burryin' time termorra," said Alonza Casteen.

"Will you go get him, Solomon?" asked Em.

"Yassuh."

"Will someone else get a horse and go get the Smiths."

"I will," said Julian Barnes.

Hyrum came up acting as innocent as all get out.

"Well, Mistuh Em, I guess we'uns will hav' ter move'n ter de new house."

Em was unmoved by their predicament. "I said when they were all finished, we'd all move in. And that is exactly what I meant. You set fire to this house and don't bother to deny it. You were seen leaving just before the fire started. Now you can sleep under the trees for all I care."

"He mite ketch his death cold doin' thet," said Abner Tootle.

"I jes' mite," nodded Hyrum in complete agreement.

"Under the circumstances, that doesn't bother me one bit," snapped Em. "I should run you off the place, so don't tempt me."

The Smiths returned home as everyone was leaving.

"Now look whut yo' gon' 'n don', yo' dang stupid negro. Yo' aut ter b' shot," yelled Lebtia. She flew into a rage digging her nails deep into his face and arms.

"Yo' cut dat out fo' yo' git hurt. I don't aim ter tak hit." Andrew and Nancy, with the help of Hinton, separated them.

"I heered 'bout de far 'n cum ober to seed iffen I cood help out," said Noah.

"Dat onery Hyrum, 'bout barn our house down," cried Lebtia.

"He ortent don' dat," said Noah in complete sympathy.

"Maw 'n Paw auto kick him offen de place."

"Thar, thar quiten down, honey. Iffen hits all right with yer folk, we'en kin marry up cum no'nin 'n dey can sleep har in de kitchen."

Looking from one to the other, "Maw, Paw, Noah jes ax fer m' han' 'n marriage. I kin, kain't I?"

"Eva body hav' ter figger out dat fer dem self. Yo' do whut yo' wan' ter do," said Andrew hoping she would say yes.

"Do yo' wan' ter?" asked Andrew.

"Ah'm ah-feared ah do," stammered Lebtia.

"Den go ahead, Mitey nice ov yo' Noah."

"Git yore thangs, Lebtia. Yo' kin sleep in wit' Roxie ternight. We'ens kin go ter de kort house 'n git hitched termorra."

"I don' hav no dress fer marry'n yo'."

"Honey, ah'll git yo' a dress or anything yo' wants iffen I hav' money 'noughter ter git hit."

Lebtia got her few belongings together. "Har, Noah, yo' tak' thangs ober whils't I hep Maw fix thangs har 'n yo' cum bak' fer me after yo' talk wit Roxie."

"She won't ker. I'se gwine hep yo' har'n we'ens both go. Roxie'll b' pumb glad ter git sum hep."

On the way over to Noah's, Lebtia asked, "Noah, youse shore yo' wan' ter marry up wit m'. Yo' kno' whut folk say 'bout me. Yo' so nice 'n all dat."

"Iffen yo' don' demand respec' den no one gwine respec' yo'. Don' yo' worry hit'll be different once we'ens git hitched."

Hyrum, stubbornly recalcitrant, tried to sleep on the floor of the new house on a quilt. Finding the house open, Em looked inside and saw the quilt. He kicked it outside into the yard then he locked the windows and doors of every finished house.

Noah and Lebtia were married three days later. That night the tavern was an oasis of light in the deep blue of darkness. Seth hearing of the wedding headed for the café. Seeing Winnie coming out he dropped back in the darkness until she was out of sight then he turned and vanished softly into the guitar-plucking, nicotine-filled café. The room was lined with wall to wall bodies. Crowds jammed every corner. Those without chairs crouched on the floor.

He offered his congratulations to Noah and Lebtia and then stood back against the wall while the floor was cleared and Noah and Lebtia danced.

"Got tew rite feets," called out Calvin Tootle.

"Naw, don' thank so," Noah said as they finished the dance. Others started shuffling around to the music. "What a mob and stinking at that, thought Seth, as he watched them, their bodies pressed close together. Occasionally a couple would slip through the door to the privacy they so evidently sought outside.

No whiskey was sold that night. The boys all begged but Noah told each in a whispering voice, "No, I'se sleepin' wit' my bride ternite."

By ten thirty Roxie called, "All out; de door closes in ten minutes."

"Aw, No, Roxie," they all shouted.

"Aw, yes, out, out, out," she hooked the screen door when they were all out.

Lebtia started wiping off tables. "I'll straighten up ternite, Lebtia. After ternite yo' kin hep. Yo' go on with Noah, hits yore weddin' nite."

"Let's walk by de rivah 'n cool off," suggested Noah. They sat down on a log near the water. Lebtia moved close to him.

"We's man 'n wife now, Noah."

"Yep."

"Is we'ens gwine sat har all nite, or is we'ens gwine ter bed?" Lebtia asked.

"Go ter bed, I guss. But hits hot." Noah said wiping his face on his sleeve.

"Cum on den we'ens kin strip 'n tak a swim fust," she smiled. Noah started taking off his shoes and socks.

"Yo' gwine ter undress m' or do I do hit?" she asked.

"Do hit yoresef. I'se gotta undress m'sef."

He left her standing on the bank and plunged into the water head-first.

"Cum on whut er yo' waitin' fer?" Noah called.

"Yo'," she stammered.

He walked back to the water's edge taking her by the hand and leading her into the water.

"I'se de wuss swimmer yo' eva seed. Yo'll hav ter hep me."

The bright full moon was playing hide and seek with them through the trees. She looked up into his face and thought, "He is all gawkin' eyes and fumblin' hands." Lebtia realized that this was a first with him and that he wasn't sure what he should do. "I knew he was good, but I'll be damned if I expected all of this innocence. Why, we have never even kissed," she thought.

Placing his arms around her waist he pressed her wet body close to his. Reaching up she drew his face down teasing his lips with her tongue until he crushed her lips with his. Tiring of her game he made a plunge for her. They fell giggling into the water. He picked her up and carried her to the bank. Laying her down half in and half out of the water, he lay down beside her. His hands played lightly over her body. They were touching, wet and naked. Unable to stand more she shuddered in ecstasy as she pulled him to her demanding the newness of him in all his innocence.

*****

Martha was restless and couldn't sleep. She had listened to Moses slip out of the house again. At least three times a week for a long time now. If he was going out with the boys, he would say so and leave. He was gone to that disreputable woman again. "I just know he has," without realizing it she had spoken aloud.

"Who was that." James said irritated at being awakened.

"Moses is slipping out at night and going to see that Johnson woman."

"Aw, Martha, hush and go to sleep."

"I mean it, James. I've heard him lots of times slipping out and he goes in that direction."

"That doesn't mean he goes there. It's just one of your crazy notions. Now, let me get some sleep."

"It is not. I know that is where he goes. I followed him one night."

"That was a stupid thing to do."

"At least I saw him go into the side yard and she opened the door that opens onto the terrace from her bedroom. I nearly feel off old Nellie."

"Serve you right if you had. Now, hush and get to sleep so I can sleep."

"That woman is with our boy and all you want to do is sleep."

"No, that is not all I want to do. But it's all I can do," he said with a feeling of envy.

SILENT TEARS

"Don't you even care whut your boy does?"

"Nope, long as it's honest. Let me sleep now."

"I just know he's gone there now," she said.

"Good for him. I'll go get in his bed so I can sleep."

"You'll be sorry," she yelled after him. "You have a moral obligation to your church and family."

About daybreak, when Moses slipped back in his room, he was shocked to find his father in his bed.

"Son, I wish you'd be a little quieter going out nights. It wakes your mama and she won't let me sleep."

"Sorry, Papa."

"She knows where you go. She followed you one night."

"Oh, God," moaned Moses. "I wish Mrs. Johnson would marry me."

"Too old for you, son, too old. Anyway, you don't have any money."

"Now what do I do, Papa?"

"Not a thing. Just go on about your business like you always do. But be sure and use protection, son. Can't be too careful. Maybe slow down for a while. I don't think Mama will confront you with it."

"Take a peep, James. Here comes Mrs. Johnson," said William as they stood outside the church leaning against a large oak tree.

"Uh-huh, isn't that a fancied-up female. Oh, oh, here comes Martha from the outhouse. Damn woman. Only one I know of that can lick an envelope after it's been mailed. She's got more mouth than a swamp 'gator."

With a rolling movement of his eyes,

William said, "That was a mouthful. You are in one hell of a mood this morning, aren't you? Come on, we might as well go inside."

James only grunted. He was preoccupied with watching Moses slip around trying to catch Titia's eyes. I guess he wants to let her know that Martha and I know what has been going on. I sure wish he'd stop acting like a jack rabbit.

Martha sat down beside Mrs. Heywood. "Look at her."

"Who?"

"That Titia Johnson. Look at her sitting here in church like a pious old hag. She is a plague on the human race."

"I would say she's a woman that knows exactly what she wants and brushes everything else aside to get it. But you're using strong words."

"Huh, everything she touches becomes tarnished. She is a selfish, self-centered common woman."

"Come now, Martha, what has got you so down on her?"

"She has ruined my boy," hissed Martha.

"Oh, come now. I'm sure she has done no such thing."

Preacher Murray walked down the aisle to the pulpit and a hush fell over the crowd. Sena began playing the organ. She could feel Madison's eyes watching her. It made her feel nervous. "He should go away and forget me. I can never marry him now, or ever. I've seen Papa watching Julia. I know what is in his mind. I've told him I'd expose him if he touches her. How long will my threats hold him off? Run, Julia, run. Please leave, girl. Run for your life." She hit a wrong note. "Now I'll get more bruises," she thought.

Madison watching, saw her body tense. "Why

won't she go away from here. I want her. I love her and want to marry her. I don't know how many more bruises I can stand to look at or hear about."

With a falsified smile on his effeminate face, Hezekiah walked in and sat down on the back bench as was his custom. His lips usually curved ready to deliver a blast at anyone who crossed him.

His family continued living a life of self-inflicted ostracism, always afraid. Hearing more and more of the deviltry of the raiders. The air sang through the trees with rumors. They were now tying farmers to trees and beating them if they fought back.

Hezekiah eased out of the door holding his arms up and walked into the woods where Hyrum and the others were waiting. He quickly changed his clothes.

"Hyrum, you better stay out this time and have our horses ready to go. Old Man Carroll or that girl will surely recognize you."

Hezekiah entered the church and heard Preacher Murray's unctuous voice, soft in volume. "His begging voice," thought Sena.

"Brothers," looking to the left. "Sisters," looking to the right. "Life up your heads to God, look into heaven. Give him your heart. Give him your love. Empty your pockets to carry on his work. Give Saints, give. Build your home on high. Now, sons, now. Lewis, you and Jacob pass the plates. Now, boys. Saints remember him who gave us life. Oh, give, Saints, give," he said as he lowered his arms and held them out to the congregation.

From the doorway came the same voice they had heard before.

"Hey gusty, get that holy plate moving."

Slowly heads turned. The same form stood in the doorway. The noonday sun blinding them as they looked.

"You defile the most sacrosanct of places. This is the house of God. Don't you dare to drop your evil expletives here."

"Why don't you wise up, preacher. You know the pure and the sinful all have the same gloomy end. Just, kissing his fingers he raises them into the air blowing, puff into everlasting nothingness and that ends it all. Now I ask you. Aren't you ashamed to call yourself a preacher and cheat these God-loving people?" He bowed his head in mock reverence.

To call him wicked was kind, guilty of all sins yet looking like a saint. To see people cringe he only had to walk into church. It appeased him to think he was making things uncomfortable for others.

Each lady there held tighter to her purse and each man kept a hand close to the pocket that held his wallet or some choice possession. He would steal, swear, fight, gamble and associate with rough characters both men and women.

"One with your mental imbalance is sick and should be put away. You're like a subcutaneous parasite making your living from others." Said Preacher Murray in a mad shaking voice.

"You're talking about yourself, aren't you, preacher?"

"Boy, you better repent of your sins and study the decalogues and live by them. You better know wickedness is never happiness."

Hezekiah said, raising his voice, "Pass the plate please while I give thanks for my blessings. Every one of you turn around and kneel in front of the bench. Bow your heads and say your prayers. Since you're all so religious you do need a reason for living, so get to praying. Move!" he shouted aiming his gun at the preacher.

The only noise was the shuffle of feet as they arose, turned and knelt.

"Yea, brothers, you pray for my soul while I fill my pockets with your hard-earned money."

"Was that Hyrum with him this time, Didge?" Em asked on the way home.

"No, Papa, I don't know where he was. It was Hezekiah though. I know those eyes and that voice. I'm surprised he had nerve enough to try it again."

The next day Em reported to Sheriff Ply. "'Bout ten people already told me 'bout hit. But I've got to have proof."

"Didge said it was him and I believe her."

"Can she prove hit?" asked Sheriff Ply.

"As an artist she has very perspicacious sight. If she looked into a person's eyes, she remembers them."

"Eyes alone ain't much ter go on, Mr. Carroll. If the judge don't believe her then yo' gonna stand guard over her the rest of her life. Cause thet man would get to her."

"I hadn't thought of that possibility," said Em.

"You go think on hit. I've got to go check on Roxie's place. I think they makes whiskey there."

"How did he ever get to be sheriff?" thought Em as he walked off. An anger boiled within him like the surging tide beneath the rolling waves of the ocean.

Ply is right. I can't place Didge's life in jeopardy. But why doesn't he do something. Everyone knows it's Hezekiah. The bigot, standing there with a gun in his hands making everyone fear him. People can't even enjoy going to church.

When he drove up in the yard, he saw Seth leaving Thankful's.

"Good morning, Mr. Carroll."

"Same to you, Seth. If you are going by Roxie's, you might mention I just left the sheriff and he said he was on his way there. Said he thought they made whiskey there."

"I don't think there is any need to, but I'll tell her. Thanks, Mr. Carroll."

"Need ter mak' any soap or warsh clothes ter day?" Noah asked Roxie. In case anyone was around this was his way of saying their supply of whiskey was low.

"When yo' ready, let me know' 'n ah'll start de far 'round de pit. Lebtia, 'cum heat up dis grease 'n strain hit good for soap-making."

Roxie was stirring the soap when Seth brought the message.

"Thank yo', Seth, I shore wisht dat sheriff would stay away frum har."

"Noah's around sum place 'n Lebtia. Yo' run along. I'll be alrite."

As soon as Seth left, Roxie hit the pot three times and Noah came out.

"I just got word de sheriff is on his way. Speak ov de debil, whut you wan' sheriff?"

"Not a corkscrew, baby. Don't you eva leave here boy?"

"Nope, m' job is ter b' her' whin Roxie needs m' 'n hep with de café work."

"What 'bout thet wife of yourn. Don' she think hits queer yo' hangin' 'round yore sister all the time." The sheriff cut his eyes toward Noah.

"Nope, she's rat har all de time 'n she heps out too."

"Noah, yo' don' hav' ter explain ter him."

"What is that? Witches brew yo' stirrin?"

"No, but iffen I thought hit would work on yo' I'd shore try hit. Yo' kno' damn well whut hit is."

"Yo' sure are one stubborn black gal." the sheriff threw back his head laughing. "What you got ter eat in there?"

"A little meat, beans, potatoes and corn pone."

"Dish me up a plate."

The meat was deer which Noah had killed and dressed out two days before. Roxie and Lebtia had ground up most of it for patties except some steaks and roasts. One roast she sent to Mr. Heath. Then gave each of his tenants a mess keeping only what she thought they could use before it spoiled.

"That meat ain't done," said Lebtia.

"Who cares," answered Roxie dishing it up.

"Sure smells good, gal. I'm hungry enough to eat a mule." Taking a bite, he added, "I believe that's whut it is." Roxie broke out laughing.

"Yo' ate sum didn't yo'?" asked the sheriff.

"Nope."

"Then try it gal," he urged.

She went in the kitchen and turned the pot roast and came back into the café.

"Yo' rite, hit's tough. Just pay half price fer de meal 'n leave."

He choked on the hot coffee. "Why can sum people drink such hot drinks. Dey just burn 'm mouth up."

"Shariff, yo' talk so much yore mouth gits sunburned thet's why anythang would hurt hit," Roxie said dryly.

"Yore the worst tempered gal I eva saw,

whut do yo' mean pay half?"

"Whilst I wus in de kitchen yo' eat de vegetables 'n braid 'n yo' drunk de coffee. Dar's yore pie, yo' mite as well eat hit. Yo' gonna pay half."

"Damn if you don' git the best of me eva time I cum in heah."

"Den, Mista Shariff, why don' yo' stay away?"

"I'm gonna eat thet pie. Then I'm goin' in thet kitchen and all ova dis house. I'm goin' ter ketch yo' whiskey makin' yet."

"Yo' go messin' up 'm kitchen again or any part ov dis house yo' pot-bellied lummox de ground hogs gonna deliver yore wanted posters." She glared at him.

"Yore heads gonna go caput one of these days. You do in one of dem rooms wit me 'n I'll fergit all about searchin' dese premises, gal."

"How many times do I hav' ter tell yo' my name is Roxie 'n m' brother is Noah. We'se not boy an' gal. Now put the money on de counter Shariff 'n in de future, iffen yo' don't wan' ter pay, stay away. I'se tired ov tellin' yo' dat." She walked into the kitchen.

Noah had come in and was listening. "Lebtia's tendin' de soap, Sis. Do you thank yo' auto say whut yo' thank ter de Shariff lak dat?" He walked on into the café.

The Sheriff finished his pie, put his money on the counter and went into the kitchen. All he saw was a neat pantry and kitchen. He started back to the pot of soap. Nothing there but soap making. He turned back.

"I'm goin' ter search the woods good."

"Hep yourself seem ter m' lak yo' lookin' fer sum way ter waste yore time. Tak your harse with yo'. Dere's no free parkin' 'round har either." Roxie quipped.

He looked at her abashed.

"Jes don' wan' any reminders ov yo' round heah. That's all."

He shrugged then laughed. "I'll be back."

"Don' hurry." Yelled Roxie. "I hopes de ticks 'n red bugs eat yo' up," yelled Roxie. "I shore do," she said with firm finality.

Moses missed his rendezvous with Titia. He was afraid to go because of Martha. His mother said nothing but sat up late every night darning or reading the "good book."

He finally sent his cousin, Isaac. "Oh, no, I'm not going to knock on her door and say I've come to pleasure you."

"Aw, you go on. I had to miss last week and if I don't go tonight, she is going to be mad as hell."

"How did you ever get on to this to begin with?" asked Isaac.

"Just being at the right place at the right time," grinned Moses.

"Go on now, she is an explosive fireball. You'll enjoy every minute of it. Be there at ten o'clock and tell her I'm sick and sent you. She'll take you on."

A timid knock at the door brought a smile to Titia's lips.

"It's about time…" she said as she flung the door open. Seeing the strange boy there the smile vanished.

"Yes, what can I do for you?"

He was short, rather thin with dark hair. A slight scar near the left temple. He smiled, showing yellowish uneven teeth.

"Moses sent me to take his place. He's sick and can't come."

He hadn't meant to speak so forward; it

just came out that way. Now he shifted from one foot to the other.

She was angry and embarrassed. "How dare that…that garrulous, miscreant, degenerate cur exploit me like this. I'll fix him. I will. Who are you?" she yelled.

"I'm Isaac, his cousin. Moses said, tell you he'd see you again as soon as he could."

"All right, you come on in and you tell that Moses Sholar to never let me see his ugly face again." She wanted to rant, rave and curse, but would not lower herself to use profanity. Titia just wrapped her soul in truth as Isaac walked through the double glass doors and she closed them.

Seth sat on Didge's thinking stump as she painted. He consumed her with his eyes and surrendered to the pure sensation of feeling the nearness of her whom he loved more than life. Only physically, could he love her more. She is a woman sweet and intelligent enough to make a man feel at ease and comfortable in her presence.

Looking up from the easel she saw he was taut.

"Take a break, Seth, you look tired," she smiled into his eyes. She was suddenly obsessed with inescapable feelings of hopes, fears, and helplessness. Her feelings for Seth were as absorbing as breathing the air of life. She had a sinking feeling of shame for having such feelings. She knew she could never marry Seth. There was family to consider as well as laws and social prestige. "Well, damn the laws and the other people too," she thought, "But I do have to respect the wishes of the family that has raised me."

Her feelings were united with his. They both knew it. But would never dare voice such emotions. "She is too naïve to understand the twist of nature," he thought. "It is what it is, Didge. Let's leave it that way. It has to be."

She dropped her eyes, too nervous to paint. "I would have. I wanted to. He knows it. Oh God, he knows." The cracking of the underbrush made Didge jump.

"It's just a curious deer to your right," said Seth. "Are you all right, now?"

She noticed lines deepening around his mouth and along the jaw as he looked at her.

"Yes, of course."

She started packing up her oils, slowly cleaning her brushes in turpentine. Like a cat, Seth disappeared over the pine straw unheard, unseen, lost in the coniferous forest.

The sweltering summer weather caused her to look out over the water. "It's early. I'll take a swim," she thought. She went into the hut and took her suit from the nail and slipped it on. She walked to the water's edge and looked down at her reflection and thought. "Who am I? I am a human being living with a family. Loving them, knowing they love me in their way which is enough for now. I am me. I have a life ahead of me and must make it take form."

"I can't understand why Papa is so stern with me. He wasn't with Lucinda and Meda. There must be something wrong with me. But what?" She slowly ran her hands over her body bringing her hands to rest on her breasts. They are really growing and feel firm, yet soft. She wondered what it would be like for a man to touch her there. She immediately thought of Seth. The unbidden shameful thought rushed through her mind and she felt delirious. She plunged into the water.

"Didge may have her thinking stump, but I

have my watching tree," thought Seth feeling guilty of invading her privacy. "I'd kill anyone else I caught doing this." As he watched her now he did so because he thought to see her safely home.

He didn't know she was going to change her mind. He watched now as she swam to the overhanging tree limb and slipped out of her suit jumping up to reach the limb to hang it on. His strong arms and large hands corded with tension. "She is bathed in beauty," he thought. "If I can't have her then there will be no one. No one exists for me but her."

She swam with the sun shimmering and sparkling over the water around her. How I'd like to be as open as the river, she thought, and each thought was filled with Seth.

"Well, well, well, look what we have here," called Hezekiah from the river's edge. "I couldn't get near Meda but you're here all alone and much prettier."

"You rotten beast, you leave here."

He started unbuttoning his shirt. She swam wildly toward her suit. She jerked it down and slipped it on just as he reached her. She ducked under water heading for shore. When she surfaced for air, he grabbed her pinning her arms to her side. She kicked digging her nails into his thighs.

"You contemptible louse. Leave me alone."

"Come on, baby, be free and easy. I'm going to have you."

"Like hell you are. You scum." She finally extricated herself swimming as fast as she could for shore. "Why in the world didn't I go home while Seth was here to see that I got there all right." She started screaming just as Hezekiah reached for her again.

SILENT TEARS

"That is enough," thought Seth as he raced toward them.

"What's wrong, Miss Didge?"

"He, he's trying to attack me," she cried.

"Get lost, negro, while I have some fun," yelled Hezekiah.

"Sure, muscle mouth," said Seth smashing Hezekiah's teeth with his fist.

"Get going before I kill you, you half-white bastard," yelled Hezekiah.

They grabbed each other. Seth tried to pull away. Hezekiah had his fist full of Seth's shirt and cursing like the devil out of purgatory. He ripped out a sleeve. Seth was sure he took half of his arm with it. He turned quickly and twisted out of reach.

Hezekiah grabbed a big stick making a clear cracking sound as he struck Seth on the shoulder. Didge picked up another stick and tripped Hezekiah. He fell to the ground striking his head on a tree root.

Tears were running down Didge's cheeks. She was shaking and scared. Exhausted, Seth sank to his knees, then with great effort he pulled himself to his feet and leaned against the trunk of the tree. Sweat and blood ran down his face and dripped off the end of his nose and chin. He gingerly massaged his aching arms.

"I feel like I'm hung over and I've never been drunk in my life."

"Oh, Seth, I'm so sorry," cried Didge.

"It's all right as long as you're all right," he managed weakly.

Didge ran to the hut and got a flour sack, wetting it in the river, she cleaned Seth's face and arms of dirt and drying blood from scratches where the splinters of the stick had dug in his flesh. Washing out the sack, she gave it to him to hold to his face and neck. Then she went back to the hut and changed into her clothing. Wetting another sack she went to Hezekiah and rolled him over placing the wet sack on his forehead. He soon groaned and sat up wiping his face with the sack. He threw it at Didge. "Thanks for nothing."

"You just...you just get up and go home and stay out of our woods and off Carroll land."

Hezekiah picked up his clothes and went, all fight drained from him.

"We'll settle this score. I'll get you," he flung at Seth murderously.

"You just clear out," Seth said glaring at him.

Didge picked up the sacks and was washing them out when the Carrolls, Hendersons and Sena came up.

"What is going on here," demanded Em.

Didge came to the bank and told them what had happened.

"Someone will fix that Hezekiah yet. You should have killed him." Miles said in disgust.

"Miles, stop such thinking," said Lukatie as she turned to Seth. "Are you all right now? Is there anything we can do for you?"

"I don't believe so, ma'am."

"Seth, we thank you for what you did for Didge," she smiled. "This reminds me of the first time you ever saw her. Do you remember, Seth? You looked in the cradle and said, Miz Carroll, I am going to take care of her when I grow up so you can rest."

"Yes, ma'am, I remember saying it. I thought then she would always be a baby," he laughed.

"Maybe we can help you home?" asked Em and Miles at the same time. They laughed, "two great minds, you know."

"I can drive him in the buggy," offered Titia.

"No, thank you. I'll be all right as soon as I get my second wind," he said with emphasis.

"If we can't help, we're going swimming," said Miles. "Join us, Didge?"

"I don't think so. I was having a swim when Hezekiah came up. Seth heard me screaming and came back." She turned to Sena. "Glad you could come."

"Thank you. Miss Titia asked me over for dinner and the afternoon and Papa let me come. I was shocked."

Didge raised her eyebrow. "Why so?"

"He usually makes me cook for the family," Sena recovered with a quick answer.

Em was disturbed over the dastardly act. But what could he do about it that Seth hadn't already done?

All the women went in one side of the hut while the men went on the other. Titia hurried to change hoping to flaunt her perfect figure in front of Seth. She was wearing one of New York's latest fashions in bathing suits. A one-piece sunback. She moved ostentatiously to display herself brazenly as she emerged from the hut.

"She is dangerous and cunning. She inflicts me with evil." Seth said frowning.

"Why, Seth?"

"Excuse me, Didge. It's time I left. I just can't stand that woman."

Before Didge could reply he was gone silently. His leaving was no louder than a twig cracking in the autumn wind as it fell to the ground.

She gathered up her art supplies and went home. Ever since beginning Seth's portrait, she had gone home and worked feverishly on a second portrait while his features were fresh enough in her mind to easily copy each day's work. She planned to give him one and keep one for herself. Next week she would only take the finished portrait and give it to him.

Sena and Madison tried to be careful and hide their feelings for each other or so they thought. It was apparent to all present that there was definitely a strong attraction between them. Titia and Miles knew and with nothing better to do watched them.

Miles had encouraged Madison to take her away. He told Miles he had begged her to go but she wouldn't. Deep inside his searching impatient nature he sought for her reasons. She was ready for him. He knew that by her kisses that shook them both with passion. Often when she met him on Wednesday nights she was in tears. He would hold her close until the tears quieted.

On such nights she was late because her father had insisted on a double lay. "Dear God, how I hate him. Would it really be a sin to kill him. If only Julia would find someone and get married, then I could run away. But everytime I threatened to leave he would tell me to go ahead, there is always Julia."

After supper, the next evening as Sena did the dishes alone, he walked up behind her and began to stroke her breast. She cried out in open defense shaking his hand loose.

The boys were out and Julia had gone to the Heywoods. Finding no one home she had walked slowly back and was walking up on the porch when she heard her father's voice.

"I suppose you'd rather young Madison Henderson or is it Miles Carroll you'd prefer having you," he sneered.

"I'd rather lay with anyone, even a negro,

than you." He slapped her and she threw a bowl of dish water in his face and ran toward the door. Catching her and beating her while dragging her to her room. Ripping her clothes off, he threw her on the bed falling on top of her.

"You animal," screamed Sena.

"I'm your father, you whore."

"I'm what you made me."

"If you don't stop fighting, I can always take Julia, you know."

"You leave Julia alone. You'll not ruin her life like you have mine. Damn your soul to hell. You are the lowest form of creature and don't you dare to dirty the word by ever calling yourself father to me again."

With his clinched fist, he knocked her unconscious.

Julia slipped from the house, the tears streaming down her cheeks. She ran to the church and sat down on the steps. The words she had just heard resounded over and over until she became sick. Holding her head over the side of the steps, she began to vomit. She was remembering all the beatings Sena had had.

"Oh, dear God, Sena took it to spare me. What she must have gone through. Well, there is no other girl in this family. I'll talk to Sena tomorrow and we'll run away. He can't take the boys' virginity or can he? When I'm through with him, he won't take anything from anyone again."

The night air began to chill her. She rose from the steps, turned and looked at the church. All the pride she had felt in her father, Preacher Murray, had been stripped away leaving her bare. The chill still in her, she picked up a rock and threw it against the door with all her strength.

When she entered the house, her father was

sitting at the table reading his Bible. She went straight to her room. "The sanctimonious hypocrite, strike him dead! Oh, God, kill him! Kill him, please." She cried silently.

Revived, Sena lay in her room for hours trying to decide what to do. Without giving her reason she wouldn't be able to talk Julia into leaving. She tried writing a letter to Madison and Julia but gave up in despair. "Without the truth what can I say. Truth…what a big, meaningful word." She tore the half-written letters up. There was only one thing to do. She left a short note to Julia.

She waited to leave her room until the early morning hours. Her father's door was ajar and she could hear him snoring. She listened at the other bedroom and heard the even breathing of Julia and her brothers. Goodbye, darlings, her eyes filled with tears that she quickly wiped away. No time for tears, she thought. Thanks to the full moon she could see to move easily about the house.

In the kitchen she picked up a long butcher knife and eased back to her father's room. It would be easy to plunge it through his heart because she knew he always slept on his back. "But he must know," she thought. "Oh, yes, he must know."

Once in the room she moved silently to the bed and around to the right side where he lay. She placed the point of the knife over his heart ready to plunge it through him. With hands on top of the handle she quietly called him.

He mumbled as he awoke from a deep sleep.

"It's me, Sena, Papa dear. I just wanted to tell you, you'll never hurt me again or Julia." He saw the gleam of the knife and felt the sting of its point.

"All right, girl, all right, I won't."

"I know you won't, Papa." She plunged with all her might. He floundered and lay still.

She had never felt such joy and freedom as she left the room leaving the knife in his body. She moved quickly to her own room and filled a basin with water. She cleaned herself. She wanted no part of the attack he had on her to be found on her body. Then she took a razor from the dresser drawer and got on the bed. "Not her father, not anyone, would ever know he had gotten her pregnant," she thought as she cut deep into both her wrists.

Julia awoke early. I have to talk to Sena before the others are up and make our plans. She dressed hurriedly and went to Sena's room. Her screams woke the boys.

"Oh, dear God, no!"

"I'll get Papa," gasped Lewis as he ran from the room.

"Julia," he screamed.

She and Jacob went into their father's room and saw the knife plunged through his body. As the boys started to him, Julia grabbed them.

"No," she cried, "Don't touch a thing. Lewis, go get Mr. Carroll."

Within the hour they were all there.

"Miles, you better go get the sheriff. Julia, do you have any idea how this happened?" asked Em.

"No, sir, when I went to bed last night, Papa was sitting at the table reading and Sena was in her room."

"That's the way it was when we came in and went to bed, too," stated the boys. They could tell the sheriff no more than that when he got there.

"Looks like murder and suicide." The

sheriff found one folded piece of paper on the dresser. The contents were brief.

"Julia, I had to do it. Take the boys and go to Aunt Ida's. I love you, Sena."

"That clinches it," said the sheriff. "I jest can't understand why she could do it. Such a lovely girl with so much to live for. I'll get the coroner."

When the bodies were taken away, Em, Lukatie and Didge cleaned up the two bedrooms and took Julia and the boys home with them. Em sent wires to the only two relatives, a brother of Preacher Murray and a sister of Charity Murray. It was after the funeral services that the boys left with Aunt Ida. Julia stayed with the Carrolls to finish her senior year of school.

A month later Julia broke down and told Lukatie all she had heard. "It's eating me up. I don't want to place my burden on your shoulders, but I have to talk with someone. I'm so sick of everyone saying, your poor father, how could Sena have done such a thing? It's poor Sena, what she was going through all that time. I remember when Papa started beating on her probably over two years ago. He used me to keep her in line. She protected me." Julia sobbed; heart broken in Lukatie's arms.

"What is wrong?" Em asked entering the room.

"Woman talk," said Lukatie.

"Tell him, Mrs. Carroll. Everyone should know. I want them to know the kind of man he was. He doesn't deserve their worship at Sena's expense."

Miles was the one to tell Madison the truth. He listened with the solemn face he had worn since Sena's death.

"I'd kill him myself if he wasn't already

dead," he swore. "Why didn't she tell me."

"For the reason you just gave, I suppose."

Two days later, Madison left for New York.

"I'll be back when I've had time to think," he promised.

As a ranking lay member of the church, Em always drew the job of conducting the services during the absence of a minister. He knew from the buzz throughout the congregation they all knew the truth at last. His remarks commanded their attention. "We must realize the church cannot be blamed for human error. Preacher Murray has paid for the unrighteous and evil acts of his life. He will also face judgement for what he did and the action he caused his lovely daughter to take. We should think more upon God and his teachings and know the truth of the scripture. Don't judge or compare them with the actions of one man's failure." For a second his eyes lingered on Lukatie. "Remember, the flesh is weak. So, do as the scriptures say. Judge not that ye be not judged. Whether we're willing to admit it or not, most people constantly pit their own finite judgement against that of the Lord's in judgement. If you feel your wisdom is superior to God's, then follow it. We must use our God given intelligences and think and ponder over this thing that has touched our lives. Let the Lord touch the eyes of your understanding and judge not. Let us live the Golden Rule. We can't do this with a closed mind. The only way to gain further intelligence is through application of the intelligence already gained. All the knowledge in the world not tempered with common sense is useless."

He closed his remarks with a promise of trying to find a new minister and inviting them all to keep up their attendance at church. They all hugged Julia and said how sorry they were. Within a month they had all started attending other churches and the church doors were closed. The property reverted back to the Carroll land.

PART THREE

1933-1934

"Em, don't go under that ladder, it's bad luck."

"Horsefeathers, Lukatie, that's just plain foolishness and superstition. I'm surprised at you."

"Guess it's old age. I worry more."

Em walked over to her and they stood looking at the house.

"It is a beautiful house. I can't wait for you to finish it. Too bad all of this couldn't have happened before I became old so I would enjoy it." She said good-naturedly.

"Don't worry, you're ageless, dear. I'd better get back to work so we can move in before cold weather."

"Now that the negroes' houses are finished, will they work as hard on ours?"

"Harder, I think. They have an itch to move in. The houses are locked, and I have the keys. And they will stay locked until our house is completed."

"Today will be another hot back-breaker and spine-cracker climbing up and down ladders. I'll be so glad when this building is done and everything cleaned up. But I can't complain. Everyone is excited."

It was late after supper one evening when they were all sitting on the porch when Fountain drove into the yard looking for Lucinda. They were all surprised to see him. He had written to Lucinda there, and as instructed, they had returned his letter unopened. Lukatie had taken the time to write and tell him she wasn't there.

He looked dejected and tired.

"I came to…"

"To refute my word," broke in Lukatie. "I'm sorry for you, Fountain, but she is not here and she hasn't been here. She asked that we not let you know where she was and we've honored her wish."

"You could have forwarded my letters on to her."

"She asked us not to."

"You must all think I'm a cad. What in the world has Lucinda told you? I'm sorry for all of this. Please tell me where she is. I love her."

"I'm sorry, Fountain, we can't do that."

"I admit I was wrong. I loved her selfishly and drove her away from me. Ask her to write me and give me another chance. I really miss her. I promise I'll change. We've been together so many years and suddenly she leaves." His voice was low. "I'll be going now." He looked over at the new house. "I see the house is coming along fine."

"Yes, we hope to soon be moving in."

"It's beautiful." He walked slowly to the car, got in and drove away.

"I can't help feeling sorry for him," thought Lukatie.

That night she wrote to Lucinda about Fountain's visit.

About ten o'clock Didge yelled for Lukatie and tore out of the house running to the mailbox.

"What do you think you're doing," she screamed at Fountain.

"Getting my wife's address," he said, throwing the letter back in the box and driving off. Lukatie and Julia had seen from the porch.

Titia drove by while Didge was standing in the middle of the road yelling.

Titia brought the car to a halt. "I might add a few words for you, Didge. Who was that?"

"I could drop plenty of words that are positively horrid if Mama wasn't listening, I'm so mad. That was Fountain, Lucinda's husband. We wouldn't tell him where she was yesterday and Mama did just what he thought she would. She mailed her a letter this morning and he slipped back and got the letter out of the mailbox and got her address from it."

"Come on, we'll telephone her."

"Mama, we're going to telephone Lucinda," she called out as she jumped in the car. They waited half an hour to get the call through only to find out from Mrs. Cox that Lucinda had left the day before with no forwarding address.

"Good," said Titia. She told Mrs. Cox what had happened. "He will probably phone or go there. Don't let him upset you." She dropped the receiver on its cradle.

Two days later Fountain was standing at the door of Titia's home explaining to Mrs. Cox who he was and why he was there.

"You may come in, sir, but she left here about four days ago."

"Where did she go?"

"She wouldn't say, sir, said she didn't want anyone to know where she was. Such a lovely sad lady."

"You're lying. You do know where she is," he glared at her.

Instant dislike for Fountain flooded Mrs. Cox.

"I don't lie," she stated indignantly walking to the door. "Leave this minute."

"I suppose I can thank you that she's

gone." He said.

"I don't know what you mean by such a remark. She was a lovely girl and we enjoyed having her here."

"We? Who is we?"

"My husband and I. We take care of Mr. Madison's and Mrs. Johnson's home. It was your wife's decision to leave and I resent your insisting I know where she has gone. Now please leave," she said in a raised voice.

"I'm sorry and apologize, Mrs. Cox." He left and with no place else to look he returned to Richmond.

Lucinda wrote one letter home when she left New York saying she would write again when she had settled someplace where she would be safe from Fountain. She exhorted them not to worry if they didn't hear from her for a while. She went by to see Meda leaving a note when she'd found she had gone out. Then she went to Grand Central Station and bought a ticket for California. She had decided some time ago just what she was going to do and wanted to go far from home to do it. She started attending Mass in the Catholic Church with Mr. and Mrs. Cox and soon joined the church to better work out her plan.

*****

Toward the last of September, the temperature plunged downward in one of its freakish unusual cold spells."

"We'uns kno' hits gwine warm up agin 'n a day or two like hit allus do. So we'se jes gwine take sum days off," Hyrum said brightly.

"We's too near finished Mistuh Em. We'ens will wok," said Clay Golden with emphasis.

"I'se gwine warp yo' head," snapped Hyrum.

"Don't fret me now, boy," Clay said, his skinny dim eyes snapping. "Jest gentle down."

"Ma' bak kin't stan much mo' ov dis bendin'," complained Hyrum.

"Yore jest too lazy ter ker' 'bout anything."

"Wal, jes heah ol mouthy takin' charge. By godly ye tak de cake."

"Aw shet up, Hyrum, and do yore wok."

"All right, boys is you want to work get the icicles out of your rears and hit that nail. We'll work inside today." Em's voice was soft and gentle as he spoke. Turning to Miles, "You never know what's cooking under your own nose. Who would have ever thought they would want to work in this kind of weather."

"Possession is the motivating force. They see better living conditions within reach if they continue working," Miles said.

"Why don't we try out that furnace and see if it really works, son."

Soon the house was comfortable.

"I'm going up to check Didge's studio."

"She's very proud of that room, Papa. It was a nice thing you did fixing that room up for her."

Em only grunted as Miles watched him leave the room. He wanted to confront Em with her true identity, feeling with all his heart she was his half-sister instead of an adopted sister. Too bad she didn't favor her mother so it wouldn't look so obvious. "With Meda gone maybe people won't notice the family resemblance so much," he thought.

The weather had warmed and with Seth's portrait in her hand, Didge was running along the cart path to the river. Regal II was prancing around her when she stumbled over a root and took a wild, undignified dive to the ground. She gathered herself up quickly finding her ankle wouldn't support her. She looked around frantically for the portrait of Seth. She saw it laying against a yaupon bush. Thank goodness it landed wet side up. Picking up the portrait she hopped to her thinking stump and sat down, leaning the picture with the face against the stump. "I wish it was dry but if I don't give it to him now there is no telling when I can."

Rubbing her ankle, she soon felt drowsily quiet. She was shaded by the great century old oaks that curtsied like ancient old ladies she had read about. As the wind caressed them gently, Regal II lay at her feet, his ears lay back alerted. Didge reached down to quiet him as an inquisitive deer inched closer. "How proud and graceful he looks. I wish I had my sketch pad." The skittish deer darted away. Didge jumped, aware that someone had come up behind her. Turning, she saw it was Seth.

Their heartbeats were as wild as the deer just frightened away. To cover his frustration, Seth reached down and picked up a mixture of dried leaves and soil, letting it sift slowly through his fingers, "What good mulch going to waste. Did you hurt yourself when you fell?"

"You saw that?" she was embarrassed.

"Just as you were getting up."

"Twisted my ankle."

"The unveiling," she laughed, handing Seth the portrait. "She has created a true to life image of me," he thought. He looked for what seemed like ages and Didge finally blurted out, "Well?"

He looked at her tenderly. "Just how do I say it's beautiful without sounding conceited. It's like looking into a mirror. You should get paid well for this kind of work. You've even painted in a corner of the hut and that large oak. The bark looks so real I think I could peel it off the tree."

She laughed. "You very well could with just a rub. The picture isn't dry so handle with care. I brought it to you now because I didn't know if I'd have another chance to give it to you before you left for school."

"Give it to me?"

"Yes, Seth, please accept it as a gift from me that says I wish you all the luck, success and happiness in the world."

"How can I refuse such a gift? Thank you, Didge. But I have nothing to give you."

"Oh, you already have."

He raised a quizzical eyebrow.

"You gave of your time to sit for me. I went home and copied each day's work and have a portrait exactly like it for myself at home," she grinned impishly.

He was pleased that she wanted one but said, "You really like to paint, don't you?"

"Oh, yes. Art has been a passion with me ever since the days I drew pictures in the sand. Now when I paint, I'm always excited, but not nervous. I just know what I want to paint and can't wait until I capture it on canvas." Seth was silent as she talked. "One thing that I think has helped me enormously is that I paint as I see it and I'll fight for my right to do so. I'm never totally satisfied. I know what I'm capable of and would like to always improve."

Seth had sat quietly on the ground near her feet as she talked.

"It's getting late," she remarked as her eyes scanned the sky. "I'd better go. I think I can walk now." She stood up testing her ankle.

Seth picked up a stick with the end curved like a cane. "Here use this to help keep the pressure off the ankle or I'll pick you up and carry you."

She looked into his eyes and laughed.

"I'll watch to make sure you get home all right. And, Didge, thanks for the portrait." Before she could answer he was gone. As always, she felt safe knowing he was near if she needed help.

She would never do the things she'd like to do she thought disconsolately as she hobbled along the path trailing along behind Regal II or I'd marry Seth and be damned.

That night Didge drew back her curtain and raised the worn shade before going to bed so the morning light would wake her early. She listened to the katydid and locust shrill their goodnight and jumped into bed.

By six thirty she arose and went to the window. The sky was clear. She quickly dressed in white ducks, oxfords, and a long-sleeve shirt to ward off mosquitoes. Again, looking out the window she saw the early sun softly kissing the treetops. She stretched her arms out as if to gather them to her.

She walked up the hill at the river, looked around and took a deep satisfying breath. The lazy haze of morning with the mist hanging heavy over the river was just what she wanted. Occasionally, she could see a trout or bass flip out of the water as if grabbing for the sun.

"This will be Papa's picture for his study." She hoped he would like it. Lukatie knew her plans to paint it and Miles would frame it as a surprise after the house was completed.

By the first week of November the houses were completed.

"Just think about seven months ago we were an utter wreck. No hopes. Not knowing what to do or what was to become of us. Now look at all of this," Em said with a sort of incredulity in his voice. "I did it all with a bunch of double damn idiots."

"Em, that was an in the privy remark," said Lukatie.

"I don't mean that like it sounded. It's just that they have no initiative to do anything on their own."

"Just don't break your arm patting your back, dear. Don't forget Miles. Jump down off your cloud and we'll go look at the finished house," said Lukatie.

"What do you mean? I'm not suspended."

She put her hand on his arm. "Nothing really, let's go. Let's walk in the front door."

"It's an aristocratic looking house, Em." She glanced at him. He was handsome in his youth. Even now in the late autumn of his life it still showed. The years had left him a distinguished and gaunt looking man. Tanned from many outdoor hours. The cool blue eyes had changed very little over the years. He turned to her and smiled as they walked up the curved steps.

"Shall I carry you across the threshold, my dear."

She laughed, "After all these years, we'll skip that formality." As they walked through the completed house it was like being someone else and entering another world. It was a big moment of accomplishment for Em. He straightened to his full height and looked nearly ten feet tall to Lukatie.

"Thank you, Lukatie, for being here beside me. Let's go to town and tell Mr. Wilson to bring out our furniture. Think we can find our way out of here?"

"Heaven must be something like this," she said happily.

That evening, sitting on the steps of the old house, Em looked at the new homes. We should also thank Benjamin for the insurance money that had accumulated in the bank. I'm not one to feel greedy or wish for something belonging to another. I've always felt happy for those that had nice things. I've wished for better than I had for my family." He arose from the steps and got the whistle off the nail and blew, its shrill musical sound sending a signal through the air.

The men of each family came with the wives and children trailing behind. "Come on you, you're all families," he called. "You've worked well. You've built fine houses. You've also built new bedsteads for your houses. Today I ordered new springs and mattresses for you. So, leave the old ones to burn. Here are your keys and papers saying that each head of the family has their lifetime right to the house. Otherwise, we'll go on as we always have."

"I've sold enough lumber to give each family a hundred dollars. I know the ladies will want new oil cloth on their table and shades at the windows." The men stuck out their hands.

"Oh, no," teased Em. "This is for the ladies." When he came to Lovie and Zarilda, he paused. With a slight movement of her head, Lovie indicated Zarilda.

"Well, I guess you're the matriarch of this family." He handed her the money. Her round face beamed. She had never had so much spending money in her life.

"Just remember there is a winter ahead of us," cautioned Em.

The next four days were the busiest Lukatie

could ever remember. The whole farm was cleaning and moving. Some had so little to move they were through in a day or two and Em hired them to help straighten his house once Mr. Wilson delivered the furniture.

"Now we need a married couple to cook and take care of the house and yard," said Em. Lukatie looked at him in a state of shock.

"You knew the apartment was being built for that reason. You didn't think you were going to kill yourself trying to care of a house this size, did you?"

"But Didge and I can do it. Just how are you going to pay for all this service?"

"Lumber, dear, until the crops start paying off."

Lovie and Winnie were there sewing velvet drapes for the windows and glass doors that opened onto the terrace. Some of the younger men were cleaning windows.

"There is a front bedroom for you, Miles, and one for you, Didge."

"If you don't mind, I'd like the one near the stairs to the studio," said Didge.

"Why, of course, dear, if that's the one you want."

"That front one would be ideal as a guest room for Uncle Kinyon and Aunt Jane since it has an adjoining bath," said Didge.

"I think I'm going to enjoy the bathroom more than any other room," laughed Lukatie.

"Miz Carroll," called Thankful. "Do you wan' dis table thet wus 'n de dinin' room throw'd out?"

"Indeed, I do not. Never."

"Why in heavens name don't you?" asked Em, puzzled.

"I've got my reasons," she said decisively.

"Clean it and place it in the kitchen."

Em knew it would go there but felt forced to ask. "Can you give me one good reason why?"

"Un-huh," she walked over and pointed at the dent in the table. "Pretty silly, huh?"

"It sure is," he said.

"Well, my dear Em, that is the decision dent that changed our lives."

"Oh," was all Em could say as he remembered. He chuckled at the memory. "Put the table in the kitchen, Thankful."

"Yassuh."

The occasional nickel Em had continued slipping to Gick made him decide that there was money in work and since he was going to school he might as well take a lesson from Seth and leave childish things behind and start learning to become a man.

The big grandfather clock that belonged to Em's grandfather was ticking away in the entry of the new house. Em felt a profound sense of relief with the houses all completed. But a new worry was forming in his mind. "How do I keep them up?"

He was busy in the living room placing the plush blue velvet sofa and chairs when Stewart stuck his head in the door.

"Need another strong back?"

"Sure," chuckled Em. "Grab hold of this sofa. We'll place it against the wall where the sun won't fade it."

"It's a long one," said Stewart.

Just as Lukatie came through the door, Em said to Stewart, "This is a sexual sofa." Then pointing to the matching chair, he said, "and that is an occasional piece." He slapped his thighs in a big hearty laugh at his own joke as Stewart joined in.

Lukatie whirled around and dashed from the

room.

"Her face sure was red," said Stewart.

"I'm sorry, Stewart. I didn't see her come in." He followed Lukatie.

"I'm sorry, dearest."

"Are you?" she quipped.

He looked at her with searching intensity. "Yes, I am."

She smiled, "I knew you didn't see me."

Em went to town to see Sheriff Ply about burning the old houses.

"Got insurance on them?"

"No," Em assured him. "They've never been worth it."

"When you gonna burn them?"

"Over a period of time starting Monday. There are seven of them."

"Why not tear them down 'n use the lumber for something else?"

"Not worth it. Too rotten. I'm hoping to rid the place of a lot of rodents and other insects and pests."

The sheriff handed Em a paper. "Here is a permit in case any questions are asked. Yo' really don't need it."

"Thank you, Sheriff."

They poured kerosene around the first house and set fire all around making it next to impossible for any rodent or insect to escape.

The men surrounded the house ready to fight fire if any escaped. The billowing smoke made a dark blue apostrophe in the clear autumn skies as black smoke streamed from the burning house. Everyone was exuberant as they watched the blaze reach high into the sky. Neighbors from all around came to watch the blazes destroy the ugliness that was like a cancerous growth on the Carroll land.

With tears streaming Zarilda watched the fire leap around her old house. She cried out. "I'se gwine tell yo'ens hit wus a pure joy ter git outen the place. Thet ungodly house. I'se glad ter seed hit burn. Praise b' de Lawd. Mite eva dadburn rat roast alive n' de red-hot ashes. Oh, praise de Lawd."

All the other negroes joined in. "Amen, praise de Lawd. Thank yo' Jesus. Thank yo', Amen." They sang together in chorus throughout the evening.

It was delayed gratification when Hyrum approached Em as the last house was burning.

"Dis is worth all de hard work, Mistuh Em."

"Glad you see it that way, Hyrum."

They looked at each other as one man measures another and Hyrum turned and walked off.

Thankful walked over. "Mistuh Em, who yo' gonna put 'n that apartment ter do yore housekeepin'?"

"I don't know, Thankful. I haven't had time to think about it. Why? Have you got someone in mind?"

"No 'zactly. I just had a idy yo'd wont young folk. N' sum ov de young bucks around har got married up 'n der all a'hopin' yo' gwine choose dem'."

"I know, but I can only take one couple. Say, Thankful, tomorrow let's get about three pigs and dress them out and have a barbecue for everyone on Thursday. We'll put tables out under that big oak back of the house and have a feast. It will be Thanksgiving and we've all got a lot to be thankful for."

"Shore sounds good, Mistuh Em. Yassuh, we'en shore has got a lot ter be thankful for."

"The beginning of a new age," thought Em as he walked over to the new house and entered.

That night Didge gave Em the painting for his study. They all laughed at his surprise.

"Why, thank you. It's beautiful, Didge. It will look good in my study."

"Why can't I put my arms around her and kiss her like any other father would?" His eyes were moist as he picked up the picture and took it to the study. But Didge saw and felt better. "He just doesn't know how to demonstrate his thanks to me." She excused herself and went to her room.

The day of the barbecue was fair, beautiful Indian summer weather. Lukatie hated staying indoors to make the barbecue sauce for Em and Thankful to use on the three pigs they had dressed out. Tables were being set up under the big oak. The air was charged with excitement as the women busied themselves in their kitchens making salads, cooking vegetables, hot breads and desserts.

Lukatie liked the new oil range Em bought. Cooking in the summer would be so much cooler. The wood range was still present for winter use.

"Didge, take this sauce out to your papa. Julia, you get out those large platters and that long oil cloth for the table while I mix this salad. Let's hurry so we can get outside. It's too beautiful to stay inside with winter closing in. I would love to ramble through the woods today."

"I used to come over here when I felt I had to get out of the house. Now where do I go?" she thought.

The young children running around the fire throwing in sticks and kicking up a plume of grey dust.

"Cut out the shenanigans, or do you want your meat full of sand?" Em was saying as Didge took him the sauce.

"They're a bunch of Indians on the war path," laughed Didge. "Why do I feel so foolish and find it so hard to even try to carry on small talk with Papa?" she thought. Em watched her as she walked back to the house.

The inflection in his voice was and always had changed when he spoke to her if he spoke at all. He was stern, hard and solid as stone. He had to be and knew it. He knew he must not relent, not even while he slept. If he did his world might crumble. Unknowingly this was the one thing that held Didge. Because of her talent he gave her more than he had given to Lucinda or Meda by seeing to it that she always had art materials.

Since becoming a man, Seth didn't feel as free to go to the Carroll's as he did as a child. So, he did the next best thing, he went to Thankful's where he could watch the house for a glimpse of Didge. It wasn't as easy now with the new houses farther apart.

He stuck his head in the door. His nostrils cringed at the odor that greeted him.

"Well, well, what a fancy house," knowing the answer he asked. "What are you cooking that smells it up so bad?"

"Crazy yo' shoon't say dat 'bout m' pot ov collard greens dey don' smell dat bad." Laughed Zarilda. As they looked through the house, Seth recognized a few pieces of furniture from the old Carroll house. The whole farm had taken on a new look of rich abundance.

"I'se gotta tak' m' greens up dat frost we'en had a while bak' sweeten em rite up." She picked up the long-handled fork, lifted the lid off the pot and started taking up the collards.

"Hum-mm dey smell lak a hot fart. Sho' glad

dey don' tast' lak dey smell."

Seth laughed and went on the porch to talk with the old man.

"What is going on over there?" He was watching the crowd around the tables.

"Dey's havin' a barb'cue fer all ov us ter cel-breate buildin' de new houses. It being Thanksgivin' 'n all."

"That is nice. Guess I'll run along. They're gathering around the table. I see Thankful and Gick are coming probably for you and Zarilda."

"Yassuh, he say he cum fer us. Sta' 'n go wit' us."

"Thanks, I've got things to do. I'll see you later."

"De collard greens 'n hot braid air ready ter tek ova dar. Whar's Seth?"

"Runt along. Got things ter do."

"Granmaw, got your cookin' don? I'll tak it ova fer yo'."

"Hits on de table, Gick. I'se gwine start on ober dar with de plates. Whar yo' maw?"

"She hepin' with de barb'cue. Deys 'bout ready ter eat. Hit shore do look goodern' all git out. Dey cuttin' up two ov dem hogs. Don' thank dey need de other one."

Em blessed the food and circulated around trying to taste each one's cooking showing no partiality. Congratulating each. He teased Myrtie Barnes' food. "Now I know why Abraham is so fat."

She snickered, "He is plumb fat as all get out, hain't he?"

Em picked up a biscuit. "Hum, who baked these?"

"Dey's Patience's biscuits. Lite as a biddies down dey air."

"Oh, yes, she married Lubby Freeman, didn't

she? Smart fellow. I understand he finished school."

Without waiting for confirmation from Myrtle he picked up a biscuit and took it to Lukatie.

"Taste this."

"I'm so full I don't know if I can or not."

"Try, go ahead." She ate it all.

"Who?"

"Patience, remember she married Lubby Freeman about three months ago. What do you think of them moving into the apartment?"

"If she cooks everything as good as these biscuits, I say yes."

"I tasted her vegetables, beans and some salad and it was just as good. She salts just right to bring out the sweetness."

"She and her husband might not want the job."

"We can find out." He turned to Thankful. "When you get a chance will you tell Patience and Lubby I'd like to see them?"

"Yassuh, Mistuh Em."

"After they finish eating, Thankful."

Half an hour later they approached Em and Lukatie.

"You wanted to see us, Mr. Carroll, Mrs. Carroll."

Em spoke. "Yes, we wondered if you two would like the house job. Of course, you'd live in the apartment. Between the two of you, you'd do the cooking, keep the house and yards clean. The pay would be two dollars apiece a week plus your living quarters and food."

"That is, if the two of you get along well. I'll have no quarreling and fussing," said Lukatie.

"Ah, he treats me like a queen," smiled

Patience.

"Well, I know of a king that cut off his queen's head," laughed Em.

"All right, Mr. Carroll. We'll try to give good service if Patience wants to," said Lubby. Patience nodded in the affirmative.

Em took a key from his pocket and handed it to Lubby. "Move in as soon as you like."

"Thank you, Mr. Carroll, we'll move in this evening and start work in the morning."

Gick was leaning against a nearby tree listening. "They talk so nice and polite like Seth," he thought. He vowed again to get a good education so he could get the better, easier jobs.

Em and Lukatie walked over and spoke to the old man.

"How are you making out, old man?"

"Mr. Mathias," he corrected. "Dis shore am good. Hit shore wus a fine bate ov barb'cue, Mistuh Em. Folk allus sayin' better times a cumin' jes wat 'n see. Now I'se gwine believe dem."

Hinton Smith walked up, "Wan tang fer shore dey kint get no worser dan dey wus unless us dies."

"Den dey shore gonna be gooder. Preacher say heaven de place ter goz'." Said the old man.

"Who say yo' goin' dar?"

"I'se good. I'se goin' dar. Don'an spect ter see yo' dar dough." Said the old man making a broad sweeping motion upward with his hands.

With his wrinkled broad face beaming, Abraham Barnes walked up to them. He stuck his hands in his pocket and reared back strutting around well filled.

Em laughed and walked on among the others. Telling them all he wanted to talk with them over at a nearby stump when they finished eating and covered up the left-over food.

Em never felt covetousness or greed in his heart but he did have a lot of pride in his accomplishments. He stood on the stump looking at the folks that gathered around him.

"All women are rich in their dreams," began Em "and I'll bet all you women want running water in your houses and bathrooms. But I can't put them in until we find a way for you to pay your electric bill. And that is what I want to discuss with you now."

"This winter is a time for us to prepare for a new beginning. These trying times have kept us all on edge." They were looking at him blankly. "What he talkin' 'bout?" asked Earthy Tootle looking enigmatic as she turned to Abner.

"I don' kno' jes listen 'n see."

"The fullness of the earth is yours to use for a better life. I'm offering it to you if you're willing to work for it."

"Heah we go agin," called out Hyrum.

"Before you get lathered up why don't you wait until I finish talking," Em said, his patience wearing thin.

"We'en won' nice things fer our houses too," Hyrum dryly remarked.

"Then stop wanting and wishing and start working and get them. Our basic need is the changing and directing of the hearts. I'd think by now we might have learned to work together," Em was saying when Hyrum interrupted again.

"Whut I'se wan ter kno' is who gwine pay us fer all dis wok we'en haint heered 'bout. We's don' nough wok fer nuttin'."

"You've got a good home to live in, haven't you?" Em was so mad his face was motted with red patches.

"Hyrum, you're nothing but a cull, now you shape up or get out," shouted his father.

Hyrum stood there with a faint smile on his face.

"I hope we can be imaginative enough to try new methods and new crops. We'll till the land and plant it in tobacco and peanuts giving us more money crops."

Hyrum laughed aloud bitterly. "This is too much, man."

Em went on stoutly. "It would be sheer waste to just let that cleared land lay there."

"Yo' got fedders fer bra'ans de 'hole thang sounds lak' week ol' fish," injected Hyrum.

"Since we have to accept the childishness of children, I'll pause a minute for Hyrum to get over his tantrum." Em was silent.

Andrew moved over beside Hyrum. "Son, I'se tellin' yo' fer de las' time. Shut up," he wheedled out the side of his mouth. "Yo' neber wus wo'th a damn."

Em wished he knew something to say to spark their desire to work. With Hyrum silent, he continued. "You all know a person reaps what he sows. We always feel apprehensive when we attempt something we feel is too large a job. We'll just do it and not think of the ramifications. If we work hard you'll be surprised at our growth and accomplishments. Work got you new homes and work can put money in your pockets. I believe we have to do something to enrich our lives or be guilty of serious omission."

"Look around you. Look how your number has increased. Do you think that corn and cotton crop is going to support all of us and keep up these new houses? If they aren't kept up they will soon look like the old ones. Is that what you want?"

"No!" they all chorused.

"Thankful, do you think we can build tobacco barns and dynamite stumps this winter, when the weather permits, and plant tobacco by early spring?"

"Yassuh, yo' bet we's ken. Yore de boss."

"Yassuh, yo' bet we's ken." Mimicked Hyrum. "Yo' shore air de boss. We'en place our fate 'n yore kin' han's suh." Hyrum bowed smiling.

"S'cuse m' Mistuh Em," said Andrew. "I'se gwine do whut yo wan' me ter mor' ways dan one." He grabbed Hyrum by his overall bib. "Yo' cum' wit' me. Yo' got no rite har. Sumthang mitey wrong with yo' boy. Dey's no need ter cause unpleasantness among us all de time." They reached the house and Andrew pushed him inside. They all turned back to Em.

"That's about all. We'll start next Monday. Let's clean up the tables and all go home."

Em walked over to the barbecued pig they hadn't cut up and cut off a ham.

"Thankful, divide the rest of this among the others and don't forget your share. There is more left over that's cut up." He walked on to the house not waiting for his family or any remarks from Thankful. He was tired.

Miles helped his mother and the girls gather up their dishes and pans. Didge watched Miles and Julia fascinated as she caught the looks that passed between them. "Everyone can have romance but me," she thought. "Even so Miles is too old for Julia. Why he's eleven or twelve years older". She remembered the time she had overheard him and Madison talking about the girls they dated. "I sure did get an earful," she thought.

*****

Saturday night and the evening was in full swing at Roxie's. They were singing, dancing, and slipping out for a drink. If anyone started a fight he was eased toward the door and pushed out while the rest went on singing. Sometimes some of the white folk would go and sit around to listen and talk.

Roxie could usually keep peace with threats of closing up. The sheriff and one of his deputies came in talking to first one and then another trying to find out where they were getting their whiskey. Even Hyrum swore he didn't drink and didn't know what they were talking about.

"It's a fact they's gettin' it. But air they gettin' it heah or before dey get heah?" he asked the deputy.

"I don't know, sir, but it's happening. Man, they're ripe. They're getting it someplace. That Kirby fellow is the only one in here not drinking."

Ira asked Lebtia to dance. He was tall and lanky with arms flailing loosely like giant wings ready for flight. His upper teeth protruded and his eyes, set too close together, were inclined to blink constantly.

"Rat face," she thought. "What did I ever see in him?" She looked at Noah. He nodded his approval. Once they were dancing, he brought his hands up folding their arms against their bodies with their hands against his chest. Letting go of her hand his slipped down to rest on her breast.

She stopped dancing raised slowly upward to her full height. She swiftly slapped him a stinging blow across the face. He raised his arm to strike her when from the corner of his eye he saw Noah straightening up. He dropped his arm quickly.

"Yo' duden't use ter mind. Whuts he got thet I hav'nt got?"

"Decency! Sumpin' yo' wudden't kno' 'bout!" She turned and walked back to Noah.

Roxie let out a sigh and watched the young couples dancing and falling in love. She felt left out of things. Love was either passing her by or she had been too busy to look for it. She danced occasionally but most of her time was in the kitchen, or behind the counter, or running from one table to another.

Seth would tease her sometimes. "Come on Roxie and let's dance." She was the only one he ever asked to dance.

"You know if I was fifteen years older I'd marry you," he teased.

"N iffen I hadden't jest 'bout reared yo' I mite say yes. Do yo' suppose we'se either one will eva get married, Seth? Sum how we'se not lak de others."

Seth had taken the portrait Didge had painted of himself by to show Roxie.

"Very good," she had exclaimed. Then she had looked long at Seth. She saw shining in his eyes the answer to every question she might have asked him.

"Hit's a good thing yore goin' away. Mite b' yo'll forget her. Dey'll talk ter us n' tease with us, even go ter bed wit us iffen we'se allows hit. But gettin' hitched up with us wudden't work'. Both sides would be madder 'n hell."

Seth had sat looking at the portrait saying nothing. "Guess yo' hav' ter figger thangs out fer yo'self." She had said.

Winnie came in the café before the dance was over. Leaning against the wall like some kind of sprite she watched Roxie and Seth.

SILENT TEARS

"Dar's a good girl fer yo'. She's 'n tune, Seth, all keyed up with whut's happenin' 'n lovin' yo' more'n a man needs lovin'."

"I guess if I just wanted to take a woman it would be Winnie. But I don't want just any woman and I'm not messing up her life." The dance ended. "I guess I'd better leave before she starts something."

Winnie blocked the door as he started out. "Dis is our dance, Seth."

Roxie laughed and went behind the counter.

"Yo' still gonna leave har, Seth?"

"Yes, Winnie."

After a moment she said quizzically, "Why don't yo' marry up with me 'n sta' home?"

"I don't want to get married, Winnie. I want a better education."

"Seth?"

"Yes?"

"Yo' got 'nough education 'n Seth I'se prayed 'bout us 'n prayed 'bout hit 'n de Lawd tolt me yo' wus de one fer me."

"Oh, he did. Well, I'll wait until he tells me too." He opened the screen door and walked out.

She yelled at him. "Iffen yo' don' agree with de Lawd yo' better thank 'bout hit til yo' do." She stamped her foot, a petulant pout on her moist lips.

Smiling amorously at Winnie, Finney Patchett walked over and said, "Forget hit, Winnie, cum on 'n dance 'n I will walk yo' home."

The work of clearing out the stumps and cutting logs for the barns started Monday morning. By nine, Mr. Heywood was there wanting to buy more lumber. The Atlantic and Pacific Tea Company wanted lumber to build one of the red front stores in Campton.

Em sold, cleared land and built tobacco barns. He started paying the negroes weekly much to their delight.

Alonza was busy at the job he loved. He could run a jack rabbit even with his peg leg as he gathered wood and water to keep the firebox fed when they worked the sawmill.

Gradually one by one, they came to ask Em for the plumbing for their houses. They were ready to have their electricity turned on.

"What?" exclaimed Mr. Heywood, "You're going to put plumbing in the houses of your tenant farmers?"

"That's right."

"Why, when you own all of this?"

"That is the answer. I own all of this. It hurts me none to make life a little more comfortable for those around me. After all, the tenants made all this possible."

Em's friends discouraged his decision to plant tobacco, but the more he thought about it, the better he liked the idea and he stuck to his decision.

Kinyon, Jane, their children, son and daughter-in-law, and the grandchildren were all coming for Christmas. Lukatie's cup runneth over when they received a Christmas card and letter from Lucinda saying she would be thinking of them and would be home to visit in early summer. She gave no address, but the postmark was from California.

"Em, could we get extra help for Patience and Lubby with that many people coming?"

"Yes, she can probably get her sister and her husband, Furney. Maybe Lovie and Winnie can come in and help in the kitchen and straighten beds."

"Thank you, Em. It will be so nice to have

my time free to enjoy my company for a change."

"I'm glad, too. Why don't we have a party Christmas Eve for everyone and invite the neighbors. We haven't had a housewarming yet. We can take the rug up in the sitting room and dance. What do you think?"

"Oh, Em, that sounds wonderful!"

A week before Christmas, Em told Lukatie he had something in mind for their Christmas present but wanted her to see it before they decided.

"I certainly wouldn't want to buy something you wouldn't like."

"What is it? Why so secretive?"

"Not saying until you see it. Miles, you better come along. We'll be back before Didge and Julia get home from school." They got in the truck and went straight to the automobile dealer.

"Mr. Doyle, have you still got that four-door Dodge sedan?"

"Sure have, Mr. Carroll, right over there." He said with a nervous twitch in the muscle of his cheek. They all walked over to it.

"Well, what do you think, Lukatie?"

"What do you mean? What do I think?" With realization she stammered, "Do you mean this car? Buy it?"

Miles was laughing outright.

"Sure," he exclaimed winking at Miles.

She looked at him abashed.

"Well, do you like it for our Christmas present?"

"Em, we have more Christmas presents than I ever dreamed of."

"What? Oh, you mean the house. Don't you think that house needs a new car to go with it?"

"It would be nice, but…" she tugged at his arm pulling him to the side. In an undertone she said quickly, "Can we afford it?"

"We sure can, dear. I've done very well with the lumber and after selling the crops next fall, we'll be so far ahead you won't believe it."

Without realizing it, Em in doing so much for her all at once was stripping Lukatie of the driving force that had kept her active. Someone to keep her house, do her cooking...she sank into thought.

"Don't you like it?" He questioned. She nodded. "Yes, it's nice. I suppose you do need a car."

Patience and Lubby proved to be such good housekeepers that in desperation Lukatie insisted on keeping the master bedroom straight. The idleness was maddening. She started sewing, making everyone presents for Christmas. She made dresses and shirts of fine linen for the girls and guys. For Jane she had stitched a beautiful white tablecloth and napkins. She made a slipper satin dress of pale green for Didge and a silk one for Julia. For Kinyon and Jane's children she made handkerchiefs, crocheting dainty lace around the ones for the girls. She wouldn't waste time thinking about what she would do after Christmas to occupy her time. She didn't forget Patience and Lubby either, making a dress for her and a shirt for him. She made stuffed dolls for Kinyon and Jane's grandchildren. She mailed a dress and a music box to Meda and included a shirt for Briant. Her heart broke because she had no address and could not send Lucinda anything. All the things she had made for Lucinda she packed away.

It would be the first Christmas Lukatie had ever been able to give each of her family a gift. It was also the first time they had ever planned a Christmas tree. Christmas had always been just another day with dry beans and collards for dinner and maybe a chicken if they could spare one. Em would manage to get a little fruit, candy and nuts for little stockings hung at the mantle handy for Santa Claus. Lukatie would make rag dolls for the girls and Em made carts for the boys. Now to have so much so fast was more than Lukatie could fathom.

Didge spent every spare minute from her studies painting. She painted portraits from pictures of Lukatie and Em. And Miles' horse for him. She did landscapes for Kinyon and Jane and their married children and made a linen handkerchief and a scarf for Carlton. She was becoming very adept at sewing. More and more her many talents were surfacing.

Julia was excited about going to the Christmas dance at school and asked Didge if she thought her parents would mind if she went.

"Are you going?" she asked her eyes sparkling.

"I haven't been asked. But I see no reason why you shouldn't go if you want to."

"I didn't know if your parents would object."

Didge shrugged her shoulders, "Ask them I really don't know."

That evening Julia asked if it was all right to go to the school dance. Lukatie looked to Em for the answer.

"Sure, if you like, a little fun would be good for you." Didge noticed Miles face blanch beneath his ruddy complexion. "Why, he cares that she is going out with someone else."

"Didge are you going?" asked Lukatie.

"I haven't been asked."

The following Thursday, Leroy Wilson invited Didge to the dance. He was a tall handsome boy with clear, chiseled features and a pleasant personality. Any girl in the room would have gladly slept with him for the chance to be his date for the dance. He was popular, and the most sought-after boy in school.

"Thanks for thinking of me, Leroy, I'll have to ask my parents."

"I think of you a lot more than you realize. Tell me, why does a girl your age have to ask? Just tell them you're going."

"We don't do that in our family. We try to please each other. I'll let you know first thing in the morning if that is all right. Otherwise I'll just have to say no now."

"In the morning it is then. I'd better get to class before the old hen misses her rooster." Watching him walk away, Didge wondered if he really was the teacher's rooster.

Going home that afternoon, Julia and Didge were full of plans for the dance. As they were finishing supper that evening and Julia had punched her ribs for the third time, filled with doubt Didge listened to her tremulous voice as she asked to go to the dance with Leroy.

"How wonderful, Didge, you..." Lukatie's words were cut short when Em said stoutly, "No, you may not go."

Didge shuddered openly.

"Why can't she go?" defended Miles.

"You stay out of it, Miles," snapped Em.

Miles and Julia left the room.

"Why is it I can never go any place like the rest of the family has and does? Do I have to be a nothing? Can't I fit in this family someplace? If you didn't want me why wasn't I put in an orphanage? Or did you keep me just to see how miserable you can make my life." Stabs of self-pity needled her into dashing out of the room.

She leaned against the wall and heard Lukatie's voice.

"Why can't she go, Em?" demanded Lukatie. "She's entitled to some fun too. Lord knows she doesn't have any around here."

"She's to stay away from that boy. He has a rough reputation."

"Why didn't you tell her that instead of sounding so cold and unfeeling."

"I don't think I have to explain my reasons to anyone. I felt the less I said the better."

"You really don't have to say much. Disapproval oozes out without you uttering a word."

"I'll decide what's right for her."

"As you always have." Lukatie was clearly agitated.

"What's that supposed to mean?"

"I mean, you can't treat her as some object you can lay on the shelf and say stay put until you move her. For gosh sakes, give her the right to use her own mind. And the chance to defend her own virtues. Let her grow, Em. She's a fullgrown woman. Let her live."

"It won't hurt her to miss a dance. Don't give me an argument about it, Lukatie."

Didge grabbed her coat and ran out of the house. She continued at a fast pace as she ran down the river thinking "What is wrong with me? Mama and Papa are quarreling. They shouldn't do that. Does Papa know something about me that Mama doesn't know? The dance really doesn't mean that much to me. I only wanted to act like other young girls my age."

She approached the river and sat down on her stump. It was here that she could always find peace and tranquility. She looked out over the shimmering water with the sun casting its last elusive shadows through the trees.

She arose and walked to the edge of the water. "How beautiful each minute of the day brings a change," she thought. "It looks like the trees are growing in the water and I'm over the top of them looking down." The water looked a hundred feet deep. She didn't notice her own reflection as she spoke aloud. "What an illusion."

"How right you are," said Seth as his image joined hers. She thought he meant the trees reflected there as she did. Even so she didn't miss seeing their reflection there together. Looking at the beauty of the picture they made in the water, Seth said, "This is the way it should be."

The picture was marred by the ripple of the water as she threw in a stick. "But that is the way it is."

"What are you doing here, Seth? You're supposed to be away at school." She said with a wan little smile in her voice as she slowly turned catching her breath at the same time. She felt like she was still running hard as she looked at him. It was always a surprise to her seeing how light of skin he was. She felt drawn to him. Looking into his face she knew he felt the same. He broke the force that was drawing them together by saying, "I'm home for the Christmas holidays. I was at Thankful's and saw you rush out of the house. I followed you. I could tell you were upset, and it was too late for you to be down here alone. May I help in any way?"

"I might bend your ear a bit. But I shouldn't bother you with my problems."

"I've real tough ears. Try and see. Talking

often helps." He was silent as she told him about the school dance and Em's refusal to let her go.

"Oh, Seth, sometimes he almost makes me hate him. If it wasn't for Mama I'd run away. I don't understand why he's so good to me in some ways. Maybe it's to make up for the lack of love he doesn't feel for me. You should see the studio he built for me in the attic. It's so light and airy with built in cabinets to put away all my supplies. I've everything an artist can need up there."

"Didge, don't hold onto grief, or hate those who inflict it. You're young with time ahead for dancing. Just be grateful for any good that might come your way. Come, we'd better get out of these woods."

Her eyes clouded as she looked at him. "I think I've had the loneliest life in the world."

"I promise you that will all change for you one of these days."

Seth had a brilliant mind with a dream and hope to realize fulfillment of that dream before long. For now, caution was part of the dream. There was much he felt he could tell her but that must wait.

He listened well when he was around the old folk. He had listened to the old man. "Anyone taking a good look at Meda and Didge couldn't help but notice the resemblance. Mr. Carroll couldn't let go 'cause it might reveal his guilt."

He left her at the edge of the woods and Didge walked on home. Her joy over seeing Seth blocked out all thoughts of the dance until she entered her room and found Julia waiting for her.

"I won't go to the dance either," she blurted out.

"Don't be silly. Of course, you'll go."

SILENT TEARS

"It isn't right for me to go when they won't let you go."

"It isn't they, it's him. Julia, I really don't care." Her heart was singing. "Seth is home!" "You go have a good time and tell me all about it. How else will I know anything at all about it?"

Leroy was leaning against the door at school as Didge walked up the steps the next day. She smiled, "I'm sorry, Leroy, the family had other plans."

"Yep, well, I'm sorry, too." He really wanted to take her to the dance. She was the prettiest girl in school.

She went on to her class as Nicholas Heywood, Jr. walked up to Leroy, "Is she going with you?"

"Nope," he said as he thoughtfully watched her walk away.

"Maybe my image preceded my asking her," he laughed.

"I'm not surprised. They say her father really keeps an eye on her and she seldom goes anyplace unless he or some member of the family goes too."

"Too bad. It must be rough on her. Some think he had a personal interest. You know she is adopted. No blood ties there."

"Nicholas, you have a darker mind than I have." He walked on to class and noticed Didge was reading when he sat down at his desk. "She's far superior to the average run of the mill girl. I really don't think I'd know how to get out of line with her. Yep, she has dignity," he sighed and opened his book.

Miles had saved his money while working with Em and was ready to buy his own Christmas present. Em took him to town and got last minute groceries for the holidays.

"Where is Miles? Thought he was with you?" asked Lukatie.

"He had some business in town. He'll be along soon."

Miles paid Mr. Doyle for the Model A Ford Coupe he had ordered.

"Fine car," praised Mr. Doyle.

"Well, it isn't a Pierce-Arrow, but it is nice."

He noticed the time and thought that if he hurried, he could catch Julia and Didge at school and take them home. He blew the horn and waved his arm out the window as he saw them standing in line to get on the bus.

"Look, Julia," squealed Didge. "It's Miles."

Sticking his head out the window he called out, "Tell the driver I'm taking you home."

"Go on, Julia, I'll tell him."

Miles was holding the door open when they got there. Didge nudged Julia in first.

"Whose is this?" Didge inquired.

"Mine. A Christmas present to myself."

"It sure is spiffy," praised Julia. "I'm firmly convinced that the horse has had it."

"Oh, I don't think we'll ever see the day people won't enjoy going horseback riding. Then there is plowing. Didge, I'm very sorry about last night," offered Miles.

"It's all right, Miles, I really don't care if I go or not. I just don't understand why Lucinda and Meda had such freedom and I'm not allowed to go anyplace. Papa should know I'd never do anything to shame our family."

"I think he knows that."

"Then what is it Miles?"

"Honey, I just don't know."

He drove up in the yard blowing the horn. Lukatie and Em came out on the porch.

"Come, see my Christmas present to myself, Mama."

Lukatie cut her eyes at Em. "You wouldn't even tell me."

"I couldn't take the joy out of Miles' surprise," laughed Em.

"He sure doesn't mind taking the joy out of things for me," thought Didge. To avoid passing him on the steps she ran to the back of the house, entered the kitchen and went to her room. Leaving her things, she went on up to her studio.

At least this is one place I can be alone. She started wrapping her presents feverishly wanting to squash each one in revolt. When she came to the portrait of Em she felt like taking a knife and slashing it to shreds. Instead she sat down and cried. She couldn't destroy a painting.

As Lukatie looked at Miles' car she did so with her mind on Didge. Even Em realized, too late, how his remark sounded. In my over-protection and thoughtlessness, I've really made her hate me. With shoulders drooping he walked around the house and over to one of the tobacco barns they had completed. Leaning against the wall, he covered his face with his hands and wept.

"I'm sorry, Miles, I have to go to her."

"I understand, Mama."

"Or should I go to him," she wondered. "No, too much might be said and at this late date, I don't want it spoken between us." She knew where Didge would be and went to the studio. She knocked softly and went in taking Didge in her arms.

"Oh, Mama, why does he delight in hurting me? I've tried so hard to please him."

"I can't say, dear. I don't think he really means to. It was just a slip of the tongue. He's never known how to reach out to you."

"All he has to do is hold out his hand and just treat me like a daughter. He did adopt me, Mama."

Her words startled Lukatie. She felt stunned as she searched for some reassuring words. "I'm sure he loves you. He's just a stern man that doesn't know how to show it."

"Don't, Mama. Don't defend him. He shows it to the others. Why did he adopt me feeling this way? I was old enough to know and feel. It was you, not him. He never did want me. I think I should leave here. I can support myself with my painting. I do have a little saved from the ones I've sold."

"No, Didge, put that idea out of your mind. I couldn't take that. I need you, dear."

As they talked, they were looking at the portrait of Em. "Wrap it up dear. We'll decorate the tree tonight and put our presents under it."

"I think we ought to open our presents now," teased Miles. "We've never celebrated Christmas before. What do you think, Julia?"

"I think we ought to make it last as long as we can. It's my first real Christmas too."

They had decorated the tree immediately after supper so Julia could enjoy helping.

"Now, I'd better hurry so I'll be ready for my date. I really don't want to go. This is so much fun. I'd rather stay here," she said wryly.

"Papa has promised some of his wine. You'll miss that treat," Miles smiled smugly.

"It's a healthy bet I won't be gone long," she laughed as she left the room. When she dressed, she returned to the parlor with her own gifts, and paused in the doorway.

"How beautiful," she thought, admiring the tree recessed in the bay window. It was piled to the lower limbs with gifts. She walked slowly over to the tree and laid her four gifts with the others. She had so little to spend. After the funeral of Sena and her father, there was very little left to divide between her and the boys.

She had bought two lovely vases for Lukatie, and had made linen handkerchiefs for Miles, Em and her uncle and aunt. She added a lace edging to her aunt's. She had purchased a set of paint brushes for Didge and sweaters for her brothers.

A knock at the door brought Julia back to the present.

"I'll get the door," said Miles. "I wouldn't miss this."

Julia swung at him as he passed her.

"Now a girl looking as pretty as you do doesn't want to get into a fight." His ingenuous smile flashed behind him when he opened the door.

"Come in, Franklin, and meet the most wonderful people in the world," she said stepping in front of Miles. "You know Didge and, of course, this is Mr. and Mrs. Carroll and their son, Miles."

"Have a good time at the dance, dear," Miles said in a sugar-coated voice as he saw them out. He had a startling revelation as they left. He felt jealous. "Why, she has been like a new sister. I could tease and joke with her. Maybe even flirt with her a little, but she is too young. Damn, damn, and double damn. This is preposterous."

Back in the room Lukatie was discussing sleeping arrangements for the company.

After the plans which also included use of the vacant parsonage had been made, she stated,

"That takes care of it. I've put cots in two of the bedrooms for the children to be with their parents."

"That's why my room feels so crowded all of a sudden," laughed Miles cheerfully.

"Could be," smiled Lukatie. "We'd better all get up early in the morning and go clean up the parsonage."

"It was cleaned up after the Murrays all left," said Miles not too anxious to tackle a cleaning job.

"Don't you think by now it might be pretty dusty?"

"I suppose so," grunted Miles, his cheerfulness clearly gone. "Well, I think I'll go out."

First stop, he thought, was to clean out all evidence of having used the house on dates with some of his playmates.

Christmas Eve everyone arrived in a festive, joyous mood dumping more presents under the tree. Gaiety was definitely the theme of the holiday.

"Kinyon practically had to tie me to keep me in Landridge until the house was finished. Now, I don't intend to wait another minute to see it," announced Jane.

"Don't come empty handed," said Em to all the men as they started upstairs. "Bring your things on up to your rooms."

"I do love the way you've picked up the blue from outside into the vestibule and spilling over in your drapes in the living room. Come redecorate our house for us," Jane suggested.

"You probably couldn't live with what I might do to it." Laughed Lukatie.

At lunch time Em suggested they might like to rest in the afternoon because they were having all the neighbors in the evening for a party.

"Sure glad we have some good strong backs around to take up the carpet in case anyone wants to dance. Oh, there will be a buffet supper for everyone," said Lukatie with enthusiasm.

"How was the school dance last night, Julia?" asked Miles.

She was a little shocked at him for asking in front of everyone and blushed prettily. "All right, I guess. I suppose you had a nice evening too. Wasn't it almost daylight when you came in?" She added quickly while everyone laughed.

"I guess that's our clue to take our things over to the old parsonage, Carlton. Then no one will know what time we get in." Miles said soberly.

Just as they finished eating, there was a knock at the door.

"Sure that is for us?" Lukatie heard Em saying as she went to the door.

"Yassuh ordered ova ah month ago ter 'b brung out ter day."

"Bring it in here," Em said leading the way into the sitting room. "Where do you want it, Lukatie, and close your mouth before a fly gets in it," he laughed. She just pointed to the wall at the end of the room.

It was a radio in a beautiful mahogany cabinet with a ribbon around it and a large beautiful bow on top. Reading the attached card, it was signed, "Merry Christmas with many happy years ahead, Our Love, Kinyon and Jane."

"Thank you," said Lukatie to Kinyon and Jane. "This is just too much!"

"We both thank you," said Em quietly. "Come on Kinyon, let's go check with Thankful and see if that barbecue is about done. I also want to see if he got the boys together to play for our party this evening."

"Be right with you, Em."

"Did you really enjoy the dance?" Didge asked Julia later when they were dressing for the party. "We've been so busy we haven't even talked about it."

"It was nice, but I think my mind and heart were here."

"Oh, with all of us or just Miles?" teased Didge.

"I'm not sure, but I think it was all of you." She said frankly.

By seven o'clock the children were fed and put to bed. The party started with supper. Two large tables loaded with food were placed against the far wall of the dining room to make room for an overflow of dancing.

Didge overheard Em tell Lukatie that Seth would come in by eight to serve the wine. "He is working to put himself through school by getting a group together and catering at clubs and private parties. He's worked out a deal with a café that cooks all the food for them. He picks it up and they serve it."

"He's smart," she concluded wearily.

"You're tired."

"Not really. Maybe too much happening too fast," she replied watching Didge dance with Mr. Heath and then Stewart.

"I'm glad Didge is having a good time," she said testing Em.

At Em's invitation Stephen had brought a business associate along to the party. Entering the door Em and Lukatie turned to greet them.

"Mr. and Mrs. Carroll, this is Major Street."

"Glad to have you join our party," said Em.

The room was filled with glib introductions

and everyone continued dancing or grouping in corners talking.

Titia, a creature of impulse, was eyeing Major. She seemed to attract and keep the men held captive around her. She could angle for compliments from men and was successful in getting them.

Lukatie watched her from across the room.

"I believe Titia is having a good time, Stewart."

"If she is surrounded by men, she is."

"Stewart!"

"Well, it's the truth."

"I think you've had too much of Em's wine."

"And I think you are by far the best-looking woman here," he said with his characteristic chuckle and twinkle in his eyes.

"And you," Em walked up as the dance ended, "Let me dance with my wife to stop you from filling her head with your silly nothings."

"That is a very becoming dress you are wearing," Stewart laughed into her eyes as he released her to Em.

Major, a double-minded man unstable in his ways, was making his way toward Didge as she finished a dance with Carlton. His squarish face topped by curly light brown hair that he made no attempt to control caused every woman in the room to wonder whom his first choice for a dance would be.

"May I?" he extended his hand to Didge.

"Of course, Mr. Street."

"Well," said Martha to James. "I guess that showed Mrs. Johnson."

"Don't know that it did. I don't even see her in the room," he said taking the joy out of her remark.

She added, "Just look at this house."

"I've looked."

"Well, all I've got to say is I hope they don't fall flat on their face."

"Glad that's all you've got to say. No reason why they should it's all paid for."

"Humph!"

Good clean fun and frivolity held sway as Em noticed Didge dancing with Major. An instant dislike flooded his features. When the dance ended, he told her to tend to the refreshments and leave the dancing to the others.

"You're the hostess," he added to soften the blow.

"Hostesses dance too, Papa. You're dancing, Mama too. As long as I dance with family and old men, it was all right, wasn't it?" She turned and fled the room. It seemed she was always running from Em's stinging words.

"I'll leave here. I'm through," she vowed. Instead of a father he's more of a stranger or jailor. She sat on her canopied bed and wept. Hers was a troubled sad heart. So much gaiety around and none for her.

"How often I've told myself I'd leave, but repetition gives lie to its sincerity. After all, where would I go. Yet, how can I take much more." She thought of Seth downstairs and having the quality of resilience needed to bounce back. She freshened up and went back downstairs to the party.

Titia noticed Major alone and approached him.

"Like a drink?"

"Yes, bourbon and water, please."

She laughed and took a sparkling crystal wine glass from the tray Seth was passing around. He tasted it and frowned.

"Guess you didn't know all you'll get here

is Carroll's homemade wine." Her voice dropped softly.

He looked into her eyes as she continued, "If you care for wine, it is as good as France's muscatel."

"You've been to France?"

"Lived there awhile. I love the north part of Paris. The Montmartre is a beautiful hilly section. Artists go there a lot. You can get beautiful paintings for a song."

"Oh, you sing?"

"You know very well, I mean a cheap price." They laughed.

"This party is not one you might say is filled with maniacal glee, is it?"

"Depends on what you want. I'd say we want something stronger than Em's wine," whispered Titia.

"I've got something in my car." He offered half-jokingly if she wanted to take it that way, but half not if she wanted the drink. She turned to Major. "Let's go get that drink."

Outside she turned up the bottle he offered to her and took a deep drink.

"Your mouth is a lovely sponge," he joked feeling concern for his whiskey. "Better take it easy. They will think you're drunk."

"The southern, genteel magnolia lady is dead, Major. When she discarded her corset and shortened her dresses, she up and died." She inhaled another drink and handed him the bottle with a bow.

Major exploded with laughter, "Come on back to the party, lovely, before they talk."

"Let them run their nasty tongues. I answer only to myself. I'm the one that counts and I don't give a damn about public opinion."

"Come on, in we go," urged Major.

"If there's anything I hate, it's a quitter," Titia quipped. Her verbal thesis on morality was as interpretive to Major as a minister's condemnation of sin. She was standing on the running board of the car. He picked her up and walked into the woods.

Later when they went inside everyone was in a state of happiness unaware of Titia entering the room. She walked over to the table and picked up a couple of hors d'oevres to nibble on as she looked around the room.

Stephen was near the door when Major came in. Looking toward Titia, he remarked, "To pleasure a woman is every man's right and this is my pleasure. It's the staff of life, man." Shaking his head. "What a fleshy earthy being." Then he noticed Didge on the stairs and felt like molasses was all over his face. He knew she had heard. His face colored as he left Stephen and followed Titia.

"Feel like dancing?" he asked putting his arm around her.

"She's made another conquest," snorted Martha.

"Hush your sharp tooth mouth, woman. Guess he knows what he likes. Look there, Mrs. Johnson has got a dimple when she smiles," James said to aggravate Martha.

"Humph, you mean she's got a wrinkle in a larger wrinkle."

Titia saw Seth go out on the terrace and excused herself from Major. "I need some air, this is unusually warm weather."

"Come on out on the terrace with me," he suggested.

"No, you better stay here. We shouldn't go out together again."

"Why not?"

"I think not, that is why." She went out and followed Seth.

Seth was leaning against a tree feeling very tired. The only reason he had agreed to serve the wine was to be near Didge and he had only seen her from a distance all evening. He was startled when he saw the faint form of a woman approaching him. Hoping it was her he straightened up.

"Hot in there, isn't it, Seth?" Titia said warmly.

"Yes, ma'am, and I'd better get back to my job," disappointment echoed through his voice.

"Why do you dodge me so, Seth?"

"Do I do that?"

"Yes, you do. Given a chance I could teach you a lot. Or did you learn more than you care to admit at college. We could start with a kiss."

"Sorry, Mrs. Johnson, I can't kiss you."

"Well, damn man, why not?"

"I have a fever sore. Wouldn't want you to catch it."

"Catch hell. The only fever I catch is for you and you're not man enough to do anything about it. I can't even interest you in that."

"Right, like I've told you before I'm not interested."

"You...I'll fix you. I'll go in there and say you raped me."

"Go ahead and I'll have to tell what actually happened then you'll have to explain why you left the party alone. I've been outside five minutes and they know it. I'm going back inside now. I imagine a lot of glasses are empty. You'd better go back inside too Mrs. Johnson."

"With that bunch of heathen piss?" she spat.

"You just remember one thing, I couldn't

SILENT TEARS

possibly undress, redress and rape you in five minutes."

She lashed out at him wishing she could exterminate him from the human race. Sexual excitement was like the spring of life to her. To have that damn Seth look upon her unfavorably stripped her self-esteem bare.

"Who is she that you can't see me?" she screeched.

He walked quickly back into the house and went straight to the pantry for a gallon of wine. Winnie followed him. "Where yo' ben?"

"None of your damn business. Now get the hell out of here and tend to your own job." He brushed past her into the dining room and poured the wine into the punch bowl.

Didge saw Seth enter the house. "Gosh he looks mad," she thought. She walked through the room and saw Titia entering the front door so mad she was mouthing words with fierce intensity. Yet no sound escaped the depth of her throat.

Stephen went to Titia. "Something wrong?"

"No, of course not!" She snapped as she brushed him aside and went looking for something to drink.

"Haw," laughed Martha, "Some jerk must have told her no. She just came in foaming at the mouth."

"Then he is a jerk, a fool at that," growled James.

"Humph, she devours men. You old fart and you're jealous."

"Could be, could be, Martha."

Didge stood just inside the doorway watching Miles and Carlton as each tried to see which one could get the most dances with Julia. From the corner of her eye, she saw Major coming toward her. To save embarrassment she quickly disappeared up the stairs to her room. She sat down on her bed and lay her head over on her pillow.

The next thing Didge knew, Lukatie was patting her on the shoulder and the house seemed very quiet.

"Merry Christmas, dear."

"You, too, Mama."

"Everyone has gone, honey, and the family has decided to open the presents now and sleep late in the morning."

"You just give them mine, Mama. I won't go down. I'm too sleepy." She lay her head back on the pillow. "I can't dance so why should I watch them open presents," she thought.

"Please, dear."

"I'm sorry, Mama, but I can't."

"All right, dear, I'll say you've already gone to bed."

"I have, Mama."

Later when Julia slipped into bed, Didge said, "You don't have to be so quiet, I'm not asleep."

"You should have come down. It was so much fun."

"I'm glad you enjoyed it."

"They all loved your paintings. Do you know there were tears in your Papa's eyes?"

"How could I know, Julia, I wasn't there."

"He said, 'This takes a place of honor in this house.' He went and got a hammer and put it over the mantle in the parlor. Then he hung your mama's over the mantle in the sitting room. Oh, Didge, I wish you had come down. They all did."

"Well, goodnight, Julia." Didge turned her back to the middle of the bed. She was up around seven and went to her studio and painted while everyone slept late.

Lukatie found her there around ten in the morning. "I'm so ashamed for sleeping so late especially on Christmas."

"You needed it, Mama."

"Yes, I do think I did." she walked over to see what Didge was painting. Then looking out the window.

"I didn't realize you could see the Henderson house so well from here."

"Yes, look out the other side, Mama."

"Why, I can see all the tenant houses, Roxie's café and the end of the Heath house," Lukatie exclaimed.

"When the trees leaf out in the spring you won't see a thing."

"Didge, will you come down for dinner, dear?"

"Of course, Mama. I just didn't feel like going back down last night."

"Everyone loved your presents. You should have seen how proud your Papa was."

"Julia told me when she came to bed."

"Then you didn't rest much either."

She walked over and took Didge in her arms. "You did a beautiful job on the portrait of me and I thank you."

"Mama, I can never repay you for all you've done for me. For taking me in as a baby and loving and caring for me. I behaved very childish last night and I'm sorry."

"That's all right, dear. Oh, I put your gifts in your room to keep the children out of them."

Didge went to her room and opened her gifts then went down and thanked everyone.

"Thank you, Papa, I believe I can put that to use." She hugged no one since she couldn't hug Em. He had given her money. I'll add it to my bank account, she told herself. "One of these days I'll have enough to leave here."

At dinner Em rose, cleared his throat for attention. All eyes turned to the end of the table. "While we're all together, I want to thank each one of you for the Christmas presents and for spending your Christmas with us. Now, I have one more gift to give while all of my family are present, since it's one we all voted on. I might add that this particular gift would have been given years ago if I had known there was any desire for it. A little bird innocently let me know. So here it is." He took a long envelope from his pocket and started to hand it to Kinyon. "No, I think I'll hand it to the lady of the house. If that isn't adequate, there is more."

She opened the envelope quickly reading its contents. "Oh, thank you! Look, Kinyon, the land to build a summer cottage on the river." All the children applauded.

"There is a clause that the land is never to be sold out of the Carroll family."

"Who would ever want to sell such a beautiful spot?"

"That is the land on the left of the path, Jane."

"Oh, the hill is on the right, isn't it?" She said looking a little downcast.

"You will have a very good view looking down the river from the left side. Anyway, the hill is where Didge paints. I always think of that as her spot."

This tidbit of news was a surprise to Didge.

After dinner while the children were having a nap they walked down to the river. Jane was already full of plans for building a summer home.

"Thank you, Em. You've made her very

happy," said Kinyon placing his arm on Em's shoulder.

The next morning after breakfast, they all left and the Blue Bird quieted down to welcome a New Year.

*****

In the Henderson home Titia was feeling lonesome for Madison. "Perhaps if Stewart were here, I wouldn't feel so alone. I shouldn't have told Isaac to stay away, or Moses, he's better."

Hearing a knock at the door she walked slowly to open it. "Oh," her features fell.

"That is an exuberant welcome padded with joy, I must say."

"What did you expect, you weren't invited. Come on in if you like, Stephen, if you came to see Stewart, he isn't home."

"As a matter of fact, I came to see you."

"Whatever for?"

"I was in hopes of a warm reception. One that would encourage me to ask you to marry me."

"Marry you!" Titia laughed so hard tears were running down her cheek. It took more to satisfy her than Stephen could offer. He hurt her once, that was enough.

"If I have to support myself, I'll do it alone, thank you." She stated.

"I'm not exactly a pauper, as president of the bank," he said acidly.

"That two cent bank! I could buy it ten times and not even miss the money. Or is that what you're after?"

"I'm not interested in your money. I just wanted to make an honest woman out of you. Call it in memory of the past if you like."

"I'll never marry a man that can't support

me in my accustomed style, without using my money," she said with emphasis.

"Stephen is the one man that will never touch me again. He will never know he is Madison's father," she thought as she stared at him.

"You're enough to make a man climb a wall backwards." He started walking toward Titia, thinking she may as well pay for her insults.

"You stay away from me!"

He continued walking toward her. Feeling panic she raced around a divan and zig-zagged between chairs to escape the advancing Stephen. He was like a gun loaded and ready to explode. Once was enough for her and she wanted no more of him. "I haven't the patience for this," she told herself as she gasped for breath. "Why in hell can't a man leave a woman alone, damn it, what am I running for." She stopped short and turned on Stephen her blond hair falling to her shoulders, her green eyes snapping in anger. "I've had enough of this. You get out of here and leave me alone or I'll scream my head off and swear you were trying to attack me."

"Do and I'll tell them how we celebrated your sixteenth birthday."

"I'll say you are lying to cover up your actions."

He tipped his head to the side as he watched her.

"You've no way to prove differently. You can bet I'm the one they will believe," she flung at him.

"I really came here with the best intentions to ask you to marry me. I never did stop caring for you regardless of the reputation you've acquired."

"Oh, you! Get out of here!" she screamed.

"I'm going, just wanted you to know I wouldn't marry you now even for your money. You're too flighty to suit me. You're nothing but an ass pusher! Always peddling it." His voice was caustic. "I hear plenty about you." He turned on his heels and walked to the door.

"Have you ever seen my oldest boy?" Not waiting for an answer, he said, "You should, he looks enough like Madison to be his twin brother, just not as old. But then, of course, everyone knows he's Elda's son, don't they?" He walked out closing the door behind him.

She felt more degraded by his words than by any act she had ever committed. She watched him through the window as he walked to his car. "He walks like a castrated ram, the damn fool," she cried out. She sat down beating her fist on her knees, tears falling as Zelphia came into the room.

"Law me, whuts de' matta wit m'baby?" She put her arms around Titia pulling her over on her big soft breast.

"M' li'l mis'able chile. Yo' tell yo' Zelphia n' she fix hit rite lak' whin yo' wuz a young'un. I seed dat man leabe har. Perzactly whut he doin'?"

"Nothing, Zelphia, he didn't do anything."

"Den whut yo' cry fo' yo' wants him bak'?"

"No! I don't want him back," Titia straightened.

"Wal, whuts dis cryin' all 'bout den?" asked Zelphia puzzled.

"Oh, he just said some mean hateful things."

"Den we'se gwine tell Mistuh Stewart."

"Oh, no we aren't, Zelphia. No need to stir up more trouble. Promise you won't tell Stewart."

"A'co'se ah will iffen dats whut yo' wonts.

Lift yo'self 'n pride, chile, 'n warsh yore purty face 'n git ready fo' dinnah. We'ens got some good hot braid 'n ham 'n taters 'n greensalat acookin'. Hum-m-m, shore gwine be good. Yo' git ready fo' Mistuh Stewart gits ter home."

A week later a nervous unhappy Titia was pacing the floor. Her thoughts on Seth. "In a few days he will return to school. Then I'll have to wait until summer. I intend to have you Seth Kirby." She threw down the book she was reading. Her desire for Seth had become an obsession. She walked over to the telephone and gave the operator the number of the Heath residence, hoping with all her heart Seth would answer the ring.

"Hello, Heath residence," answered Seth's clear voice.

"Hello," she said and hesitated.

"Mr. Heath has retired for the evening, I'm Seth Kirby. May I help you?" he asked hoping to make it easier on the hesitant caller.

"It's you I want to speak to, Seth."

"Oh."

"This is Mrs. Johnson. I wondered if you'd do some work for me in the morning?"

"Don't you have boys there that could do it?" asked Seth.

"Most of them are busy clearing new ground and I thought you might use the money for school."

"Yes, Ma'am, I could."

"Then why don't you come as early as you like in the morning. Just knock on my room door off the side terrace. No need to disturb the whole household."

"All right, Mrs. Johnson, I'll be there early." He hung up and went back to his reading.

"Warm again," thought Seth the next morning

as he saddled the golden buckskin to ride down to work for Mrs. Johnson. He was glad it was warm since he would most likely be working outside. He hadn't seen Titia since the night of the Carroll party. As he knocked on the door he wondered, "What do I say to alleviate our last unpleasant encounter? Maybe it's her way of saying she's sorry."

Titia had just finished her bath when she heard Seth's knock. The room was warm so she got back in bed pulling just a sheet over herself as she called out.

"Come in," there was nothing more satisfying to Titia than performing perfectly with a clean healthy man.

Seth opened the door and stepped inside. "You have some work you want me to do?" he said, feeling very embarrassed, and hesitant about being in her bedroom. "You might call it work, Seth, but there is nothing more enjoyable than taking a good bath and getting between a couple of clean white sheets, with a good-looking clean man. I've had my bath. You go take one." She pointed to a door.

"I've had my bath this morning, thank you."

"Then undress and crawl in."

"No thank you, I came to work."

"What do you make of this?" She lifted the sheet revealing her nude body.

"I have a highly stimulating nature. I promise you won't be disappointed. Think of it as work if it makes you happy. Interest you?" she asked.

"No!" Seth said gruffly with a mixture of surprise and defiance.

"You! You don't want me?"

"No, and don't offer yourself to me again. I'm not interested in you. I thought by now you knew that."

"There aren't many men that get this chance."

"Oh, you had me fooled."

"Are you a queer, homosexual or something worse?" she blurted out.

"No!" he said fiercely as he glared at her.

She had never felt so rejected. "Haven't you ever loved a woman?" she barked.

"Been in love, yes. Your kind of loving, no, so just stop pushing yourself on me."

"Well, are you asexual?" she flung at him.

"No." his voice was heated. "Your mind is sure filled with trash."

"You mean you don't want a woman, Seth?"

"Not just any woman, Mrs. Johnson."

"Then there is a woman. Man, if you can't get her any other way, marry her."

"Can't do that either."

Titia was becoming interested as Seth realized he was saying too much.

"And why not?" she demanded.

"Just wouldn't work, not now anyway. But until I do marry there will be no other woman. I'd appreciate it if you'd leave me alone."

"You think you're such a hell of a good man, get the hell out of here," she yelled.

Didge awoke early and hurried to her studio to paint. She was working on the Henderson house and wanted to finish the painting of it before the holidays ended. She had just started when she saw Seth leave through the terrace door.

Thoughts began running wild and stumbling over each other. "Could it possibly be that Titia and Seth? Oh, no!" She tried to push these thoughts from her mind which quickly began to catalogue the past. She was remembering Titia's curiosity about Seth. The look in Titia's eyes when she saw Seth at the fair. Her actions at the swimming hole. The party when she had come in looking excited, even flustered. "At the time I remember thinking she was just having fun, probably out with Major. Have I been wrong all this time?" Didge asked herself. "Can it be Seth and Titia are…?"

Didge watched more closely as Seth drew near the house. "He's mad, he's really mad. Why, she's using every trick in the book to push herself on him, and he won't have any part of her."

Seth looked up just as she turned from the window and thought, "Damn, she saw me leave there. What will she think? She may even think I spent the night there. Oh, dear God, why won't that woman leave me alone?"

That afternoon Seth walked to the river. As he walked along the bank, he checked the traps that he had given to Gick. He had tried to teach him trapping as he himself had been taught by Mr. Heath.

In the woods he felt as hard as the great oaks surrounding him and as soft as the tall pines. His memory reached back to the warm summer days when he would find Didge sitting on her thinking stump with the soft summer air playing with her hair, and Regal laying at her feet. Life had been so simple and uncomplicated. Then his vision came true and he saw her sitting on the stump with Regal II at her feet. "That picture will be imprinted on my mind when I'm away, Didge," he called out.

She looked up smiling. He had on a red sweater and a white shirt collar open at his throat. How handsome he looked.

He plunged ahead, "I was hoping I'd see you. About what you saw this morning, Mrs.

Johnson telephoned me last night and asked me to do some work this…"

"Seth," she interrupted, "What I saw this morning was a very mad man. What I should have seen was Titia." Didge began to laugh. "The brash hussy, I'll bet she is still cussing you out. I'll admit I was puzzled at first, but not after I saw your face. I went back to painting. I didn't know you saw me."

"Yes, I saw you turn away and felt you were turning away from me. I couldn't leave in the morning without making you aware that she means absolutely nothing to me."

"I know that, Seth. I know that even if you had stayed with her. I know what she is. Not many men would walk away from her." Abruptly changing the subject, Didge said, "You're leaving in the morning?"

"Yes." He dropped to his knees, sitting back on his heels, and scratching Regal II behind the ears.

"Will you be back in the summer?"

"That depends on the catering service I've started. I had eight parties set up over the holidays."

"How could you leave? Do you have enough men working with you to handle it when you're away?"

"Sure do, I get the checks and pay the men. It's paying rather well. We give good service and that's what people want. I'd like to save enough to open a restaurant."

"I bet you will, too, Seth. I hope so if that is what you want."

"Yes, I want direction, Didge. I wouldn't want to be a thimit."

She broke out in a big laugh. "I never have called you a thimit. What kind of group do you serve?"

"Parties like the other night. Business, religious groups, office parties, large and small ones, conventions and ethnic groups in general. I very seldom do the actual serving. I make the contact, plan the menu, check out the place to see that everything is in order, and make sure our service is good. I don't have to worry about that end of it anymore. The men I hire don't drink. You'd be surprised how many problems that solves. Let's talk about you now. Are you doing much painting?"

"As much as school will allow. I'd much rather hear about you and New York."

"Oh, New York is just big, you'll have to go see it."

"Me, go to New York. Can you imagine Papa ever letting me go to any place unless I'm guarded like Fort Dix?"

"I couldn't help seeing Mr. Carroll when he stopped you from dancing."

"Can you tell me why he treats me like that?"

He could hear the anguish in her voice.

"Seth, art can reach into the imagination, the spirit. It's cousin to writing a book, I guess. I don't know what I'd do without it."

In his soft well-modulated voice, Seth said, "Don't let your hurt lash out and leave you with a bruised heart that won't heal. The secret of true happiness is being at peace with oneself. Hold on to your high ideas and create your own happiness."

"Pretty words, Seth, but how does one create happiness in a prison?"

"I think there will be a way out if you just hold on a while longer."

She looked long and deep into his eyes.

They were so direct, so understanding, so full of love. She wondered if he would run from her as he did from Titia. Their very souls were shining through their eyes. "Dear God, help me not to love Seth, but if it's right, let me know. Let me know what to do; let it be right and wonderful to reach out and touch his face," she prayed silently. "I want…oh, I want…Seth, oh Seth." She jumped to her feet and ran down the cart path, Regal II dancing joyously along with her. "It can never be," she cried aloud in agony to each tree she passed.

Seth dropped his head on his folded arms as they lay across his knees, angry, vexed and disheartened by the trick nature played on him. He sat waiting for the pain and loneliness to wane.

His desire had been to attend the Johnson University in Charlotte, North Carolina, "but I'd have trouble there because of this white skin that I've had here all my life and I just didn't feel like fighting my way through college. I don't like living a lie either." No questions asked, no questions to answer, he thought. He sighed, got up and went home to pack.

Two days later Titia packed and returned to New York. Stewart went along to make sure she didn't change her mind and turn back. He wanted her gone, but safe.

*****

The warm Christmas season had changed abruptly by New Year's Day. The days would be cold, warm and cool, ever changing days until spring. Em and Miles sat in the library before a warm, crackling fire.

"Papa, what do you plan to do with the

church and parsonage house?"

"I don't know, son, I really hadn't given it any thought. Have you?"

"Yes, Sir, lately I have. I don't think I'd ever be a good farmer or love the land like you do."

Em was startled, "You had me fooled; I always believed you wanted to farm."

"I didn't know what I wanted so I've stayed with it."

"Are you saying that now you do know?"

"Yes, Sir, if you can hear me out."

"Go ahead, talk."

"Well, Sir, I'd like to convert the old church into a seed and hardware store. Put in a glass front and counters and fill the yard with farm machinery including tractors. I'd like to renovate the house so it will look completely different to live in or tear it down and build over."

"What is the matter with living here?"

"Well, Sir, I was thinking of marriage, so Mama will stop calling me her bachelor son," he chuckled softly.

"Not much of a reason to marry."

"No, Sir, the real reason is I want to if Julia will have me."

Em almost lost his balance as he was picking up a back log to throw on the fire.

"Julia! Why, son, she couldn't stand living in that place."

"I know, that is why I want to completely change it. She shudders every time we pass there."

"Guess you better find out if she'll have you before you do too much planning; she's kind of young, you know."

"I still want to do it. At least the

hardware store. I could do the house over and rent it if you'd like."

"What will I do now?" thought Em as he watched Miles leave the room. "I depend on him so. He is so full of energy and quick to know what needs to be done. I suppose he has his own life to live." Em sat there gazing at the fire and thinking of the church. In his mind he began to throw out the church pews and tear out the walls that divided classrooms. He then built counters, a new store front with plate glass. Hardware to the front, seed and fertilizer to the back with tractors out under the trees. Taking all of ten minutes to do the job, he thought, "Miles might have something there." His head rolled to one side and he fell asleep.

Julia became very quiet and thoughtful as she listened to Miles outline his plans. She knew a little about it since she saw them working on the church as she passed it on her way to school. She also heard discussions at the table, but hating the place as she did, she couldn't ask questions about it. Finally, it lost the church look. It made her happy for surely old Satan himself had been dwelling there. "In a little over three months I'll join my brothers and never look on that God forsaken place again. Anyway, it is much nicer going with the Carrolls to church in town," she thought.

She suddenly turned her head to look at Miles as they rode around on this brisk Sunday afternoon wondering if she heard him right. "Did I hear you right? Did you say, marry you and live in that…that…that, place?" she said in hurt anger. He turned off the road into a cart path and stopped the car. A gentleness was in his voice as he spoke. "Listen, Darling, don't you know I love you with all my heart, and I want to protect you. The rest of my life is wrapped up in your answer. There is nothing wrong with that house, and I mean to change it. You won't know it was the same place. We'll even change the approach to the house." He moved closer to Julia. Capturing her hands, he pulled her to him. Julia yielded and Miles gathered her hungrily into his arms and kissed her. She drew back and looked at him.

"May I take that kiss as yes?"

"I don't know. I have school to finish."

"I know that and believe me I don't mind waiting," he cut in.

"I want to go see my brothers. Their letters sound so lonely. Miles, I can't live in that house. It's still the same location and you can't change that."

The memory of what had happened in that house flashed through her mind and grief shook her very being. She began to shake and Miles put his arms around her again to hold her close. "Darling, time and youth are on your side. The memory will dim. That house is perfect for running the store. I'd be near all the time if you needed me, and you could help in the store if you'd like to. It would be our business and I believe a good one. Won't you think about it?"

"Yes, Miles, I will. You're good and I like you a lot. I love your family too."

"Reach deeper than just being liked, Darling. I want your love coming my way."

"I'll promise to think about it, Miles. That's all I can promise now."

Summer came and Julia insisted that she needed more time to think. She had been working at the five-and-ten-cent store and was saving her money to make a trip to see her brothers. She tried to give half of her earnings to the

Carrolls but they refused it.

Miles was selling every tractor he could get in and had back orders that needed filling. "Ma' tractor cum in yit, Miles?" asked Mr. Tartt almost daily.

"Not yet. It will be here any day now."

"Whut air dey shippin' hit on, a snail train?"

Finally, the day came when Miles could respond to Mr. Tartt's question by saying, "Your tractor is at the depot, Mr. Tartt. It just came in."

Mr. Tartt's old face broke into a toothless grin. "Now, I kin have time ter garden 'n run m' gee-rage, too."

*****

Lucinda planned to come home shortly before Kinyon, Jane and their family was to visit. "At least I will have two weeks with Lucinda before their arrival," thought Lukatie.

LuKatie waited impatiently. She hadn't seen her daughter is so many years.

"My great God in heaven," she cried, her feet glued to the floor as she watched Miles help Lucinda from the car so she wouldn't trip over her nun's habit. Em placed his arm around her to steady her.

"As much as I wanted to see her, I feel like running out the back door. Oh Em, why has she done this."

"I can't answer that. Get control of yourself, dear, and let's welcome our daughter home. Come on, smile."

In the warm glow of welcoming her home, Lukatie could already feel sorrow.

"Miles, will you take Lucinda's things up

to Didge's room."

"Where is Didge?" Lucinda asked.

They heard feet running down the stairs. "Here she comes, make room," called out Miles.

"Still hasn't slowed down," laughed Lucinda nervously. She really wasn't prepared for the shock her presence was going to give the family any more than she was prepared for the beautiful young girl that paused in the doorway. Her face broke into the prettiest smile Lucinda had ever seen. "God! She is beautiful," thought Em as he watched her walk toward Lucinda with outstretched arms.

"Oh, Lucinda, you're beautiful; it's so good to see you. May I paint you while you're home?"

"Our baby has grown up. I still think of you as the little girl I last saw," said Lucinda as they embraced. "Of course, I'll pose for you if you like."

Turning back to the family, she said, "I'm truly sorry. I just didn't think my being a nun would shock you so. I should have told you in my note."

"Why, Lucinda?" Lukatie asked.

Lucinda hesitated a moment, a sadness filling her face. "A convent was the most secluded place I could think of to get completely away from Fountain."

With her sensitive inner ear, Lukatie heard the cries of Lucinda's heart and knew she had to have this peace. "Out of one prison into another," she thought but said nothing.

"Do you hear anything from him now?" asked Lucinda.

"No, not since his surprise visit. Did you get the letter about his coming here?"

"Yes, it arrived the day before I left New

York."

"I wish you had come home, Lucinda."

"You know I couldn't, Mama."

"Come, let's sit down while we talk," suggested Em, leading the way to the sitting room. They told Lucinda about Didge catching Fountain at the mailbox.

"That sounds like something he would do."

The Kinyon Carroll clan arrived two weeks later. They concealed their surprise by greeting Lucinda warmly. Each in his own heart was wishing she wasn't there. To a degree, it dampened their bubbling spirits. Kinyon soon suggested to Em that they walk to the tobacco field.

"Em, I've been thinking about something, but if you say no then that is the end of it."

"Oh? Out with it."

"Jane approves of what I'm about to suggest. It's about Didge. She's a fine artist, but more schooling wouldn't hurt her. What I'm proposing is that I take her home with us for a year and let her study art under a new teacher that has opened a studio in Landridge. They say she is marvelous. She studied in France and Italy."

"Why is someone like that in Landridge," Em wanted to know.

"She married a local guy and they're making their home there."

"I don't mind her having more training, but I don't let her date and you know why. Do you think if I let her go you can control her?"

"I think I can. We'll have that understood if she goes."

"Does Jane know?"

"No."

"Then we'll leave it up to Didge. You can make the offer at dinner tonight."

On the way back to the house they met the others on their way to the river.

"Come on, we're all going swimming. I have your swimsuit, Kinyon." Called Jane.

After swimming they picked out the spot for the summer home to be built for Jane and Kinyon.

"In the winter, the tenants might be able to start it for you after they finish some work they are to do for Miles." Em said. Eyebrows raised. Em hurriedly added, "he's going to tear down the parsonage and enlarging the store with the lumber."

"Oh, we thought for a minute," started Penny Sue.

"No," put in Lukatie. She felt she had to defend Miles since he was at the store.

Didge had worked feverishly on the portrait of Lucinda. Completing one in charcoal to work from if Lucinda had to leave before she could finish the one in oils. Didge reached over playing with Regal II and remembering Seth playing with him. She buried her face in his fur.

"Do you love me as much as I love you, old boy?" She rubbed his back as he wagged his tail and thumped it on the ground, his big soulful eyes looking into hers.

"I do believe he does. I'll bet that means yes," laughed Lucinda.

"You're so pretty when you laugh like that," Didge said warmly.

Back at the house they walked around the yard. "The gardens are so pretty, just beautiful," beamed Jane.

"The longer warm day and light hours cause plants to grow so fast."

"Horse feathers," said Em interrupting Lukatie, "she trims, weeds, hoes, powder puffed and pampered this yard for so many years that all we needed was a house."

"Sounds like you're too modest, Lukatie," they all laughed.

At dinner that evening Kinyon told Didge about the art teacher in Landridge and invited her to spend a year with them so she could study under her. Jane nodded her approval.

"Thank you both, but I don't see how I can go."

"Didge, Kinyon and I have talked it over, and you may go if you like and if Lukatie doesn't object," said Em.

"I can go, you mean I can really go?" She was dumbfounded. She looked at Kinyon. "Suppose I go and she won't take me as a student?"

"She will, Jane and I took the painting you gave us for Christmas, also Penny Sue's and Everett's down to show Mrs. Howard and told her about you and your love of art."

"What did she say?" asked Didge eagerly. Kinyon and Jane exchanged glances.

"Was it that bad?" grimaced Didge.

"No, no," said Jane. "She said and I quote, 'her suppressed nature is revealed in her work, she is good. I do believe I can help her loosen up.' End quote."

"I think I know," Didge said docilely, "Mama," she turned to Lukatie.

"Yes, dear, I think you should go. It will be wonderful for you to train under someone so capable."

"Then it's settled. We'll leave Monday morning at seven o'clock so I can get to the mill by nine thirty," said Kinyon adding, "Didge, pack a few of your best paintings. Maybe you'll have a chance to sell some."

Before Didge could realize to the full extent what was happening, she was telling everyone goodbye. When she hugged Lucinda, she whispered, "Please forgive me for running off, but maybe this is my chance to start a new life."

"It's all right, darling, I understand. Mama has told me a lot. I'm leaving tomorrow anyway. Just study hard and make the most of this opportunity."

"I will, oh, I will."

Carlton grabbed her by the arm, "Come on, you can wave goodbye from the car."

*****

Lukatie put her arm around Lucinda's shoulder.

"It will be so lonesome around here tomorrow after you leave. Julia is leaving to join her brothers tonight." Lukatie sighed. "What will it be like?" she wondered.

"I thought there might be a romance between Julia and Miles. Then you would have grandchildren and fill the house up again," Lucinda's face was sad as she continued talking. "I wish my baby had had an opportunity at living."

"God often disguises our opportunities dear. We have to search them out to find out what they are. From the day of our birth we have a destination. Your baby's destination was not out of his world. God had his reason for taking the baby. Someday you'll understand. You know you could have had more babies."

"Not with Fountain, I couldn't. Mama, you have no idea what it was like living with that man, that family. I felt like I had to ask if I could go to the bathroom. I'll admit his jealousy was funny, even flattering at first, then it became horrible. My life became a living nightmare, a prison. You and Meda made it possible for me to leave. Mama, please thank Mrs. Johnson and Uncle Stewart for providing me with a place to stay. I left a gift there for her and wrote a thank you note but never felt that was enough. Is she as beautiful as Meda and Mr. and Mrs. Cox say she is?"

"Her looks are flawless, dear. She is a beautiful woman."

Lukatie thought of Titia who wasn't happy unless her body was touching that of a man.

"Mama, speaking of Fountain, I want you to know I have no regrets about leaving him. Life with him was hard. Emotionally the strain was too much."

"It was up to you to determine if your life was hard or easy. You have to scrutinize closely the reward it brings. Only you know if you were giving as much as you were receiving to make your marriage a success."

"I was at first, Mama, I tried very hard."

"The best marriage is a hard road to travel but if it gives you strength of character, faith in God and trust in others then it's worth it. Things never come easy, if they did, I wonder if we'd recognize them. Tell me, Lucinda, how did you, a married woman, become a nun?"

"I wasn't married when I entered the convent. When I left New York, I bought a ticket to California. Then I went to Reno, Nevada and worked as a secretary until I could get a divorce. Then I went down in southern California and entered a convent."

"Does Fountain know about the divorce?"

"Yes, Mama, he was sent a copy by the lawyer."

"I guess that is why he never bothered us anymore. May I ask again, dear, why a nun?"

"I got the idea when I was with Mr. and Mrs. Cox. I sometimes went to church with them, they were Catholics. I decided it would be a place I could go to get out of this world, so to speak. I don't like the way most people are. Fountain and his family mostly. The only things worthwhile are here. But they would have never let me live in peace here. He would have hounded me to death."

Lukatie was a woman with a straight-forward set of personal values and could not applaud the step Lucinda had taken.

"But a nun, Lucinda."

"Oh, Mama," she cried, "It's the next thing to death to me, but it's too late now. It was my only refuge, my change to get completely away from them. At least I can escape the mechanical and meaningless life I was living through my service to God and others."

"Is it a lonely life? I do want you to be happy, Lucinda."

"As I walked the long hall to the novices' wing, I was never lonelier. Others had family there to bid them farewell. I had no one. We lived a life of poverty, chastity, and obedience. After six months we took our first vows and got our nun's habit. When we first entered the monastery, we decide if we want to live a cloistered life or tend to the outside business. I chose the outside. I had already spent too many years closed in." She paused remembering the room to which she had been assigned to share with another nun. The nun had looked Lucinda over and smiled.

"You're so beautiful and built so well. The last one in here didn't have much to offer. You and I will get along fine together. Here, let me help you change clothes. I'll bathe you if you want me to."

Lucinda had turned around and had run from the room. She knocked on the door of the Mother Superior. A small sounding voice called out for her to enter.

Lucinda hardly noticed the bare room and walked straight to the desk, thinking the tiny diminutive person seated there was the smallest person she had ever seen.

"I may as well be honest and come straight to the point," she blurted out.

"By all means do that," said the Mother Superior, a concerned look on her face.

"I cannot share a room with that nun you assigned me to. I'll sleep out in the courtyard first or just leave here now, and Mother I'm not saying this to be a troublemaker. You will find I am a very easy-going person."

The Mother raised a curious eyebrow. "Yes, yes, go on."

Lucinda quoted word for word what was said to her. The Mother Superior picked up the phone. "Sister Esther, would you please come to my office."

Shortly a stout elderly nun limped into the room. Lucinda ran to her, "Let me get you a chair, Sister."

"That's all right, dear, I'm really all right. Just a slight club foot. You're new here, aren't you?" Without waiting for Lucinda to answer she went to the desk.

"Sister Esther, I wonder if you would share a room with Sister Lucy and tell her I want to see her."

"Oh, trouble again." She turned to Lucinda, "Get your things and come with me."

"Yes, Sister." Lucinda had stayed as far away from the frosty stares of Sister Lucy as possible. Two months later Sister Lucy was gone. Lucinda relaxed and never bothered to inquire about her.

"It doesn't bother you to live a chaste life?"

"Sex, Mama? No, people give sex a mystique status that is highly overrated in my opinion. Most people think that achieving orgasm is the most important satisfying accomplishment in the world. I don't happen to agree. It's the most over-acted, over-played, over-worked and over-emphasized act in the world."

Julia ended their conversation by coming into the room. "I'm all packed, Mrs. Carroll. I do thank you for all you and Mr. Carroll have done for me." She broke into tears. "I just don't know what I would have done without you."

Lukatie took her in her arms as she had her own daughters. "We have done nothing dear. It has been our pleasure to have you and we hope you will come back often."

Miles closed the store early so he could take Julia to the train depot. They left immediately after dinner.

When Lucinda left the next morning Em and Lukatie stood waving until the train was out of sight.

"I wonder if it will be over ten years before we see her again," Lukatie was in tears.

"Don't worry, dear, you've still got me." Em put his arm lovingly around her shoulder. "Come, Miles, let's take Mama home."

"Disgusting, isn't it?" Miles said speaking with mock fever as he lifted his pants legs and sashayed behind the disappearing train.

Lukatie laughed, "You're wonderful, with just the right amount of good humor to lift my spirits."

During the warm summer months, the Carrolls often sat late on the terrace when there was enough breeze to keep the mosquitoes away. All lost in their own thoughts.

"Papa," said Miles one evening. "Do you mind if I push a road down the property line so I can build a house behind the store?"

"No, I don't mind. Has Julia said yes?"

"Not yet, but if she doesn't, I'll find someone else. I've wasted enough time playing around."

"I can't help noticing you get three or four letters to our one. Naturally, we thought things were serious between you," said Lukatie.

"Speaking of building, Miles, have you noticed the headlines in the papers lately?" asked Em.

"No, Papa."

"Stocks are dropping or rising too fast, sounds unstable to me. Banks are emphasizing danger of inflation as speculations rise. They are saying a depression is inevitable. Just between us, I'm thinking seriously of putting my money in my own safe instead of the bank. The interest the bank gives isn't enough to risk losing what money I do have. I plan to sell the crops as early as I can and put the money in my safe."

"Do you think the banks are going to close, Em?" asked Lukatie with concern.

Em cleared his throat, "I remember hearing my father talk about the financial depression of 1873. The west flourished while the east suffered. Many lost their homes and lands because they couldn't pay the high tax. I guess you've heard how hard times were in 1893 and continued with us until now. If I hadn't sold timber, there would still be hard times with us."

"What do you advise me to do, Papa?" Miles wanted to know.

"Save every cent you can, keep out of debt, keep your money in the safe for a year or two and wait and see what happens. But whatever you do, keep it to yourself."

"Then you think I should forget building a house."

Em thought for a minute, "Go ahead and push in your road. Find a house plan you like. Move the sawmill over there. You can use the timber for the house that you cut when clearing the land for the road and house site. When you tear the other house down to enlarge the store there will be timber from that you can use."

"If you should marry, you can always stay here until you build," offered Lukatie. "Lord knows there's plenty of room."

"What surprises me is how all my vegetables are selling at the market now." Em laughed shaking his head. "It's hard as hell to believe this big house is making the difference. But Lubby tells me that people ask if they come from the big blue house and they won't buy others until ours are all sold. Oh, by the way, Miles, have you thought of getting in some of those electric washing machines? Kinyon writes they are selling like hot cakes in Landridge."

"Thanks for the thought, Papa, I'll look them up in my catalogue."

"You do that, I'll take one."

"Great," Miles slumped down in his chair. "What do you hear from Lucinda and Didge?"

"Lucinda writes she is being sent to central China for a while. And Didge is thrilled with her art classes. She feels she will learn a lot under the tutorship of Mrs. Howard. I sure do miss her." Lukatie said.

"I thought she was pretty good. I take it other people thought so too the way she was selling paintings," Miles injected.

"Practically giving them away you mean." Said Em disgusted.

"Papa, beginners never get top price no matter how good they are. And I still think she was all right."

Jane had taken Didge to see Mrs. Howard to arrange for art classes. Mrs. Howard wasn't sure what kind of girl she expected to see, but was totally unprepared for the lovely, gracious girl that stood before her. Her beautiful hands with long tapering fingers could only belong to an artist or a musician.

"Looking at you and having seen some of your work I don't think it's necessary to say I won't tolerate or waste my time with sloppy work. I'm looking forward to working with you, Miss Carroll."

"Thank you, Mrs. Howard." Smiled Didge as the inner storm in the pit of her stomach relaxed. "I'll try my best to do good work."

"Well, thank God, you didn't say you'd try to please me. Could you come Monday at 10:00 a.m.? We'll start with pencil and sketch pad."

"Yes, ma'am, I'll be here."

As Didge left with Jane her mind carried her to the riverbank where she used to sit on her thinking stump. How she wished she was there with Seth.

"Pencil and sketch pad indeed," she said aloud to Jane.

"I'm sure that's the golden key to get you to relax, a get acquainted time."

Didge worked hard. She was thrilled to find that the library in Landridge carried many books on art. She read them at the library or carried them home to study. Art became her world.

Dates were offered and refused. She had been told the trip was for learning not dating and she wouldn't put her Uncle Kinyon on the defensive by asking. Keeping busy was her escape mechanism. Seth often crept into her mind and every time he came with such great force into every feeling of her heart. She had to fight and fight hard to close him out.

*****

Mr. Bradley knew Seth wanted a chance to spend the summer with the big-league baseball team. So unknowing to Seth he invited Coach Hardison to see Etherton's last game before summer vacation. It was a totally beautiful spring day with a light breeze as Seth went to the field early to get in some extra warm-ups before the team arrived to practice.

Tension ran strong in the grandstand as the boys left their bench and walked out together, then fanning out to their positions. Playing against Etherton College was a fresh team from Florida that had a rough reputation. "These kids," thought Seth, as he looked around feeling the tension himself, "are really keyed up. Maybe that's what we all need to keep us on our toes." Seth had the ability to communicate with each player as he turned his head looking at each one before a game.

Outwardly he was strangely calm and was breathing deeply. "Bradley thinks I'm best, now I must prove it." He then turned to face the first batter.

"I thought for a minute your pitcher had gone to sleep," breathed Coach Hardison from where he stood just outside the dugout.

"Don't fret over that boy, he has the fastest ball of any man to ever throw one." Laughed Coach Bradley.

As Seth ripped fast ball after fast ball past the batters, the crowd was going wild, screaming, throw it, baby, throw it, make it a curve, aim the ball below the knee.

"He really does have more power in his arm than any pitcher I've seen; he's accurate too. Where is he from, Bradley?"

"North Carolina, small placed called Campton."

"Wonder if he would be interested in working for me this summer. He can be work-out man. Why haven't you told me about him, keeping your smug mouth shut?"

"Just wanted you to get a damn good look on your own. First time I saw him I got this feeling, well, it's hard to explain," said Bradley, "but I knew I had found a damn good ball pitcher if I could get him to sign up."

"So, you meant me to use him this summer, you crazy drabbletail," they both laughed.

It was a great game; not a single Florida runner reached home plate.

When the game was over, Seth raced off the field with his jubilant teammates. Once in the locker room he quickly showered and dressed and was about to leave when Coach Hardison walked in.

"May I have a minute with you, young man," he asked.

"Yes, Sir," replied Seth thinking, "Just so you make it fast."

"You don't know me."

"No, Sir."

"I'm Coach Hardison with the Ruthland National League. Coach Bradley told me you're Seth Kirby." They shook hands as Seth said, his interest quickening, "Yes, Sir, glad to meet you, Sir. What can I do for you?"

"I was wondering if you would be interested in working for me this summer."

"Yes, Sir, I would."

"I guess that is a straight enough answer."

"What would I do?" inquired Seth.

"Work out with the team. Fill in where you're needed and be a relief pitcher."

Seth worked hard that summer. The pay was small and the training was hard. He slipped home a week before school was to start. If I can only get a glimpse of Didge maybe I can make it until Christmas. It was as if someone had pulled the props out from under him when Roxie told him Miss Carroll was in Landridge. In fact, she had left on the same day he had left for school last fall.

"Don' let hit shock yo' so, she kin't sta' heah always," said Roxie watching his pained expression.

He left Roxie's and walked away. The weather was warm, but he felt a bit chilly. Without realizing it, he found himself moving along the riverbank to the quiet, private place that Didge called her thinking spot. The translucent water of the river was smooth and shimmering. He paused and looked at the tall giant trees along the bank and wondered if their roots ran inland or into the water. He walked over to her thinking stump and sat down. He had a maddening re-run of the scene that was etched in his soul of the way Didge looked at him. It was frozen there for eternity. "Nostalgia is not what I feel. I ache with love unfulfilled. Is she coming back or gone for good?" Like a flash he thought of the old man, "He will know." He rose and headed for Thankful's.

Seth paced back and forth in front of the

old man, his hands rammed down in his pockets.

"Sum'thang worrin' yo', boy?"

"You know there is. Is she coming back?"

"A'co'se she air."

"Any time soon?" asked Seth.

"Kin't say thet fo' shore, left fo' a yar' with Mistuh Kinyon, but gwine sta' longer, har' dey gwine hav' one ov dem art showins fo' her. I tol' yo' ter fergit dat gal, boy."

"Wish to God I could. I'm sure God had a purpose for everything he created, but why in the name of God did he mix us all up?"

"Face up boy, who don' de mixin' not God, jest don' blame him fer de mess folk find demselves 'n."

"You're right, of course. I sure do reveal myself in my true color at times."

"Son, de lawd ain't heah ter down yo' he's 'round ter help yo' iffen yo' lets him. He sho nuff kin't iffen yo' don' tek yo' mind offen dat gal."

*****

On the farm everyone was busy hoeing cotton. Em told Thankful to put Hyrum in charge of all the children old enough to kill a boll weevil or tobacco worm and to keep a record of each day's work. He also told Thankful that Hyrum was to work along with them.

"Yassuh, Thankful," grinned Hyrum when he received the message. Once in the field he took over.

"Alrite yo' chillums I am yawls boss. Yo' work or yo' don't git paid. Now git de worms offen dat cotton 'n watch fer eggs. See who kin kill de most."

"How we'ens kno' who kill de most, yo'

gwine count 'em," spoke one small voice.

"Sing songs, den."

"Who gwine brang us water?" spoke another small voice.

"Yo fill up fo' yo' start woek, den yo' go one-time ter git sum fo' dinnah den yo' fill up agin 'n go one time in the afternoon dats all. Now start workin' 'n singin'. I'll see yo' down yander at de end ov de row." Hyrum walked to the end of the field, sat down and leaned against a tree. He slept until the singing of the children awakened him.

  Sing holy hell ter wipe out evil
  De hot hot sand burns our feet
 As we'ens walk de rows 'n de sun's heat

  We'se makin' money ter buy sum shoes
 So's we'ens kin hav' 'em ter wear ter school
  We'se kinda thank we'ens mite be fools
  Ter work lak dis while Hyrum drools.

"Hit's nigh on ter impossible to kill all dem damn weevils," grumbled the children glaring at Hyrum. "We'se hared Thankful. Yo' supposed ter work wit us."

Hyrum began doing his work walking from one end of the field to the other. His nights out on raiding parties with Hezekiah left him with little energy to do more.

The first week of July they started cropping tobacco, handing and looping it on a stick to be hung in the barn. Lubby had worked in tobacco all his life before he married Patience and came to the Carroll farm to live. Em put him in charge of teaching the other men how to work and handle the tobacco. He then asked Lovie to help with the housework.

After dinner Em said he was going to walk out and see how Alonza was doing with the fire.

"I'll walk with you," said Miles leaving the table.

Alonza was going from barn to barn taking the night shift. Clay Golden would fire the barns during the day. Em was beginning to see where flue cured tobacco would be a nuisance to keep a constant heat. They talked with Alonza awhile.

"Remember not too hot, Alonza, we don't want to burn the tobacco," said Em as they left.

"Yassah Mistah Em, I'll tend hit rite."

Em had a porch covered the length of the old slave quarters for the women to sit under while grading and tying the cured tobacco.

It turned out to be the most productive season Em could remember. The earth's yield far surpassed anything he had ever dreamed of. "I love the earth it is so good," he thought as he looked out from the window of Didge's studio on the golden autumn of contentment. He turned and looked around the studio, everything orderly and in place. "Will she come back?" he wondered. "Yes, she will because Kinyon will bring her, but will she stay? Will I ever be forced to tell her the truth to make her stay or would the truth run her away? Dear God, who knows?" His eyes glistened with unshed tears as he left the room closing the door.

In October Em and Thankful started hauling the tobacco and cotton to the warehouse.

Em's prophecy proved true with the stock market crash the last of October 1929. He had sold the cotton and tobacco, with the cotton selling higher than in any year since 1920.

"Thankful if you will put a table and chair out under the big oak in the morning, I'll pay everyone at ten o'clock."

"Yassuh, Mistuh Carroll, I'll do thet 'n I'll let em know."

By nine o'clock the next morning Em was at the bank to draw out the money from the sale of the lumber.

Stephen was surprised. "Do you think it's safe to keep that money at home, Mr. Carroll?"

"I've got to pay the men and women for their summer's work."

"But you sold cotton and tobacco."

"I know, Stephen, just give me the cash in small bills. I know what I have to do."

"Yes, sir, if you say so."

At ten o'clock Em was at the table with his cigar box of money. Thankful started calling the names telling each one how many hours he had logged and what it amounted to.

*****

Meda walked the streets of New York, window shopping to pass the lonely days. Often, she walked in dress shops and tried on dresses with no real thought of buying. She had often been asked by sales ladies if she was a model. Suddenly the idea became implanted in her mind that she could become one. With Briant traveling for months at a time, it would fill the many lonely hours.

Her only friend, Milissa Hill, lived in the apartment across the hall from her. They had met one day when they bumped into each other on the steps of their apartment building, each with both arms loaded with bags of groceries.

"Go on," said Meda, "I'm not in that big of a hurry."

"Well, I am," snapped Milissa as she pushed ahead causing Meda to drop a bag of groceries.

"Oh, damn, can't you hold anything?"

"I was doing pretty well until you came along," Meda replied stonily.

"I'm sorry," she set her bags down. "I'll help you pick them up."

"No need to. I'll get them myself. Anyway, the bag split."

"I'll run up and get another one. Just wait a minute." She gathered up her own things and disappeared through the door.

"That's the end of her," thought Meda as she started picking up the tins of food trying to get them in with the other bag of groceries putting small items in her pockets thankful she had put on the navy dress with the big pockets that morning.

"You look deformed," laughed Milissa as she came through the door holding open a bag. "Here, empty your pockets."

"Lucky for me the glass of jelly and eggs were in the other bag," said Meda.

"Sorry I snapped at you. My only excuse is I'm tired. I'm Milissa Hill."

"I'm Meda Roberson," she smiled. "Thanks for bringing back the bag."

"That was the least I could do for being so rude. Here, I'll take that bag up for you."

"Oh, I can manage."

"Sure, you can. Come on, lead the way."

"You live here?" exclaimed Milissa when Meda stopped at her door.

"Sure, come on in for coffee. Where is your apartment?" Milissa just pointed two doors down the hall. They burst out laughing and a new friendship was born.

"You an artist?" asked Milissa looking at a painting on the wall.

"No, my sister did that of our home on the

farm down in North Carolina."

"What! You leave a home like that for this kind of living. Not that your apartment isn't nice, but…"

"But," interrupted Meda. "When you marry you make changes. Anyway, I never lived in that house. I married and left before the house was completed."

"Oh, a husband, huh," she wrinkled up her pert freckled nose, shook her short windblown hair, turned her short five-foot two inches frame around and headed for the door. "I'd better run. You've probably got to prepare dinner."

"No, no, he's out of town. A salesman. Please stay and tell me about yourself. I take it you aren't married."

"I was. It didn't work out."

"Oh, you share the apartment with another girl?"

"No, thank goodness. I can afford to live alone. I own a bookstore I inherited from my father."

"I'm sorry you lost your father. Where is your mother/"

"Passed away when I was fourteen. I am an only child. Do you have a family besides a husband and sister I mean?" Milissa asked.

"Yes, father, mother, two sisters, and two brothers. Lost the oldest brother in the war and the youngest sister is adopted, the artist." Said Meda as she nodded at the painting.

Milissa turned her slate blue eyes again to the painting.

"Come on, let's fix some supper. I mean dinner. See the country is still in me. And Milissa, home was not always like that." Meda turned and went into the kitchen. "Come on, you can help."

As they did the dishes, Meda asked, "What happened to your marriage? Of course, don't answer that if you don't want to."

"I don't mind. When we were married, I thought it would last forever. Inside of one year he went from a size thirty-eight suit to a forty-eight. I started spending every night climbing a hill to stay on my side of the bed. When I did get to sleep, he would wake me up telling me to get my knees out of his back. I asked for twin beds and he wouldn't hear of it. Then when I got the bookstore and was making twice as much as he did, he was jealous and started drinking. When I said anything he would say, 'you make plenty and don't need my money; any smart woman like you can take care of one man.' Things got worse and worse until I hated to go home, and I was always tired. Then he quit his job. He just sat around eating and drinking and getting fatter until I finally exploded and moved out."

"That was rough. Haven't you seen him since?" Meda asked.

"He came to the bookstore full of promises. When that didn't work, he begged and pleaded. Then he threatened to burn the store."

"Didn't that frighten you?"

"I'm not sure. I just told him to go ahead then I'd collect the insurance and go to Europe like I've always wanted to."

"That was fast thinking, or did you really want to go to Europe?"

"I'd never given it a thought, but found it wasn't a bad idea in case he did do it."

Meda had told Milissa about Briant as they ate. Now Milissa asked, "Meda, isn't it hard on you being alone so much?"

"I get very lonesome, so I walk and window shop, sleep late, go to bed early and listen to the radio or read."

"I think we should go to the movies one evening," suggested Milissa. "How about next week?"

"It's a date if Briant doesn't come home." They saw several shows before Briant returned a month later.

He was depressed. Sales hadn't gone too well. Meda tried to cheer him.

"Maybe the depression will end soon and things will get better," Meda encouraged.

"I only hope we can save the factory. It would help if we moved out to the house and saved this rent."

"Why didn't you live out there before we were married?" Meda wanted to know.

"It wasn't necessary then; I had plenty," he said, impatience creeping into his voice. "We haven't the means to live here much longer and we'll be forced to move out there. You may as well make up your mind. The sooner the better."

Briant had met Milissa and liked her. He was glad that Meda had a friend her own age. He knew she was lonesome. He loved her and found it hard to be stern with her. His time at home was always so short that all he wanted to do was make love. "Why can't I feel like he seems to and respond to his love making. He's good-looking, very sweet to me, even Milissa jokingly said she could almost envy me. Only she is sour on men."

Meda was glad when Briant left again. His long goodbye was beginning to bore her and she teasingly pushed him out the door before she could find herself back in the bedroom.

The idea that had lain dormant in her mind the past few weeks surfaced and became so active she ran to Milissa's apartment as soon as she heard her open her door that evening.

"Something wrong or right?" Milissa asked noticing the excited look on Meda's face.

"Right, I hope. Briant wants me to move out to his parent's home."

"You call that right?"

"No, no, I don't want to, so I'm going to look for a job so I can pay the rent."

"What can you do?" Milissa asked. "Can you sew dresses in his father's factory? Are you a secretary? Have you had any training of any kind?"

"No, no and no. Oh, I had a year of commercial, but I thought I would try for a modeling job." Then she told Milissa about the comments of the sales ladies in dress hops.

Milissa's face showed doubt, then she said, "With this depression on, you'll be very lucky to find any kind of work. I'd suggest you try the factory. With the commercial training you could learn office work and they could let the secretary they have go and keep it all in the family, as the saying goes."

"Work with them, live with them, no, Milissa, I'd feel smothered."

"Would you like to work at the bookstore part-time? I've been thinking of hiring someone part-time."

"Is business that good?" Meda wanted to know.

"Surprisingly, yes. It seems that people don't have the money for a lot of entertaining, the movies or the theater. A book lasts much longer than any of them, so they are reading more."

"Thanks, Milissa, but I would still like to try my luck at modeling."

"All I can do is wish you luck then."

Early the next morning when Meda got up,

she dressed very carefully, and left the apartment with high hopes. She went from one agency to another, dreams slowly crumbling. She was about to give up when she walked timidly into Sumner's Model Agency. Just inside the door she hesitated and looked around. No one was in the room. Comfortable looking white velvet chairs were placed attractively around the room. The floor was carpeted in a deep rich green, with drapes the same shade at the two windows at the end of the long room. A mahogany desk and chair were placed near a door on the far side of the room, with tables and lamps placed at intervals among the chairs. Beautiful paintings of landscapes and still life adorned the walls. She found the room cool and attractive not at all like the offices of the other agencies.

She stood there wondering if she should leave, when the door across the room opened and a girl walked over to the desk. She looked up as she sat down, and seeing Meda, smiled. Meda thought her pretty even with her dark brown hair in a bun and glasses over her pretty eyes.

"May I help you?"

Meda decided that this was nineteen thirty instead of eighteen thirty and as the Grimke sisters had done, she too would speak out. With some effort she got her tongue out of her cheek and said, as she walked forward smiling, "I hope so; I came to find out about a job as a model."

"Well, we have plenty of girls, but I don't do the hiring. You'd have to see Mr. Sumner and he's tied up at the present time." Meda took a seat to wait.

The door burst open and in walked one of the most attractive, handsome men Meda had ever seen. He spoke to the secretary, Onedia, "Get one of the girls over to Harris Studio within the

SILENT TEARS

hour. One with good hands. They have to do a handcream ad."

"Mr. Sumner, you know every girl is out on assignment except Liddia and her fingers are too short and stubby for such an ad." Sumner groaned.

Onedia looked at her own hands. "Nope, won't do. Say," she pointed the pencil she was holding toward Meda, who was walking toward them, thankful she had polished her nails that morning wiping the tips clean and leaving perfect moons.

"This young lady just came in looking for work," Onedia said.

"One thing for sure I don't want to hire another girl," he thought as he turned from the desk and saw Meda walking toward him smiling, her hands outstretched. "What a crazy business," she thought. He thought, "What beautiful hands, the kind you'd like to have caress you." Then he looked at her face. "Beautiful too in a country fresh way." His quick mind was working, "Maybe I could use her this once and then say she won't do."

"What are your measurements?" he asked matter-of-factly.

She blushed and hesitated.

"These are routine questions if you want to be a model," said Sumner starting to turn away.

"Thirty-seven, twenty-three, thirty-four, Sir."

"Humm, is that dressed or undressed?" Sumner asked.

"Undressed, Sir."

"Where are you from?" he asked having noticed her accent.

"Campton, North Carolina, Sir."

"Sure wish you had worn your best clothes, but guess you'll do since it's just for hands."

"But this," Meda stopped, it's not any of

his business that this is my best dress.

"Yes, you were saying?" he raised a quizzical eyebrow.

"It was nothing, Sir."

"Do you think you can get over to the Harris Studio? It's only three blocks down the street. Here's our card and their card." Picking up the cards from the desk he handed them to Meda.

"When you're finished come back here for your pay of ten dollars."

"Yes, Sir." Meda smiled at Onedia and left.

Ward Sumner threw his hands to the ceiling in a gesture something like despair. "Why does she want to work. Doesn't look like she needs it."

"Sure, I don't know," replied Onedia.

At the studio Meda was looking at in wide-eyed wonder as she walked in. Harris broke away from a group and walked over to her. Without a word she handed him the cards.

"What's with Sumner this afternoon, Richard?" Harris spoke toward the group.

"Handcream ad," called out a short stout man in his early thirties.

"The man called Richard might be tall if his legs were as long as his body," thought Meda.

Harris was speaking again, "Give these back to Ward when you return to the agency." He was careful to look at her hands as he handed her the cards.

"Yes, Sir."

Harris continued to watch her hands as she placed the cards in her purse.

"You have a name?" he asked.

"Yes, Sir, Meda Roberson."

"Just call me Harris. Everyone else does. Rose," he called out. When the tall thin woman appeared, he said, "Take Miss Roberson…"

"It's," Meda started to say, it's Mrs. but again she fell silent. Maybe they didn't hire married women, she thought.

"Prepare her for the whole."

"Yes, Sir," said Rose. "Come with me, Miss Roberson." Meda followed the thin woman. She was tall, her eyes seemed to be colorless, but Meda was to learn she had a heart of pure gold.

They entered a room full of costumes, mirrors, and tables full of makeup. Rose went to a rack and looked at several dresses choosing a deep yellow one with a square neckline. It was a little lower than Meda liked, but she allowed Rose to pin her into it anyway.

Harris put his head in the door, "Let the hair down, Rose," the door closed.

"Does he do things like that when girls are dressing?" asked Meda.

"Oh, he's like a doctor. He pays no attention to a half-dressed girl."

"I sure care. He has no right to do that."

Rose was pleased that Meda had some modesty. She could see that the girl was not the usual run of girls around there, and she liked that.

As Harris walked away from the door, he thought, "She's a lovely creature, yet she seems so sad."

A few minutes later Rose led Meda back to the studio. Her hair fell softly around her shoulders. Harris' fast eye took in the cascade of hair, face, curve of her breast and hips. All feminine. What a good model she'll make.

"Miss Roberson, walk over to that table, pick up the jar of cream and say, "sit on my lap."

"Whatever for," she broke out laughing,

relaxing. Her eyes caught the lights and sparkled like mischievous agate. "That lucky son of a gun Sumner gets all the beauties. I would snap her up if he didn't already have her," thought Harris.

"Miss Roberson, the words will help your facial expression. Say the words over and over, silently if you like as you pick up the cream, open the jar, take out some cream and rub gently into your hands. Then hold your hands in front of you as if you are admiring them while Richard takes pictures."

He found her to be natural, poised and ingenious. Turning to Richard he said, "When you finish the hand cream do the shampoo ad while she's here."

"But I thought that was to be done by…"

Cutting in, Harris snorted, "Never mind what you thought, use her." He walked to his office entered and closed the door. Boy, oh boy, Harris rubbed the palms of his hands together and reached for the phone. The operator cut in on his thoughts.

"Number please."

He drummed his fingers on the desk while he waited for Sumner's voice.

"Ward, Harris here, I just wanted to know where you found her?"

"What in the devil are you talking about?" Sumner's voice had an edge to it.

"Miss Roberson, of course." Harris' voice had just as much edge to it.

"Oh," guess I'd better play this by ear, Sumner thought, puzzled. "She's from some small place in North Carolina. If she isn't satisfactory send her back and I'll send another girl. I just thought she would be perfect."

"Perfect? Man, she's terrific, a natural, just wish I had found her first."

He listened to Ward a minute, then, "Yes, I know I don't usually hire girls, but I would like this one in a minute if you didn't already have her."

"Dear God," thought Ward, I hope she didn't say she hasn't signed a contract with me.

"Listen, Ward, I'm doing a shampoo ad while she's here. How about sending her back tomorrow for a face cream and jewelry ad."

"Hunky-dory, if you want her."

"Want her, by cracky, I'd marry her if I wasn't already married."

Ward shook his head as he hung up the phone. "Damn, sounds like she could be very hot property. She could free-lance if she comes on that strong with Harris. I'd better take another look at that girl."

"Onedia," Ward yelled, "Onedia."

"Yes, Mr. Sumner," she walked slowly into his office.

"Get some axle grease in your rump and move, girl," snapped Ward.

"Yes, Sir, cream puff."

"And cut that out. Listen, have a contract ready for that Miss Roberson when she returns. Make it a long term one and send her in here with it signed."

"If you say so."

"I do say so now move." Her dejected look made him speak quickly. "Sorry Onedia, I didn't mean to speak sharply, but if I don't grab that girl fast, Harris will. I only hope he will keep thinking I've got her signed up."

"So that's it."

"Yep, just have that contract ready."

Ward was young, impatient, demanding and forceful. His drive was felt by all those associated with him.

Three hours later Meda walked into his office. It was much like the outer office only a row of file cabinets was against the end wall and the colors in the room were softer. A framed photograph of a lovely girl set on the desk.

Ward was watching her. Her hair, now down, seemed to float as she glided across the room. "Why didn't I notice it before? She's ideal, the perfect type. She will be one hell of a beautiful model." Meda was eyeing the photograph on his desk.

"Your wife?" she asked.

"Was, she's dead. Childbirth five years ago; the baby was lost too."

"So sorry, I wasn't trying to pry."

Ward held out his hand for the contract. "Did you sign this?" He asked while reading the information Onedia had typed in.

"No," answered Meda.

"Maybe you'd better if you want to be a model." He held out a pen to her.

She hesitated.

"Well, are you going to sign?"

"That depends on how much I'll make."

"Oh, here's your ten dollars for today," Ward said. Opening a drawer, he took out a ten dollar bill and handed it to her.

"This is for the handcream ad. I also did a shampoo ad while there. Mr. Harris said he called you about it."

"Smart ass woman," the thought, taking another ten dollars from the drawer and handing it to her.

"Satisfied?"

"Not really."

"All right, I'll pay you top rates."

"Put that on the contract then I'll sign."

As she signed, he said, "I see you're a

Virgo."

"How did you know?...Oh, my birthdate."

"Girls shouldn't be virgins you know."

"And why not?"

"It sounds too pure. And what girls want to be one?"

"I'm afraid a lot of them do. Me for one."

"Guess I'll have to go easy with this one," he thought as he watched her leave.

Once inside her apartment Meda leaned against the door thinking, "I've got a job, I've got a job, imagine me with a job." She danced around the room taking the twenty dollars out of her pocketbook. Fun money. A knock at the door startled her into dropping the money. She watched it float to the floor.

"Meda," called Milissa.

"Come on in," Meda grabbed the door and opened it.

"That radiant look says you got a job but is that the reason to throw money around." Teased Milissa.

"I dropped it. I'll take you to supper to celebrate." She paused and took a deep breath. "Well, aren't you going to ask me about my job?"

"I already know. It's modeling." They both broke out in a big laugh.

Milissa asked, "What is your boss like?"

"Very tall, blond curly hair that insists on falling down on his forehead. He's really a giant of a man with sea blue-green eyes. He looks all right."

"He sounds yummy."

"You know something, Milissa, when he looked into my eyes, I felt stripped. I'm sure he was seeing all the way to my toes," Meda looked flushed.

Milissa felt concern for her friend, "Tread

carefully, Meda, a man like that can be dangerous."

"I'll be careful, but a man like that would never notice me."

Meda worked like a bubble that wouldn't burst, enjoying every minute of it. She was exquisitely sensitive to all around her, trying to please. She was sure she was right to take the job and was happy in it, and happiness she wanted.

Ward arranged to have her work late to give him an excuse for asking her out to dinner. She always had an excuse. Dinner probably wouldn't hurt, but he'd expected to take her home afterward and that could never happen. She couldn't have him coming to the apartment. She'd have to explain Briant's things laying around very much in evidence. No one had asked and she would never volunteer her marital status, they might fire her.

Ward's insistence was wearing her down and it frightened her. She wondered if he was a scoundrel who would back an innocent girl into a corner and try to take advantage of her. "Mama has always warned me there were such men, that I should always keep a man at arm's length to be on the safe side. I must remember that."

Ward dropped in to see Harris one day while Meda was modeling a swimsuit. It was molded to her figure like skin. He felt his skin prickle sending a tingling sensation through his whole being. She was turning slowly in front of an ocean backdrop when she saw him watching her. She became conscious of a new feeling, not an unpleasant one, but an excited nameless one. It was like the feelings she had on a real hot day and someone tempted her with a tall frosted glass of lemonade with mint leaves floating on top.

"I don't care how we pose her, she always comes out looking good." Harris shook his head. "It's unbelievable, only one in a lifetime comes along like that."

"Yep," said Ward indifferently.

"You want to sell her contract?" asked Harris.

"Nope."

"Then what in hell's wrong with you?"

"Who in hell said anything was wrong with me." Glared Ward.

With a little laugh, Harris said, "What's the matter, old boy, did she tell you no?"

"Damn you, Harris, I haven't asked her anything." He stomped out of the room, "but I will and I'll have her too," he swore to himself.

When Meda reported back to the studio, Ward was waiting.

"I'm taking you to dinner and you needn't say no." After dinner he asked if she'd like to go to a movie.

"No, Mr. Sumner, I'd better go home."

"All right, I'll take you home then."

"Oh, no. A taxi will do."

"I said I'd take you home," Ward said firmly.

"No, Mr. Sumner, you can't do that. You…you see, I live with a young girl who is a partial invalid and when I've tried to date she is so unreasonable. Her jealousy is unbearable. She can't go out on dates and have fun and can't stand to see anyone else enjoy themselves."

"Then move out."

"I can't. Her mother pays the rent for me to stay with her while she is in Europe."

"Then how do you manage to work?"

"She can get around on crutches a little, even that is hard on her. She doesn't think of work as pleasure. I just stopped dating and don't allow any fellows to go there, and things are pretty peaceful."

"All right, Meda," He hailed a taxi and kissed her lightly as he helped her in. She waved goodbye and settled back. The lies had started. She was surprised how easy it had been. She was beginning to see herself in magazines and wondered what Briant would say or think if he saw one.

"Aren't you afraid your success will cause the other girls to talk about you?" asked Milissa one day.

"No, why should they? I don't criticize them so why should they say things to hurt me?"

"One's worst enemy often turns out to be the one they thought to be their best friend. They know too much about you. You should never let the right foot know what step the left one is about to make." Milissa said seriously.

"I'll remember that, Milissa."

"Remember too that you have stepped into a jealous, self-centered, selfish world 'n baby hit ain't lak hit wuz down on de farm," laughed Milissa trying to mimic the southern drawl.

*****

Kinyon had arranged an art showing during the holiday season for Didge, soon after Mrs. Howard announced she had taken Didge as far as possible. "I think she can teach me now," she had laughed adding, "She will work on one subject with different light and shading quickly avoiding reality if it's weak in substance or too subtle. She's a very talented and gifted unusual girl. She should go to France and study."

They wrote Em and Lukatie they would bring

Didge home on New Year's Day instead of Christmas. She had been gone a year and a half. Em never mentioned her absence and no reference to it was made by Miles or Lukatie.

Miles wrote, inviting Julia to come for the holidays. "Please come help liven up our home and lift my spirits," he pleaded. "Since Christmas falls on Sunday, I could drive up over the weekend for you. Didge will be home New Year's and you will get to see her. I've driven up a couple of times to see her, but Mama never goes. She never leaves here. Aunt Jane has pleaded with her to go for a visit, but Mama says Campton is far enough away from home."

Julia was happy to accept the invitation. Life with her Aunt and Uncle was stale. It took patience and endurance to live the oppressed, suffocating, choked life within which she found herself. They were completely lacking in interest in political or religious affairs. They were inactive and dull, any small joke floated over their heads as if to laugh was an overstrain.

"If he asks me one more time to marry him, I will," she thought. The boys didn't need her anymore. Lewis was out of school and gone. Jacob had finished school last June and was working. Her Uncle had managed to keep his job through the depression even at a large cut in salary. "I've helped the boys now to help myself," Julia thought as she wrote accepting the invitation.

Lukatie met them at the door, "Oh, Julia, Julia, let me look at you. It's been so long. How happy I am to see you."

"And I you," Julia smiled as they embraced. Turning to Em, "I shall hug you too," she declared as she laughed happily.

"Julia, I think of you so often. Are you all right now, dear? I mean does coming back here bother you?" asked Lukatie.

"I don't think so. Miles once told me time and youth were on my side and I believe he may be right. I hardly realized I was passing the old place a few minutes ago. All the building Miles has done on the ch…store, and the house gone, it's like a completely different place. I can't connect it with that horrible nightmare anymore."

"I'm so glad," said Lukatie.

As usual the holidays were warm and quiet for Lukatie. Miles and Julia were on the go all the time and Em was outside or reading. How they found so many places to go she didn't know. Lukatie stood by the azalea bush absent-mindedly picking out the dead oak leaves that had bedded down to spend a restful winter among its evergreen leaves and thought of tomorrow when Kinyon would bring Didge home. It would be New Year's Eve. She was glad there would be life and people in the big house again. She hadn't found the joy in the Blue Bird she had hoped for. Comforts and the feeling of security were here but would gladly give these up to have Em back as he was in the early days of their marriage.

Lukatie looked up when she heard the mailman stopping at the box, and started to walk the curved drive just as he turned in to stop beside her.

"A telegram for you, Mrs. Carroll. Sure hope it isn't bad news."

"Thank you, I hope it isn't, but they've always been a bad omen to me."

She watched him drive on around the curved driveway in his old secondhand model T Ford and thought of the years he had delivered mail in a horse drawn buggy. As she looked down at the telegram, she felt a cold chill spread through her body. Oh, dear God, not Lucinda, too. They had heard of the earthquake in central China over the radio and read of it in the papers. They had been so hopeful it had not been in the section Lucinda was in. "It was, it was oh, I just know it was," she thought as she rushed into the house.

"Em, Em," she called her voice breaking. He came from his study.

"Here," she handed the unopened telegram to him. "I just can't open it. I don't need to."

"Calm down, dear, you aren't sure what is in it." He opened it and read. He felt so inadequate to comfort her. "Two of our children are gone, but she went through the pain of bringing them into the world, and would feel the loss more, if that's possible."

"You're right," he sighed tensely as he put his arms around her. "There is no trace of her or three other nuns." Their hearts were melted in grief, but Lukatie didn't faint this time as she had when Benjamin was killed. Lukatie had the feeling she had already suffered the loss of Lucinda once. Lukatie knew Lucinda was unhappy, and had she lived a long life, it would have been a sad one. "Please, dear God, let our girl be happy now," moaned Lukatie.

The next day when Kinyon and Jane came to bring Didge home, their joyous expressions fell as they saw the sadness etched on the faces of those within the house.

"Oh, Mama, something is wrong," cried Didge as she hugged Lukatie.

"What's wrong, Papa?" she asked over her mother's shoulder.

"It's Lucinda, she was lost in the earthquake in China. We just received word yesterday. She and three other nuns just swallowed up in the earth." Didge continued to hug her mother as she held out a hand to Miles and Julia, then looking at Em she just said, "Papa," and buried her head in Lukatie's shoulder and cried.

Kinyon and Jane went to Em and embraced him, then to Miles and Julia.

"Carlton didn't come?" asked Miles.

"No, he was married two days before Christmas and they are off to Europe on their honeymoon. It was so fast we didn't have time to notify anyone."

"We had no idea he was even serious about anyone," said Em.

"The girl, did you know her?" asked Lukatie gaining some composure.

"Yes, we did. That is the funny part about it. We've known the family. For years she and Carlton have fought each other, then all of a sudden Carlton asked her to a dance about two months ago and came home with the most puzzled look on his face. We asked him if anything was wrong, and he just laughed and said, no fighting. They continued seeing each other. Then three days before Christmas Carlton walked in and said "We're getting married tomorrow." The minister from their church came over and with just the two families present they were married in their living room. That's the whole story," said Kinyon.

"The old son of a gun," laughed Miles, glad that the news had gotten their minds away from Lucinda.

Didge gave them one of the paintings left from the showing. "All but two sold. We're so proud of her," Jane said.

"All of you can be proud of her, she's good," Kinyon said smiling.

"We are and we thank you for all you've

done for her," exclaimed Lukatie.

That evening as Miles and Julia left the movie the lights from the marquee added sparkle to Julia's hair to match the sparkle in her eyes.

"You look lovely," Miles said as he took her arm, "Come on it's time we talked."

He drove along silently until he reached the road he turned into once before when he proposed to Julia. He turned in again and brought the car to a stop.

Julia had on an oxford gray sport coat with the collar turned up at the back of her neck. Miles reached over and took hold of the tip of the collar and pulled her over to him dropping his arm around her shoulder. With his left hand he gently touched her chin turning her face up to his kissing her gently.

"Julia."

"Yes, Miles."

"You know I love you, but I'm only going to ask you once more to marry me. Will you?"

"That's putting it on the line, isn't it?" She turned her face away as if weighing the thought from deep within, then looked back at Miles.

"Ask me twice, I may say yes."

A fiery feeling engulfed him.

"Julia," he said, impatience edged his voice. "This isn't the first time and it isn't necessary to ask again, you aren't hard of hearing."

"You really won't ask again?"

"No, I'll look for someone else. There's a cute little filly over…" Miles laughed as he reached into his pocket and drew out a small box.

"You'll accept this, I hope."

Opening the box, the moonlight glittered on the diamond within.

"It looks like cold ice. I think it will be warmer on my finger," smiled Julia.

She handed Miles the box and held out her finger.

"Will you set a date, darling, soon I hope."

"Won't you have to build first?"

"Nope, we can stay at the Blue Bird. That way you can supervise the building of your home."

"With this depression can you afford to build?"

"Believe it or not this depression has hardly touched us. Thanks to the wisdom of my father, I'm not broke. Now while labor and materials are cheap will be the best time to build. Now set a date, please."

"You won't do, Miles."

"Give me a chance and I will."

He chuckled as he grabbed her and kissed her. One hand slid down to rub the small of her back. He kissed the nape of her neck as her head fell over on his shoulder. She felt a quickening within her that was frightening.

"Don't," she cried, and tried to pull away from him. He turned her lips back to his placing a hand on her knee as he gently caressed it.

"Stop," she said, pulling away again.

"Stop it now! We'll be married next week. No, tomorrow, but until we are, I have to live in your parent's home and I won't live there in shame."

"I'm not going to hurt you, darling. Don't you know I love you and have wanted you for years. Julia, there's no shame in love."

"There is shame in the act before marriage. Let's go tell your parents. Miles, they might not want me for a daughter." Julia tried to laugh, but it was plain she was shaken and trembling.

They rode home silently.

"Miles, are you mad at me?" asked Julia as they drove into the yard. "I hope not. I want your love and your respect."

"Having you now would not cause me to disrespect you. I'm proud of you. I know you were right to stop me when you did. Satisfied? Come on let's tell the folks."

Everyone was sitting around talking about farming or the operation of the Mill, because there was little else to talk about, unless you include the weather and since it was here to stay and only changed its temperament or temperature, there was little to be said about it. Kinyon was talking when Miles and Julia walked in.

"Think we will get any snow this winter?"

"If we do the bright glow on those two faces will soon melt it," said Em.

Miles took Julia by the hand leading her into the middle of the room. Holding out her hand, he said, "I finally got her to say yes." Miles looked at Julia and winked, "That is if Papa and Mama will accept her as a daughter."

Julia burst out laughing as Lukatie jumped up, "gladly," she said as she hugged Julia.

"Guess I get to play clerk in the hardware store while you go on a honeymoon," said Em.

"If you don't mind, Papa."

"I don't mind just so you get it over with before planting season."

"How does next Friday morning suit you. Then we'll leave for places unknown," Miles said with emphasis.

They all laughed. Kinyon and Jane congratulated them and went upstairs to bed. Didge had gone to her room earlier to unpack and put her things away. She had taken her art supplies to her studio then stood at the window and looked out at the Heath place for a long time. "I want to see him so bad it hurts." She heard voice and turned to go down to her room. Miles and Julia were standing at the door of the room that would have been Meda's had she stayed home until the Blue Bird was finished.

"I'm walking her to her room to make sure she doesn't slip away during the night. I think I'll lock her in," teased Miles.

"Gosh, it's good to have you home, Sis." He held out an arm to her the other one was around Julia's shoulder.

"Congratulate us, Julia has said yes." Didge squealed with delight as she hugged them.

"I'm so glad, so happy for you both," said Didge.

When they were alone Miles said, "Julia, you know you haven't said you love me."

She turned her face up to his.

"The words you mean. Oh, Miles, I didn't think, that is, I thought acceptance of the ring said it." She threw her arms around his neck. "Oh, Miles, I do love you. I think I did when I was living here. I just had to be away to know it and know how much. Yes, I love you."

"Then say it every day, I'll never tire of hearing it."

When they returned from their honeymoon, they gave a travelogue of their trip.

"We decided to go south since there would most likely be snow on the highways in the north. Imagine my surprise when I was called by name in this five and ten cent store in Jacksonville, Florida," said Miles.

"Well, who was it?" asked Didge excitedly.

"I'm getting to that. This strange man, at least I thought he was a stranger, walked up to us. You are Miles Carroll, aren't you? I said yes, still not recognizing him. Then he said, "I'm Fountain Rue." We shook hands, I told him I was sorry I didn't recognize him. To shorten the story, he was transferred there about a year after Lucinda left him. He never did get the divorce papers, he said. Somehow, I couldn't believe they weren't sent on to him. We told him about her becoming a nun and her death. I thought he was going to start crying standing right there in the middle of the store," Miles said.

"I guess he never did get over Lucinda," said Lukatie.

"He looked awful," said Julia. "Like a broken, self-condemned old man."

"Well, dear, we'd better get our things up to our room," Miles said, turning to Julia.

"I've fixed the guest room for you since it's large," said Lukatie.

"Thanks, Mama," said Julia. "I may call you Mama now? I always wanted to."

"I wouldn't have it any other way," smiled Lukatie.

"And?" Julia turned to Em.

"Papa, please," Em answered her unvoiced question.

Julia went to Didge and hugged her. "How wonderful to have a sister again," she said.

Julia loved staying at the Blue Bird and was in no hurry to start building their own house. She turned down plan after plan. In desperation Miles told her she must make up her mind or they wouldn't have time to build before Papa needed the men to farm. Then it would be in the fall before they could start.

"Good," Julia had replied. "That will give us plenty of time to find just the right house." In a house of her own she would have to cook and clean; here it was all done for her. She loved this lazy life and meant to hold on to it as long as possible.

One night in February as Didge turned out her bedroom light, she noticed a white glow of light that seemed to sparkle like fairyland as it danced over her room reflecting through the window and across the floor. How light it looks. She got out of bed and walked to window. One of the rare snows was falling softly disturbing no one, covering the earth in all its brilliance. Excitedly she grabbed her robe.

"It's snowing, it's snowing, so beautiful," she called out as she ran down the stairs. "There's a big beautiful new world outside all fluffy white." Everyone gathered on the porch to see this rare new night almost as bright as day. They stood in silence watching the soft flakes drift slowly to earth. What words would be said to compare with so much beauty.

The next day everyone was out enjoying it, making snowmen, throwing snowballs, faces were washed in it and snowcream was in the making to satisfy the palate.

Didge was busy laying in the dark colors of her canvas, then put dabs of white, blue and yellow for sparkle and light with a touch of red for warmth on her palette to paint this world she so seldom saw. In all of her life she could barely remember two or three light snows.

If anything, it was always freezing rain that made the tree limbs heavy with ice, breaking them so they would thunder to the ground and break into splinters to rot during the long hot summers.

*****

Didge came in loaded with art materials

which she took directly to her studio. "It sure is a beautiful cool spring day," she remarked to Em and Lukatie when she came back downstairs. "A lot of people were in town. Campton really is a place of pastoral beauty, so quiet and clean. I'm glad Miles took me in with him. I saw Leroy Wilson. He asked me to the movie with him. I'd like to go if it's all right."

"It isn't all right and you may not go," stated Em flatly.

"Why shouldn't she?" asked Lukatie.

"I've told you before she's not to go out with that boy and I mean it."

"I think I'm old enough to take care of myself. I do know right from wrong. Don't you think I want a full life? I'm old enough and ready for love and marriage like Miles and Julia, and Meda, yet you won't even let me date. Why? Is there something wrong with me? I feel like I'm in a prison, in fact, I'd rather be in one. I'd have more freedom."

They were forced to appraise each other as though they were complete strangers. The father, the daughter who knew not to be a daughter only by adoption. A fire burned warmly in the huge fireplace. In spite of the warmth, Didge felt a shiver of the unknown. She left the room. Perhaps she could run away from the feeling. A miasma of self-pity filled her as she left the house and started walked to the river. She seemed to be born into a world of perpetual loneliness.

Walking along slowly she thought, "I know absolutely by heart every hole and root on this path." She was trying hard to keep her mind off the things that were probably being said between Em and Lukatie. "I'll never mention a date again and one day I will leave here." She vowed.

*****

It was a pleasant morning in May when Didge walked the curving driveway to the mailbox. The early blooming flowers made the air smell so sweet. She found a letter addressed to herself and one to the family from Meda.

"Who in the world can be writing to me," she wondered. "Maybe someone wants a painting or portrait done. How nice it would be to have a friend writing me. An honest-to-goodness true friend I could share secrets with. Huh! I have no secrets. But we could talk, talk and exchange ideas. It would be so wonderful." Walking into the house, she handed Lukatie the letter from Meda. Laying down her knitting, Lukatie opened the letter.

"A carriage cover," exclaimed Didge. "Could it be that Julia is expecting."

"Not that I know of, just anyone that I might need to give a gift to. It will soon be too hot to bother with yarns," said Lukatie as she started to read the letter.

"Well, Meda has been working as a model for some time now. Said she had a chance of this job and took it since she was so lonesome with Briant away so much. You haven't opened your letter, dear."

"So, I haven't." She carefully tore off the corner of the letter, slipped out the single sheet and read it.

"Dear Miss Carroll. At a recent team social, I met a Mr. Bush, a publisher. He explained the meeting saying he had orders from Coach Bradley to attend. People like that…good publicity for the team…so be there…I went." As Didge read, she noticed his beautiful bold handwriting and thought of the scratches in the sand of their childhood play. She read on. "He needs someone to do illustrations for the books he publishes. I told him as much as I knew about your work. He was interested so here is his card. If you are interested, drop him a note to set up an appointment. You're to pick out five books you've read and do an illustration on each as you think it should be done for the jacket of the books that will attract attention and get more sales. You might be interested in knowing that once you have the interview and get the job, you can work at home and mail it in."

The note was short and to the point and signed, "Regards, Seth."

Didge handed the letter to Lukatie. When she finished reading, she looked at Didge. "Do you want to set up the appointment and go to New York?"

"I'd love to try, but I don't know if my work would measure up to what they want. Papa wouldn't let me anyway."

"I'll speak to him. Suppose you let him read this note from Seth. This is a great opportunity for you. You have enough money for the trip from the portraits you've done and all those paintings you sold at the art showing in Landridge. You could stay with Meda."

"Mama, you'll have to sell Papa on the idea, he's the one that never lets me do anything."

Lukatie's pride in Didge was unbounding. She wondered if Didge's mother had been a talented artist. She felt sure that her father was not. A thought that never failed to deaden her nervous system and start the painful headaches. She took a couple of aspirin and went to talk with Em.

"What's this?" he asked, as she handed him

the letter.

"Read it and see."

After he read it, he sat thinking for a few minutes. "How long will she be gone?" he finally asked.

"Not more than a week or ten days. She can stay with Meda."

Didge walked timidly into Em's study.

"When will you be leaving?" he asked her.

Didge dropped into a chair, shock written all over her face.

"I'd have to write for an appointment and do all of that work."

"Then get started on it so you can get back. No need wasting that fine room upstairs."

"Thank you, Papa," she smiled at Lukatie and rose to leave the room. Oh, how she wanted to hug and embrace them both in thanks.

At the door she turned, with an expectant smile on her face.

"All right if I look at the books here in your study to see if there are any published by Bush Publishing Company?" she asked.

"Sure go ahead," said Em.

Didge wrote to Mr. Bush and started working on the illustrations. As she worked, she became dubious and was living in a private dour of doubt.

"Calm down, honey, relax, you can't reach that destiny by imperfect preparations. Do the best you can and stop worrying," said Lukatie one day.

"Suppose he doesn't like my illustrations and I do all this work and take the trip for nothing," said Didge.

"Stop worrying about all of these uncertainties and go to New York to see this publisher. You'll never know if he likes your work if he never sees it," answered Lukatie.

"Of course, you're right, Mama."

Misfortune of birth, renewed faith in herself and determination to succeed teamed up to drive Didge to her work on the five paintings. She realized how nervous she had been since hearing from Mr. Bush.

Meda read the note from Didge and ran down the hall to Milissa's.

"Here, read this. My sister is coming."

"So, I get to meet the artist at last."

"Yes, in two weeks like she said. I can hardly wait." Meda danced around the room happily.

"You really have missed her, haven't you?"

"Oh, yes, I've missed all the family," Meda said quietly.

"Then why haven't you been to see them, or they to see you?"

"I hadn't thought of going. As for the family, they just don't care to travel. Mama says Campton is far enough away from home."

"How far is that?"

"Oh, walking distance," laughed Meda. "Well, I've got to run. I have to work tonight."

"Oh."

"Some fashions for a department store that they want done after hours when the store is empty."

"Sounds crazy."

"Yep, but they pay plenty for it, so here goes." She rushed to her room to bathe and dress carefully. Then went to the department store.

Ward was there with Harris as picture after picture was taken.

When they finished Ward said, "Come on, Miss Roberson, after all that work you deserve a good dinner."

"Thank you, Mr. Sumner, but I'd better hurry home to Milissa. She might need something."

"I'm sure she has had her dinner by now and can wait a few more minutes. Come on now," Ward urged. "It won't take long to eat."

Meda ate slowly. She enjoyed her frequent dinners with Ward more than she was willing to admit even to herself. Glancing up from her plate, she found him watching her. The look in their eyes was not just the glance of one person at another, it was flashes charged of deep desire. A tingle passed through her again as it had in the studio. She had felt it many times since, only this time it reached deep within her.

"Meda, this might come as a surprise to you, but I love you, and I think it's time we talked. I can't help thinking you have some feeling for me too," said Ward.

"Why would you think that?" Meda gasped.

"The way you fight being with me as if you're afraid to. Yet when you're forced you seem to enjoy it, and the look in your eyes when they meet mine."

Meda had a feeling of frightening despair as she listened to Ward.

"Will you think of marriage, Meda, I…"

"No! No!" She cut him off, jumping to her feet.

People at nearby tables turned and looked at her. Ward rose quickly and took her arm leading her from the restaurant.

"Call a taxi for me, please, Mr. Sumner," pleaded Meda.

"I will not," he walked her to his car and opened the door. "Get in."

"Where are we going?" she asked as he drove along.

"To my place, Meda."

"I'm not going, I'm not going," Gathering courage she went on, "Take me to the corner of my block and let me out. Please, Mr. Sumner."

"Don't you think that after nearly two years you could call me Ward? I said we'd talk."

In front of the apartment building he opened the door and led her to his apartment. Meda walked to a sofa and sat down. The room was straightened, clean and in good taste.

"This is a lovely room," said Meda weakly. "But really, Ward, there is nothing to talk about so please call me a taxi."

He pulled her to her feet and put his arms around her. Looking into her eyes he kissed her lips softly, unhurriedly.

"Don't," Meda cried out and tried to pull away.

He put her head against his shoulder and stroked it gently.

"I'm not going to hurt you, darling. I love you too much to ever hurt you." He kissed her again and all reason escaped her. She found herself responding to his kisses, opening her lips to respond more deeply. He picked her up and carried her to the bedroom. Laying her on the bed his caresses were soft as he slowly undressed her. Watching her he felt elated as she responded to his touch. Later she slept curled in Ward's arms.

Ward gazed at the ceiling until she awoke. "Who was he? I'll kill the skunk," he swore.

Meda sat upright as one awakening from a bad dream. Gathering the sheet around her in embarrassment, still not fully awake she managed, "Whatever are you talking about?"

"You know what I'm talking about! All this display of innocence for two years."

"Ward!" then she faltered, fully awake.

"Stop it, Meda, you know damn well I'm not the first man you've slept with. How many, Meda?"

She looked long at Ward, the color draining from her face. the moment of truth, she thought.

"Only one, Ward, my husband of four years." With a flicker she continued. "There is no girl that I live with. I pay my own rent so I wouldn't have to go out to Long Island and live with his parents. He is a salesman working for his father. They have a factory—women's dresses. He's gone so much I had to do something to pass the time." "Ward, no one ever asked me if I was married, so I saw no reason to volunteer the information. But, Ward, I know even if you don't, in a sense you really are the first man."

Ward was silent as Meda gathered up her clothes and went into the bathroom. Completely dressed, she came out and picked up her purse.

"Goodbye, Ward, I'll find another job."

Ward reached the door one step ahead of her. Gathering her in his arms. "Meda, Meda, why didn't you tell me before I loved you so fully."

"I guess I was afraid I'd be fired and I loved the job. I was also learning to love you. I tried so hard to keep this from happening Ward."

"I know that now, and I'm so sorry, darling," he held her tightly as if he'd never let her go. "Then Milissa is non-existent," said Ward.

"Very much alive. She's my best and only girlfriend in New York. She lives down the hall from me."

Ward threw back his head and laughed happily as he held her tightly.

"You have to get a divorce, you know that, don't you? In the meantime, continue work as you have been doing…saying nothing."

"Ward, my sister is coming soon and I can't

think of doing or saying anything that would make her think anything was wrong. A divorce takes years, you know."

"No, my sweet, it doesn't, you can go to Reno, Nevada. I'll send you."

Meda sat back in the taxi thinking as she rode home. Ward was in her blood; she knew she would go to him again and again for the emotional release she didn't achieve with Briant. "Do I want to give up a dress factory for a model agency?" she wondered. "One day the big house and factory will be ours. When the depression ends, we'll probably get very rich. The model agency does well too. Guess I'll have to think it all out and that takes time. But I don't think I could ever give up Ward now that I've found him."

Arriving at her apartment she was shocked to find Briant home and waiting for her.

"Where in the hell have you been all night," he asked.

"I did write you about my work, well, one of the girls got sick and I went home with her. She ate something that gave her food poisoning. She was really sick for a while."

"And now she is alright," Briant replied stonily.

"Sure I gave her some salty water...Mama's old remedy," laughed Meda.

"What time did you get in?" she asked.

"Wish I had known. I would have come on home anyway. I am sorry, Briant. Did you get your dinner?"

"Oh, sure Milissa prepared me a nice one. She's a fine girl. Too bad her husband was such a rotten egg. I like her."

"Yes, well, I'm glad you weren't alone."

Meda went on in the bathroom and took a bath. When she came out, she said, "I'm going to lay down for a couple of hours. I'll soon have to get up and go to work."

"Go ahead," said Briant, "I may as well stay up, I'm not sleepy."

Briant thought of the conversation he had with Milissa the evening before.

"Why does Meda feel she has to work?" he had asked Milissa.

"She needs something to do while you're away. It's hard to sit in the apartment all day, every day, with nothing to do. She often said she was beginning to feel like a thimit," said Milissa.

Briant laughed, "That is her youngest sister's expression for someone she feels has no direction."

Milissa loved to see Briant laugh. "I'd be happy to sit and wait for him." She mused.

Briant was home for a week. Meda was glad to see him leave. The pretense of being a good wife, accepting his lovemaking was working on her nervous system. She let him hold her tight and tried to respond. It was hard. "I'm glad Didge is coming, dear, she will be good company for you while I'm gone. Maybe you can talk her into staying," said Briant.

"I'll try," Meda promised, "but I doubt Papa and Mama would let her."

"I hope I won't have to stay away so long this trip. I know it's lonesome for you."

"Yes," She wished he'd stop this trivial chatter and leave. "This is all nice," Meda finally said, "but I've got to get ready for work too."

"I'd like to take you to bed again before I go," he groaned.

She hugged him tight and opened the door. "Bye," she smiled as she closed it behind him.

She leaned against it for a second as she breathed a sigh of relief.

It has been hard, seeing Ward daily, and acting as though he was only a boss, then going home to Briant. "Now I can spend the night with him," she sang happily as she dressed for work.

It was three days later before Milissa caught up with Meda as they entered the apartment building.

"That happy look on your face must mean you got a bonus or something, or is Briant home again, or still home," teased Milissa.

"No, no, and no. Oh, Milissa, what am I going to do?"

"About what?"

"I'm making such a mess out of my life," Meda said.

"Then stop it," suggested Milissa.

They had reached Meda's apartment. "Come on in for a minute. I've got to go soon," Meda said.

"Working late again?"

"No, having dinner with the boss."

"Think you should so often? It could breed trouble," remarked Milissa.

"Oh, Milissa, it already has," she blurted out.

"Oh." Was all Milissa could say. For a minute Milissa hated the unknown boss for what he had done to Briant. But maybe that opens the way for me, she thought. I won't tell Briant, I'd lose him for sure, but I'll sure be around to sweep up the ashes, when he finds out he will surely burn. He deserves to have Meda return his love, he works so hard for her. Dear God, how I wish it was me.

*****

Em and Lukatie took Didge to Campton to catch the train to New York. Didge hugged Lukatie and as the conductor shouted, "ALL ABOARD," she wanted desperately to hug Em, but only smiled and said, "Bye, Papa. See you both in a week."

Lukatie waved as long as the train was in sight then hurried to catch up with Em. He had already walked to the end of the platform. She was rubbing the back of her neck. The beginning of the headaches she had lived with so many years now.

"Em, stop by Doctor Wesson's and let me get something for this awful headache."

While Em waited for her, he thought how strained and formal their relationship had been for years. He guessed her feelings but since she never brought it up, he certainly wasn't going to. He loved her and knew he had never loved Didge's mother, Milla. It was she that searched him out. It was only physical attraction too overwhelming to be denied.

Waiting for Doctor Wesson to see her, Lukatie thought of Stewart. "Why is it when I reach an impasse in my life, I need so desperately to be comforted by him," she told herself. "I do wish he was home."

Ward drove Meda to Grand Central Station to meet Didge. He watched the happiness shown by the two girls as they met. Both talking and laughing at the same time. As he watched the truth of Didge's identity was apparent to him. "Adopted, my eye," he thought. "She is every bit as lovely to look at as Meda. I'd better make sure Harris doesn't see her." At that moment Meda, looking beyond Ward, burst out in a gleeful laugh.

"Come, Didge, you must meet my boss and my photographer." Meda added.

Ward swung around, "You old snooper," he

yelled at Harris. When introductions were over, Harris thought, "boy, another one, she glows, golden hair, brown eyes, full glorious mouth and shaped as well as her sister."

"Miss Carroll, I'll hire you, will you model for me. If there are any more at home like you, I'll hire them, too." Harris said seriously.

"What?" teased Meda, "and knock me out of a job."

"Thanks, but no thanks," laughed Didge. "I am the last one at home except Mama, she's beautiful. I've a one-track mind where work is concerned."

"I understand you're an artist," said Ward.

"At least trying hard to be," smiled Didge.

"I'd like to see some of your work," said Ward and Harris at the same time.

"When we get to Meda's apartment, you may see the paintings I brought to show a publisher," said Didge.

"We're going to the studio, dear, not my apartment," Meda said.

"Oh," said Didge as they left the platform and walked through Grand Central Station to Ward's automobile.

Harris stood on the sidewalk, "Well, come on," said Ward, "You might as well ride back with us. No need to take a taxi."

At the studio, Ward asked again to see the paintings and Didge consented. Like Meda, she was impressed with the studio and looked around while they looked at the paintings.

"You are good. Meda said you were, but I had no idea you were this good. You've a couple here I'd like to buy," said Ward.

"Sorry they aren't for sale," said Didge.

"I understand but after you've seen the publisher, maybe they will be. These are just to show what you can do, aren't they?" asked Ward.

"Right," said Didge.

"Meda, why don't you take the rest of the day off and show your sister around. We'll see you in the morning."

When the girls left, Harris turned to Ward. "All right, fellow, if they are sisters why the different names."

Ward hedged, "Didge was adopted."

"Adopted, my ass, they came from the same stem, and they'd still have the same name," Harris said firmly.

"Exactly my thoughts, old boy. All right, I guess you're entitled to the truth. But keep it to yourself, Meda has been married for four years."

"Well, I'll be damned. You mean no one knows," laughed Harris.

"No."

"So that's why she always gives you the run around." Bending with laugher, Harris walked out of the office.

With a sigh of relief Ward sat down behind his desk, "Whee, that was easier than I thought it was going to be."

After leaving Didge's suitcase and portfolio at the apartment, Meda showed Didge around New York. Pointing out Bush Publishing Company, the art gallery, the Empire State Building and department stores, she could get lost in. The late hour forced an end to their day.

That evening they sat up late talking with Milissa. Meda had to know all about home and the family, especially her mother. They spoke of the tragic death of Lucinda. As Milissa listened. "No wonder Briant loved this family," she thought.

Meda insisted that Didge spend the next day

shopping. Looking at dresses Didge tried to keep Meda's comment in mind, "You don't want to look like Campton when you go to see Mr. Bush. Neither do you want to look too New Yorkish."

She bought some clothes and a newspaper, then hurried back to the apartment. She opened the paper to the sports section, less to follow sports than to search for some news of Seth. Finding it she read with interest. The reviews were unanimously jubilant ranging from an unknown to an overnight sensation to one of the greatest baseball pitchers of the season. His strong arm can hurl a fast ball with excellent control. Any game he was in spoiled the season for any opposing team. Didge was bursting with pride as she read about Seth.

Seth telephoned Mr. Bush to inquire if Miss Carroll had written for an appointment and learned she had one the following Thursday. Now to find her.

With the money Seth had made catering he had opened his own restaurant, enlarged his catering service, and soon added two more restaurants. He then converted rooms over one of the restaurants into very comfortable living quarters. He meant to have a large chain of seafood restaurants one of these days. Seth entered the restaurant business with a brilliant uncompromising courage. People from all around came to savor the snapper soup and seafood delicacies that his chefs prepared.

At the game, the day before Seth had accepted the slaps on the back…the accolades silently, barely managing a slight smile. He couldn't help wondering how much praise he would get if they knew his true origin. "How about a rubdown, pitcher?" someone called out. "Don't need it," he answered. He quickly showered, dressed and left the building. Seth for all his challenge was a mystery to all. He wasn't interested in their small talk. He was only interested in working hard, pitching a good game and resting. The team invited him everywhere and no one ever questioned his race. It was taken for granted that he was white and he saw no reason to tell anyone differently. He had power in his arm, a fast ball he could command, and a curve that seemed to move at a ninety degree angle.

As if drawn by gravitational force, Didge walked along Fifth Avenue. She hadn't planned on buying new clothes and didn't bring much money so she shied away from places that cost too much.

Didge liked the feel of newness, good cut and becomingness of the suit she had bought the day before. It had a surprising effect, making her feel new and wonderful. The white organdy ruffled blouse framed her face, the accordion pleated skirt of the green linen suit that complimented her golden hair and complexion made her look as fresh and alive as the summer day. She strolled nonchalantly along looking at the beautiful shops and beautiful people that were soon hidden by the whirling doors of the department stores. Didge felt that she was in another world lost in the mystery and splendor of the big city. "How exciting," she thought as she walked block after block. Her neck ached from looking up at so many tall buildings. "Taller than our straight pines," she thought and for a second her mind carried her to the river's bank where she sat on her thinking stump. "How I wish I was there, no…no…I'd miss all of this if I were. I've the rest of my life for that."

"What an interesting looking church," thought Didge as she walked past the St. Boniface Roman Catholic Church on the corner of 47th

Street. She was glad when she reached the art gallery. It would feel cooler inside. She felt she must have an idiot's glare on her features as she stopped to study every painting that caught her fancy. The magic of the art lined walls in their crusty frames. Didge filled her eyes and soul roaming through room after room while the works of mysterious painters looked down at her.

A book could be condensed, changed, mutilated and still be a book, not so with a painting. It would always remain the same as the artist created it, unless deliberately destroyed. Thus, she spent her day and found it all very rewarding. "Someday I'll come again," she thought.

Seth had phoned Meda's apartment several times without an answer. "Where can she be?" he wondered. "Oh," he snapped his fingers, an art gallery of course, how dumb of me.

Seth walked up to Fifth Avenue, three blocks later he saw her. Could be perfect blendship between us he thought as he looked at her reflection in a store window. It was a moment flavored by seeing a vision of her in the water as he stood on the riverbank.

She saw his reflection in the glass window as he walked up behind her. Her eyes met his in the glass and her face lit up in a rapturous grin. She whirled around and started talking, her words racing together.

"Never talk too fast for when you do the impact of your effectiveness is lowered," teased Seth. She stopped, tears of happiness welling up in her eyes.

"I'm only teasing you, Didge. I'm so happy to see you, I could do cartwheels down Fifth Avenue."

"I can't imagine you doing that," she

laughed.

"That's better," Seth said with a steady penetrating look. "That was a bad start. Let's begin again."

"I was only trying to thank you for putting me in touch with Mr. Bush. And upset because you didn't put a return address on your letter so I could write to you. I finally figured out you didn't want any thanks."

"I didn't know if you would be interested or not and thank me to mind my own business. It's getting late. Come on, I'll take you to dinner," said Seth.

"But Meda," she paused remembering Meda had said she would be out rather late. "Oh, she's to be out late. Dinner sounds fine," smiled Didge.

While they were eating, they talked mostly of home, art and what each was doing.

"This seafood is delicious Seth. How did you learn of this place? The Fish Box, I like the name, it sounds homey, too."

Seth threw back his head and laughed pleasantly.

"What's so amusing?" Didge asked, puzzled.

"I'm glad you like it. This place is mine. I have two more like it, plus a catering service."

"Yours! No wonder everyone in here has been looking at me so strangely and seems to know you. I guess I'm one of many girls you bring here, and they're wondering who this time. Do you ever tell them?" laughed Didge.

With a sober expression, he said, "You're the only one."

"Oh!" She felt a moment's embarrassment as she gazed at him with the deep fire of womanhood shining in her eyes.

Abruptly he rose. "Let's walk."

"I'm sorry, Seth, I shouldn't have said that. It was really fishing. You should have told me it was none of my business who you took there."

"I haven't wanted to take anyone there. If I did, I would."

"We have really gotten off to a bad start. Perhaps you'd better take me to Meda's apartment," suggested Didge.

"Didge, I'm sorry. It was me that started wrong. I guess I was so happy to see you and put my big foot in my mouth. Please, am I forgiven?"

"Sure," said Didge quietly. The sting of his first words had been with her all evening.

They turned on Fifth Avenue again pausing now and then to look in shop windows. Seth felt proud as he walked beside her and protected her from the buffeting of the crowd which seemed to be on the streets day and night.

"I wonder where so many people come from. They are always here," said Seth.

"They need our forests to wander around in," smiled Didge looking up at Seth.

The light, soft evening breeze that gently blew her golden hair made a lovely picture as they walked along. They were indeed a handsome couple and many heads turned for a second look. As they neared 42nd Street, a man came hurrying around the corner and almost collided with Didge.

"Sorry," he stammered. "Oh, hello there, Seth," and as he looked at Didge, he uttered, "My, my, my, so this is your secret."

"Miss Carroll, this is a team member, Hubert Merritt," said Seth reluctantly.

"Pleased, I'm sure," grinned Hub Merritt. He curtsied kissing the hand she had extended.

Hub was looking at Didge with joy and an ache in his heart for something he immediately felt to be beyond his reach. Seth knew the look; he had worn it many years himself.

"Come, you two, the team is having a party around the corner and I won't take no for an answer. It was a quick decision. We tried all afternoon to reach you, Seth, and couldn't. Now I know why." Hub stepped between them taking each by the arm and propelled them around the corner. Didge was thinking, "Thank goodness, I bought the new clothes as Meda had insisted."

A collective moan went through the room as Hub pushed them through the door.

"Look what I found, people. No wonder Seth dodges us all the time."

While Hub introduced Didge, Seth watched noticing her engaging enthusiasm for all she met and how she listened attentively to all they said sometimes kidding back very much at ease. He was almost glad she would be going back home soon. He had placed her on a pedestal and felt his soul fill with black despair at the thought of another trying to pull her from the high pinnacle he had placed her. Hub, the most egotistical of men, would try his best to project Didge into his realm of living, given half a chance. Seth didn't care to go out with them after games. It was sickening to listen to them brag about the women they had slept with, and the amount of liquor they could drink. Seth fully believed a man's affairs should be private. What right do they have to degrade a woman that cared enough for them to reward them?

A radio was playing and Hubert led Didge into the middle of the room. Her only dancing had been at the river alone or with Meda when they could get the old graphophone to play. Sometimes they could tease Miles into joining them; it was such fun when he did. Then there was the time at the Christmas party, I'd just as soon not think of that, she thought shifting her mind back to the present.

"I really don't dance, Mr. Merritt," laughed Didge.

"An angel like you doesn't dance. No, I guess not, you just float along, and call me Hub, please."

"Really, I don't," laughed Didge. "I'm too busy with my art to learn."

"An artist! Tell me, angel, what makes a great artist?"

"It takes the gift, the feeling, plus hard work and study, a lot of practice and a bushel of mistakes."

"Are you a great artist, angel?" Hub asked.

"Of course not, just hope to be." Didge couldn't help adding, "I have had a showing in North Carolina and all but two of paintings sold."

"Best average, I've heard of, but then I know little about art. You are really serious? You like painting?" asked Hub.

"Oh, yes, I like being able to express myself in oils. My aim is to convey to others what I see."

Her speech bore a beguiling southern drawl. As she talked, she looked up into Hub's face. Her smile complemented her deep-set dimples, lifting up her laughing deep brown eyes. Everything about her fascinated him. Hub had easily started dancing and without realizing it Didge was following like she had danced forever. His arm tightened around her, she felt so desirable to him.

The new suit gave her a fresh soft demure look. She felt gay and floaty; she loved the flouncy feel around her legs of the pleated skirt giving her a feminine sensation. When the music stopped, Hub looked at her and said, "Honey, you're like a breath of fresh air in my life. I knew you'd dance like an angel and I do love the way ya'll talk."

"We are inclined to draw our words out while you yankee's chop yours off," her smile contained a touch of pepper.

"May I come calling? I'd really like a date with you."

Didge laughed, "I hardly think so since I'll soon be returning home to quiet North Carolina."

Seth walked up, "You're in a rather rare mood, aren't you?" he said in a voice raw and tortured. "We'd better go; you have an early appointment in the morning."

"Oh, that's not until eleven in the morning," she said quickly.

"Goodnight, Hub," said Seth.

"Oh, no, you don't leave until you've danced at least once," said Hub pushing them on the floor as 'A Pretty Girl is Like a Melody' blared forth from the radio.

Seth was forced to touch her as his arms slowly went around her very lightly and her hand rested just as lightly on his shoulder. Didge laughed, tossing her hair she looked up at him.

"Seth, smile, we're being watched. Please don't be tenacious. Don't begrudge me the first fun I've ever had. I just bared my soul, didn't I?"

"I'm sorry, I am acting like a jealous fool," he tried to laugh.

As they looked at each other there was a desperate intense desire that plunged deep into the soul. Didge felt she was drowning, and if so, prayed it would last forever. She swayed and

Seth's arms tightened to steady her. Realization of self-betrayal flooded her. The air between them sent out electric vibrations as they looked at each other. She quickly withdrew from his arms just as the music ended. Trying frantically to think of something sane to say. Her thoughts were tormenting her, and she felt exquisitely terrified by what she saw revealed in Seth's eyes. She had always felt he loved her, and now she knew how deeply. And to what extent he had gone to suppress himself. Oh God, why couldn't he have been white or me black. Seth vowed to never let his feelings show again.

Didge turned to Hub, "It has been fun, but we must run. Perhaps we'll meet again."

"You bet, if I have anything to say about it, we will." Hub said walking them to the door.

"Lucky stiff that Seth," Hub had seen the look between Seth and Didge and knew he'd never have a chance with her. "I'll be damned," he thought, "with that much exposed feelings I'll bet she's a virgin."

"Seth, the interview tomorrow frightens me," Didge said as they walked to Meda's apartment.

"Don't let it. Mr. Bush is only a man and seems like a nice one."

"Suppose I don't please him. With no experience in commercial work he might not like me or my work. Maybe I shouldn't go." As she said it, she knew she would. Why else had she come all the way to New York.

"He will definitely like you, and I believe he will like your work otherwise I wouldn't have told him about you. Just don't act afraid of him; he's just another person and all he can do is say yes or no," said Seth.

Seth suffered the agonies of the damned

every time he walked away from Didge as now when he said goodnight at the door of Meda's apartment, parting with words always left unspoken between them. The valour within Seth gave him the strength, courage and determination to do what he knew to be right. He would not touch Didge; she would have to take that giant step herself.

Promptly at eleven o'clock the next morning a nervous Didge walked into the office of Bush Publishing Company. She approached the girl seated at the reception desk.

"I'm a Didge Carroll. I have an appointment with Mr. Bush."

"Oh, yes, Miss Carroll. He's expecting you. Come with me, please." The receptionist took Didge down a hallway and stopped in front of a door with Bush Publishing Company painted in bold gold letters on it. "Mr. Bush, Miss Carroll is here," announced the receptionist and closed the door behind her.

"Come in, come in," said the small man behind a huge desk, while he continued reading the paper in his hand.

"The moment of truth is about here, am I good enough or not," thought Didge as she waited.

Mr. Bush rose extending his hand. "Thanks for coming and waiting until I finished reading the letter. Please be seated. So, you're the young lady our pitcher is in love with," Mr. Bush said with interest.

Her lips broke into a surprised grin over white even teeth brightening the pretty smile that activated her face. Surprised that he spoke so openly. "I couldn't say that, Sir. We're friends that grew up together. He's a fine person. He was always like a protector."

"As you say. I'd like that job myself"'

thought Mr. Bush. "May I see your work?" He reached for her portfolio.

A sheet of paper naming a book and page number she had developed the picture from lay on each painting. She was careful, he noticed, to choose books he had published and would be familiar with. Smart girl.

Didge studied him as he looked at her paintings. He was a small wiry little ferret of a man, with a sharp nose and penetrating eyes topped with a bald head. When he lowered his head, his chin seemed to disappear into his neck. What little hair he had was straw colored and on a level with his pouchy eyes. All Didge could think of was "bird man," and felt ashamed for thinking such thoughts. But he was funny looking. With all his work, he probably doesn't get any rest. She didn't know why, but she felt pity for him.

Mr. Bush found her paintings to be fresh and unaffected. Without looking up he asked, "At what point do you consider a painting finished?" With little hesitation she replied. "There is no method per se, I paint as I feel it…see it…I look for reality and depth in a subject. I feel my paintings are like stories, they have something to tell. It's like writing a book. When the author gets the story told, it's finished. My paintings tell a story. It's painted thoughts as my mind sees it." She smiled as if at some private joke and continued. "I have to observe, watch, even listen sometimes a sound can build into an idea and once I capture it, I have to work fast or lose what might have been one of my best paintings. Call it a birth from my imagination."

"I see. Would you consider staying in New York?"

"No, Sir, I can't. I'm needed at home. My father built me a lovely studio in our attic. I'd be foolish not to use it. The paintings you have there, Sir, of the young couple in the lane of the house…well, Sir, that is our home and those windows across the top is my studio. Perhaps I shouldn't have used that, but it seemed to fit the story."

"Now tell me how we can work together so far apart?" asked Mr. Bush.

"I was hoping you would send me the manuscript…I'll read it…paint a scene for the jacket…then mail it back to you. That is if my work is satisfactory," said Didge.

"Satisfied with your paintings," he thought, "Good heavens, they're great. Somehow the commercial look was missing. But I must not overreact."

"Yes, Miss Carroll, I think we can work something out," said Mr. Bush finally looking up at her.

He was pleased with the innocent expression of delight shining in her eyes.

"Could you come back tomorrow and sign the contract, and then let a lonely old man take you to lunch?"

The twinkle in his eyes made him look like a mischievous leprechaun. Didge liked him. He was everything Seth had said he was.

"Thank you, Mr. Bush. It would please me to lunch with you. What time shall I come?" asked Didge.

"Make it eleven thirty. My secretary should have the contract ready by then."

Mr. Bush turned back to the paintings as Didge left his office. "She has a lot of feeling for figure composition," he thought, as he looked at the colored man standing in the middle of a field, his arms uplifted baring his soul in a desperate cry of silent agony because of crop failure. Mr. Bush looked at the title of the book she had chosen for this painting, "Tired Hour of Shadow." This one will be very good for the "Fall of Summer" that will soon go to press. The one of the aged man walking a curved driveway with the sun casting elongated shadows toward a large blue house would be perfect for "The Gathering End." Didge had only used a different angle of their house for this painting.

Didge was very happy the next day when Mr. Bush handed her a very generous check for the three paintings he had chosen. He included a manuscript to take back home with her.

It was after lunch that Didge signed the contract. She left his office feeling the happy aura of success. "Joy…is that what I feel…it must be…I feel so happy, never in my life have I felt so happy."

Later as Didge entered Meda's apartment the telephone was ringing. It was Meda.

"How did it go this morning?"

"Fine," Didge talked excitedly as she told her of the lunch with Mr. Bush, and the paintings he bought.

"Great! Now Mr. Sumner can buy those that he wanted," exclaimed Meda.

"Mr. Bush took the one that he wanted."

"I'll tell him he can pick another one. I'll bring him tonight when I come home. I have to rush now. I've lots to do!"

Seth telephoned just as Didge settled down to read the manuscript and asked about her day. He hadn't called the day before. Now Didge wasn't sure she wanted to tell him about her interview and the contract. "How childish of me," she thought. "He said he had some business he had to take care of."

"My day was nice, I had lunch with Mr. Bush. He took me to a fabulous restaurant, everybody knew him and hurried to serve him. The head waiter drew out my chair and helped with the menu telling us what was good. There were exotic plants and waterfalls. Mama would have loved it as I did. All the attention made me feel like a celebrity," she smiled ruefully into the telephone.

"That's fine," said Seth, "but how did your interview go?"

"Great! He bought three of my illustrations and I signed a contract today. He is the fine person you said he was, Seth."

"I'm so glad for you Didge. Now that is taken care of, how about having dinner with me to celebrate, I can pick you up at seven."

"Sorry, Seth, I have plans with Meda tonight."

"She could come along," offered Seth.

"Her boss is coming over. He's interested in buying a couple of the paintings, so I have to be here," explained Didge.

"Oh, what about tomorrow?" disappointment sounded in his voice.

"I had hoped to see the Empire State Building and see a good movie. I have to go home the next day."

"May I take you tomorrow?" asked Seth.

"Yes, Seth, you may." She was about to ask him over tonight and remembered that Meda might have to go back to work and they would be there alone, so she kept silent.

To be with Seth was very stimulating, too stimulating, there was no need to play with fire.

"What time should I come for you?" asked Seth interrupting her thoughts. "Would ten in the morning be too early?"

"No, Seth, that will be fine, I'll see you then, bye." Didge added a silent "darling" as she hung up the receiver. How she wanted to love him and wanted his love. "We could stay in the north," she reasoned, "but there could be children, then what…what color would they be. As long as they were his she didn't care. But what about the children? What would their life be like? Would it be fair to them?" She thought of how Seth had fought his way through school to get an education. It hasn't been fair. She knew she couldn't do that to a child.

*****

Didge and Seth stood on the 86th floor of the Empire State Building. "I never dreamed I'd be so high in the sky," laughed Didge. "Come on, let's go to the top."

She grabbed his hand as she pulled him along to the elevator. She became aware of the grip of his hands and withdrew hers.

"I'm acting like a ten-year-old, Seth."

"You're acting like a happy girl interested in seeing all she can." Replied Seth.

Didge was looking down, "Look, Seth, the streets below look like miles and miles of dark blue-gray ribbon stretched out. The automobiles look like ants crawling along. Oh, Seth, this is wonderful. I'm so glad you are here to share it with me," Didge said breaking into a sudden deep flush.

"I'm glad too Didge; do you know you're glowing?"

She was glad Seth was no phony. He was a man that spoke his mind forthright and honest. She had brought a camera and took picture after picture. "This is to remind me that all this is real and not just a dream."

"Do you have plans other than the movie, Didge," asked Seth when they were back on the street.

"No, why?"

"Come on, I'll show you what five cents will do." They took the Ninth Avenue elevator train and rode from station to station, never passing through the gates and changing train often. They passed the Polo ground in the Bronx. They went to Battery Park. They rode the Fulton Street line and he told her about the Fulton Street Market. In one of the large stations they walked through tunnel after tunnel to change trains and rode to Coney Island. They stood on the platform of the station and watched the people and saw a part of the amusement area.

"Want to go over and try the rides?" asked Seth.

"Sounds like fun but I don't think I'm dressed properly to enjoy it. I should have pajamas on like those two girls going there."

"The fat one or the thin one?" laughed Seth.

"Crazy, the only difference is the size. They are cute with the white ruffles and large polka dots in red and white," said Didge.

They left the train at 42nd Street near Sixth Avenue.

"Thanks, Seth, that was really fun and quite an experience. How time flies. The afternoon is gone. Do you take those train rides often?" asked Didge.

"Yes, every time I feel I have to be alone to think."

"Can you think in that noise?"

"Yep," he put his hands in his pockets,

bent his body forward then rocked back on his heels. "Sounds silly, huh, but I do. I close out the noise." Seth laughed.

"In that noisy train."

"And I thought you enjoyed it," teased Seth.

"Oh, I did, I did, but I wouldn't pick it for a thinking place," Didge said firmly.

"Well, I don't have a thinking stump here."

"Oh, Seth, I'm sorry."

"Me too, I wish we were there now, together," Seth said softly. "Say shall we have dinner before the movie, or would you rather see a stage show? All we've done is eat candy in the subway station."

"Neither, let's have dinner, afterwards we can walk and talk or sit in the park and talk for a while. I'll have to pack my things tonight. At least I've only one illustration and the manuscript to take back beside my suitcase."

"Then Meda's boss bought one of them?"

"Yes and paid a good price for it. Even more than Mr. Bush paid. He insisted I take it, said it was worth even more. I would have gladly sold it for less."

"Didge, never undersell your work. The hours you spend on one painting is worth plenty," Seth warned.

The evening ended too soon. A whole day with Seth was more than Didge ever dreamed of. As they neared Meda's door Seth spoke, looking long at her.

"Didge, you may never know what this day has meant to me."

"Or to me Seth. It is one I'll long remember, and thought could never possibly happen. Seth, I've known this moment was coming all week, now I find it hard to say goodbye and leave."

"Not goodbye, Didge, just goodnight for a while. I'll probably go home at the end of summer."

Didge smiled with delight. "That will be nice." She was glad he saw fit to let her know he would be going home. Such a little thing yet to her it would be a secret something to look forward to.

Didge lay her hand on Seth's arm lightly, "Then I'll say goodnight until the end of summer and thanks for a wonderful day."

Seth placed his hand over hers and looked down into her eyes. "Goodnight, Didge." He turned on his heels and walked away his passion so aroused just being near her filled him with anguish.

The next day Meda stood on the platform and watched the train until it was out of sight. A sadness filled her. Meda loved Didge and being with her filled her with a desire to go home and see her family. It had been so long.

Meda started, walking fast, and turned her mind to the things of the day. "No lies now to Didge about working late. I can be with Ward, oh, how I love him." The thought filled her with euphoria and her steps quickened.

The next few months were happy ones for Meda. She was with Ward every free minute. Milissa tried to caution her.

"Be a dear and phone me if Briant does come home, please, Milissa," pleaded Meda.

She didn't have to phone. Meda had come home for clean clothes when Briant walked in with his suitcase, so she knew he was just getting in.

"Hello stranger," Meda said allowing him to give her a kiss she couldn't return. "I must ask him for my freedom," she thought. She was thankful that her period had started that same morning and ruled out sex.

"You must be starving, I'll prepare dinner," Meda said as an excuse to withdraw from his arms. She pecked him on the cheek and headed for the kitchen. Briant's eyes followed her lovingly, longingly, happy to find her home. He hadn't said a word, just held her tight. This, his wife, the woman whose face, body or hands he saw in nearly every magazine he picked up. He picked up his suitcase and he went to the bedroom to unpack. He was a meticulous person and put everything in place even though it was only for a few days. He could only have her twice before leaving again.

"Onedia, when Miss Roberson comes in send her into my office," Ward said to his secretary.

"Yes sir, Mr. Sumner, I'll do that."

It was only a few minutes before Meda walked into his office. "You wanted to see me?"

"Yes, Meda, I've a very special favor to ask of you," Ward said.

Meda started to walk around the desk to him.

"Meda, please, just sit down."

"Of course, Ward, but I must say you're acting very strange."

"I don't mean to, darling, I'll come directly to the point," said Ward.

"I do wish you would," said Meda anxiously.

"Right, right, I need a girl to pose nude for me. There will be a tremendous profit in it for both of us." Explained Ward.

"Us! You mean for me to pose nude?"

"Yes, you're the best model I've got. The only one with a perfect figure."

"Thanks for that. You say you love me, yet you say you want me to do this thing. I don't understand that kind of love, Ward."

"Look, honey, this is where the real money is. It's not bad. It's art, that's what it is…art."

"Then get another girl. I won't do that," said Meda almost in tears.

"It's you they want. After all, we aren't angels anymore."

"I don't know about that kind of thing. You say you love me, and I know you wouldn't shame me or make me do anything wrong. All right, if you tell me to, I'll do it."

Meda went to Milissa feeling that she had to discuss it with someone. She wished Didge was still here but she wasn't nor Briant, but she knew what Briant would say. Meda knocked softly on Milissa's door wondering just how to tell her. When the door opened Meda blurted out the whole proposal as quickly as possible.

"What should I do, Milissa?" pleaded Meda.

"Well, everything is becoming modern and absurd. It's called art. Which is supposed to mean something, and it can be awful sometimes." Milissa dropped her head and thought of how Briant would feel.

"Meda, as I see it, it is trash, a cheap exploitation of the body. I wouldn't have it in my bookstore." Milissa felt sorry for Meda as she sat quietly listening to her. She hadn't interrupted since her first outburst.

"Meda, if you don't feel right about posing in the nude, then don't do it."

"Mr. Sumner will fire me if I don't. Then I'll have to go to Long Island and live with Briant's parents."

"I wouldn't worry about that," said Milissa, "He is too crazy about you. He won't let go of you that easy. The question is, will you get as many job offers after posing nude? You know it will probably hurt your fresh country girl image."

"I hadn't thought about that." Said Meda.

"Think about it if you do it, it may be the last posing you ever do, unless it's always in the nude. Having an affair with him is one thing, but exploiting your assets to the public is something entirely different. It's entirely up to you, Meda, a decision you'll have to make, just think it over seriously," advised Milissa.

"I will, and thanks for the advice." Meda said.

Meda finally decided that she would go through with it. She just couldn't chance losing Ward. He made the preparations and took her to Harris' studio himself. The crew were all excited even as Sumner tried to explain it was only another day's work to them. It was done at night so everyone else would be out of the building. Rose was asked to stay with her.

"Honey, are you sure you want to go through with this?" asked Rose. Meda was one of the few models Rose cared anything about and hated what she was about to do.

"No, Rose, but I'll try to."

"Don't do it if you don't want to. I wish you wouldn't."

Before Meda could answer there was a knock on the door and Ward's voice called out, "Come on, Miss Roberson, we're ready. Let's get it over with." She clutched her robe tightly as Rose opened the door and walked out of the dressing room with Meda. Meda's face was frozen, her body stiff.

"You don't have to, dear, it isn't too late to back out," whispered Rose.

Meda hesitated a moment then unfastened her

robe taking her position in front of the camera. As her robe began to slide from her shoulders the room became tense. Filled with panic she jerked the robe tightly around her and ran to the dressing room, she was shaking violently.

Meda cried out, "I'm sorry, I'm sorry, but I can't, I just can't do it."

"Crazy woman," said Ward looking at Harris. "Wait, I'll get her back."

Without knocking Ward walked into the dressing room. "Don't be a silly prude. Come on, darling, let's go back and get it over with. It's only a photograph."

Meda turned still clutching the robe tightly around herself. Her eyes mirrored the love, hurt and shame she was feeling as she looked at him. Ward put his arms around her to block out her gaze. No girl had ever looked at him like that before. He felt flooded with guilt for trying to use her love to get gain. He knew that men would love it, and that women would snicker. Meda's life would become shady.

Meda broke away from him, her voice quavering and small. "You can't have very much love for me to want this of me."

"You don't believe that; you know I love you, and this will make no difference to me," pleaded Ward.

"I'm convinced that your love for me is only for sex," Meda said vehemently. "I wish you'd go now and let me dress and go home. You can fire me if you like, but I won't do it."

Ward looked at her and his countenance softened.

"So, I lose a contract but I'm glad. I'm glad you wouldn't do it, but I would have let you. I just don't look at it like you do. Now get dressed and I'll take you home." He walked to the door and turned, "No, Meda, you aren't fired. The day I fire you is the day I marry you." The door closed softly behind him. He walked slowly back into the studio.

"Sorry, Harris, she won't do it. I'm taking her home," said Ward.

"Have you fired her?" asked Harris.

"Hell, no," roared Ward. "You'd like that, wouldn't you?" Then he laughed, "See you around. Goodnight, Rose, and thanks for waiting."

Ward went to the back and knocked on the dressing room door. "Ready, Miss Roberson?"

A disgruntled crew swore and stalked out of the building feeling cheated to the bone.

Ward broke the silence as he drove Meda home. "Honey, Didge has gone home now, so don't you think it's time to ask for that divorce so we can get married?"

"You really aren't mad at me about tonight?" Meda asked.

"Nope, that's my body and I really don't want other men gawking at it."

Meda flooded with relief and moved closer to him.

"That's better," Ward said. Patting her knee, he let his hand slide up to rest on her thigh, his fingers playing lightly.

For the first time Ward went into the apartment with her. Milissa had knocked on her door and finding no one there had gone back to her own apartment. She heard footsteps just as she was closing her door and left it open a crack to see if it might be Meda. Seeing Ward with her, she worried, should I just go over there and stay until he leaves or should I mind my own business. I'll just wait a few minutes and see if he leaves.

Milissa must have dozed for suddenly it

seemed the building was coming down around her. She opened the door as Briant was throwing clothes and shoes at a naked man. She wanted to laugh but didn't have time as she could hear chains slipping on the other doors.

"In here, Sir, quick before other doors open," urged Milissa.

Having no other choice Ward jumped inside the apartment. Milissa stayed outside and closed her door then quickly sat on the floor as doors opened. The neighbors came to assist her.

"Sorry, I disturbed you. I turned my ankle. These spike heels aren't much support to a woman."

"They certainly aren't," spoke up one woman.

"Women should wear sensible shoes," said the woman's husband. "Let us help you to your room," the couple offered.

"Oh no, that is, I mean I'm all right. The fall didn't hurt me." Milissa walked around to show she was all right. "Thank you all very much, and I'm sorry I disturbed you." She let herself into her apartment and continued to pace the floor as she whispered, "Are you dressed?"

"Yes, and I want to thank you. You must be Milissa," Ward said.

"Yes, I am."

"That was quite an act out there, young lady."

Milissa turned around looking at the man. "And you must be Mr. Sumner."

"An embarrassed one. That was a nice thing you did for me." Indicating the hallway with a nod of his head.

"Not for you, for Meda," said Milissa.

"Oh, yes, of course," agreed Ward.

"You might as well tell me what brought

Briant home since he just left a few days ago," Milissa asked.

"Sick with a cold, all this rain we're having wasn't helping him, so he came back home and found us. Meda was going to ask him for her freedom when he did come home." Said Ward.

"I guess she will get it now without asking," Milissa said.

"I'll leave now and thanks again. I wonder if I should go back over there. I'm worried about her." Ward looked directly at Milissa and said, "I do love her very much."

Ward stood outside the door a minute, then left. He was to regret it the rest of his life.

After Ward left, Milissa continued to stand at the door filled with a dreadful feeling of helplessness. "How can I go to Meda? What earthly excuse could I use for bursting in there now?"

Milissa heard the door of Meda's apartment open and cracked open her door. "If Briant is leaving, I can go to Meda." She thought. Milissa was startled to see that Briant had Meda by the arm and was pulling her along the hall, and down the stairs. Milissa walked to the end of the hall and looked out of the window and saw Briant push Meda into the automobile. When they drove off, she walked slowly back to her room.

Once the automobile was in motion, Briant turned on the windshield wipers. He did wish the rain would let up.

Briant turned to Meda, "Why Meda? Just tell me why. I did everything I could for you. I gave you my heart, my love, and would have given my life if necessary."

"I'm sorry if I've hurt you, Briant," Meda hesitated a moment. "I was going to ask you for my freedom. I've never said I loved you. I thought I could learn to, but you were always gone for such long periods of time and when you did come home it was sort of like a rabbit, hit and run. There was never any romance. I began to feel like I was your wench instead of your wife. I even wondered if you had one in every town."

"Hell, no, I didn't. There was never anyone but you. In another year I would have had things arranged so I could stay home all the time, but you couldn't wait. I had to work. I couldn't sit at home and hold your hand all day. I thought you understood. I was trying to build us a good future. I'll own the factory someday. We had so much going for us. We could have stayed out to the house then you and mother would have been company for each other but you wouldn't do that," his voice broke.

"No, I wouldn't; one roof is never big enough for two families," screamed Meda.

"You needn't scream so. Mother had a lonely life too, but she didn't run off and get a job and get involved with the boss," Briant said stonily.

"Don't hold your mother up as a good example to me. She's a fine woman and I love her but I had as fine a woman as there is to set examples for me. Anyway, how do you know what your mother did. She must have done something drastic because she sure controls your father now. She's got him walking a tight rope and he hasn't got sense enough to know it. And she was thirty-six when you were born. So how do you know what she did with all of her time? Were you sitting up above peeping down from heaven?"

"My little bitch of a wife, you needn't get sacrilegious."

"Who are you to condemn me. How do I know what you do on your long trips. Oh, Briant, can't we talk this over without getting nasty?" Meda asked pleadingly.

Briant made a turn and she realized they were headed for the Holland Tunnel.

"Where do you think you're going?" Meda asked.

"I'm taking you back to your parents."

"Oh, no, you're not!" Meda yelled.

"Oh, yes, I am."

Meda grabbed for the door. Briant jerked her back causing the automobile to slide on the wet pavement. Getting control he yelled at her, "You leave that door alone before you kill yourself."

"Then you take me back to my apartment. If you don't want to live there, you leave! Go to Long Island and live, I don't care!" she said with a flip of her hand.

"I'm taking you back where I got you from, then you can do what you damn well please."

"Just what am I supposed to tell my parents showing up there like this without even one suitcase of clothes."

"I don't give a damn what you tell them, but you could start with the truth!" Briant said emphatically.

"I'm not going back to that farm. I married you to get away from farm life, and I'm not going back. I'd rather die first." Meda yelled and grabbing the steering wheel she tugged with all her strength. The automobile went out of control and skidded sideways into the path of oncoming vehicles. Meda was killed instantly.

"Something has to be wrong," thought Lukatie, as she walked from room to room. That persistent foreboding premonition, so depressing a feeling that she felt the world was ending. This helpless feeling that she had felt a few times in her life was crushing her. "Maybe I'm just getting old and the hot flashes are getting worse."

Didge brought the news. She had taken the telephone call from New York. Meda was in an automobile crash, killed instantly and Briant is in serious condition. Briant's father had called.

"Oh, Mama, Meda was so full of life, so happy with her work." cried Didge.

Lukatie screamed, "Oh, God, why? All my children are nearly gone." She continued to scream as she ran upstairs and fell across her bed. Unable to control the flood that poured from her eyes and heart.

Em ran from his study taking the stairs two at a time. He burst into the room, "What in heaven's name is wrong with her, Didge?"

"It's Meda, Papa, she was in a wreck."

"Well, is she going to be all right?"

"No, Papa, she was killed. Briant is in serious condition at the hospital. Mr. Roberson called. He wants you to call him back as to what arrangements you want to make. He suggested their family cemetery on Long Island. Their automobile was hit on the side Meda was sitting. Briant has a broken leg, head and chest lacerations and has been unconscious ever since it happened last night," Didge stammered. She was shaking so bad she could hardly talk.

"Of all the terrible rotten news," Em sat down on the bed gathering Lukatie in his arms ignoring the grief-stricken look on Didge's face as he comforted his wife.

Didge left and went to her own room where she suffered alone. When the pain eased, she went to the telephone and called Miles at the store.

Em and Miles went to New York. They visited Briant at the hospital. Then brought Meda home to be buried in their own cemetery.

PART FOUR

1934-1938

The soft green shoots of grass refused to die and return to earth as long as summer lingered on. "The south is like that," thought Seth returning home in the warm early fall.

One of his first stops was to see Roxie and Noah. "Dars ma big boy all grow'd up." Roxie threw her arms around Seth's waist as he lay his arms around her shoulders.

"Have you shrunk, Roxie?" Seth laughed happily glad to be home.

"Nope, yo' jes grow'd taller."

"Roxie, I think you should go to New York and manage one of my restaurants," said Seth as he shook hands with Noah and Lebtia.

"One ov dem, how many yo' got, Seth?" asked Roxie.

"Five now, and planning another one in Washington, D.C.," Seth said hopefully.

"I'se happy fo' yo', but I coodn't lebe har. Dis air home ter me," smiled Roxie.

"Yo' gwine ter b' de richest man in de worl," said Noah.

"Not likely," laughed Seth.

Winnie burst into the café. "Whar is…oh…" she stopped short just inside the door. "Hello, Seth."

"Hello, Winnie, I was just leaving. I'll see you later, Roxie, Noah…"

"He won' notice me atall," pouted Winnie.

"No man likes ter b' chased after, Winnie."

"I don' do dat." Winnie blew her nose.

"Oh, yes, you do 'n listen ter how yo' talk. Whyn' yo' finish yore schoolin' so's yo' cood larn ter talk proper yo' mite hav' more ov a chance wit him."

"Yo' don' talk as good as I do 'n he lov's yo'," cried Winnie.

"Thets true, but lik' a sister," said Roxie.

"Oh!" Winnie stormed out of the café.

After the summer heat the cool quiet autumn breeze and rustling of crisp dry leaves of Indian Summer gave Didge the true feeling of joy. She raced with Regal II down the river path. Just being here and knowing Seth was home was reward enough to be happy. At the river, the sunlight was hitting the water just right to wake it up, it was smiling bright and beautiful. She hated to blink her eyes. It would be like drawing the blinds on so much natural beauty. The falling leaves added music to the beauty of the moment. The breeze blowing through the branches added the strumming of guitars with the rustle of leaves and warble of birds filling out a melody.

Didge sat down on her thinking stump leaning backwards to look up at the tall straight pines and spreading oaks. They whispered to her, but she knew it was the soft breeze caressing their limbs. Regal II barked and she reached over to pat and quieted him as she looked in the direction he was staring. The dog continued to bark while they watched bewitched as a large black snake slid around the limbs of an oak tree as graceful as a swan glides across a pond, looking for bird eggs and lizards to satisfy his appetite. Didge sighed as the snake disappeared. Her thoughts returned to the trees. She wondered what secrets they held. Would they speak to her if they could? Surely they would. Maybe they are as lonely as I am. In a virgin forest like this, they must be as old as eternity, perhaps even the creation. If they could tell their dreams and the things they've seen it would probably be quite a revelation to us all. I must paint them, especially the gnarled twisted one full of burls. It holds so much interest.

"I can see the seed of a painting that is about to be born being planted," Seth said standing behind Didge.

Didge whirled around to stare into Seth's eyes. She caught her breath quickly.

"Oh, yes, oh, yes, yes, I must do exactly that. I need a swamp scene for a book and with a little imagination I think I can get it right here."

"Didge, I've never seen anyone find so much joy in doing their work."

"Painting is like being in love, Seth, it…"

"And have you ever been in love, little Didge?" interrupted Seth.

Her face drained of all color as she gazed at him, raising slowly to her feet. It was a scene to rend the heart and surrender the soul.

"I'm sorry, Didge, just tell me to mind my own business."

In the shadow of her mind, Didge wondered as she looked at him if she put out her hand to touch his would his response be savage or gentle or would he withdraw. Every fiber of her being wanted to fade into his arms. The ache within her was filled with desire for him.

With an effort to control her voice, she said, "How long will you be staying this trip, Seth?"

"A week or two. I've quit playing baseball, so I'll come home often now."

"That will be nice," said Didge.

"I say home just like I had one here. I really never had a home."

"Of course, you have, Seth, both you and your grandmother. Mr. Heath expects you both to stay there, he is very fond of you."

"I suppose so, he has been every good to me and helped when I had no one to turn to. Didge, you were always my friend and helpful, but you couldn't help as he did and still does. I guess I feel sorry for myself because I didn't have a family like you have. Maybe I've envied you a little, but I'm very happy for you. A girl has to have a family for her well-being," said Seth.

"You think so," she flung at him. "You're welcome to mine. I'll keep Mama, you take Papa and good luck."

"I'm sure you don't mean that."

"Oh, yes, I do. He acts like he hates me. I'm still trying to figure out why he adopted me. Personally, I think Mama made him do it, and I'm always asking myself, why? They were so very poor. They could have put me in an orphanage. I don't like to talk about him, but you know how it has been."

"Yes, but you've still had protection and have been taught correct principles. Why don't you leave now? You're independent with a good income," suggested Seth.

"I've thought of it. Then I look at Mama. Miles and I are all that she has left. I don't think she's well, but she doesn't complain. I just can't bring myself to leave, not yet anyway."

By the middle of November all the crops were sold, and Miles came in excited with a house plan that even Julia couldn't deny was perfect. Work started on the house.

The idea of giving up her soft life living at the Blue Bird was making Julia irritable, ill-tempered and easily provoked.

"Is my girl pregnant?" asked Miles hopefully.

"No, I'm not pregnant, thank God," Julia snapped.

Bewildered Miles stated, "Then something is eating at you. What is it?"

"Nothing! Nothing is wrong," Julia said falsely, "Why?"

"If nothing is wrong then stop biting off everybody's head," said Miles.

"I haven't bit anyone," she yelled.

"You're getting impossible," Miles walked out of the room slamming the door behind him.

Julia refused dinner that evening begging off with a headache. "Nothing will ever be the same again," thought Julia, "when I move into the house. All the housework to do, the cooking and babies could come along to tend. I just don't have the will for all of that. I must think of something or someway to handle this."

Next morning at breakfast they all showed concern, asking about her headache.

"I'll act better," she thought. "They don't' know how I feel. It is silly to build a house when this one will belong to us one of these days. He's the only one to inherit it now. Didge is only adopted but of course she can stay on with us. Anyway, she makes good money and can take care of herself."

In their own way each knew what was eating Julia. They said nothing, but Em changed his mind about deeding over the property that the house and store was on. He'd wait and see…let him inherit it.

Gick had finished school, the only one of

the negroes on the Carroll farm to do so. Some had gone through the ninth grade and quit.

Seth was Gick's idol, and he told himself that if Seth could do it so could he. Gick continued on for two years of college at Smith University in Charlotte, North Carolina studying business and working to pay his expenses. Thankful helped all he could, and Em slipped Thankful extra money at times. Send it to Gilbert he would say.

When Gick returned home, Miles offered him a job in the hardware store. Thankful encouraged Gick to learn everything he could about the business.

"Mebbe sumday yo' kin open yore own store," said Thankful.

"Negroes don't open stores, Pa, even if they had the money. People wouldn't trade with them." Gick informed Thankful.

"Yore wrong, son, people trade whar they kin find whut they wonts," Thankful said. "Enyway times air changing 'n things will git better."

Gick liked working with Miles. They had a good understanding, and Miles could leave him in complete charge, if necessary. Em could read the prayer in Miles eyes when he looked at Julia and tried to tell her of his happiness in building the house for her. Julia was so noncommittal Em wanted to shake her.

"It's all so foolish, this building a house," Julia argued with Miles each night in their room.

"We should get a place of our own and leave the folks their privacy."

"Have they said for us to leave?" Julia pouted.

"Of course not," said Miles, his voice heated.

"There, there's no need to move out. I'm perfectly happy here. Anyway, the Blue Bird will be ours someday, and we might as well stay here."

With a feeling of exasperated reprimand, Miles said, "Listen to me, Julia, we are building, and we are moving, and it isn't likely we will ever call this house home again. Visit here all you like, but we will live in the house I'm building where we can start a family," said Miles firmly.

"A family be damned," Julia yelled, "I'll not raise a family to be hurt as I have been."

"I pray to God you don't place me in the same category as your father," Miles shook his head sadly.

"Miles!"

"Well, you asked for it, honey. You're against everything I try to do. Come here." Taking her by the hand he led her to the bed. "I know exactly what you need."

Didge was up early, watching the sunrise. It was almost a ritual with her to watch it rise each morning and set every evening. Slipping on a pair of old white ducks, and an old discarded shirt that belonged to Miles she gathered up her art material and headed for the river to paint the old gnarled tree with the lazy river showing just enough to look like swampland. She worked through lunch and could hardly believe the day was gone when she realized it was getting dark. So dark, she thought, I can hardly go on painting, my brushes are dripping with color, and gummed with oils, yet I do want to get in a few more touches.

Looking around, Didge realized that the darkness was because of the clouds. "Looks like rain," she thought. "In fact, it is raining." She brushed the hair out of her face with the back of her hand and started cleaning her brushes with turpentine and packing up her supplies. Didge arose reluctantly from her thinking stump and walked toward home. "Still so warm," she thought. The rain started peppering down harder, so she turned back and left her art materials in the old bathhouse.

A noisy confrontation of blue jays startled Didge and she turned abruptly to see one of them do a nose dive and peck Regal II on the rump as he raced yipping through the woods toward her. Didge dropped to her knees to comfort him and laughed as the blue jay flew away to sit innocently on the limb of an elm tree while squirrels barked and raced to safety.

"All right, old boy, I'll race you home." Regal II was getting very old and walked all the way. The blue jay had sapped him of his remaining energy.

The night was restless as the big drops of rain fell. Tension filled the air. A staccato pounding hit the roof and shouted against the windowpanes finally merging into sheets of rain as it lashed out against the house and upon the land, washing gullies through the now empty fields. Fireworks of lightening played continuously in the heavens reaching long flashing arms to earth to tantalize, frighten and destroy anything in its path as thunder rolled its anger through the air. Ruthlessly the wind stripped the trees of their last glorious color. Like the very wrath of God, it blew and howled breaking limbs and uprooting trees. The earth shook, the rain fell in torrents, trees twisted or bowed to the ground. It looked like the new house would be left in the same ruins as the old one had been. Lightening flashed recurrently never ceasing, while the moon stayed comfortably hidden in the heavens.

The torrents of rain provided the earth with tears to cleanse itself, or so it seemed to Lukatie as she walked from window to window looking out. "Wind...wind...wind...thank goodness I can't see you. You're so terrible in your wrath." She felt fascinated as she watched, wondering what pleasure the wind got out of destroying or whipping everything in its path. She wondered if her Blue Bird was going to fly away on such a wild wind.

The next morning Regal II was found dead under the house. "Poor fellow died of old age," they thought. Didge felt crushed.

"We can get one of Clay Golden's puppies. They are off-springs of Regal II we could call him Regal the Third," offered Lukatie.

"I think in this case you can call him Jr.," said Em. "I guess that act was the old boy's undoing."

A week after the storm Stewart returned home. "How I've missed him," thought Lukatie as she greeted him at the door. The smile on her face was not forced as she held out both hands to him.

"You have been gone so long, so very long," Lukatie said.

"Yes, I have, much too long," Stewart took both her hands holding them tightly as he smiled into her eyes. His eyes teased her as he said, "It strikes me as how one so beautiful can also be so good. Let's change that." He pulled her against him and kissed her full on the lips for the first time.

"You're all scoundrel," she laughed, "but I love it."

"You're an honest, tender and lovely person, Lukatie Carroll, and I still wish you were mine."

"At my age?" teased Lukatie.

"My dear, you mellow with age. Just keep that twinkle in your eyes, dear, and you'll stay young forever," Stewart's eyes were serious.

"What's this," cut in Em as he walked down the hall from his study. "You still trying to fill my wife's head with foolish notions?"

"Of course not," chuckled Stewart, "Just telling her the truth."

"Come on in and tell us about your trip," invited Lukatie. "You certainly aren't one for writing."

"I stand guilty as accused." Stewart hung his head rolling his eyes.

"You're forgiven," laughed Lukatie.

"Well, I did try to phone Meda when I left New York. I couldn't get her. The operator said the number was disconnected. I figured they had moved."

"Meda is dead, Stewart," said Em quietly.

Stewart looked from one to the other at their still faces.

"I'm sorry, I didn't know."

"We know you didn't. It was an automobile wreck. Miles and I went to New York and brought her body home. We tried to telephone you, but never could get in touch," Em said.

"Didge tried to call you when she was in New York, too, but couldn't get you either," said Lukatie.

"Didge was in New York?"

They quickly filled him in on her trip and job. "She had barely been home a couple of months when Meda was in the accident. We lost Lucinda too, Stewart," said Em.

"Oh my God, no. What you two must have been through."

"The hurt has turned to numbness now Stewart, or otherwise we couldn't bear it," said Lukatie.

"Was she with Meda?" asked Stewart.

They told him of the life Lucinda had chosen for herself in order to hide from Fountain, and of her death caused by the earthquake in China.

"I didn't realize I was gone so long. A lot has happened, I'm so sorry."

"Tell us about yourself," begged Lukatie.

Didge walked in and saw Stewart, "Oh, Uncle Stewart," she ran to him as he rose from his chair and they embraced.

"I hear you've become a famous illustrator now. I'm very proud of you."

"Thank you. Tell us about yourself, please," Didge begged as she sat down at his feet.

"To begin with, Titia has married again to another foreigner in Europe."

"What is he like?" Didge asked eagerly.

"He's a Duke. He's a fine old nobleman. I really like him," said Stewart.

"A ruler of a duchy, huh, that makes Titia a duchess," grinned Didge.

"That about sums it up," said Stewart.

"When did she marry him?" asked Lukatie.

"About six months ago," said Stewart.

"Everytime I called you, you were out. I'll bet you were busy dating all those beautiful smart looking New York ladies," teased Didge her eyes laughing into his.

"I could write you a book about some of those beautiful, smart-looking New York ladies, but it wouldn't be for your eyes to read," Stewart teased back at her.

"Oh," Lukatie raised her eyebrows.

"Oh, don't get me wrong, I did meet some nice ones, one in particular. A very lovely lady, we spent a lot of time together. Say, I do remember Mrs. Cox saying a young voice called me several times, but wouldn't leave a name," smiled Stewart.

"No, I wouldn't. I wanted the pleasure of surprising you. Did you bring the very special lady home with you, Uncle Stewart?"

"No, Didge, I didn't."

"She wasn't so smart to let you get away," declared Didge. "Any woman should be happy to get you for a husband. I hope someday I can find a man as good and fine as you to marry."

Somewhat embarrassed Stewart smiled, "That is a nice compliment dear, and I'm sure you'll find the right one."

Em cleared his throat trying to catch Didge's eye but she wouldn't look at him.

"I hope you're right, Uncle Stewart, because one of these days I do intend to marry," Didge said, feeling Em may as well know it.

"Didge," Em spoke sharply, "Go bring some coffee and muffins."

"Yes, Sir," she answered cooly rising to her feet. She glided easily, smoothly across the room and through the door.

Em watched her go, thinking, I never noticed her walking like that before. She is indeed her mother's daughter.

Returning to the room, Didge set the tray on a table beside Lukatie.

"Excuse me, please, Uncle Stewart, I'd like to finish the painting I was working on. You know I'm a working girl now."

"Sure, honey," said Stewart.

Em breathed easier, he felt he had nothing to worry about when she stayed in her studio.

"Maybe I should lock her in then she wouldn't get killed like my other two daughters," he thought.

Lukatie was happier than she had been in a longtime knowing Stewart was home. He made her laugh but more he made her feel like a woman.

Lura was strolling aimlessly across the field soon to be planted. Suddenly she became aware of some unusual commotion in the woods. She paused to take a better look then walked on into the woods. Drawing nearer she saw Winnie butting her stomach against a tree as hard as she could throw herself against it.

"Winnie stop dat, whut 'n tarnation air yo' doing' thet fer?" asked Lura.

"Whut air yo' followin' me fer," Winnie said acidly.

"Don' yo' git sassy, young lady, yo' hain't too big fer me ter tan yo' hide," Lura said confused.

"I didn' say anythang sassy, Maw."

"Hit hain't whut yo' said, hit's de tone yo' said hit 'n, chile."

"Oh, Maw, why did yo' hav' ter cum along rite now. Oh, Maw, I'se a tryin' ter git rid ov dis chile dat I'se hung up wit'." Tears brimmed out of her eyes sliding down her cheeks as she looked at Lura.

"Oh, Gawd," moaned Lura.

"I'se sorry, Maw, I'se so sorry. Yore allus haranguin' me not ter mak' mistakes cause yo' allus had such great plans fer me 'n I'se let yo' down," Winnie buried her face in her hands and cried.

"Wal yo' don' hit 'n no young'un ov mine is gwine ter turn murder. So face up ter hit."

"Maw, yo' asayin' I'se got ter hav' dis chile?" asked Winnie.

"Dat's whut I'se asayin' chile."

SILENT TEARS

"No, Maw, no, I don' wan' dis chile, dis is no love chile. Hit's a spite chile. I'se got ter rid m'self ov hit, Maw, I'se jest got ter," pleaded Winnie.

"Yo' will hav' hit," Lura said emphatically. "Yo' kill hit 'n de Lawd Gawd 'lmighty will sand yore soul straight ter hell."

"No, Maw, no," cried Winnie dropping her head on Lura's shoulder.

"Yas, chile, now yo' cum on home 'n fergit dis notion ov riddin' yo'self ov dat young'un." Lura put her arms around her daughter and led her home.

At the supper table that evening Chauncy asked Lura, "Whar is Winnie?"

"Sh' acryin' 'n 'er room."

"Whut sh' acryin' 'bout," asked Chauncy.

"Mite as well know'. Yo'll be' aknoin' fo' long anyhow."

Clarkey and Levi were listening, but didn't slow down in their eating.

"Kno' whut, woman, say hit," said Chauncy clearing his throat.

"Winnie gon' 'n got 'erself wit' chile, dats whut," sniffled Lura.

Clarkey and Levi nearly choked on a mouth full of food. Levi in worse shape ended up with Clarkey pounding him on the back while Clarkey asked, "How sh' do thet, sh' neber hang 'round wit de negroes."

Winnie ran in the kitchen. "Whut yo' go 'n tell fer, Maw. Ain't I got 'nough troubles?"

"Dey gwine kno' soon, mite as well git hit ober wit'."

"Who hit belong ter, girl? 'N sit 'n eat yore vittles," ordered Chauncy.

"Kin't tell 'n I hain't hungry," cried Winnie.

"Yo' got ter feed two, yo' betta eat. Den yo' git ready yo' gwine marry up wit dat chile's pa." Chauncy informed her.

"Kin't do dat Pa, I don' lov' em," cried Winnie.

"Yo' hav' ter figure dat out fer yoreself. Look's lak us collored folk 'ud larn sumpin' sum'time. 'N I thought dis fambly had," said Chauncy.

"Den, Maw 'n Pa yo' tell me why I'se so much lite'r den yo' 'n m' bro'hers."

"Tain't nuttin' wrong twixt me 'n yore Pa," snapped Lura. "Yo' cum by hit natural lak m' maw wus lite 'n yore pa's maw 'n pa wus lite. Nuttin' wrong gal. We's had ourself a good honest life marrin' up. Iffen yo' keep dat chalk offen yo' face yo'll see dat yo' hain't as white as yo' tink yo' air. Yore de one dat's lettus down." Hurt and angry, Lura left the table.

Winnie jumped up from the table and followed Lura, "Maw, Maw, I'se so sorry. I is, Maw, I is." Cried Winnie.

"Go warsh yo' face 'n col' water 'n stop dat cryin'," said Lura.

"Yassum, Maw."

By the end of spring it was quite evident that Winnie was pregnant. Some of the black men had placed bets on who the father was. Winnie spent more and more time at home unless she thought Seth was around. Then she ventured out to Roxie's looking for him.

Finny Patchett was always waiting and would beg Winnie to marry him. She looked at his acne scarred face and wanted to vomit. "At least it was darker that night and I couldn't see him," she thought.

"No, thank yo', Finny," Winnie said.

"Yo' kno's I love yo' 'n m' baby yore

acarrin', please, Winnie."

"Wal, I don' loves yo' 'n I hain't amarrin' yo'."

"Winnie, we's did enjoy 'n iffen we's marries up we's kin do hit allus wants ter, please, Winnie."

"I said, no Finny, now lebe 'm alone. 'N I shore as hell dudden' enjoy hit." Winnie looked like she was about to strike him.

The next day Winnie met Seth on the path. He was headed for Thankful's.

"Why, hello thar, Seth," said Winnie.

"Hello, Winnie," Seth continued walking.

"Kin yo' holt up, Seth, I'se thangs ter talk 'bout ter yo'."

"I'm in a hurry, Winnie," Seth said tersely. He could see Didge walking in the yard and wanted to hurry. *Maybe I can walk over and talk to her.*

There was a numbing feeling of futility as she looked at him.

"Seth, please, we's culd marry up 'n I'd mak' yo' a good woman."

"No, Winnie, you marry the baby's father." Not one to mince words, he added. "I don't love you and I won't marry you."

"Don' fret 'bout dat, I loves yo' 'nough fer both ov us," declared Winnie.

He scowled saying nothing. Winnie looked in the direction he was looking and switched her role like a flash with a harsh accusative question.

"Why air hit yo' look at thet damn white gal so dandified 'n yore eyes kin't see 'm atall." Winnie glared at Seth hotly. Her wrath so strong she was shaking.

"Cut it out, Winnie, and behave yourself. You go on and marry that baby's father like you ought to and get it through your head I'm not marrying you or anyone else. I don't want to be a married man. Do you understand?"

"Yes, yo' will marry up wit 'm cause I'se tellin' eber one hit's yore child I'se a totin'."

"You know that's a lie, Winnie."

"I kno' dat but no budy else gonna kno' hit. Dey shore gon' kno' yore dis chile's pa." Trying to act coy Winnie said, "A-co'se yo' marry m' I'se gwine say yo' shore goodern any man alive ter marry up wit m' 'n give dis chile a pa."

Seth strode off before he completely lost control of himself and struck her.

Winnie's breath came in little sobbing gasps. Pulling herself together she dashed home to start the rumors that Seth was the father of her child.

When Seth walked away from Winnie, he drove all night returning to New York to take care of business. Perhaps leaving he could stop Winnie's tongue. He certainly didn't like clashing with her. Seth's desire to see Didge was so strong that a month later he headed home again. Just seeing her from a distance was better than not seeing her at all. Seth was beginning to regret putting her in touch with Mr. Bush. Even when he was home, he hardly ever saw her since she was so busy all the time.

Mr. Heath kidded him, "Couldn't stay away, huh?"

"What are you talking about?" Seth asked.

"Oh, you know, can't say I blame you, she's a cute wench."

"Mr. Heath, would you please be a little more explicit?"

Seth's grandmother was working around the room listening. She hadn't liked the accusations made against Seth.

"I'm talking about that Winnie, the stories she's spreading around about you being the father of the baby she's expecting."

Seth leaned against the doorfacing feeling numb, "She seems to have been busy. I didn't get her pregnant, Mr. Heath, she's trying to force me to marry her by telling these lies, and I won't do it."

Seth's grandmother gave an audible sigh of relief.

"Well, somebody did it and it certainly wasn't a coon," declared Mr. Heath.

"And it certainly wasn't me," said Seth angrily.

Seth left the house and walked through the woods to the river. His dark thoughts were penetrated by the barking of a dog. He went to investigate and found Didge crumpled in a heap her head rammed against a tree. His quick eyes took in the roughed up bark on a large root exposed above ground. Tripped, he thought. Seth felt her neck to see if it was broken. "No, thank God," he spoke aloud. He carefully picked her up making sure her clothing was straight. He was careful not to touch the skin he loved to look upon as she swam in the river. He must leave her all the modesty she deserved. Seth dropped his head and kissed the top of her head thinking it surely wouldn't hurt to kiss the hair.

Didge felt suspended, drifting in space as Seth carried her. "Dream on, little Didge," her thoughts tumbled down like flashes of strong bright lightening a whirlpool of memories that refused to surface. "Dream, baby, dream, this is all so beautiful."

Em saw Seth as he walked into the yard with Didge in his arms and Regal Jr. at his heels. He was shocked at seeing her carried so tenderly in a man's arms. It disconcerted him momentarily.

"Put her down and keep your filthy hands off of her," Em shouted. His shouts brought Lukatie running to the door.

"Didge is hurt, Mr. Em and I don't think you'd want me to leave her laying on the path near the river." "Thimit," thought Lukatie looking at Em.

"Em, open the door and show him to Didge's room," she yelled.

"Bring her in, Seth, you must be exhausted bringing her that far," she said with concern.

"Yes, ma'am, my arms are aching." Seth followed Em into the house and laid Didge gently on the big four posted bed. Lukatie came in with cold compresses and lay one on Didge's brow then wiped her face with a cool wet cloth.

"What happened, Seth?" asked Lukatie.

"Ma'am, I heard a dog barking, and I went to investigate. Regal, Jr. was circling around Miss Didge and wouldn't let me near her until I could calm him down. It looked like they had been running and she tripped on a large root and struck her head on a tree. She was out cold just like she is now. I suggest getting the doctor. It could be a concussion. Ma'am I couldn't leave her alone in the woods to get help. So I just picked her up and brought her home. If you think I did wrong, I'm sorry."

"You did exactly right, Seth, and I'll always be grateful to you. Some wild animal could have killed her. You probably saved her life."

It was the first time Seth had ever been in Didge's bedroom. He had been through the house many times before its completion. While he talked he was taking in every detail of the large room with the built-in clothes closet, big comfortable looking bed, large marble top dresser, the deep green carpet picked up the floral pattern of the bedspread, with pale green curtains that crisscrossed the window. "The room is perfect for her golden beauty," Seth thought.

"I'll go along now if there is nothing more I can do, Mrs. Carroll. I hope she will be all right," said Seth.

"I've called Dr. Wesson," Em said as he came into the room. "Seth, I want to apologize for the way I spoke. It was uncalled for. It was just the shock of seeing you holding Didge. I would have said the same thing to any man. I do hope you know it was nothing personal. I do know you would never harm her."

"I understand, Mr. Carroll," said Seth.

"If you want to come back and see how she is getting along, please feel welcome to do so." invited Em.

"If it's all right I'd like to sit on the steps and wait until the Doctor comes and hear what he says." Said Seth.

"Now, Seth, there is no need to sit outside in those mosquitoes; go in the parlor. Maybe you'd like to read the paper while you wait," Em suggested.

Seth went outside. Regal, Jr. was on the porch waiting. "It's all right, boy, she is going to be all right, she's just got to be all right," Seth said as he sat down on the steps and petted the dog.

Doctor Wesson confirmed Seth's diagnosis saying, "About all we can do is wait until she comes to."

"How long do you think that will be?" asked Lukatie.

"I've no way of knowing, it could be an hour; it could be days," said Doctor Wesson.

"Days!" cried Lukatie.

"Yes, I've no way of knowing how hard the blow to her head was. There are no bones broken so I think she will come to with a very bad headache. I'll leave some pills for her aches." The Doctor said.

"Isn't there something we can do?"

"Sure, have someone with her at all times. We could take her to the hospital, but I don't think that will be necessary unless we find there is more wrong than the concussion when she awakens."

Em listened, a helpless look on his face. Wishing he could do or say the right thing, he noted that the death-like paleness didn't detract from her beauty. She looked so peaceful and pretty lying there.

"I'll go tell Seth," Em said.

"He is the one that found her and brought her home," Lukatie said to Doctor Wesson by way of explanation as Em left the room.

It was getting dark and starting to rain when Seth thanked Em and left. It was pouring rain when he ran up on Thankful's porch.

"Hit ain't a fit night ter b' out," said the old man sitting in his chair leaning against the wall.

"Sitting out in the dark, huh, good way to hide your sins, Mr. Mathias."

"Cum on 'n sit Seth 'n mak yer'self home whar yo'ought ter b'," chuckled the old man.

"You're right, you old coot. I should be somewhere besides around here. May I talk with you a little?" asked Seth.

"Yo' kin talk all yo' wants ter. Yo' hav' thangs on yore mind yo' wants ter git offen hit don' yo'?"

"I guess so; it seems it doesn't make any difference where I go or what I do, I feel it's all wrong, Mr. Mathias."

"We'se don' git by wit out havin' troubles or worries sumway or tuther. Eber one has dem. Whut's yore troubles, son?"

"I found Miss Didge on the path down near the river; she had fallen and hit her head on a tree. She's out cold and I'm worried sick," said Seth.

"No need ter worry won' hep none, son."

"Sometimes I think I'll find the blackest girl there is and marry her. Maybe then I could get Miss Didge out of my system," muttered Seth.

The old man let him rant and rave as he spent his pent-up emotions. Then softly said, "Ter do thet wud ma' a lie outten yore life 'n yo' wouddn't wan' ter do thet."

"But how do I get over the ache, the want, the feel of her warm body in my arms when I took her home," said Seth.

"Don' thank 'bout hit; turn hit offen yer mind."

"I can't turn off something I live and breathe daily. She feels it too. I know it. I can see it in her eyes."

"Son, yo' kno' de way she's been raised. Sh' kin't cross ova no matter whut sh' feels."

"Oh, I suppose you're right. I'll run along home. See you soon and thank you, Mr. Mathias, for listening."

Em and Lukatie sat with Didge all night. They talked constantly thinking that their voices would rouse her. Stewart came over and offered to sit with her while they rested.

"We couldn't sleep so we'll sit with her," said Lukatie. "Maybe later if she doesn't improve, we'll need you."

"Then I'll go if you promise to call when I can help," said Stewart.

"Sure," said Em and walked outside with Stewart.

The next morning Lovie came over to sit with Didge. "My poor baby," she moaned. "My pore, pore baby, lak m' own sh' shore is. Jes look at dat lump biggern airy egg I'se eber seen on m' pore baby's haid." Cried Lovie.

Curiosity caused Winnie to go over to the Carroll's to see if she could help.

"I kin cum set wit 'er ter night, Miz Carroll."

"Thank you, Winnie, that will be a big help. Can you come about nine o'clock?"

"Yas'm, I kin b' heah."

"We'll look for you then," said Lukatie.

Winnie was there on time. "Miz Carroll, yo' go 'n git sum rest. I'se go'en ter tak' good kar ov Miz Didge fer yo'."

"All right, Winnie, but if she starts to come to you call me." Said Lukatie.

"Yas'm, Miz Carroll."

Winnie sat beside the bed looking at Didge, thinking, she's so purty. I wish sh' dead. If sh'd jes die I could git Seth. Maybe sh' die while I'se sittin' here lookin' at 'er. Sh's good to me, but I wants Seth. I do.

Winnie watched Didge's even breathing for hours, hoping each breath would be the last one.

"I kin jes hep 'er outten 'her misery wit' dat pillow, I kin," Winnie mumbled out loud.

She picked up the pillow was about to place it over Didge's face when the door opened and Em walked in.

"Jes thouten I culd mak' 'er more comfitaball, Mistuh Em," said Winnie, pumping and fluffing up the pillow she exchanged it for the one under Didge's head.

"I woke up and thought I'd look in,

goodnight, Winnie," Em walked slowly back to his room. The look on Winnie's face had puzzled him.

Em got back in bed, but couldn't go back to sleep. He kept seeing Winnie's face. he went back to Didge's room just as Winnie was reaching for the pillow again.

"Winnie, you go on home. I'll sit with Didge," Em told her.

"Oh, no suh, Mistuh Em, I'se ter sit wit 'er."

"No need for both of us to lose sleep. I can't sleep so you go on home, now Winnie, go on and thank you." Em sat down beside the bed.

"Yassuh, iffen yo' says so."

"So insensible a person," thought Em. "She wouldn't know what to do if Didge did regain consciousness. In fact, I wonder if she ever would if Winnie had stayed." Em couldn't rid himself of the expression on her face. "She won't stay again. I'll see to that." He told himself.

The next afternoon, Didge tried to open her eyes and they wouldn't obey. "That just isn't right. They're supposed to look at beauty, even ugliness and make beauty of it. For goodness sakes, open eyes, open so I can see." A wave of fear engulfed her. "Am I dead, it's so quiet. Somebody, please help me." Didge thought she was screaming yet no sound escaped her lips. "No, I'm not dead. If I were, I wouldn't be having this awful headache." Her hands spread out by her side with arms straight, she fingered the sheets. "Are they Mama's colored sheets?" she wondered, "or new black ones, black sheets for the dead," she giggled trying in vain again to open her eyes.

"Em, she is moving her hands." "Didge," a voice said softly.

"That I am," thought Didge hazily. "I'm laying down too in bed. Is it my bed?" She couldn't ask, couldn't look, and who in hell is Em. "Oh, oh, I don't talk like that. Oh, yes, Em is my father. No, he is just the man I was forced on that the nice lady, Lukatie, wouldn't let him get rid of me. I like calling her Mama."

"Mama."

"Yes, dear, I'm right here," Lukatie said softly.

"There, I said it," she thought as she drifted to sleep again washed about by the turbulence of her dreams, running, running. "I was running," Didge cried out.

"There, there, dear, rest now," said Lukatie's soothing voice. "You've been through some bad times, just try to rest and sleep, you had a bad fall."

Two hours later, Didge snapped her eyes open and closed them quickly. In that quick glance the room she knew seemed to shrink so small she and all those swimming craggy, distorted faces around her would be crushed.

"Didge, open your eyes, young lady," urged Doctor Wesson.

"Everyone will be crushed if I do."

"No, they won't," he forced her lids open and shined a light into them. He felt her forehead, checked her reflexes and her pulse.

"The knot on her head has gone down a lot. I'd say a couple of days she will be fine. Give her those pills I gave you for a headache. Mrs. Carroll, you can do as much now as I can for her. Just let her rest but try waking her every hour or so during the day and let her sleep all night until she's herself again. Patience, you can keep cold compresses on her forehead."

"Yes, Doctor Wesson," Patience said, glad to be of service.

A week later Didge was completely

recovered. She called upon Winnie and asked her to make a couple of smocks. "Can you get them ready in about a week?" Didge asked.

Winnie shrugged and turned away from her with the material in her hands.

"Yas'm I rackon I kin."

"Winnie, I want to thank you for sitting with me when I was hurt."

"Yo' welcum," she flung out over her shoulder.

Didge couldn't miss the scathing hate in her voice and wondered why. That wasn't like Winnie, maybe she doesn't feel like it.

"Winnie, please, just a minute. If you don't feel like sewing that is all right. I can get someone else. I just thought you might want…"

"I do wan' de money 'n I'se gwine ter do it, Miz Didge," cut in Winnie.

She walked into the house, the screen door slamming behind her.

Didge was puzzled as she walked home.

Winnie flung the material across the room, the thread followed the pattern, then anything else within reach.

"Maw, Maw," yelled Levi. "Thet Sis gon' plumb crazy 'er maddin' up 'n a-cryin' 'n throwin' tings eber whar."

Winnie turned on Levi fighting and scratching. "Whut ho' maddin' up at me fer, Sis?" When Levi couldn't hold her off, he slapped her across the room.

"Doan yo' pounce onter m' lak' dat yo' dang black negro," Winnie screamed running at him wildly. Levi grabbed her and pinned her arms to her side and Lura came in.

"Whut's go'en on 'n har," Lura wanted to know. By then Winnie was crying in Levi's arms.

"Hits all right now, Maw, Sis wus upset."

"Wal, sh' better git dis room sot 'n order agin 'n I means hit," emphasized Lura. Stoically she turned and walked back outside.

Seth was tired of the rumors spread by Winnie that he was responsible for her pregnancy. Her family didn't believe it, thank goodness. But there is always that element of society that believes anything, especially if its derogatory to others. Since no one won any bets as to the father of Winnie's child, bets were placed on the color of the skin it would have. Seth's denial only caused laughter or rebuke. He was a dang fool or a lucky dog in the opinion of most. "I could go back to New York, but that would make me appear guilty. I'll just go ahead and have it out with her and force her to tell the truth."

"Wal, whut yo' har fo'?" Winnie asked.

"Winnie, I want you to stop telling people I'm responsible for your pregnancy, you know it isn't true."

"Yo' marry up wit m' 'n I tells de truff."

"How can you debase yourself so. No, Winnie, I'm not going to marry you. I don't love you. I just want you to leave me alone."

Winnie glared at Seth, "damn yo', yo' kin larn ter lov' m'." She struck out blindly, fighting; she had to hurt him.

"That is enough, Winnie." Angrily, Seth grabbed Winnie by the arms holding her off.

"Why don't you tell the truth? You, oh, what's the use. No one can reason with you," Seth released her.

Winnie yelled at him, "Why don' yo' beat m', go on b' a man or hav' yo' got so much ov thet sof' wite blood 'n yo' thet yo' kin't eben b' a man?"

"A man is a gentleman which I'm trying very hard to be right now," said Seth. "Winnie it's your bed, now you lie in it. And tell the truth."

"I bet yo' wish I wus daid."

"No, I don't wish that. Just tell the truth that is all I want," said Seth.

Unknown to either of them Didge had left her house walking over to see if Winnie had finished her smocks. Didge paused on the steps when she heard Winnie's loud voice saying.

"Ov co'se I kno' hit's not yore baby 'n yo' kno' hit, but jest try 'n prove hit. I'se tolt yo' I'se gwine ter git yo' 'n I will," glared Winnie.

Didge spoke from the door, "I guess Seth has his proof. I heard every word you said." She stepped through the door looking calm, yet with an almost uncontrollable turmoil raging inside. Didge felt like she could shake Winnie until she fell apart.

For a minute Winnie was stunned, her hands dropped to her sides and she stood rigid with her feet slightly apart. She needed time to think. She tucked her chin down; her eyes shot up looking first at Seth then Didge. Then she thrust one hand forward pointing at Didge but looking at Seth. Winnie said between clenched teeth. "When yo' look at 'er yo' hav' de look ov lov' 'n yore eyes, but whan yo look at m' hit's gon'." Switching to Didge Winnie said, "Yo' tink yore bettern anybudy else, but yo' ain't. Yo' kin't tell m' dere is no goin's on betwist yo two. Wal, Miz Didge I'se seed how he watched yo' 'n iffen yo' says one word I'se gwine swear dere is sum goin's on twist yo'. Der jest got ter b' sum rasin yo' hain't a courtin' 'n marrin' up lak' yore sisters did. Now, Miz Didge, I'se don' wan' ter hurt yo', yo' good ter m', but I'se got ter fight fo' whut I wants."

Didge looked from one to the other, nothing

the mulatto skin of Winnie and the white skin of Seth. "Indeed, there has been some goings on as Winnie said, but certainly not between Seth and me."

"Winnie, I came to see if my smocks were ready and to bring your money," Didge laid the money on the table.

Winnie picked up the smocks and thrust them at her, "Hare."

"There is no excuse for ill manners," said Seth as he walked out the door, leaving the charged air behind.

"Winnie, I won't bother you for anymore sewing, but I warn you to tell the truth about Seth. And if I ever hear of anything you say about Seth or me, I will put you in jail so fast for defamation of character you won't know what hit you. There is nothing between us, never has been and never can be, not that it's any of your business," Didge said stoutly. Turning she walked out leaving Winnie stammering in the middle of the room.

Winnie kept quiet. She didn't clear Seth of her pregnancy neither did she say anything against Didge. She only succeeded in losing her opportunity for sewing jobs. She needed the money badly. "Will I end up having to marry Finny," she wondered. "No, I can't stand him, I'll never marry him."

To Seth's surprise the next two weeks passed quietly. Then on a beautiful moonlit night as he left Roxie's café and walked along the road he saw Finny Patchett trying to pull a woman into the woods. This was surprising since they usually went willingly. With a few exceptions their morals were nothing to them. They had pleasures whenever they chose, without conscience. This was one thing about his people that worried him.

Seth hurried and saw it was Winnie. Why in heaven's name does it have to be her. He could hear Finny talking.

"I wan' yo' 'n I wan' yo' now, cum on fo' sumbudy see us," Finny urged.

Winnie screamed at him, "Yo'll not git me. 'Cause I don' wan' yo'."

"Winnie, do you want to go in the woods with Finny?" Seth asked as he drew near.

"Hell, no, I don't."

"Yo' shore hav' changed, Winnie, look at yo' carrin' m' baby 'n sayin' yo' dudden lak hit." Finny looked down his nose at her.

"Damn yo' Finny, I'se larned better. 'N tryin' ter hurt him," indicating Seth. "I'se let yo' ruin m' now, yo' lebe m' alone yo' black bastard, yore de baddest man 'round yo' varmin."

Finny's mouth was open baring his teeth and gums like some feral animal about to pounce on some defenseless mammal. He grabbed Winnie and knocked her down. Impulsively Seth hit Finny and knocked him down. He came up fighting. Then they were down rolling on the ground like wild cats. Finny was trying to get at his pocketknife. Winnie was rigid with fright as she watched the fight. "Watch out," Winnie yelled, "Watch out, Seth, he's comin' unhinged." Back on their feet, Seth hit Finny with a swift right on the jaw, with a left in the stomach as Finny's head bounced on the ground, he doubled up and lay still.

Seth leaned against a tree while he mopped his face and caught his breath. Then he walked over and checked Finny.

"He's all right, Winnie, I suggest that you go on home."

"Seth, yo' fights fo' m' 'n yo' say yo' don' lov' m' yo' mu skar," pleaded Winnie.

"You are confusing the issue. I wasn't fighting for love. It was the principle. Shall I spell it out for you?"

"Yas," Winnie said meekly.

"You damn dumb foolish woman," Seth swore under his breath. "Listen, Winnie, if you had wanted to go in the woods with Finny I would have gone on. Since you didn't want to go and he was forcing you, I stopped him. I would have done the same for any woman, understand?"

"I gess so, but I shore wist yo' lov' m'."

Understanding a thing, and accepting it were two different things to Winnie. She wasn't about to give up on Seth.

"Well, I don't. Now get on home," said Seth.

The tenacious Winnie begged and pleaded with Seth to stay with her.

"I wuld go in ter woods wit' yo' Seth," Winnie pleaded.

"I'd rather rot in hell first," Seth said and left her standing there. "I'll sure avoid her like the proverbial plague," he told himself.

Winnie turned furious, looking down at Finny a second or two. She kicked him in his genitals and walked off. She had gone only a few steps when she heard someone coming and ducked behind a tree. It was Hezekiah. He stopped when he saw Finny stretched out in the road slowly coming to. "It looks like somebody gave you a good going over. I'll just bet I can help out." Taking the knife out of his pocket he plunged it into the prostrated body of Finny.

Winnie's skin pricked and instinctively she pressed her hand over her mouth. Oh, my Gawd, she thought, I'm going to spew, and he'll find me and kill me too. Then she was spell bound as Hezekiah slashed him across the throat several times severing the jugular vein and larynx. A circular slash through the stomach eviscerated him then he kicked him in the face knocking his teeth out. Hezekiah wiped his hands and knife on Finny's shirt. "There's no common place cliché between us is there old boy?" He laughed and walked on down the road.

Seeing the knifing caused Winnie to start shaking violently. She sank silently to the ground. Controlling herself as long as she could, she screamed, jumping up and ran stumbling into the cafe.

Winnie pointed down the road, "Seth, Seth, he, he, Finny dead he…" she crumped into a dead faint.

"Whut's wrong wit yo', Winnie?" asked Roxie going to her. Failing to revive her, Roxie was worried.

"Levi, yo' 'n Clarky, git Winnie home jest as fast as yo' kin. One ov yo' run 'n git Miz Carroll ober dare 'n hurry now. Calvin Tootle, yo' go down de road 'n see whut 'er wus talkin' 'bout. Go wit him, Jesse."

Stewart was at the Carroll's for dinner. Afterwards they were all sitting around talking when a loud knock sounded at the door. Clarky was standing there with sweat running down his face.

"Miz Carroll, Maw say kin yo' cum quick," Clarky was panting as he talked.

"What's the matter Clarky?" concern showed in Lukatie's face.

"Hit's Winnie, Miz Carroll, Maw says 'ers losin' 'er chile, 'ers bleedin' sumpin' arful. Paw's got de hot watah boilin'."

"Run on back, Clarky, and tell them I'm coming."

"Yas'm."

"Let them call the Doctor," said Em.

"Take him too long to get here. You can call him, but I'll go over. She's about to abort, and needs someone now," said Lukatie.

"You really aren't thinking seriously of going over there, are you?" questioned Em.

"I don't think about it, I just do it, Em, you know that," said Lukatie.

"I'll go with you, Mama," said Didge.

"Here, Didge, take my car since it's already out front," said Stewart holding out the keys.

"I'd better not, Uncle Stewart."

"Go ahead, Miles said you were a good driver."

"It isn't that, I just don't know how long we'll be gone," smiled Didge.

"That's all right. I'll sit here and talk with Em." affirmed Stewart.

"Well, all right," Didge accepted the keys and ran out the door behind her mother.

They found Winnie hemorrhaging and within half an hour the fetus delivered. Wrapped in newspapers, Levi took it into the woods and buried it. It was a black boy. Winnie only moaned at its birth, the delivery was reasonably easy. She was built wide through the pelvis, a very healthy woman that recovered quickly.

Lovie got word and went over to help. Seeing that Winnie would be all right Lukatie left everything in Lovie's capable hands and went home. "The negroes thought Winnie was saying she had seen Seth kill Finny." She decided to let them think it. Thinking if he decided to marry her, she would tell what had happened, otherwise, he could hang. She relished the sympathy shone by those around her.

"Pore chile, whut 'er mus hav' gon' through hit's kno' wonder 'ers lost 'er baby," said

Molitha Casteen bursting with understanding.

"Oh, lawdy, yas, pore baby whut 'er seed 'n 'er so crazy 'bout dat Seth, oh my."

"Dey goin' ter put dat Seth unner de jail house, yas dey air," said Nancy Smith knowledgeably.

Didge stood by in case she was needed, but there was plenty of help. She really didn't care to be in that house. She waited on the porch for Lukatie. "Mama has either brought or assisted in bringing every child that has been born on this farm into the world since her marriage to Em. It's time they gave her a rest and got someone else," thought Didge, peeved at their use of her mother's goodness.

Others gathered around talking excitedly, and Didge listened and learned that Seth was being accused of the murder of Finny Patchett.

"Who said such a thing about Seth?" Didge asked.

She was told Winnie had seen it and that was what brought on all her misery.

"I don't believe it, Mama," said a mad Didge. "That is an unjust accusation against Seth," she was saying as they walked back into the house. "I just don't believe it. Winnie was lying or mistaken."

"Don't worry about it dear. I'm sure when she can be questioned tomorrow, it will all be straightened out," promised Lukatie.

"What is going on?" questioned Em.

"Winnie lost a baby boy and they're saying it happened because of the shock of seeing Seth kill Finny Patcheet." Lukatie told them.

"Seth would never do a thing like that," said Em.

"Of course, he wouldn't," agreed Stewart.

"At least we all agree," said Didge. "Here

are your keys, Uncle Stewart, thank you. If you'll excuse me, I'm going to my room."

Didge stood at her window and looked out at the flickering fast flashes of the fireflies as they darted spiritedly through the trees and around the yard. She watched them, fascinated, wondering what turned them on and off. Her ears were deaf to the hum of the night spirits as she thought of Seth. Would they prove him guilty and end his life? The thought was more than she could bear. Didge fell on her knees by her bed and prayed as she had never prayed before. There would be a trial and Didge meant to go even if she had to fight Em. "I will go to town and buy a car tomorrow. If Titia can own one so can I. I've enough money, nearly all I've made is in the bank." Without consulting Em she had opened an account at the bank and had enough for three maybe four cars saved up. "I will walk into town and drive one back home," she thought.

Didge went downstairs the next morning dressed for town.

"No work today?" Lukatie asked.

"Not this morning, Mama, I'm going to town."

"Good, we're going so we'll all go right after breakfast."

*****

Seth paced the floor of the jail cell still in a daze. He had read of such things happening, but never believed they could happen to him. "Not a very good way to start a new business, or keep one going," he thought. In anger Seth hit the wall with his fist and skinned his knuckles. "Why! Why!" he screamed at the wall. "Why indeed, guessing, guessing, guessing, that is all I can do." He winced as he rubbed his knuckles.

Winnie walked into Roxie's café letting the screen door slam behind her.

"Whut air yo' doin' out ov bed, Winnie?" asked Roxie.

"Beds air fer old folks, Roxie, I'se not old."

"Den, w'en is yo' gwine down ter de jail 'n tell de truff 'n git Seth outten dat jail?" Roxie was getting mad at her.

"Whut yo' think I kin do, dey wus fightin', dey wus fightin' ova m' Roxie," Winnie raised her head high and strutted over to a table and sat down.

"Winnie!" Roxie raised her voice, "Yo' kno' Seth duddn't kill Finny 'n yo' auter b' 'shame ov yoreself fer allowin' as how he did," she glared at Winnie.

Winnie looked at Roxie as if she were something menacing. "Huh, I don' hav' ter set har 'n listen ter yo'," Winnie rose and strutted out of the café as fast as she could.

"Git 'n don' yo' cum back' har til yo' clears up Seth's name, yo' schemin' wicket gal," yelled Roxie.

"Now, Sis," comforted Noah, coming out of the kitchen, "don' talk lak dat. Yo' is purple in de face."

"I'se mad, dat Winnie kno's more 'n sh' atellin'," said Roxie.

"Yo' don' kno' dat, Sis."

"Oh, yas I do. Sh' atryin' ter pull sumthang off 'n I kno's hit. I, I, oh, Noah, yo' kno' dat boy ain't hurt no one."

"Co'se I kno's hit, Sis."

"Den whyn't sh' tell de truff?" Roxie was very worried.

"Mebbe sh' will, Sis, jest mebbe sh' will,"

Noah said hopefully.

Instead of going home, Winnie headed for town. She walked slowly, thinking, twirling the beads hanging like a rope around her neck. She turned them loose and absentmindedly rubbed her stomach. "It wasn't bad having a miscarriage. Sure glad I lost it. It left me with a better figure, looking more womanly now. Maybe Seth will like my looks now. I'll go to the jail and see him. If he's good to me maybe I'll clear him. I can and he knows it," she thought firmly as the pace of her steps increased.

Winnie stood in front of the jail cell looking at the cot in the tiny bare room enclosed with bars. She felt like crying as she looked at Seth.

"Hello, Seth," Winnie said her voice wavering. "I've got to get all untongue tied," she thought.

"What are you doing here, Winnie?" Seth asked.

"Cum ter vist yo', but I sees no wecum 'n yore eyes."

"No! You're not welcome unless you've come to tell the truth. And the sheriff is the one to tell it to. I know what I did. I know that when I left you, Finny was all right. You go tell the judge the truth about what happened after I left. Now get out of here."

Seth grabbed the bars as if he would come through them, glaring at Winnie as Roxie had earlier.

Winnie threw her hands up in despair. "Den yo' hang, rot 'n jail or hut eber dey do wit murderers."

Swiftly he answered, "I'm no murderer."

"I kno' dat, but dey tink yo' is."

Coldness settled over him as he turned

abruptly away from her, walked to the back of the cell and leaned against the wall. He folded his arms against his body embracing himself against the chill that ran through him.

"Yo' kin b' sot free iffen yo' marry up wit m'." Winnie's words stung him. Seth looked at her in disbelief.

"Duddn't yo' har I'se lost de chile ona count ov whut I'se seed," she patted her stomach.

"Sorry you lost your baby, Winnie…"

"Sorry air yo' crazy man. I dudn't wan' no chile frum dat Finny. Now I'se free ter marry up wit yo'."

"You're selling yourself; you're not fit to be a decent man's wife." Seth grabbed the door shaking it making a raucous sound.

Winnie jumped back, "Stop dat, Seth, 'n doan't yo' say bad thangs 'bout m' jest 'cause I'se mad' one mistak'." Softening she said, "I'se gwine tell dem yo' duddn't did hit iffen yo' jest marry m'."

"I'll dwell in hell before I marry you, Winnie, I've told you that."

"De choice is yoren, but I sugges' yo tink hit over."

"No thank you," Seth said through stiff lips, "the price is too high. I wouldn't want to be indebted to you. You be the usurper and see what it gets you. Live with it if you can. Now, get out of here and don't come in here again," his voice was hard.

"Yo' go ter hell, man, yo' gon'ter burn till yore de sam' color I b'," she blazed in hurt anger. "Huh," she thought, "He gwine tak' m' befo' he'll burn. Iffen he don' he gonna hav' ter burn." Winnie rushed out of the jail looking hurt and flustered. "I jes got ter do whut I says," she told herself. Winnie walked around town looking in store windows before going home. She window shopped for things she would need for her home with Seth.

With the aid of his cane and the arm of a friend, Mr. Heath had been to see Seth several times and had sent his lawyer to talk with him. The lawyer was taken to Seth's cell about an hour after Winnie left. Seth was still seething with rage from her visit and in a raw mood.

"In case you don't remember me, I'm Arthur Quinn, Mr. Heath's lawyer. He sent me to talk with you. After we talk, I'll decide if I'm going to take your case."

"I haven't asked for you," snapped Seth. He felt like pitching Quinn out. "You're intruding on my privacy. Just get out and leave me alone. Furthermore, I don't need you."

"That depends on what you have to say."

"I've told all I know to the sheriff. Go talk to him. Then go to Winnie Brown. She's the only one that knows the truth."

"She fainted and doesn't know anything," said Quinn.

Seth looked irritated. "Yes, she fainted, but when? Before she saw Finny killed or after," he flung out.

"You have a point. I'll check it out I promise." Said Quinn.

Seth just looked at the tall pale lawyer whose flinty eyes stared from behind his glasses and said nothing.

"First, let's see what I can do for you."

"What can you do? Someone set me up. I haven't a chance unless Winnie tells the truth," Seth shrugged. "Just go away," he said with a condemned expression on his face.

"Why don't you tell me what happened, and we'll see what I can do. I certainly can't if you won't talk or do you choose to remain silent and help the one trying to frame you?"

Seth stopped pacing the floor and stood in front of Quinn, his tension easing. Seth told him all he knew from the time he walked down the road and saw Winnie until he left her standing in the road looking at Finny.

"Then you hit him first, Seth."

"Yes, after he knocked Winnie down, then we fought, and I knocked him out. I checked him and he was all right. I told Winnie that he was, and to go home. Like I said, I left her standing there, but I don't believe she would do a thing like that. All I know is, I didn't do it. I could never kill anyone," Seth's voice raised with sincerity.

"I believe you and I'll try to prove it in court if you'll have me as your lawyer," and for the first time Quinn smiled.

Seth liked him better and sat down. Far too good natured to be uncomfortable and unhappy all the time, he relaxed.

"Could this Winnie have done it, Seth, to make it look like you did? I've heard she tried to blame her pregnancy on you."

Seth raised his eyebrow in surprise, "No, I told you I don't think she would go that far. But I do believe that after a situation presented itself, she would take advantage of it." Then he told Mr. Quinn of her visit leaving nothing out and also of her other attempts to talk to him into marrying her. "She knows I'm innocent and she could clear me and said she would if I'd marry her, but I'm not about to. She didn't hesitate to blackmail me to force me to marry her to save my life."

"She was all right when you left her?" asked Quinn.

"Yes, she was."

"Then she must have seen who did it before she could get away," suggested Quinn.

"Right," said Seth, "and the one who did it knows she saw him which jeopardizes her life."

Mr. Quinn rose from the cot. "Guess I'd better go talk to Miss Brown. I'll see you later, Seth."

Sheriff Ply came to open the cell door and let Mr. Quinn out. He looked at Seth as he locked the door.

"That court ain't gonna turn you loose, boy. They gotta have sumbody to act law on 'n you're it. That lawyer man will shout 'n yore ear as to how much he's gonna hep yo', but ain't nuttin' he can do. That jury will burn you a new one. Yo' better make up a likely story 'n stick to it."

Without speaking, Seth turned his back on him and walked the few steps to his cot and sat down. His mind was a collage of memories as he sat there thinking, always ending with thoughts of Didge, the baby, swinging her, watching her grow up, swimming, swimming, swimming. Oh God, Seth dropped his head on his arms, his heart pounding mightily. "What must she think now."

*****

Didge watched the back of Em's head as he drove to town. She stared at his straight white silvery hair that had been carefully combed back. She suddenly realized that she hadn't noticed it's turning. He was blond naturally and had always worked bareheaded. The sun kept it bleached almost white. He was often asked how he kept himself in such good physical condition. Em would say, "Work keeps my legs strong and my back straight."

Didge's eyes strayed to the back of Lukatie's head. "I love her," she thought, "she's so good. She's the one that keeps me here. I wonder what keeps them together. I don't know what it is, but something is missing. I feel the chain broke years ago. Was it me, her wanting me? I'm sure he didn't."

Em was stopping the automobile in front of the bank. "We'll be here when you finish shopping. Getting some art supplies, dear?" asked Lukatie.

"No, Mama, I'm shopping today for an automobile," Didge said casually.

Em whirled around and went in the bank. "She's gradually slipping away," thought Em. "But what can I do or say. Admit everything after all these years? It would kill her. I can't hurt her like that."

"Marvelous," responded Lukatie. "May I come along and look too?"

"Oh, yes, Mama, I'd like that," said Didge, pleased.

They walked around the corner. Mr. Doyle's automobile agency was only a block away.

"Howdy, Mrs. Carroll and Miss Carroll," greeted Mr. Doyle as they walked in. "May I show you some automobiles today?"

"You may show one to Didge, Mr. Doyle," said Lukatie.

"Sure thing, buying your own automobile, are you?" asked Mr. Doyle. "Any kind you're particularly interested in?"

"A good one. A late model," said Didge.

"I have a 1932 Lincoln V-S over here." They looked the automobile over.

"No, that isn't my car," said Didge.

"I've a sporty job over here." It was a

Packard, straight eight 1931 model. Front and back windshields. "Look at this trunk and spare tire on the side, Miss Carroll."

"It's nice but used, I've seen his son driving it around," Didge whispered to Lukatie. "No, not this one, Mr. Doyle."

"Then how about a brand new 1934 Chrysler Air-flow. It's a beautiful new blue automobile, just got it in late yesterday."

They looked it over. It was a roomy sedan, Didge liked that it would be snug, dry and warm in the wintertime.

"Oh, I don't know." Didge could see Lukatie liked it. "How much?" asked Didge.

As Mr. Doyle was quoting the price, Em walked in.

"Too much," he said flatly. "Sharpen your pencil, Mr. Doyle."

"Excuse me," he said as he walked into his cubby hole of an office and shuffled through some papers. Coming back, he said, "I find I can cut two hundred off that price."

"Thought you could," mumbled Em.

"Sir?" said Mr. Doyle.

"Nothing, nothing at all," said Em. "Do you want the automobile, Didge?"

She was dumbfounded, she would have paid the two hundred more.

"Yes, I suppose so. I do need something to get around in so I can find new scenery to paint if I intend to keep my job. I'll go to the bank and get the money out of my savings for it," said Didge.

Mr. Doyle had her papers ready when she returned.

"You'll have to go get a driver's license," Em told her.

"I've had that a year, Papa. I got it right

after Miles taught me to drive. Come, be the first to ride in my new car, Mama, you too, Papa, and you drive."

"Well, I...go ahead," said Em. "I've a few more things to do."

"All right then, come on, Mama, we'll do our shopping and go on home," Didge paused, "Thank you Papa. I would have paid the two hundred dollars."

"Oh, Didge, I tried the automobile out while you were gone to the bank. It's a good automobile. Just remember always try one first before buying," cautioned Em.

"I'll remember, Papa."

It handled beautifully. Didge was well pleased. Now she could go and come at will. She parked on Main Street near the bookstore to finish her shopping.

"Mama, while you're in the department store, I'm going in the bookstore and see if they got my order of art supplies in."

"All right, sure glad you're not spending all your money in one place." Lukatie laughed and stepped into the store.

"I won't," thought Didge. Coming out of the bookstore she saw Winnie walking down the street. Stepping in front of an empty store Didge waited for her.

"Winnie, what in the world are you doing out so soon after the miscarriage?"

"Had ter see Seth, Miz Didge."

"Couldn't that wait until you were well?"

"I'se well, feels alrite now."

"What do you want to see Seth about? Since you're the one that got him in jail."

"Kin't ritely say hit's any ov yore business, Miz Didge."

"Winnie, Seth is in jail because of you and

you know there is not one bit of truth in what you are saying." Didge was trying hard not to show the anger she was feeling toward Winnie.

"I don' kno' what yo' means, Miz Didge, but I'se jest got ter git whut I wants de best way I kno's how."

"Winnie, Seth has integrity."

"He do?"

"I mean Seth is a nice person with high ideals. He doesn't do mean spiteful things. You know he didn't kill Finny, and I believe you know who did."

Winnie was silent staring at Didge.

"You let him die for revenge and you'll die in hell. It's not going to do you any good to hide the truth. Either way, you will probably lose him. One thing for sure you won't have a chance if they kill him. Saving him isn't giving him to me if that's your worry. For goodness sake girl, think, he's negro, I'm white. There's nothing between us and never can be." The old doubtful look spread over Winnie's face. Helplessly Didge continued. She was having trouble controlling her voice.

"You let him die in the electric chair and old Satan will rejoice over your soul." Said Didge.

"Ain't nuttin I kin do," shrugged Winnie.

"You stand by and let the law take his life and you're guilty of murder."

"Iffen yo' don' wants him why yo' care?"

"There's a thing called justice, Winnie, and you had better think about it before it's too late."

"Oh, there you are, Didge. Are you ready to go home?" asked Lukatie.

"Yes, Mama."

"Hello, Winnie, are you feeling better?"

"Yas, Mam, thank yo' fo' heppin' m'."

"You're welcome. If you're going home, we can take you. Didge just bought a brand-new automobile," said Lukatie.

They were all silent on the way home. Didge was filled with resentment. While Lukatie sat back and enjoyed the ride, Winnie was looking out the window, fascinated with the fast-moving trees. It was her first automobile ride.

On the day of the trial Didge dressed and came downstairs.

"Where are you going?" asked Em, a worried expression on his face.

"To Seth's trial," answered Didge.

"No, you aren't going to that courthouse. It's no place for a lady."

"I'm sorry, Papa, but I will go to his trial. I owe him that much. Anyway, I promised Mr. Heath I'd take him."

"But you will stay home, I can tell you what happens. I'll also pick up William," argued Em.

"Seth's my friend, Papa. I'm the one that owes him. It was my life he probably saved, and I am going. How can you think of saying I can't? He's a fine person. You can at least let me go with you if you think people will talk," pleaded Didge.

Lukatie stood in the hall listening. "Just a minute while I get my hat," she called out. "I'll be ready to go with you."

"Bless her," thought Didge.

"Seth is innocent, you know. He's a good lad, Em." Said William as they rode along.

"I know that, but convincing the court is another matter." Em replied.

"It's all very confusing and nebulous," said Lukatie. "The evidence points at him, but I just don't believe he could do it."

"If Winnie's child was his and he saw another man pushing his attentions on her he could have done it in a passionate rage," said Em.

"The baby wasn't his," said Didge.

"Not his? How would you know that?" asked Em.

"When I went to get my smocks from Winnie, Seth was there trying to make her refute the accusation against him. I was on the porch and overheard her say he wasn't the child's father, but the only way she would tell the truth was for him to marry her."

"You heard her say that," said Lukatie.

"Yes, I walked in and told her I heard her say it."

"And you never said anything about it?" Em continued to question her.

"No, no need to, she soon had the miscarriage. I do think she saw more than she is telling about Finny Patchett's murder, and she could clear Seth," declared Didge.

"How do you know that, Didge?" Em asked.

"Oh, I can see the lie in her eyes. She's scared, too."

"Well, here we are," said William as Em parked the automobile.

"Look," said Lukatie, her voice filled with compassion, "There goes poor old Mrs. Curlee in the courthouse. I'll bet she walked all the way to town to be at her grandson's trial."

"I think she rode the wagon in with Noah," said William.

Hezekiah was feeling pleased with himself as he walked into the courthouse and took a seat. "I'll be even with that Seth for interfering with my fun with that Carroll girl. Maybe I wouldn't have raped her afterall. Once I started kissing her, she might have given in. Who knows?" He watched with surprise and interest as the Carrolls walked in. "Why would they come to a negro's trial?" he wondered, "And old Man Heath here with them. He should be home in bed. He can hardly get around. The old coot ought to drop dead." And so, the rapacious Hezekiah observed and thought his private thoughts about all those gathered to hear Seth's trial.

Everyone stood as the Judge entered. Holding the gavel in his hand his face was stern and his whole countenance seemed to stand out above his black robe. The judge spoke to all in the court.

"I don't know what sort of sadist would do a brutal thing like this, or what joy can be found in the killing and mutilating of another human being. I intend that justice shall be carried out in this court. The prosecutor will now start this case."

Seth felt like wheels were running around inside his stomach. "Why do I feel like this when I know I'm not guilty." He had seen Didge and didn't like her seeing him like this.

For two days witness after witness was called. The case seemed to hang. Winnie stared at Seth and stuck to her story that she had fainted.

The judge noted that no one believed Seth guilty, but they couldn't find enough proof to prove him innocent. Even the prosecutor could find no hostile witness. "Damnedest case I've ever seen," mumbled the Judge as he recessed for the weekend with a warning.

"This is the most violent crime perpetrated in my term as Judge, and I assure you this court does not condone this. I will get to the truth of this detestable act."

On Monday morning Gick went to work at the hardware store while Thankful, Lovie and Zarilda left for the courthouse in Em's old truck. The old man was left alone sitting on the porch.

"Wal, no budy ax'd m' but fo' dis goes any fudder I outen't ter dress 'n go 'n ter town n' tell whut I kno's. Mite help Seth," the old man mumbled aloud. He got up and walked to the edge of the porch to spit out his tobacco. Then he went to the back porch and washed himself making sure to wash out his mouth good with soda water. Dressed in a clean shirt and overalls he picked up his cane and walked over to the Carroll house just as Didge was coming out of the door.

"Mr. Mathias," she called, "are you all right?"

"Yassum, Miz Didge, I'se alrite. S'cuse m' ma'am fer ax'in but wuld yo' tak' m' ter town. I hafta git ter de korthause 'n tell whut I kno's dis mo'nin. I jest kno's Seth is innercent."

"You know! Mr. Mathias!" said Didge bewildered.

"Yassum, shore do."

"Papa, Mr. Mathias is coming with us," announced Didge when Em and Lukatie came out of the house.

Em helped the old man in and sat down with him in the back seat of Didge's automobile. The weekend rain had left the road humped and rutted. The leafy branches of the oak trees hanging with moss shut out the sun leaving a gloomy feeling as they bounced along the rough road.

"Am I going too fast for you, Mr. Mathias?" Didge asked.

"Nope, de faster, de better, mos' fun I'se eber had." They all laughed.

"Tell Papa what you saw, Mr. Mathias," said Didge.

"Saw!" echoed Em and Lukatie as they looked at the old man's crinkly face.

At the courthouse Em spoke to the officer at the door. Soon Mr. Quinn joined them and listened to the old man's story.

"Will you repeat that on the witness stand, Mr. Mathias?" asked Quinn.

"Dats whut I'se har fo', Sir." The old man looked completely at ease. He was the first witness called and sworn in.

"Give your name, please," said Mr. Quinn.

Looking out at the sea of faces, he stammered for the first time. "Ah, a…a…a…"

"State your name," the Judge demanded. "We'd like to get this case over with."

The old man called out, "Zarilda, whut's m' name?"

The whole court broke out in laughter. The Judge beat his gavel. "Order, order or clear the room. This is no circus."

Zarilda in shock ever since the old man walked in regained partial control and stood up.

"His name is Gilbert Mathias, yore Hono'."

The old man's face looked like dried up fruit as he sat in the witness stand.

"Your Honor, I would like for Mr. Mathias here to tell the court in his own words what he just told me," said Mr. Quinn.

Didge wore a hopeful look as she listened, praying that the court would believe the old man.

"Does the prosecutor object?" asked the Judge.

"No, Your Honor."

"Then proceed, Mr. Mathias."

"Wal, yore Hono' hit wus hot 'n I wus up late a'sittin' on de poch hit wus a brite moonlite, Mistuh Judge, suh 'n I seed dis man flash ah nife blaid…"

"Seed, seed, seed," ran through the courtroom, "dat old man..." The room became quiet instantly as the Judge reached for his gavel.

"Ah' decla'ah seed dat yore Hono' lak' hit wus ah religious ritual de moonlite kotched onter de blaid 'n I shore seed hit 'n he said, now yore hono' I heered him talkin' ter hisself. Only de ol' devil do dat..." Quiet giggles ran through the courtroom. "He talk crazy he deed yore Hono'."

"What did he say?" prompted Lawyer Quinn.

"He say, yo' did ah good nite's wark ol' nife I kin allus depend on yo', yo' shore put dat Finny 'n his place. 'N he walk on down de road flashin' dat nife."

"I've been told you are blind so how can you see all you say you have?" questioned the Judge.

"Secon' sight yore Hono' don' see clos' up lak', but I culd see ah rooster on ah fence spit iffen he wus far 'nough away. 'N I seed dat man good cause ov de brite moonlite he stood out mity plain, yore Hono'."

"If that building across the street was on fire could you see a man in the window?" asked the Judge.

"Shur'. Whut air yo' talkin' 'bout I culd see ah warn onter his nse dat far a'way," the old man said.

"Could you identify the man for us if I have some stand?"

"Yassuh."

"Is the man in this court room?" asked the Judge.

"Yassuh." The old man assured him.

"I shall point out several men in the room. Will you please stand and line up against the rail there?"

The judge pointed out five white and five

black men including Em, Stewart, Hezekiah and Hyrum.

Obliquity in his thinking, Hezekiah knew all the deviltries of man and the devil. His smile was smug as he stood indifferently in the lineup. "Who could or would even dare identify me? That Winnie hasn't, I don't think she saw me, but she sure saw what I did to Finny," he chuckled. "I shall look her up after this is all over," Hezekiah thought.

"All right," said the Judge, "Point him out."

Without hesitation the old man pointed to Hezekiah.

"He's crazy!" yelled Hezekiah.

"One more burst like that and I'll hold you for contempt of court."

The Judge had the men change positions again and again. Each time the old man pointed to Hezekiah.

"Yo' needn' twist dem up Jedge danged iffen I kin't seed 'em rite eber time. I eben sees dat bird on dat lady's hat bak' dar 'n de kort room," the old man pointed his bony finger to the left of the room where a red bird sat atop a woman's hat.

Stifled giggles ran through the room again invoking a very stern look from the Judge.

"Wormy old man just full of facts, aren't you? Why can't you keep your damn mouth shut and stay on your front porch where you belong?" Hezekiah shouted.

"Kin't do dat, gotta hep justice. Sorry yore Hono'," apologized the old man.

"You're jes' a lyin' ol' crank," yelled Hezekiah.

"Wal whu yo' kno' 'bout bein' a ol' crank, son. Yo'll b' m' age fo' yo' eben kno' 'bout bein' young. Jes tank how much I'se already forgot. Sorry, Jedge."

"Such flagrant disregard for the courts will not be tolerated, young man. Find Hezekiah Bolton for twenty-five dollars, no make it fifty dollars," said the judge.

Hezekiah became loud and impudent yelling that he was innocent, and the fine wasn't fair.

"You haven't been proven guilty," said the Judge. "I remind you again this is a judicial assembly and we will retain order."

"Well, that old coot is a bald-faced liar, Your Honor," said Hezekiah.

Seth could feel the old string of fear tighten around his heart getting tighter and tighter. They would just laugh at the old man and throw his testimony out. "Why, oh God why did he pretend to be blind all these years? The old malinger."

If there was anyone other than family and Seth that Winnie loved it was the old man, and for that white fool of a Hezekiah to talk like that to the old man was more than she could sit still and take. She rose slowly and walked down the aisle.

"Yore Hono', Mr. Mathias he don' lie, he spoke de truff," said Winnie.

The Judge nodded at Lawyer Quinn. "All you men be seated, but Hezekiah Bolton don't leave the room. Mr. Mathias, you may step down if there are no questions from the prosecutor."

"None, Your Honor."

"Take the stand, Miss Brown," said the Judge.

Out of habit Zarilda started to rush to her father just as Thankful pulled her back to her seat.

"All right, Miss Brown, tell us what you

really saw on the night of Finny Patchett's murder and don't leave anything out this time," said Mr. Quinn.

Winnie told exactly what she saw happen before going to Roxie's and fainting. She dropped her head. "I wus tryin' ter tell dem at Roxie's whut rilly happen. How Seth faught fer m' wen't nuttin' 'rong wit Finny when Seth left him. See," she stuck her hand showing where she had bit it to hold back the screams when she witnessed the black deeds ov thet Hezekiah! "I wus hiddin' behind a big oak tree yore Hono' plum scairt outten m' wits. He wuld ov kilt m' too iffen he'd a'seed m'dar," cried Winnie.

"I sure would have and I'll be back and get you," yelled Hezekiah as he ran for the door.

A deputy cut him off at the door. Hezekiah hit him and pulled his knife. Noah rose from his seat like a huge bear and leaped with a speed that belied his size. He grabbed Hezekiah's arm with one huge hand and forced the knife to fall to the floor. He then wrapped his arms around Hezekiah and held him aloft.

"Arrest that man," said the Judge. "And get him out of here."

Unhurt but crushed by defeat Hezekiah started crying and calling the old man names angrily shaking his fist at him. "I'll get you, you damn deceiving punky old crud. I'll get you too, you useless whore," he flung at Winnie.

"Yo' better go say yore prayers, boy," said the old man.

"You pray for me, old man, and see if you get any answers," Hezekiah stated in a bland and beaten manner as he was led from the courtroom.

"Miss Brown, you may step down," said the Judge.

After speaking with Quinn and the

prosecutor, the Judge cleared his throat.

"Seth Kirby has been unjustly accused of the murder of Finny Patchett and this court dismisses all charges against him. The defendant is released from custody with an apology from the court. The Jury is excused, and this court is adjourned until tomorrow morning at ten o'clock."

Everyone stood as the Judge rose to leave the room.

Seth couldn't remember feeling so relieved in his life. He thanked Mr. Quinn, the old man and then Winnie.

"Why did you wait so long to tell the truth, Winnie?" asked Seth.

"Wal, Miz Didge, she say I'se guilty of murder iffen I don' tell de truff 'n lets de law tak' yore life."

Seth looked up, his eyes meeting Didge's, where she stood with her family, Mr. Heath, and Stewart in the rear of the courtroom.

"William, please tell Seth we're very happy for him. Come, dear," said Lukatie, "I believe your father is ready to go." She had seen the look in Seth's eyes and the smile in Didge's.

Lukatie was puzzled. "Have I missed something all these years or has this trial started it. Em's a fool not to let this girl date. Without realizing it he is pushing her toward the only young male she's ever associated with. How would he like it if she ran away and married a Negro?" Lukatie's quietness conveyed her thoughts to Didge.

"Don't worry, Mama, it's his way of thanking me for making Winnie tell the truth. I'm just happy he's free."

"How did you do that?" Lukatie asked.

"I just told her if she didn't tell the truth about what she saw, and they sent Seth to the electric chair then she was guilty of his murder. I told you she was hiding something," said Didge.

"Maybe we can't blame her for trying in her way to get what she wants," Lukatie said.

"Well, I do blame her for being so inconsiderate and letting him be put in jail in the first place," declared Didge.

Zarilda waddle up to the old man, "Pa, why yo' fool us all dem yars?"

"Wal, yo' mad' hit mitey easy. Jest cause I says I kin't seed ter read de good book eny more or look at dem pactures on de slide, fo' long ya'll starts ter leadin' m' 'round 'n sayin' I kin't see, fust thang I kno's folk sayin' I'se blind. I gess all ov dat attention wus kinda nice. So I jest sit 'n sit. Shore wus a hinderance sum time w'en I wanted ter go fishin'." The old man said shaking his head.

"I auto tak' ah piece ov stove wood ter yore bak' side. Yore de onliest critter I eva hared ov. De ol' devil gonna git yo' 'n I hopes he do," cried Zarilda.

"Me! Mebbe he will." The old man plumped his cane on the floor and walked out of the courthouse as unruffled as a banker.

Hezekiah's trial was held a month later. He implicated all the other men that had been on the raiding parties with him. Hyrum and the others were given stiff sentences. Hezekiah, sentenced to die in the electric chair, was sent to Raleigh for the execution. His parents and sister changed their name and left quietly in hopes that Mary Ann could find love and marriage, and joy in a life free of embarrassment and fear.

The old man went out on the porch as he did every evening to sit until the heat of day was eliminated by night's mist. He thought of the ride to town and back in Didge's automobile.

"Ah mitey fine ride hit wus. Gess I auto go inter bed, but dat riddin' so nice," his voice whispered into the night as his mind drifted blissfully down the road.

The next morning, he was found still sitting in his chair, his head against the wall; a slight smile was on his craggy old face.

"Oh, Pa, Pa, Pa, I duddn't mean hit. Pa, I duddn't," cried Zarilda. "I duddn't wan de ol' devil ter git yo'." She gathered the old man in her strong plump arms.

"Pore ol' soul he sit out har all nite whils't we'ens lay 'n our soft beds." With each thought a new gush of tears ran down her fat cheeks to fall on the old man.

"Maw, he kno's yo' duddn't mean it. Now stop cryin' 'n be happy for him. He's had as happy 'n easy a life as enyone kin hav'. He's neva wanted fer a thang, now calm yo'self 'n tarn him loose thar's preparin' to be doin'. He's found his reward."

"Iffen hit don' dry off ter day hit will dry out sumtime," Em could hear the old man saying as he, Lukatie, Didge, Miles and Julia followed the procession to the graveyard.

*****

"Miles, I would like to go see my aunt and uncle. They are getting so old I feel I should see about them," Julia said one bright beautiful fall day.

"This comes as a surprise, Julia, you never talk of them."

"True, but I think of them. I really would like to go," she pouted.

"All right, I'll take you over the

weekend," Miles offered.

"Miles, I'd like to stay longer than a weekend," pleaded Julia.

Miles was dressing for work, as he fastened his suspenders, he paused looking at her where she still sat on the side of the bed.

"Really, dear, I'd like to pay a real visit. Maybe do some shopping while I'm there. I was thinking of a month if you don't mind too much. I do hope you won't say no."

"Of course not. Well, I'm off to work," Miles leaned down and kissed her, playfully pushing her over on the bed as he patted her rump and walked out.

Julia quickly packed everything she could into a couple of suitcases, dressed and went down to breakfast.

"You look very dressed up this morning," observed Em.

"Going to town, Julia?" asked Lukatie.

"I'm going to visit my aunt and uncle for a while." Turning to Didge, she asked, "Would you take me to catch the train?"

"Why, yes, of course, Julia, if that is what you want," said Didge.

"Will you be gone long, dear?" asked Lukatie.

"Miles and I decided on about a month," Julia's voice was shaky.

"Oh, then Miles does know, but why isn't he driving you?" asked Em.

"He's busy this morning," answered Julia.

When Miles came in for lunch, he was surprised to find Julia gone. "Didn't you know she was going?" asked Em.

"I knew she wanted to go."

"She said you and she had decided on a month's visit. So, we assume it was settled between you," said Lukatie.

"Yes, that part is right. Only I thought I was to drive her there over this weekend."

"I'm sorry I drove her to town when she asked me to," said Didge, feeling something was wrong. "She had very little to say on the way in."

A week later Julia wrote that her aunt and uncle were very feeble and she might have to stay longer. Since they had no children they needed her.

"I need her, too," said Miles. "She should be here to pick out the décor for the house. Maybe I'll go up there this weekend."

No one responded to Miles.

"Well, silence speaks louder than words. I shouldn't go, I suppose," said Miles.

"I would think not," said Em. "Whatever is bothering her let her get it out of her system first, then she will be all right."

"I think the thoughts of living in a spot where so much happened in her life bothers her. It would me," said Didge.

"Why don't you rent out the house Miles and stay on here. She seemed contented until you started building," said Lukatie.

"I'll think about it, Mama," Miles said simply.

Julia's next letter said that her uncle had passed away. Now she would have to work out some arrangements for her aunt before coming home. She also stated that she hoped to visit both her brothers before coming back. "I do hope you won't mind darling." It hit Miles quite forcefully that she hadn't said a word of love or that she missed him, or even wanted to come home.

"I don't understand her," Miles fretted. "Why didn't she let us know about her uncle? I would have gone."

"She probably thought you were busy and didn't want to worry you," Lukatie said calmly.

In desperation Miles wrote exactly how he felt, he thought she should come home and bring Aunt Ida with her if she liked.

"I can't bring Aunt Ida. She passed away two days after my last letter," wrote Julia. "They willed everything they had to me. I was very surprised; even more surprised at the amount of money they had. They were frugal even chary. I really thought it was because they had so little. Now I know they just didn't care for worldly things. I'm a rich woman, I guess. I've the house and even some rental property and over a hundred thousand dollars after all expenses were paid. I closed up the house and came home with Jacob. I've been here a week and am leaving tomorrow for Nevada to visit Lewis. Miles, don't begrudge me seeing my brothers. You'll hear from me again when I get out there. Please be patient with me, Miles…"

"Well, I don't give a damn if I hear from her or not…" Miles threw the letter across the room and stormed out of the house.

Em picked up the letter and read it. Then took it upstairs to Lukatie where she was laying down resting.

"I believe our son has a problem. What is happening to them?" Em sat down on the side of her bed.

"I'm not sure, but I've felt for a long time the train was reaching the end of the line," Lukatie said searching Em's face.

They sat thinking silently, pondering, evaluating.

Lukatie was propped up against the pillows. Finally, she spoke, "Em, I think it's that house down there. By that I mean where the house is."

"Maybe you're jumping to conclusions."

"In my mind it is a foregone conclusion. I suppose you noticed she never went to the store."

"Yes, I've noticed that. I'm just about convinced the only way she and Miles can make a life together is to start over some other place…"

"You really think that?" said Miles walking into the room. He stood at the foot of the bed. "I can't leave her. My roots are here. I love it here. I've a good business going, I can't just throw it all away," Miles said positively.

Lukatie looked at her son, her heart was breaking for him. That same foreboding possessed her. "What is it to be this time? " she wondered.

Days passed with no word from Julia. Miles searched everywhere; there wasn't an address to be found among Julia's few remaining possessions. Then a letter came. It was short. Julia wrote that she would not return knowing that she could never live in the house Miles was building. She had decided to get a divorce while in Nevada. She was sorry to break it to him this way…he would receive a copy of the divorce papers in a few days…give my love to your parents and I thank them for all they have done for me…I do love them…I love you too Miles…but it isn't enough and I won't ask you to leave a place I know you love.

Miles would spend the rest of his life in deep wonder. It was Gick that kept the hardware business together. Only in his bedroom could Miles feel the nearness of Julia. It was life's end. His place to think of her…to dream of her…to try and erase her from his mind.

"Find someone else, son. She isn't the only girl in the world," encouraged Em.

"In time, Papa, in time," Miles would say.

Misery filled his soul night and day. He

would sob in his pillow until sleep came to console him...then he could return to work his hurt buried.

The years of bottled up strain had taken its toll on Lukatie. She was sick and had no desire to prolong the unfulfilled years with Em. She would pick at her food hardly touching it. As time passed, she spent more and more time in her room. Didge was always happy when she came down to breakfast.

"I'm glad you feel better," Em would say. "How about eating some of this good breakfast Patience has prepared."

"I'm just getting lazy, I think. I've nothing to do and I need a busy mind, busy hands and body." Lukatie looked at Didge and laughed. "I feel like a thimit."

"Not you, Mama, not ever you," assured Didge.

"You need a good rest," Em advised.

"That is a good prescription for laying down and taking a nap, which I do entirely too much of." her voice raised, "It's killing me, I've never liked idleness."

"I always thought you wanted all this...this house...a way to take things easier," Em spread out his arms looking dejected.

"I sound like a complaining wife, Em. I did want a house...a good solid one, but I wanted the joy of keeping it. It seems in getting this house, I've lost everything else." Softening she said, "I'm sorry, Em, I don't mean to be ungrateful. Those first few days here were like moving into heaven. Then Patience took over the house and LeRoy the yard. I admit I was lost. All I had was a little sewing. It was nice having them there to work when Kinyon and Jane and all the children came so I could visit with them and not have to stay in the kitchen. When they leave all the loneliness crowds in again."

"Why don't we take a nice long trip. Didge may come along if she likes. It would do us all good," suggested Em.

"I don't think so, Em," Lukatie said.

"Why don't you think on it. Now eat a big breakfast and let's walk some. Down to the river maybe. If you keep on losing weight your bones are going to rattle in your skin," declared Em getting to his feet.

"That's a clue as to what I'm looking like if I ever heard one," laughed Lukatie.

Didge went to her studio as they left. She watched them from the window. Memories flashing through her mind and she remembered no closeness between them. At least not since Em came back with the sawmill and found them huddled together on the old porch trying to keep dry. "I guess there is no bonding there. I must put such thoughts away and think ahead. I suppose age changes people."

Didge wondered if Seth was ever coming home again. She couldn't blame him if he didn't. He left right after the trial. Maybe he would come for Christmas.

Didge turned from the window and started to paint. Glad Mr. Bush had allowed her to do the illustrations according to her own resolve.

*****

Winter came and passed with Lukatie spending more and more time in bed. Stewart came often. He was concerned and worried about her. Only Stewart and Lukatie knew that his concern was for the woman he had loved since the day Em had first brought her to the farm. He prayed constantly. "Dear God, I've always honored her womanhood and loved her and Thee. Please don't let her die, bless her with the will to live, but let Thy will be done in all things. Her smile can brighten my whole day. How can I live on without it."

Spring came and Didge was sitting by Lukatie's bed.

"Look, Mama, a tiny blue bird is perched on your windowsill."

"It's the same color as the house, isn't it dear?"

"Yes, Mama," Didge assured her.

"I never did get to see a blue bird against the house, only those onery jays." Lukatie's voice was weak as she talked.

"Let me prop you up and you can see him." Didge propped Lukatie up with extra pillows, and they watched the bird in silence until it flew away.

"Now I know Spring is really here," said Lukatie.

"It sure is, Mama. While you're up let me comb your hair and slip on a fresh gown," suggested Didge.

When Stewart came later Lukatie was sitting up in the huge bed wearing a pretty fresh lacy pink bed jacket. Her dark hair with very few streaks of gray was combed back from her face. "She looks so lovely," thought Stewart as he stood at the foot of the bed talking to her.

Stewart handed her a box he was holding in his hand. "Sweet to a sweetheart," smiled Stewart.

"Now I know what's inside," said Lukatie with a weak smile that broke Stewart's heart. "She doesn't feel well at all," he thought.

"Thank you, Stewart, for your

thoughtfulness, not only now but all through the years."

"If I've ever brought you a moment's pleasure, my dear, you're most welcome," Stewart assured her.

"Uncle Stewart, while you're here with her I'm going up to the studio and work. When you leave will you press the white button there on the table. The pink one is for Patience in the kitchen. Miles wired it up for Mama yesterday." Explained Didge.

"All right, Didge, I'll buzz you when I leave."

"Why didn't Mama marry him?" Didge thought as she left the room. She cried as she walked up the stairs. "Mama's leaving us soon, I just know it. This terrible malignant cancer she has won't let her linger much longer. Doctor Wesson said it could be now, next week, a month or no later than six more months. Thank God she doesn't know. She might not take the pain pills and fight it if she knew."

"Stewart, I'm so conscious of the limbo I'm existing in. It's driving me mad. I feel useless, ineffectual and invalid. I want to be up and doing things." Lukatie's eyes were pleading.

"It's time you took a rest, dear. Those things you want to do can wait."

Lukatie rolled her head from side to side in disagreement. "Rest, rest, rest! That is all I hear. It's time you took a rest, Lukatie," she mimicked. "The need to keep busy is making me ache laying here day in and day out."

"Come now, dear, it's nice to see you relaxed this way," Stewart assured her.

She smiled sadly. "I'm like a person without any spirit. I need activity before I die of boredom…"

Stewart reached over and took her hand. "I'm sure you will be up soon, but it's best to let the doctor tell you when. In the meantime, take it easy. Catch up on books you've wanted to read. And hold on to that beautiful smile. It can still lift me to the heights of heaven."

She looked into his eyes and was convinced there was no feeling in the world that could compare with that of the nearness of Stewart. He was so comforting, so understanding, he could lift her out of deep despair and soon have her laughing. "Would that have been enough," she wondered. The thought of any other man other than Em had always repulsed her.

"Should I speak my thoughts, Stewart?" Lukatie asked half-apprehensively.

"If you care to. I'm all ears."

"I was wondering if I had met you first would my life have been different?"

"It would if I'd had anything to do with it. Don't you know that?"

"You will tease me, won't you? And I've always loved it," she smiled weakly.

"I've never teased you, Lukatie Carroll. I've meant every word I've said and a lot I didn't say."

"Didn't say, Stewart?" Lukatie's eyes glistened with tears.

"That I never stopped loving you during the years. Yes, my dear Lukatie. I've always loved you and could see no other woman. And I don't want to lose you," vowed Stewart.

"Oh, Stewart, dear, dear Stewart..." Her eyes closed as her hand tightened around his finger.

"Looks like I've put you to sleep." He leaned over and kissed her, then freed his hand and rang for Didge.

"She isn't breathing right," said Didge.

She rang for Patience. "Uncle Stewart, find Papa. He said he was going to walk and stretch a little. I believe he went toward the river. He may be at the little field they are plowing down there."

"Yes ma'am," said Patience from the door. "Yo' want m'."

"Sit with Mama, Patience, I'm going to call the doctor."

Lukatie was in a deep coma and her breathing was very irregular by the time the doctor arrived.

"I don't think she can last much longer, Em." Said Doctor Wesson.

Outside the door Didge and Stewart heard the labored breathing and sudden gasping for breath, then silence. It was over.

Em sat quietly trying to condition his mind to the fact that she was gone. Weeping silently, he sat slack shouldered beside his bride. "She's gone, the woman of service is gone. My God, that's what she was, a servant to all that needed her."

Didge went to Em. She could never remember seeing him so bent gazing into space. "How are you feeling? Is there anything I can do?" she asked him, bending over his chair.

"I'm all right. No one can do anything now," he said, his mouth tightly shut. He blinked as he turned his face away.

Didge had always felt defeated, closed out, before even saying a word to Em. The feeling was strong now. Feeling helpless to help, and a desperate need for a moment of peace. She paused at the foot of Lukatie's bed wishing with all her heart she could do or say something to bring her back. She looked at the still hands laying on the coverlet and thought of the strength they had possessed, the service to others they had rendered. The hot biscuits for breakfast every morning with some left over for her homemade jelly and jam during the day. The magic of those tender hands had made life easier for all those around her. Didge turned and retreated from the room.

To Em there was no hurt in the world like looking into the lifeless face of the woman he had loved for so many years. He rose from the chair and left the room. His face was lined with fatigue and drained of all color. His eyes touched Didge and Stewart and he moved away walking on out of the house.

"Oh, Uncle Stewart," cried Didge. "Doesn't he know we loved her too?"

Stewart put his arms around her, "Of course, he knows, but his heart is full. He can't talk now. He needs to be alone."

Didge slowly walked to her own room closing the door behind her and gave way to the heartbreak she felt, releasing the inner turmoil within her she wailed unrestrained.

Stewart wanted to tell Em how sorry he was and how he felt the loss too. He could still feel the clutch of her hand and looked at his as though her hand would still be there with her fingers wrapped around his. "Will her hand always be there? Dear God, it's all I have."

Em walked to be alone. To suffer alone. "Why, oh God, why?" he moaned. Then the tears came, one of the few times he could remember crying, he felt like a lost child, that was child no more.

All the negroes were under the big oak. Waiting, praying, and waiting, endless, hopeless waiting. Sometimes they sang strange songs, some religious and reverent hymns. Some chanted voo'doo or a blending of both standing about with lowered heads or slowly moving around waiting. Their sound came inside the house with an ineffable sadness.

Stewart sat on the porch to wait for Em. "Good heavens, we've forgotten Miles." He went inside the house and called him.

"I'll be right there," Miles said. He ran up the stairs to his mother's room and stood at the foot of her bed. Stewart followed him.

"She seemed almost cheerful this morning when I kissed her and left for work. Where is Papa?" asked Miles.

"Walking," answered Stewart.

"He didn't say what we should do?"

"No, not a word," Stewart said.

"Didge?"

"In her room," said Stewart.

"I'll go to her." Miles tapped on her door and called, "Didge, may I come in?"

"Yes, Miles," she was in his arms and their tears blended.

The negros watched Em as he returned to the house feeling his grief as if it were their own. "What will become of them when I'm gone too?" he wondered.

Doctor Wesson had waited for Em. "Would you call the undertaker for me?" Em asked.

"I sure will, Mr. Carroll, and stay until they come. And if there's anything else I can do, please let me know. I want you to know how sorry I am, Mrs. Carroll was a fine woman. I believe everybody loved her."

Stewart, standing a few feet away walked over and laid his hand on Em's shoulder and patted it. Em looked up in gratitude deeply touched by his friend's presence. Then Em noticed all the negroes gathered on the porch and steps.

Their murmured prayers, the quiet stares told more than goodbye. They were giving thanks for all the love and kindness shown to them by Lukatie Carroll.

Em felt their love and thanked them for all their devotion and vigilance. He spoke quickly to them calling each by name.

Lukatie's death had wrenched the three remaining members of the family hard. They suffered alone. Neither could console the other unless it was Miles and Didge, after all what good were words. They were only tissue thin anyway.

After the funeral, Em just stood there at the graveside feeling his world closing in around him. Stewart stepped back and waited. Motioning for the others to go to the house, he quietly waited for Em.

The following weeks Didge lost herself in her work. She would leave early in the morning and drive to the ocean and paint the rolling waves until her eyes ached. Painting in the bright sunlight was quite different from the protection of her forest. Sometimes Miles would go along and lay around in the sun while she worked.

"Sis, you make the waves look so real. Are you sure they won't spill over?"

"Nut," Didge laughed.

*****

Since Lukatie's death they had grown very close. But only a small inter-change of informal conversation ever passed between Em and Didge.

Em often wondered if she would leave and prayed she wouldn't. If she ever starts to, I'll have to tell her the truth. On this thought he went to his study and wrote her a personal letter containing all the facts of her birth. He sealed it and addressed it to her to be opened at his death. Should she die first it was to be destroyed unopened. This Em had written into the new will he had made leaving the half of land with the store and the house Miles built to him, and the half of the land the home was on to Didge. With Miles to have a lifetime right to live in the house should he choose to.

The negro families were to continue farming the land with Thankful Mathias as overseer of farm operations so long as he should live and be able to do so. Those farming should continue receiving their wages according to pay scale. Miles and Didge should divide all farm profits after farm and household expenses were paid.

Em called Mr. Quinn and asked him to come to the house at two o'clock that afternoon. Em opened the door to his knock and led him past the curving staircase and walked down a carpeted corridor to the end room.

"Come on in and have a seat, Mr. Quinn." Seeing the look on Quinn's face, Em added, "this room wasn't meant for visiting. Have a seat, please." Quinn sat down in one of the straight chairs placed at each end of the desk, Em sat down in the comfortable chair behind the desk. There was a neat pile of papers in front of him. Mr. Quinn looked at Em and saw a reserved man with very blue eyes that looked openly and directly at him. Em had thick blond gray hair and heavy lines etched in his face. He was a man with dignity and outward restraint. The lawyer surmised that he must be in his late sixties.

"I've asked you to come out to make a new will," Em told him.

"Yes, Sir, I'll be glad to handle that for

you, Mr. Carroll. I hope it isn't too late to offer my condolence."

"Of course not, thank you." Said Em. "I've written out the details here that I want put into the will. I suppose you'd rather work it out in your office. When you've finished, bring it back and I'll sign it."

"Will you have witnesses here, Mr. Carroll?"

"Guess I wasn't thinking. You call and I'll come to your office," said Em.

The telephone was ringing as Em showed Mr. Quinn out.

"Here take this letter and put it with the will. Make sure it stays sealed and is never placed in anyone's hands but Didge's. You'll read it all in the will." Em closed the door and went to answer the telephone.

It was late in the afternoon when Didge and Miles came in happy and laughing. "Oh, Miles, I'm so glad you went with me today, it has been so much fun. Say, your face is red," laughed Didge.

"So is yours, Sis," teased Miles.

"Maybe I'll get freckles. The ocean is beautiful, isn't it, Miles?" her eyes sparkled.

"Yep, just about as sparkling as your eyes, little sis. Bet you're tired, I sure am."

"Then how about taking a seat at the table and let's eat dinner," said Em walking into the sitting room where they stood.

"Sure, Papa," said Didge.

"I've a couple of things I feel I should tell you both," said Em.

"What is that?" Miles asked disinterestedly once they were eating.

"I had Mr. Quinn come out to make me a new will."

"Oh," said Miles.

Didge remained silent.

"I'm leaving the half of land with your store and house on it to you Miles, with your lifetime right to live here, but I'm leaving this home and half of land it's on to Didge."

"But I don't want…"

Em cut in, "It's your right, girl." Em continued logically, "Thankful will continue as foreman as long as he lives. Then you two will hire someone else. After household and farm expenses you two will split the profits."

"That's all right with me, Papa, but don't talk like you've already got one foot in the grave," said Miles.

"I didn't pack my bag and come to stay when I was born, son. I don't like to think of it either, but it happens to all of us and we should prepare for it. Oh, well, you can both read the will when Mr. Quinn writes it up."

"Didge is not likely to leave a house that will be hers one day." Thought Em.

"William Heath died this afternoon," Em informed them.

"I'm so sorry to hear it," said Didge. "He was a very special person. Should we go over? Maybe we could help?"

"I've been over there for the past few hours. There's really nothing to do," Em assured them.

"What caused his death, Papa," asked Miles.

"Heart Attack," answered Em.

"Poor man, all alone, no family to care. Who will handle his affairs?" asked Didge.

"His lawyer mostly. Mrs. Curlee called me, and I called Stewart. We contacted the undertaker and did all that could be done. William had everything in order. How his funeral is to be handled is all in the will. Stewart and I witnessed it; we've always known what was to be done," said Em.

"We've never heard you speak of it," said Miles bewilderedly.

"That was his own personal business," said Em flatly.

"What becomes of his place?" wondered Didge aloud.

"No reason you shouldn't know now, I guess. Since some of the tenants had paid for their places, the rest will have to pay, too and it goes into the estate. And the whole thing goes to Seth Kirby." Em said simply.

Miles raised his brow, "Has he been notified?"

"Yes, I talked to him long distance this afternoon. Mrs. Curlee had the number where he could be reached. She stays on salary and keeps the place clean as long as she lives, a perpetuity was written into the will to protect her," said Em.

Suddenly Didge felt happy. She was sorry about Mr. Heath, but she would go to the funeral, and get to see Seth. She felt guilty and ashamed that sadness could bring her such happiness.

Seth stood beside his grandmother at the funeral. It was easy to see the progenitor of his whole family line had been white. Didge couldn't help but wonder if it was by consent or force during the years of slavery.

While the graveside eulogy was being given by the preacher from Campton, Didge looked up to find Seth watching her. Their eyes caressed and his moved on. Mr. Heath always said mornings were the best time of the day and wanted his funeral preached at eleven o'clock in the morning.

When the services were over, Seth came over and spoke to them. "I want to thank you for calling me, Mr. Carroll," he said.

"Glad to do it, and glad you could get here in time for the funeral," answered Em.

"I drove all night to do it. I don't think I would have made it in time if I hadn't just bought a new automobile," Seth told them.

"Then it's you with the Cadillac roadster?" Miles said interestedly.

"Yes, that was me. That automobile sure will move."

"It sure is nice looking, Seth," said Miles.

"I'm sorry about Mr. Heath. I know he was a close friend to all of you," Seth said.

"Yes, it's too bad, we shall miss him. We know you'll miss him too because he was close to you too," said Em.

"Yes, I really cared for him. Well, Sir, I guess I'd better go. I've got to make some arrangements about my grandmother today. Sir, I was sorry to hear about Mrs. Carroll. Such a fine person. I really liked her."

"Thank you."

Didge just stood there waiting, she didn't enter into the conversation with the men.

On the way home Didge said, "I take it Seth doesn't know about the will?"

"Sounded that way," said Em.

Didge waited two days before going to the river. She knew Seth would have to rest and that Mr. Quinn would have to see him concerning the will. He would also want to pay his respects to Thankful and Zarilda because of the old man's death.

Didge sat on her thinking stump all day, waiting. Not one to waste time, she painted a tree, a large tree with a trunk that was twisted and gnarled. Trampled weeds by animals made a path by and around it that disappeared into the woods. Thick tangled strands of moss hung from this tree. The deep twilight fell upon her and Didge hurried to get out of the woods before darkness overtook her. She was disappointed and hurt that Seth didn't come, but at least she had the beginning of a good painting. "I'll go again tomorrow and just sketch some," she thought as she walked into the yard.

"We were getting worried about you," said Miles. "About to send out a search party."

Didge laughed, "See."

"Oh, you finally got around to doing that old tree. That is very good," praised Em.

"Thank you, I'll work on it some more when it dries out some," said Didge.

"You mean it isn't finished," Miles feigned surprise.

"Of course not, nut," she laughed.

"Well, I'm off on a date, yaw'll," Miles grinned as he walked to his automobile.

"When I'm old enough I might go on one," flipped Didge as she walked into the house.

Her words cut Em like a knife. "She's twenty-three and right, of course. By everything that's right she should be married with a couple of children. I wish I could take her in my arms and tell her the whole story, but I can't. She'll know one day maybe soon." Em sat down wearily struggling for composure. The fight to keep his secret had been hard and long and ate away at his very being.

After dinner Didge went to her studio to stand in the dark room and look out of the window toward the Heath place. She wondered if Seth would keep the house or sell it. The house was in darkness. She turned on her light to straighten up the studio. When she turned off the light and started downstairs, she noticed lights at the Heath house. After a few minutes she went on to her room. "I could stand there all night but what's the use. I would only tire myself out and I surely can't see Seth."

As Didge approached the river the next day with pencils and sketch pad and Regal Jr. at her heels, she heard Seth playing his guitar and singing.

Didge paused and listened.

Her smiling eyes have told me it is so
But then the world will never let her go.
Please help me find the way to say
My love will come and stay.

It puts within my heart a song to sing.

The memory of her smile can touch me still,
Who knows but me the joy her nearness wills,
The aching of the smile she holds
Can reach into my soul.

It puts within my heart a song to sing.

The time has come for her to come my way,
She has so much to bring into my days
She knows I love her, Oh, so much,
And waiting for her touch.

It puts within my heart a song to sing.

Not just the words but the depth of feeling in his voice drew Didge onward. She knew he was singing about her.

"I know I wasn't supposed to hear that." She stepped over giving Regal Jr. a slap on the rump, "Go get him, boy."

Thinking she meant a rabbit that had just hopped into sight, he howled and dashed after the rabbit both sailing over Seth's legs where he sat leaning against a tree. Springing to his feet he whirled around to confront a laughing Didge.

"I guess that scare was worth it," he smiled propping his guitar against the tree. Didge placed her art pad and pencils on a stump and stepped forward stretching out both her hands to him. Seth took them bringing them together wrapping them up in his large ones. A warmth flooded her.

"I think this is the most relaxing place in the world," Didge said, withdrawing her hands and walking on down to the water.

"It's the only place I can feel attuned to nature," Seth thought as he looked once again at their reflection in the water.

"It's so nice to see you again, Seth. How have you been?"

"I'm all right. When I'm in New York I dream of us being here like this together," Seth said with a wry smile.

"I came yesterday," she said.

"I came the day before. I was busy yesterday getting Mr. Heath's things in order," Seth said.

To steer away from talk too serious, Didge asked, "Do you miss playing ball?"

"Not really. I stay so busy. Since I was here, I've been down to Washington and opened two more restaurants."

"How wonderful for you. What will your grandmother do now, Seth?" Before he could answer she went on. "People have always called her old Mrs. Curlee. I was looking at her at the funeral and she isn't old at all," she said.

"She's about fifty-eight now. I guess

people call her old because of Granddad. He was in his fifties when her parents made her marry him. She was only a child of fourteen. She was only fifteen when my mother was born."

"So young," said Didge. "Parents back then would sell their children's souls for a dollar. Thank God I wasn't born in those days," Didge said with relief.

"I'm thankful for that too," Seth whispered hoarsely.

"Have you tried to find her sister who sent you here?" asked Didge.

"Oh, yes, as soon as I got the first restaurant going. I wanted to be able to help her."

"But you didn't find her?" questioned Didge.

"No, but I did find out she died about two years after she sent me here. She wasn't well then, but I thought she just didn't want me. A child can really misunderstand," he said calmly.

"Nothing but chit-chat," thought Didge to prolong our time together.

"Seth, did you know you were to inherit Mr. Heath's place?"

"No, I didn't, Didge. I'm very surprised. How did you…oh…your father was a witness to the will. Then you've known for years?"

"No, Papa told Miles and I the night Mr. Heath died. What are you going to do with the place?" asked Didge.

"I really don't know. I haven't had time to think about it. But I will do a lot of thinking," Seth assured her.

"Do you think you might farm it?" asked Didge.

"I've too much going in New York and Washington to think about farming."

"Didn't your grandmother have a place?" Didge wanted to know.

"Yes, Mr. Heath cleared the debt against that in his will. Her working and taking care of him cleared it he said in his will."

"Seth, why don't you fix up her house for an overseer and let him tend the farm for you. That is a lot of land to lay idly. I've another idea..."

"Keep talking."

"If you aren't interested in tobacco, cotton, corn or peanuts, why not shrubbery. Nurseries are in. They are shipping shrubbery all over the world. There's a good market for pretty plants." Didge said, "Also fruit trees."

"It takes a while to get it started growing," warned Seth.

"True, but you wouldn't have to worry about meeting payments on the place, and if Mr. Heath left you his bank account too, then you could very well afford it. That would make you a pretty wealthy man. I really don't mean to say anything I shouldn't, Seth."

"You haven't said anything out of the way. And it does make things easier for me, but I'd give it all away for you." He hadn't meant to say that. It just came out. He always meant for her to step over that horrible invisible line.

"I want you, Didge, more than anything else in this world," he groaned.

"Seth, please don't," she looked into his eyes, "The song you were singing said you know it can never be."

"You heard that!" Seth chuckled, "That is some of my mess."

"Well, I liked it." While she had an opening, she quickly changed the subject.

"Do you know your land will join mine

someday. Papa is leaving me the half with the house on it."

"Then I'll never sell mine," Seth assured her.

"I'm glad. I might not like my new neighbors near as much as I do the old ones," she said with delighted gratification.

"Didge, Didge, don't you know we can't go on like this. We must talk, we have to."

"What is there to talk about, Seth?"

"Us, our future...together, Didge."

"Seth, you know there is no future together for us," cried Didge.

"Then why in the name of all that's holy should I care if that land over there grows things or not if there are no children to inherit it," Seth said bitterly. Didge could read the prayer in his eyes. But what could she do about it? "How can I talk about marriage when I'm not even allowed to date?"

"Do you really want to date anyone else, Didge?" asked Seth.

She burst into tears and ran down the path. Seth started to follow then stopped. Let her think on it. Seeing her pencils and sketch pad he picked them up, put them in the hut, and went home.

Seth was called to New York and didn't see Didge before leaving. He telephoned but no one answered. With the old man dead, he had no one to talk to, so he got in his automobile and drove.

*****

Em felt he had walked away the past two years. It seemed that it was all he had done since Lukatie's death. Often, he walked to the graveyard. Guilt and the misery that he had caused her would drive him away, yet he continued to go. As he walked home a gentle wind rustled the dry leaves on the ground making them prance playfully as they leaped around the cold earth. "Are they playing hide and see?" mused Em as his gaze drifted from the leaves to the bare branches of the trees. Even a very young chestnut tree struggling to survive was bare except a few stout leaves refusing to turn loose and fall.

"Like me," thought Em, "I won't turn loose and fall. I hang on when I should leave this place for good." His life now was spent in semi-solitude. He saw Miles and Didge at mealtimes, then Miles was off on dates, and Didge kept busy with her paintings.

Didge hadn't seen or heard from Seth since she ran from him at the river. "If I contact him it means all the way. Why, oh, why couldn't we have continued on like we were?" She was pleased that an overseer had been placed in his grandmother's house and shrubbery planted on all the cleared land. The telephone interrupted her thoughts. It was Gick. "Miss Carroll, is Mr. Carroll at home?"

"No, Gick, he's out walking. Would you like for me to give him a message?"

"Yes, Miles is hurt bad. I called the doctor and he is on the way."

"What happened, Gick?"

"He fell off a tractor and it rolled over on him."

"Dear God!" moaned Didge. "I'll find Papa and we'll be right there."

Didge drove the roads looking for Em and finally saw him in the woods. She bore down on the horn.

"What is all the noise about," Em asked approaching the automobile.

"It's Miles, Papa, he's been badly injured. Gick called." Explained Didge.

Em gasped, "Why didn't he call the doctor?"

"He did, Papa, then called us."

When they reached the hardware store Gick said they had taken Miles to the hospital.

"Is it bad, Gick?" Em asked.

"I'm afraid so. His chest is crushed and there are internal injuries. It looks bad, Mr. Carroll."

"Let's get to the hospital, Didge," Em said impatiently.

They rushed up to the desk. "My son, Miles Carroll was just brought in. May we see him?"

"That would be the man Doctor Wesson brought in…"

"Yes, yes, Nurse, we want to see him," pleaded Em.

"I think you had better talk to Doctor Wesson. Here he comes now."

"Doctor Wesson, how bad is it with Miles?" Em asked.

"I'm sorry, Mr. Carroll. Miles was crushed by the tractor. He was dead before we reached the hospital. I'm very sorry."

Didge cried silently, how in the world could she make it without Miles. He was all she had; now he was gone.

Miles was buried two days later. Heads were shaking. "All of Mr. Carroll's direct descendants gone. Just the adopted daughter left." No offsprings to inherit the place. What a shame. The family was always so close, yes, what a shame. Heads kept on shaking.

Kinyon was very feeble and unable to attend the funeral. His boys were running the mill. They had purchased beach property and built a summer cottage there. All interest in the river front lot was gone with the death of Jane a year ago and Kinyon had returned the deed to Em. I will go visit him soon, thought Em.

Thus another epoch was reached in Em's life. At least things wouldn't be hard to take care of this time. He went to the telephone and called Lawyer Quinn.

"Mr. Carroll speaking."

"Yes, Mr. Carroll, what can I do for you?"

"There will have to be a change in the will, David."

"I'm sorry about Miles, Mr. Carroll."

"Thank you. Listen, I want you to change my will leaving everything to Didge. When you have it ready, I'll come by and sign it."

"All right, Mr. Carroll. What about your brother and his children? You're leaving them out of the will? I'm only checking, Sir."

"Right. They aren't interested in the farm." Said Em.

Once again Didge was thankful for her work and painted more feverishly than ever. Stewart was in New York again and she felt there was no one to turn to. The one person in the world that controlled her destiny and kept friends away was the one that remained living. "Why couldn't it be Mama still living?" she cried.

Time would not stand still, and Didge lived each day as it came, never looking ahead. Any hopes for a life of her own had been squelched by Em years ago. All she ever really wanted was a chance to share in happy family living. She had had it in part, but Em had cheated her of its fullness.

Em went to the hardware store until he found that Gick was capable of running it himself. Everyone that came in asked for him so Em put him in full charge.

Julia stopped her automobile in front of the hardware store. "I wonder," she thought as she walked in "who is running the store now?"

People will mix up screws and nuts, thought Gick, as he looked up from the bin he was straightening out.

"So, you're still working here, Gick," said Julia.

"Yes, Mrs. Carroll, I'm manager of the store now."

"Then maybe you'd be interested in buying it," suggested Julia.

"I didn't know it was for sale," frowned Gick.

"It is," Julia assured him.

"Who is selling," Gick asked.

"I am, since Miles is dead," Julia said smugly. "What was his is now mine."

"Oh, I think you better go talk to Mr. Carroll," Gick advised her.

"I can't see where that is necessary."

"Do you have a deed to this property?" asked Gick.

"Well, no. I guess I would have to get that from Mr. Carroll. You think it over while I get my papers; I'll be back."

Gick shook his head.

Didge looked out of the window as Julia drove up in the yard.

"Papa, there is Julia."

"I thought we had seen the last of her," said Em.

"I guess she got my letter about Miles and is coming to pay her respects."

Didge ran to the door. "Oh, Julia, how good of you to come."

"Yes," said Julia as they embraced. "Is Mr. Carroll at home?"

"Yes, he's here in the sitting room; come on in."

"Hello, Mr. Carroll, I'm sorry about Mrs. Carroll and Miles, of course." Julia said as she walked in. "I just came home and found a note from Didge telling me about them. I rested a couple of days and came on down here."

"Where were you?" asked Didge.

"In Nevada with Lewis getting him started in a radio repair shop."

"He should do well in that," said Em. "What is Jacob doing now?"

"Preaching," Julia said scornfully.

"You look like you're getting along well," said Em.

"Not really, I've a little money left, but not much," Julia said meekly.

"Oh, I thought that your aunt left you well fixed," remarked Em.

"I've spent a lot traveling around," shrugged Julia.

"Don't you get an income from the rentals she left you?" asked Didge.

"Oh, yes, but it's getting hard to keep going since I financed Lewis in his repair shop."

"How much do you get from the rentals?" asked Didge.

"About three hundred a month."

Em let out a whistle. "In this day and time, you should live very well on that."

"I can't seem to keep going on it," answered Julia.

"Then I suggest you stay home and stop going so much," suggested Em.

"With my inheritance from Miles I shouldn't have to," Julia said seriously.

"What inheritance, my dear," asked Em.

"His half of the property. The hardware

store and the house. If you'll give me my deeds to it, I'm sure I can sell it for a good price," Julia said evenly.

"Miles didn't own any property, Julia," Em informed her. "Even if he had when you divorced him you automatically lost all claim to anything he might have had," Em explained.

"But I didn't divorce him," Julia lied.

"We have your letter and divorce papers that say you did, Julia."

"Then I'll get me a lawyer and we'll see. That place down there is mine and I'm going to have it," Julia said angrily.

"Well, Julia, if you want to be embarrassed, go ahead. But this has always been my property and any building on it is also mine. I will suggest you have a good talk with your lawyer and listen to his advice." Said Em.

Julia stormed out of the house slamming the door behind her.

Didge flinched and walked to the window as Julia roared out of the yard. "I hope that automobile lasts until she gets home," Didge said worriedly.

"I feel sure that is the last we'll see of her," said Em.

"I sure hope so, she sure has changed. The very idea of trying to pull off a thing like that," Didge said. "Guess I'll go paint an automobile racing out of a yard for that new manuscript that came."

"At least she got something out of it all," thought Em as she went upstairs.

Em was exclusive of others as he walked alone daily. Occasionally talking with Thankful. He walked away another year, then was found lying at the foot of Lukatie's grave with his arms outstretched.

"Sh' cum fer him," said Zarilda. "See he's holdin' out his arms ter her."

At the funeral, the negroes were on one side of the grave while the white people stood on the other side. Didge stood alone at the foot of the grave.

It was a time for tears but they refused to come. Didge could feel nothing but a cold numbness.

The next day she went in to Em's bedroom to clean it. She felt closed in by the silence. Quietness had her in its grip. "Mama always said we should try to help someone every day. That everyone needed a hand to hold. Well, all I have is the bedpost." She whirled out of the room a restrained half-cry escaping her throat, she ran downstairs just as a knock sounded at the door. Pausing a moment to gain composure she then opened the door.

"It seems I'm offering my condolence here too often, Miss Carroll. I'm very sorry about Mr. Carroll's death. He was a fine man."

"Thank you, Mr. Quinn. Won't you come in," invited Didge.

"I've brought the will since you're the only one involved, I just brought it on out," said Quinn.

"But Uncle Kinyon, isn't he in the will? He was sick and couldn't come to the funeral. He said he would come as soon as he is better," explained Didge. "Let's go in the study where Patience and Lubby won't interrupt us."

She sat down in Em's chair and felt lost. She was silent as he read.

"It isn't in the will but when Mr. Carroll came by the office to sign it, he said he hopes if you ever marry and have a son you will leave the land to him."

Didge couldn't believe Em would ever leave everything he had to her. She said as much adding there must be some mistake.

"No mistake, and here's a letter he wrote and sealed, and said I was to give it to you on his death. Maybe it will answer your questions." Quinn handed her the letter along with a copy of the will. "Is there anything else I can do for you, Miss Carroll?"

"No, no. I'm all right and thank you, Mr. Quinn." Didge said calmly.

The letter fell on the floor as she went to show him out. Some neighbors came by and left before Didge returned to the study. As she picked up the letter she wondered, "Why in the world would he write something to me? Whatever it is I'm not sure I want to know." She looked at the fireplace. There was no fire, so she dropped it in a desk drawer. When it's cold enough for a fire, I'll just burn it," she thought. Picking up the will she read it over then went to Thankful's.

"It's Papa's wish that you continue running the farm. I'd like that too, but I'd like for you to train someone trustworthy to help you so they could run things if you're ever sick," requested Didge.

"I unnerstand, Miz Didge 'n I'm going to do it doan't yo' worry eny." "Pore chile," thought Thankful as she left.

"Death ends a life but the spirit lives on," thought Didge. "I must live on and struggle to find a meaning for being me. Tomorrow I'll go see Gick about managing the hardware store." Out of habit, Didge went to her studio and started painting.

Thankful took all the crops to market. Wish

Mistuh Em had lived on to be with m'. It took him about two months to see all the crops. Then he took Didge all the checks.

"Guess you'll wan' ter tak' all these to the bank 'n git the money to pay the hands," Thankful said handing her the checks.

"Thank you, Thankful, I'll do that in the morning. If they'll all come here on the porch, I'll pay them. You'll be here with the book, won't you?"

"Yas'sum," said Thankful.

"And Thankful, will you please assure everyone things will go on just as they did when Mr. Carroll was living," said Didge.

"Hare's the keys to the truck, Miz Carroll."

"Thankful, you keep them, you know what has to be done and you'll have the truck to do it. Take your family to church Sunday and an afternoon ride."

His big broad face beamed, "Thank you Miz Carroll, they will lak' that ridin' 'n dat purty new truck Mister Carroll bought. 'Bout gettin' a fellow to train I've been thankin' it ober 'n dey's three I think kin do the job."

"Who are they, Thankful?"

"Dere's Elijah Golden, Clarky Brown, then dere's Hinton Smith. I kno's dat his brudder Hyrum was rotten, but Hinton he's a purty fair fellow."

"Thankful, try Elijah Golden. I've noticed that he's a hard-working man, and he did go to school, didn't he?" asked Didge.

"Yas'sum, he went ten years. Then I'm gonna git him. Good day, Miz Carroll."

"Good day, Thankful, and thank you." Said Didge.

Weeks slipped into months as Didge painted

and spent all her spare time reading everything she could find on farming.

Seth was busy in New York, Washington, Maryland and Virginia with his restaurants. Opening up a new one every time he found a good location. "I guess it's time I telephoned Grandmama to see how she is." He asked about her health, the new overseer, and news in general. He decided to go home before she finished talking. He told her that he would see her Easter. "Business can take care of itself," he thought as he hung up the receiver.

Seth drove the tree lined avenue leading up to the house. No river this time he thought. He looked at the tall white columns of the house behind the moss hung water oaks and wondered if Didge would be home. Walking up the steps he could see the marble mantle at the end of the sitting room through the window. Also, he could see the shining chandelier and the glittering prisms twinkling a welcome.

When Didge opened the door to his knock, she saw a wanly smiling tired Seth standing there. Their eyes met and held. "Yes, it's still there," she thought. "His eyes can still flash 'I love you' in a hundred different ways."

Seth spoke slowly, "You look the same, but prettier if that's possible. You're thinner, your hair's shorter, but still you. Yes, I keep thinking…"

"So do I," Didge broke in, her voice soft, grave. "Wondering where you are, if you knew…"

Seth was aware she was assessing him. She said sadly, "It's been a very long time. Hello, Seth, please come in. It's so good to see you."

"I'm sorry, Didge, about Miles, and Mr. Carroll. I just found out when I telephoned Grandmama three days ago."

SILENT TEARS

"Now, how are you?" Seth asked as they walked into the living room.

"All right. When did you get in?"

"I'm just getting in. I haven't been down to the house yet. Grandmama isn't looking for me until tomorrow."

"Why is it that every time I see him, I want to rush into his arms? Even without an invitation." Didge walked over to the mantle and leaned against it. "How have you been?"

"How like her to ask about me when she has lost so much...her whole family."

"You must be tired after your long drive. It's unseasonably warm too. Seth, please sit down and rest while I get some fresh lemonade. I think that might be better than a hot drink, or would you prefer some wine?" asked Didge.

"The lemonade, please."

When Didge returned to the room, she found Seth seated in Em's deep comfortable chair. His legs were crossed and his fingers laced behind his head. His eyes were closed. "He looks so tired," she thought. Even so, she had to smile. Opening his eyes, he saw her expression and sprang to his feet.

"Is something wrong?" he asked.

"No, No, please sit back down," Didge handed Seth the cool lemonade and sat down opposite him.

"I was smiling because it seems so odd to see someone else sitting in Papa's chair. It was always understood that that was his chair and no one else sat in it." Seth started to move. "Please, no, Seth, don't move. To tell the truth, it looks good to see someone else sitting there. Now, tell me about yourself and what you've been doing?"

"Have you had dinner, Seth?" asked Didge.

"Yes, I stopped in Campton and ate. Say, it's getting late. I'd better go on to the house. Look, I'll try to see you again before I leave. Remember one thing, if you ever need me, I'm just a telephone call away." Seth took a card from his pocket and handed it to her.

"Thanks, Seth, I'll remember."

He looked at her and smiled. Abruptly rising to his feet, Seth cupped her face with his hands as he smiled into her eyes.

"Didge, I'm still waiting, and I'm weary of waiting." He turned and left, leaving her room to think.

It was in the sunless hours of early dawn that Didge finally slept. Only to turn and toss and carry into her dreams her thoughts of Seth. Only in dreams could the emotions erupt that she held confined within her. She wondered if there were any comparison between dreams and reality.

The next day Didge walked to the river; perhaps she could think there. She sat for a while on her thinking stump. "I'm no more free now than I was with the family living, there is society to answer to whether I like it or not, even if it breaks my heart." She picked up a twig and threw it in the river watching the circle of ripples spread out. "My life," she thought.

"You don't have to give in to the whigmaleeries of other people, Didge."

"You think that is all it would amount to." She said turning to face Seth.

"Oh, Campton will say the Carroll girl ran off and married a negro. Then they will settle down to their own lives and forget about it."

"You're asking me to marry you, Seth?"

"Haven't I always? Yes, I'm asking, but I'd take you anyway I could get you. There has never been any other woman. Didge, I've loved you ever since I first heard there was a little baby girl left at the Carroll's and I went to see her. I looked down in the cradle at the prettiest baby ever born. I loved you then. I love you now, and I want you as a man wants a woman." He smiled tensely.

Didge felt her heart would burst. "Seth, oh Seth, what can I say?" She looked at him her eyes crowded with love. "I've loved you for so long, but I've never been free to think about it."

"You are now, Didge."

"Yes, I am now. And habit has caused me to remain in the same old rut. Now I need time to change my way of thinking. Time to adjust to freedom. I'm responsible for the farm and the hardware store. They are all mine now, Seth. I've got a lot of planning and thinking to do."

"I'll come back in the fall and hope you can give me an answer then. Think long and serious, little Didge. It will be for keeps. I shall leave in the morning."

"So soon, Seth?"

"Yes, now I'll go see Roxie and spend the afternoon with Grandmama." As Seth walked away from her, he thought, "I've given her every opportunity to cross that line; it will have to be her decision."

Didge kept busy the next few days. She went over the books at the hardware store learning as much as possible about its operation.

"Gick," called Didge.

"Yes, Miss Carroll?"

"Don't you think you should hire a helper? The books show a very good profit."

"I could sure use someone," agreed Gick.

"Go ahead and get a good man that has enough schooling to know what he's doing," said Didge.

"Yes, ma'am, thank you."

"I hear you are getting married, Gick. Miles' house is sitting empty over there. It needs to be lived in. All I ask is that you keep it up. Just consider it a raise, and I hope you'll be happy." Said Didge.

"Thank you very much, Miss Carroll," said a pleased Gick.

Later in the day, she was cleaning out some desk drawers and ran across the unread letter from Em. She had forgotten it. She held it over the trash can. Suddenly leaning back in Em's chair, she held it tapping it with her fingertips. Then she ripped off the end extricating the letter.

As she read the letter reality began closing in on her. "It's worse than a bad dream to wake up and find out I'm not what I thought I was all my life. This is lasting; the dream isn't." She was so stunned she just sat. Was Papa that cruel or trying to protect her she certainly couldn't rationalize, not now, maybe tomorrow, but not now. She only knew that she hated the words that sprang out at her. "I must move carefully," she thought, as she tried to rise and go to her mother's room. She sat down in the straight chair at the end of the desk looking at the empty fireplace. "I'm freezing. I do believe I'm freezing to death," she thought as she felt herself plummeting down, down into blackest despair. The quiet flowed around her, ah peace, peace, peace was exactly what she needed, she had to have it.

Lovie found her. She had come to clean out Lukatie's room. Em had refused to let anyone touch it as long as he had lived. The letter was on the floor beside Didge. Lovie picked it up and called Patience as she slipped it in her apron pocket. They got LeRoy to help and took Didge up to her room.

"Go on wit yore work, Patience, I'se gwine ter sit rite har wit m' baby til har cum's 'round," said Lovie.

"Yo' call m' iffen yo' needs enythang."

Lovie put a cold wet cloth on Didge's forehead and sat down beside her. She took the letter from her apron pocket, smoothed it out, folded it and put it in the envelope.

"Whut is 'n dat letter ter upsot m' baby lak dat, hum…" Lovie said aloud.

Lovie took the letter out of the envelope and read it.

"Oh, Gaed, mercy m' dat Mistuh Em he her real Pa all dis time. 'N her Maw daid 'n her a negro just lak me. He shore assayin' how sorry he b' fer all de misery he cause her all dese yars. He say her maw wus so wite he duddn't kno' sh' wus ah negro, humm, m' pore baby whut misery do lay 'heah fer her. I dassan't utter a word 'bout dis ter no one," said Lovie not realizing she had been reading the letter aloud.

"Yo' started talkin' ter yoreself, Lovie?" asked Patience sticking her head in the door.

"No jes talkin' ter m' baby," said Lovie.

"Mebbe I outten ter call de doctor," Patience decided.

"Doan't think so, har'll b' 'round fo' long, jest passed out," said Lovie. "Pore baby all alone."

"Sh' got m'," Patience said emphatically.

"Sh' got m' too," snapped Lovie laying on another cloth. "But dat's not lak fambly."

"Shet yo' mouth," said Patience and left the room. "Dat woman allus takin' ova evatime sumthang happin' 'n dis is m' hause ter run."

"Mama, Mama," called Didge turning her head

from side to side.

"Hit's Lovie, baby, I'se wit yo'."

Didge opened her eyes, "Lovie, the letter."

"Yas, love, rite har," Lovie patted her apron pocket. "I'se gwine ter put hit 'n yore drawer ober dar."

Didge started to giggle then laughing until she couldn't stop. It lasted an hour. Her face felt frozen in that crazy laughter, that gradually changed to a groan. Then she cried.

Lovie gathered Didge in her arms and held her, cooing to her as she did the baby she first held. Exhausted Didge finally slept.

A month passed as Didge sat around. The letter burning a hole in her mind. But she couldn't bring herself to destroy it. How miserable Papa's life must have been living such a lie.

Didge opened the drawer and saw the letter and once again it was raining memories through her mind. Everything that had happened since she was old enough to remember was pouring in so loud that she clapped her hands over her ears to close out the sound. Through it all Seth was tumbling in and out caught in the current of her thoughts. As she calmed, she began to feel free, free at last… "Oh, Seth…I need you so very much."

For the first time in her life she could thank Em for being stern. He perhaps unknowingly had saved her for the one she wanted most in the world, the one she knew wanted her. She thanked God solemnly for this father she never knew or understood.

With realization came a burst of hope. Didge ran to the telephone and grabbed it, putting it down she ran to her room for the card Seth had given her. She waited impatiently for her call to be placed. Didge felt weak when she heard Seth's voice on the other end of the line.

"Hello, Seth, this is Didge calling to say I've decided. I wonder if you could meet my train one week from today."

"You bet I can," Seth let out a howl that could be heard all the way to Campton. "Sure you don't want me to come there. What's going on down there?"

"No, I want to come there, and I'll explain when I see you. Please meet me."

"You can bet I will," Seth said happily.

"Good, I'll see you one week from today. And Seth, I love you. Bye." Didge dropped the receiver in its cradle.

"I guess I should say something to Uncle Stewart. But what will I say? The truth I suppose; it's better he learns it from me."

When Stewart came in answer to her call, she had the letter in her hand. "Read this, please, then you'll understand why I'm leaving," said Didge. "How do you feel about this, Didge?" asked Stewart when he finished reading the letter and handed it back to her.

"I was shocked, of course. Aren't you?"

"Not really, you were a Carroll in all ways, Lukatie and I both knew it. But we never knew who the mother was."

"But Papa?" said Didge puzzled.

"He never knew we knew it. She never confronted him, and he never told her. Em should have told her. It would have eased the strain between them."

"I always thought it was because I was here, and he didn't want me. I was old enough to know Mama wouldn't let him send me to an orphanage. I never felt any love for him at all, Uncle Stewart. But I loved Mama very much," said Didge.

"Lukatie always said you should have been carried under her heart."

Didge's eyes filled with tears.

"Even Miles guessed at the truth. I often saw him watching you and Meda."

"According to this, Uncle Kinyon knew. I wonder if he ever told Aunt Jane since the woman that gave me birth was their maid."

"I can't answer that, Didge. Anyway, she's dead so don't worry about it," said Stewart.

"Uncle Stewart, I'm leaving a week from today. I thought you should know," Didge told him.

"You're not leaving for good, are you? There's no need to leave. It's nobody's business and this is your place, and you're still my little girl, so why run?"

"Thank you, Uncle Stewart, thank you, but I'm not running. It's Seth. We've always loved each other. Now I feel free to go to New York and marry him. You know Papa would never let me date and Seth was the only young man I was ever around. The time came that I didn't want to be around any young men but Seth."

"You can date now," Stewart told her.

"No, this way if there are children and I hope there will be plenty of them if they are dark no one will be hurt."

"Didge, a child will be no darker than the darkest parent and often they are as light as the lightest parent."

"You think I shouldn't marry Seth," said Didge.

"I'm not saying that. I think you should date others to compare and be sure."

They talked late into the night, but Didge had made up her mind before she called Seth.

The next morning, she started packing

choosing the best of her wardrobe, with a day of shopping planned when she reached New York. As she looked around her, the colors were no longer cold and drab. Her season had changed and for the first time in her life the colors came alive, bright and warm.

    Didge left her packing and rushed to the window that she had looked out of ever since the Blue Bird was built. She saw the fine old oaks, the graceful weeping willow and wondered if it really did weep, even the hickory and buckeye trees…oh, carry a buckeye for luck. Didge laughed happily. I've got all the luck I need now. The fields all looked loved and needed. She suddenly realized she did love them now that she was leaving.

    At last the train pulled into the station and Didge thought, "The Lord Knoweth all things from the beginning he prepareth a way…" Her thoughts faltered then went on, "and thank you, God, for preparing my way and giving me the truth."

    She could feel the train coming to a stop. Oh, what news, what glorious news she had for Seth. She could see his smiling face above the crowd. Didge took the letter from her purse as she raced down the platform to him.

    At last I'm free! I'm coming my love. There will be children. Oh, yes, there will! What a heritage they will have!

    Didge's heart was beating joyously as they ran toward each other, her arms outstretched to him as they met for the touch of love.

THE END

Acknowledgments

A special thank you to Katherine McCafferty for her help in publishing this book. Her patience and guidance are gratefully appreciated.

Katherine also designed the back cover.

Also, many thanks to John F. Arnold for his assistance in editing SILENT TEARS.

Although Mom is no longer with us, I hope in some way, she knows her dream of having her book published has finally happened.

This has been a labor of love.

G.P.A.

BOOK CLUB DISCUSSION

This novel was written a half century prior to publishing and is set around the turn of the twentieth century. Compare and contrast between eras.

Do you agree the negroes were treated fairly in this novel? Why or why not.

How did Mr. Williams' attitude toward the negro children make you feel?

Did you agree with Em that he should make the negroes wait to occupy their homes until the Blue Bird was built?

Did you feel LuKatie should have confronted Em when Didge was left on their porch?

Do you feel Em was justified in his treatment of Didge?

What will life be like for Didge and Seth?

SILENT TEARS

thimit – unmotivated, directionless

Made in the USA
Middletown, DE
05 November 2020